OUTSTANDING REVIEWS FOR *EVERGREEN*

"Intriguing, engrossing, romantic and a definite page-turner! Not to be missed!"

—*The Paperback Forum*

"A one-sit read . . . I loved it! A uniquely fresh book with engagingly honest characters who will steal their way into your heart."

—Patricia Potter

"An exciting novel . . . Tremendous!"

—*Affaire de Coeur*

"Incredibly poignant . . . Ms. Parr is a force to be reckoned with . . . Not to be missed."

—*Heartland Critiques*

"Skillful plotting and well-realized, engaging characters . . . a promising debut . . . electric!"

—*Publishers Weekly*

St. Martin's Paperbacks by Delia Parr

EVERGREEN
THE FIRE IN AUTUMN

NOTE: If you purchased this book without a cover you should be aware that this book is stolen property. It was reported as "unsold and destroyed" to the publisher, and neither the author nor the publisher has received any payment for this "stripped book."

THE FIRE IN AUTUMN

ISBN: 0-312-95690-8

Printed in the United States of America

St. Martin's Paperbacks edition/January 1996

10 9 8 7 6 5 4 3 2 1

Dedicated to

my sons, Matthew and Brett,
and my daughter, Elizabeth . . .
for painting all the seasons of motherhood
with the wondrous colors of love fulfilled
and promises kept.

Prologue

Comfort Bend, Ohio
1850

The cradle was empty, too.

John Logan knelt down, and his fingers shook as he started to trace each of the letters of his daughter's name which he had carved into the tiny, wooden headboard: A-m-e-l-i-a J-o-y. The cradle rocked, and he held it still until he had finished, as though completing the task might somehow bring the infant back.

Tears welled in his eyes, and he swiped them away with the back of his hand. Still on his knees, he saw something glitter on the inside of the cradle atop the miniature quilt his mother had crafted stitch by stitch for her first granddaughter. He looked closer and recognized Trina's thin gold wedding band inlaid with tiny seed pearls. He drew a deep breath and picked up the ring. It nestled in the palm of his hand.

Trina.

Vivacious and blue-eyed, with hair the color of whipped sunbeams. Almost sinfully endowed by the Creator, she had been the fairest belle in New York City. When she scandalously pursued him, he let her.

Trina.

His magnificent bride thought that moving to rural

Ohio was akin to a cross and motherhood a sentence of martyrdom.

He clutched the ring in his fist and looked up. Through the half-open window, a gentle breeze carried the sweet smell of apples from the orchards surrounding the house into the room where Amelia had been conceived. He took a deep breath and detected the heavier scent of roses that blossomed in the garden his mother had planted for them as a wedding gift—a gift Trina ignored as readily as she neglected her own child.

Trina.

He swallowed hard, his gaze avoiding the bed and settling on the wardrobe. The doors were open, revealing a gaping cavern where Trina's gowns once had hung. His fist tightened around the ring before he slipped the band of memories into his pocket. His eyes scanned along the floor to just beneath the window. Standing up, he walked over and bent down to pick up the daguerreotype he somehow had missed seeing before.

He turned it over, stared at the copper images for only a heartbeat, and put it into his coat pocket. He could not bear to see the image of his family. It was an illusion, a shattered dream, now, that tore his heart into jagged pieces. Was he strong enough or foolish enough to try to put the remnants back together?

He clenched his jaw and walked stiffly out of the room. He rocked back on his heels when he reached the kitchen. "What are you doing here?" he said through gritted teeth, eyeing his sister, Grace, with fury.

She swirled around from the cookstove clutching a wet rag to her chest. "When did you get back?"

"How long has Trina been gone?" he snapped, demanding answers to the few words on Trina's terse note he had found when he first entered the house: I CAN'T BEAR LIVING HERE WITH YOU ANY LONGER.

A flush covered Grace's face. "We think that it's been a few weeks."

"You think? You don't know? You and Daniel promised to keep an eye on my family while I was in New York."

Tears spilled onto her cheeks and melted the outer crust of John's anger. He walked over to his sister and enfolded her in his arms. He held her until she stopped crying and looked up at him. "Where's Mother?" he rasped.

"Back at the farm with Daniel and Stephen. Trina sent her to us. Your wife didn't even have the decency to hide her scandalous affair with—" Grace clamped a hand over her mouth.

Bile stung the back of John's throat as he stepped away from his sister. "Trina didn't go to her father in New York?"

"M-maybe," Grace stammered as she dropped her hand and lowered her gaze.

He grabbed her shoulders as ugly possibilities slashed through his mind and shredded his pride into tattered ribbons of shame. "Where is she?"

Grace pushed his hands away. "No one knows for sure."

Taut-lipped, John glowered. "There are rumors?"

"I'm sorry. I'm so sorry," she whispered.

"A name."

A hard swallow. Quivering lips. "Welles. Clayton Welles. He's a Yankee peddler. He . . ." She stopped mid-sentence, looked around the kitchen, and walked over to a tea caddy on the top shelf of the corner cupboard. She lifted it down and handed it to him. "This is one of his wares."

John's fingers wrapped around it, denting the thin, tin cylinder and distorting the unique, delicate vine of pale yellow flowers painted on it. With his other hand, he reached into his pocket and pulled out the deed to the house in New York City he had purchased and stared at it, ignoring the daguerreotype as it crashed to the floor.

No longer the talisman that would miraculously salvage his marriage, the deed was now just a piece of paper. This ordinary legal document became extraordinary again in a single heartbeat, mocking his decision to move back to New York with his family as a desperate and foolish attempt to forge some kind of peace with Trina.

He looked away, pained further by the sepia images that stared up at him from the daguerreotype. He was tempted to stomp them away, but picked up the daguerreotype and handed it to his sister along with the deed. "I wanted to surprise Trina," he explained. "I should have told her about planning to move back to New York. I should have—"

"It's not your fault!" Grace argued. "Trina betrayed you. She betrayed her marriage vows!"

A chill ran down his spine, and he knew that if Clayton Welles had been in the room, John would have squeezed the life out of the man without a moment's hesitation. Barehanded, and fully cognizant of what he was doing. Hanging was the standard punishment for horse thieves. How should he punish a wife-stealing, child-abducting Yankee peddler?

Slowly. Painfully. Without mercy.

He put the tea caddy onto the table and picked up Grace's shawl that was draped across the back of the chair. He wrapped the fawn-colored garment around her shoulders. "I'm taking you home," he pronounced solemnly as he led her toward the door. "Tell Mother to keep the deed and daguerreotype safe for me."

"What are you going to do? What about Trina and the baby?"

His voice hardened, turning cold enough to freeze the

eternally damned out of Hades. "I'm going to find Trina and Amelia and bring them back home. If I can try to forgive Trina for what she's done, she can try to find a way to live here. In Ohio."

"You want Trina back?"

." 'Till death do us part.' Trina made that promise to me, and I intend to see that she keeps it."

Grace started to cry. "What about Amelia? Do you think Trina will take good care of her?"

Will she?

John's arms began to tingle with the memory of cradling his infant daughter close to him. "Amelia," he murmured. He could almost feel her warm little body nestled in the crook of his arm. *Amelia.* With shimmering, distinctive turquoise eyes and a tuft of red curls that were gifts from her grandmother, she was the link between Trina and himself that was supposed to keep them all together.

Close-lipped, he shut out thoughts of what might have been that all started with *if. If* Trina had waited for him to get back from New York, would she have understood that his offer to move back to the city was an opportunity to start over? *If* they had resettled there near her father and her friends, would John have been able to salvage his marriage? *If* . . . .

He ushered Grace out of the house and closed the door, wondering if he would ever be able to shut out the pain of Trina's betrayal. He drew his brows together. When, not if, he found Trina and his daughter, he would convince Trina that she had been wrong to leave him, that she had been wrong to take Amelia away from him, and that somehow they would find a way through the hurt and pain to reach some measure of contentment with one another. Here. Where Amelia could grow up protected from the frivolous excesses of the city that spoiled her mother.

He would put the pieces of their shattered marriage back together, even if he was not sure he could ever forget how mistaken he had been to confuse infatuation with love. It was a bitter lesson, but he was determined to honor his marriage vows . . . even if that meant spending the rest of his life with a woman who claimed his name, but never his heart.

All he had to do was follow the trail left by Clayton Welles to lead him to Trina. A sudden inspiration sent him back into the house. He picked up the dented tea caddy and walked back outside. It was the only clue to Clayton Welles he had to follow.

Would it be enough?

Even if it took him the rest of his life, he had to hope that it was.

Chapter 1

Branfield, Connecticut
1855

Autumn had put it off for as long as she could, praying for a miracle. Counting on Fate for a last minute reprieve. Or better yet, hoping for sudden inspiration that would forestall tomorrow's event. At this point, however, divine intervention seemed unlikely, Fate had apparently withdrawn her favors, and Autumn finally resigned herself to the inevitable.

Bracing both feet on the bare, wood-planked floor, she brought the rocking chair to an abrupt halt, stood, and walked determinedly to the open, half-packed trunk that sat next to the door. Accepting her lot, she decided that she had no choice but to finish packing. The trunk lid rested against the wall, and she peered inside the open trunk. The first light of dawn peeked down at the pale, freshly-laundered, and neatly folded apparel, and she sighed. Muted earth tones of dove gray, light brown, and faded black resembled parched or overused soil. They were quiet shades that shadowed her natural flair for vibrant colors, shades deliberately chosen to give her the dignity so important to her reputation as a decent-living, God-fearing woman.

Feeling very alone in the three small rooms she rented above the tailor shop, Autumn indulged her flagging spirit and let the tears escape slowly. As the warm droplets coursed down her cheeks, she gathered together the few remaining items that space permitted her to take. She put them into the trunk one at a time. She laid a burlap bag filled with dried flowers on top, but buried her sketch pad, replete with detailed notes, beneath her clothing so it would rest flat against the bottom of the trunk. The mortar and pestle she used to mix her own paints and a small bottle of linseed oil, each wrapped in fabric remnants, fit into the corners of the trunk.

A lifetime of memories flowed through her as she inhaled familiar scents. They evoked loving thoughts of her mother who often smelled of oil and paint after decorating ordinary tinware her father made and turned them into lovely pieces for the table. She spoke aloud quietly. "You taught me everything. How to hunt for wildflowers and select them for their color instead of their beauty. How to sketch, how to mix the paint."

Her voice dropped to a gentle, hushed whisper. "And how to dream."

Did Mother ever realize that she had given Autumn much more than just a trade or a hobby that would make everyday kitchen items like cups, pitchers, or creamers into attractive tableware?

She shook away her poignant memories, turning to glance at the two wicker baskets that held her paints and brushes. They would not fit into the trunk, but somehow, she vowed, she would find a way to take them with her. Using a bit of twine, she tied the lids to the baskets closed and set the twin baskets next to the trunk. Regardless of what Reverend Briley decreed, she knew she could not leave the tools of her trade behind.

She had earned a decent living painting designs on tinware, but her skill with the brush meant so much more to her. Tole painting buoyed her spirits and let her escape into fantasy and dreams as she mixed a world of colorful paints from the wildflowers she picked with her own hands, the petals dried and used as pigments. The flowers she created on tinware never wilted under the blaze of a noonday sun or froze in an early frost. They bloomed magnificently and forever, just like her dreams of falling in love someday with one special man and having him love her in return.

Her painting was not just an unusual way for her to earn her living. It was a lifeline between practical necessity and the dreams that anchored her world through troubled times.

Until just a few short weeks ago.

Until Zebulon Klerk, the owner of the Branfield Tin Factory, reneged on her contract, declared bankruptcy, and left her penniless and more vulnerable than she had ever been in her life. Without funds to traverse New England in search of another position, she had been totally unprepared for the devastating sense of failure that overwhelmed her pride and independence and left her desperate enough to agree to . . .

Tossing her head to shake away the past, she also refused to ponder the future she had embraced just to survive and concentrated instead on the task at hand. With a quick scan of the room that served as both kitchen and sitting room, she assured herself that all of her personal belongings here had been packed. She walked to one of two bedrooms that overlooked the main street of a still-sleeping town. The door was open, and she went directly to the small crate that served as a bed table, ignoring the freshly-ironed gown that lay draped across a chair, ready for her to wear tomorrow.

A small square tin, handcrafted by her father, sat in its customary place. With several quick steps, she retrieved the tin and headed back to the trunk. As she stooped to place it deep within the folds of one of her aprons, she paused. Against her better judgment, she carried the tin with her and took her seat, once again, in the rocking chair.

Father.

Her fingers tightened around the tin. How long had he suffered before joining her mother in a world without pain? Autumn leaned back, closed her eyes, and began to rock, allowing the rhythmic motion to block the memory of the years she had cared for her father as a wasting disease stole his life one terrible inch at a time. Instead, she tried to remember happier days when her parents were both young and vibrant, when responsibility and duty meant doing what pleased her parents. Memories of days full of laughter and joy had been stored so deep in the hope chest of her heart that it was difficult to recall them at all, now that she was the only one left.

Clayton.

Her hands trembled as she lifted the lid of the tin and gently removed a yellowed bit of newspaper. Seeing the bold headline again sent tremors through her body. Her shoulders shook as she relived the horror of his death one more time. Her dashing, irresistibly handsome older brother had been brutally murdered two years ago by thieves on a lonely road just south of Boston, along with his beautiful and adoring wife. So senseless, tragic. And so unfair! Autumn's breath caught in a strangled cry. She could not bear to read the newspaper account again, or find any measure of peace in the knowledge that the murderers had been captured and hung for their crime.

Not now.

Neither could she bear the strain of trying to reconcile the conflicting emotions she felt concerning her brother, emotions that seesawed between youthful adoration and adult disillusionment when she finally realized how irresponsible and hedonistic he truly had been.

Squaring her shoulders, she put the newspaper article back into its tin coffin, trying to bury the past by snapping the lid back into place. It was not that easy. Why did her life seem to be the accumulation of one tragic heartbreak after another? She blinked back her tears, knowing that her greatest heartache still waited for her. Tomorrow.

She was not accustomed to despair or self-pity. She had always used solid determination and an indomitable spirit to knock down every barricade Fate erected. She had survived the deaths of both of her parents, her dreams intact. She had survived Clayton's murder with her dreams still alive. And somehow, she would survive tomorrow, even though she knew she would then have to mourn the loss of her dreams, too.

Spirit weary and tired from lack of sleep, she packed the tin into the trunk and made her way to the second bedroom. She paused just outside the door to stare out of the curtainless window. *Dawn.* Golden fingers of light waved over the horizon and mottled the new day's sky with dizzying shades of blue. Pale morning blue, sparkling afternoon sapphire, husky blue-gray twilight, and midnight blue, the color of the waning summer night. All the hues that held the hopeful promise of a colorful new day.

She turned away from the window, her sadness distracted for a moment with ways to blend her paints to duplicate all the elusive colors of dawn. She bit down on her lower lip. Would she ever paint again? *Could* she ever paint without her dreams to guide her?

She opened the door and tiptoed into the room, making her way to the small cot in the corner. A ribbon of first light bathed the features of a sleeping child and nestled in the ringlets that covered her head. Large, wide-set eyes were closed in sleep, but Autumn knew that when they opened later in the morning, she would catch her breath the same way she did every time she gazed into those magnificent eyes.

"I love you. For now and all your bright tomorrows," she whispered, repeating the phrase she used in their bedtime ritual, with the child that the world now accepted as Autumn's natural child. She touched her lips to the little girl's cheek. For a moment, Autumn stood there and watched the gentle rise and fall of the five-year-old's chest. Her memories of Clayton softened. This darling child was, in truth, Clayton's very own daughter, and Autumn's heart swelled with gratitude. At least Clayton had left a child, a blood relative for Autumn who otherwise would have been left totally alone. Irrevocably bound together by nature, Autumn and this innocent little girl also shared a love that had sustained Autumn in her darkest hours.

A shadow of sadness descended over her once again, and Autumn trembled. Except for this small child, the daughter of her heart, no one knew how much Autumn needed her painting to keep her hopes and dreams alive. Would this little one also understand one day that Autumn had cast her dreams aside so that they both would survive?

She shivered, bewildered by the unfairness of it all.

"Autumn."

She could almost hear her mother call out to her, urging her to be brave and strong. Autumn was not a common name; neither was it an ordinary season, her mother had explained when Autumn asked why she had been given such an unusual name. The season of autumn was nature's brilliant annual fete that celebrated summer's bounty. The vivid, brash colors of autumn represented strength and hope, promising that even when the dregs of long, cold winter days seemed interminable, spring would return, completing an endless cycle of birth and rebirth and acknowledging the power of nature to restore herself.

For Mother, naming her daughter for this emotional season meant giving her child the same strengths, and as Autumn grew up, her mother's expectations became her own. She faced every challenge, every obstacle with a strong sense that nothing ever would defeat her.

Taking a deep breath, Autumn filled her lungs with air and squared her shoulders. She knew she had no choice but to carry out her decision and accept the fact that just as the seasons eventually changed, so did the direction of her life. Tomorrow, she would no longer be Autumn Welles, independent artisan and self-supporting "widow." Tomorrow, she would become Mrs. Norbert Briley, a minister's wife, properly subservient to her husband's authority.

Yet, if tomorrow seemed to be the winter of her existence, she had to believe that spring would eventually return. Somehow, she would find the strength to survive the barren days of a loveless marriage, clinging to the hope that spring would blossom with new and different dreams that might make her happy again.

Unless Norbert discovered the truth about her daughter and turned those dreams into spring sorrows.

Sleep, like immediate success, eluded him.

John woke up coughing in the early hours of dawn on Tuesday. He hauled himself up into a sitting position and fumbled for the bottle of medicine from Myndert's Apothecary that he had put on the bedside table. Beads of perspiration dotted his bare chest as he shoved aside a spoon and took a long swig from the bottle. The thick tonic coated his throat and eased the nagging tickle that triggered eye-watering spells that stole nearly every bit of air from his lungs.

He leaned back against the headboard, arms at his side, the bottle of medication clutched in one fist. He closed his eyes, too exhausted to move. Taking short, measured breaths, his heartbeat eventually resumed a quiet, steady rhythm. He swallowed carefully, testing the efficacy of the medicine that was supposed to temper the lingering aftereffects of whooping cough. The disease was long past the contagious stage but had an irritating persistence that left him weak and vulnerable to the slightest bit of dust or dirt in the air and woke him frequently from a fitful sleep.

As he sat there in bed, he became aware of the sounds and smells of an awakening town. Coaches and wagons began to creak and roll in the street below into another day's duty, and the smell of baking biscuits and sizzling slabs of bacon that wafted up to his room from the inn's kitchen made his stomach growl.

Branfield was not very different from any of the other myriad small towns that criss-crossed New England like freckles on an Irishman's face. A loose marriage between manufacturing and agriculture provided a fair number of opportunities for able-bodied men to earn a decent living and raise their families in tight-knit communities bound together by patriotism, church, and high moral standards as well as a strong distrust of strangers.

Unlike many others, however, Branfield had proven to be providential for John. After months of searching, he had found her.

The Tin Lady.

His heart pounded at the prospect of finally locking horns with her, and he took another swig of medicine to forestall the new spell of coughs that threatened to erupt again. The medicine soothed his throat, but he almost choked on the irony of his situation. He had found her, all right, but at his moment, he could not wage an assault against a one-legged mouse with any hope of winning.

He scowled, refusing to consider anything less than total victory. Not now. Not after being cheated out of fulfilling his vow to salvage his marriage. His heartbeat accelerated again and his jaw tightened. When he learned that Trina and her scurrilous lover had been set upon by thieves and murdered, he had been willing to spend the rest of his life searching for the miserable bastards responsible. He had wanted the honor of putting the noose around their necks. He had wanted to see the horror in their eyes . . . .

John closed his own tired, bloodshot eyes and took a deep breath. He had been cheated cruelly out of having one more chance to make his marriage successful and thwarted by Fate from exacting vengeance against the two men who had murdered his wife and radically changed the direction of his life. He had resumed his search for Amelia, vowing that no one would stop him from finding and reclaiming his daughter. As years passed, however, he knew that the already jagged pieces of his heart had hardened against any emotion.

He got out of bed and walked a bit unsteadily to his travel bag and pulled out the dented tea caddy, still the only clue he had to follow. He held it out in front of him to stare at it, his thoughts concentrating on the woman who had painted it.

Autumn Welles.

Multitalented with the brush, Clayton's sister was only one of a handful of fairly anonymous female artisans who painted designs on tinware that Yankee peddlers carried with them on routes that took them as far as the Western frontier. She was the only one, however, who had a small daughter with curly red hair and shimmering turquoise eyes. Eventually John had tracked Autumn to Waterbury, Connecticut, where suddenly the trail had gone cold. The next eighteen months were filled with frustration and, most recently, his illness.

Nearly a week ago, he had found her in Branfield and discovered that she had carved out a simple, quiet life centered on her work at Klerk's tin factory and a child she protected fiercely. Cloaked with respectability, apparently she had earned limited approval from the citizens of Branfield.

Autumn.

Even her name was a contradiction. When he first learned her identity, his mind filled with the image of an animated, energetic woman with a zest for life that rivaled the brilliant colors of fall in New England. When he first saw her, dressed in a dull, nondescript gown that matched the prim, dry expression on her otherwise attractive face, he had been unable even to utter her name without grimacing at the unbelievable contrast between his imagination and reality. With earth-brown eyes and hair, she was as plain and colorless as an autumn field of white pumpkins, pale gourds, and sun-blanched acorns.

He overheard gossiping townspeople refer to her as the Tin Lady, and the unusual nickname fit her perfectly. Weren't her expressionless features as hard as tin and perpetually hammered into prim solemnity?

In spite of his assessment of her physical appearance, however, he was actually encouraged by her demeanor and truly thought his quest had reached a fortuitous end. Expecting to find her raising her brother's child as her ward, John only anticipated difficulty in convincing her that the child was truly his. How many times had he regretted leaving the daguerreotype behind? Still, he hoped that the woman had the common decency to listen to him, and he was fully prepared to let her accompany him and Amelia back to Ohio, as much to satisfy her own doubts as for the child's sake. After all, Amelia would probably be attached to her caretaker, and he could hardly expect the five-year-old to recognize him as her father.

His hand tightened around the tin caddy as anger and bitterness soured his mouth, but he was not too proud to admit that he had been wrong. Instead of waiting for him to come for his daughter or sending Amelia to him after Clayton's and Trina's deaths, Autumn Welles had run away to Branfield, cloaked herself with widowhood, and claimed Amelia as her natural child. Autumn Welles was as shrewd and calculating as her brother had been and for reasons he had yet to decipher, she deliberately had hidden Amelia's true identity. Autumn Welles's entire persona was a polished facade that, as an outsider to Branfield, left him little chance of challenging.

Left in dire circumstances after her employer declared bankruptcy several weeks before John had arrived, however, Autumn Welles had been left as vulnerable as tin was to fire, and he had had every intention of heating up a plan to make her bend to his will.

At least that is what he thought when he quietly established himself in town as an ordinary traveler who had the misfortune of becoming ill and needed time to recover before continuing his journey west. He was quick to admit that his recent illness had at least one more advantage: he was given a private room on the second floor, banished from the common sleeping room and sequestered from the other patrons for the pure and simple purpose of assuring everyone else a full night of uninterrupted sleep. He had set up a reasonable timetable which allowed for a few more days of recuperation before he would implement a plan to lure Autumn Welles to Ohio. There he would strip away every one of her lies, layer by layer, until the truth was revealed: Autumn Welles was not a widow, and Mellie was not her daughter at all.

The child's real name was Amelia.

Amelia Joy Logan.

His eyes misted, recalling the moment only days earlier when he had seen Amelia on her way home from the schoolhouse. He knew her. Instantly. Instinctively. This was his little girl. The fruit of his loins and keeper of his heart—or what was left of it.

And John had every intention of proving it in court with the help of his family and friends.

He put the tea caddy onto the bedside table as bright sunlight filtered into his room at the Golden Eagle. Everything was working exactly as he had planned.

Until last Thursday.

Unfortunately, Reverend Briley had surprised more than the entire congregation when he proposed to the widow Welles, who had agreed to marry him and journey west to start a mission church.

Tomorrow.

Is that what his desperate, five-year odyssey had come down to—a final day to claim his victory? Or was finding the Tin Lady just as she was about to slip away again just another example of how elusive and determined she was to keep Amelia from her natural father?

He walked over to the window and pulled back the curtain to look outside. The wizened proprietor of Myndert's Apothecary swept the planked sidewalk in front of his establishment. Two small boys, their books bound together with a strap, scampered down the street toward the one-room schoolhouse as the school bell clanged a warning that their day of lessons was about to begin.

The school bell rang again, and John claimed it as a signal to begin his own lesson for the Widow Welles today, centering on the art of subterfuge. If the plan he had implemented just before midnight worked, he would not have to wait very long before the Tin Lady learned that her attempts at deception were childish and amateur compared to the scheme he had devised.

The echo of the school bell also reminded him that he had learned important lessons of his own during the past five years—lessons based on frustrating, endless experiences on the road that also changed his priorities and forced him to reconsider the life he had planned for himself and Amelia when he eventually found her. Lessons Edsel Cameron, Trina's father, reinforced with a single document: his will.

John turned away from the window and searched through his travel bag until he found the two documents that had altered his goals and made his initial plan of returning to Ohio to live seem terribly naive and plebeian. The first legal paper, a bill of sale for the house he had purchased in New York for Trina, had provided the funds to continue searching for his wife and baby daughter—funds which had dwindled to a dangerously low figure because his search had lasted much longer than he ever dared to imagine.

The second document was actually a sheaf of papers filled with legal-winded prose that translated into two important decrees: If Amelia claimed her vast inheritance from her grandfather, who had died shortly after Trina, John would have to raise her in the New York mansion where Trina had grown up. The will also stipulated that John could not marry again before Amelia reached her majority, a galling mandate meant to insure that the Cameron wealth would remain with blood descendants, and John would not be able to misuse his position as administrator to divert funds to any future children he might have.

Five years ago, John would have burned the outrageous document and sent the ashes back to Cameron's New York lawyers unless he could have figured out a way to send them directly to Cameron in hell. Ironically,

John was not the same man he was that day so long ago when he had learned that his wife had run off with her lover and taken baby Amelia with her or naively had thought he could fashion a good life for all of them in Ohio.

Not by half.

Personal tragedy and betrayal were powerful taskmasters. They taught John the full value of a fortune and the need to provide for his daughter in a way that would protect her, economically, for the rest of her life. With his role as a husband obliterated and his notion of fatherhood redefined, he welcomed the opportunity to finally lay claim to his daughter's fortune so they could settle in New York permanently. There he would carefully monitor Amelia's investments and guide her into adulthood. He would prove to everyone that he was a better father than Edsel Cameron had ever been or judged John to be, and he would make sure that Amelia was everything her mother was not.

He just had to travel back to Ohio one more time to prove that Amelia truly was his daughter . . . before he could settle in New York.

His determination reinforced, he placed the documents back into his travel bag, turned away, and started to dress. He might be physically weak at the moment, but his resolve was indefatigable.

He knew that his plan was risky, but he had little choice.

There was so little time left and so much to lose . . . *if* he failed.

Chapter 2

This was just about the last place on earth Autumn wanted to be on the eve of her wedding.

Clutching a borrowed book in one hand, she reached out and grabbed the handle of the door in front of her. She closed her eyes for a moment, gathered her wits, and wished with every faint and trembling breath she took that the voices she heard inside the converted dressmaker's shop belonged to family and friends. They would be gathered together, just on the other side of the door, anxiously awaiting her arrival so they could shower her with love and affection and share her joy at finding love and a lifemate who had the same hopes and dreams for the future that she did.

Her family, sadly, waited for her in the next world and the only friend she had in Branfield was Matsey. Just thinking about the free Negro cook who labored seven days a week at the Golden Eagle Inn brought a smile to her face. Imagining Matsey discussing Hawthorne's latest work with the town's leading citizens here at the Lyceum turned the smile into a grin. If she did not know that Matsey was as likely to socialize here as she was to put a teaspoon of salt into her tea, Autumn might have been tempted to convince Matsey to steal away from her duties. Just long enough to shock the men and women inside—a shock that would surpass the collective gasp they'd uttered when Norbert had proposed to Autumn instead of Wilma Spakes.

Heart pounding, she pushed the door open, trying to convince herself that attending a book discussion led by her future husband instead of a pre-nuptial celebration was not tantamount to cruel and unusual punishment. She fixed a placid look on her face and stepped inside, hoping she was not late enough to invoke Norbert's censure.

A quick glance around the room eased her concern. She had apparently arrived just as the discussion began. She placed her book on a table already stacked with other volumes of literature being returned and looked around for a place to sit. Instead of taking a place up front where there were still several available seats, she chose one of two remaining seats in the last row of sturdy, wooden chairs that faced a podium centered in the front of the room. She had a clear view of Reverend Briley and the audience of almost two dozen people, none of whom could ever fathom the depth of disappointment that filled her soul.

She nodded stiffly when the minister acknowledged her presence with half a frown. Sitting erect, she folded her hands properly on her lap. As the discussion continued, she tried to concentrate on the topic and to block out her discomfort. The heat of the early August day, still captured in the windowless room at night, left her gown sticking to her skin within minutes. Beads of perspiration dotted her hairline, but she refused to even consider removing her bonnet in polite company, out of deference to Norbert's strict code of propriety.

A rush of cooler night air distracted her thoughts, and she immediately turned toward the door. A man she did not recognize entered the room, looked around, and took a seat in the closest available empty chair.

Directly next to her.

Autumn pressed her lips together and tried to still her rapidly-beating heart. She vaguely remembered Matsey telling her about a traveler who had been forced by illness to delay his journey, but this stranger exuded strength and vitality. Intrigued, she studied the man out of the corner of her eye. Broad shoulders strained beneath an expertly-tailored frock coat the color of melted chocolate. Thick brows hooded large, deep-set eyes that were set in bronzed features framed by sun-streaked brown hair that just touched the collar of his coat and caught the light from the overhead chandelier.

She pressed against the back of the chair to get a better look at him, and when he smiled at something Norbert said, the man snatched her breath away.

She blinked hard, looking straight ahead at Norbert as her heart thudded in her chest. Compared to the handsome stranger who sat close enough to her that she could feel the heat of his body, Norbert looked like a scarecrow who had stalked straight from the corn fields to the podium, even if that was an unkind comparison—for the scarecrow. Ill-fitting garments emphasized his rawboned frame. Thick spectacles that hid a clear view of his eyes softened his angular features, but a prematurely receding hairline, which he had explained was a family trait, made him appear much older than his twenty-eight years. Or was it the fact that even now, his lips never fashioned much more than a permanent frown?

Heart pounding, she clenched her jaw. Coming here had been a mistake. Maybe worse, she realized as her curiosity pressed aside her better judgment, and she tried to get a glimpse of the stranger's eyes to discern their color. In a man as attractive as he was, they would not be an ordinary shade of brown. Perhaps sable, flecked with gold. Or more likely, his eyes were blue. Which one of the various hues that had colored this morning's dawn would they be?

"It doesn't matter," she mumbled half out loud, convinced that her reaction to this stranger was proof that she had yet to give up her foolish, romantic dreams and face reality which, unfortunately, was marriage to a scarecrow with a rigid sense of Christian duty.

"I beg your pardon?"

His question, delivered in a low, seductive voice, snapped the thin thread of her composure, and she felt a warm blush stain her cheeks. She linked her fingers together to keep them from shaking and tried to pretend she had not heard him.

"I didn't hear what you said. Were you speaking to me?"

She turned and stared at him.

They were blue. Midnight blue.

She dropped her gaze before she took her next breath. "I'm sorry. I didn't mean to distract you from the discussion," she whispered, trying to still the pounding of her heart.

He chuckled, pausing briefly to clear his throat. "Fascinating topic."

She nodded, praying that he would turn his attention back to the discussion at hand before he drew unwanted attention to either of them. She listened politely as the minister answered yet another question, thankful that the man followed her example.

"Hawthorne chose Hester Prynne to symbolize sin in *The Scarlet Letter,* but he was using adultery only as an example of what happens to us when we choose the forces of darkness over light. Sin isolates us. From our neighbors, from loved ones, from God."

A high-pitched voice, one that Autumn knew could

only belong to Wilma Spakes, her self-proclaimed rival for Norbert's name, rang out. "Some people argue that there are different degrees of sin. Adultery is a horrible sin of the flesh, a betrayal of promises to man and to God. Is there really any difference between that sin and others less vile, like cheating or lying?"

The minister shook his head. "Not for God. Sin is a violation of His Word. You can't put sin into different categories and say one is any less displeasing to Him than any other. Adultery is a sin. Cheating is a sin." He paused to adjust his spectacles. "Lying, even for good reasons, is a sin, yet all of us find one reason or another to justify our breach of faith."

Autumn swallowed hard. Aching memories blended with present heartaches as disbelief and fear raced through her body. She could not accept the idea that there was no difference between the sins of adultery and lying any more than she could deny the need to breathe. Jaw tight, her hands clenched into fists. No one had the right to judge her reasons for hiding the truth from everyone in Branfield. Not Norbert Briley. Not the smug young woman who tried to ingratiate herself to the minister. And certainly not the self-righteous stranger who nodded solemnly, clearly endorsing the minister's sanctimonious interpretation of God's Word.

In the audience, heads bent together. A quiet murmur of voices debated the issue. Irritation flashed through Norbert's expression, and he held up his hand, urging cooperation and apparently waiting for silence to reign before speaking again. Once he had the full attention of the audience, his expression grew stern, his voice patronizing. "It's never easy to follow the Word. Every day we are challenged. Forced to face our human frailty. Yet we are all called to reach deep within our hearts and feel the love of the Creator. Respond to His call and follow His Word."

Pale and stiff, Autumn's hopes for understanding from her future husband, assuming she ever had the courage to tell him about her past, crumbled and fused into dread. What would he do if he knew the truth? She forced herself to remain outwardly calm, although she had the feeling that if anyone touched her, she would splinter into brittle fragments of flint.

Was it guilt?

No.

She would never feel guilty for lying to protect Mellie.

Next to her, one masculine brow lifted in concern, as though he sensed her turmoil. The stranger looked at her, and she smiled weakly, allowing a fleeting crack in the stone armor she had practiced wearing for nearly five years. When their eyes met, she nearly gasped at the intense emotion that flashed back at her.

She forced a mask of disinterest to slip back into place. Shifting in her seat, she tried to understand her alarming response to this man. She was twenty-four years old with responsibility for a five-year-old child, not a giggling, immature schoolgirl. She was betrothed and only hours away from marrying the minister. She was not going to allow this man's compelling presence and handsome good looks to jeopardize the only chance she and Mellie had to survive.

It was ridiculous and foolish. But she could not deny that she was also intrigued by the paradox of gentle concern and cold disdain she glimpsed ever so briefly when their eyes met. She was just . . . just very upset and vulnerable tonight.

Vulnerable? If Norbert knew the truth about Mellie, if he discovered that Autumn's whole life in Branfield was an elaborately-conceived lie, she suspected that he would humiliate her publicly . . . just before rescinding his offer of marriage. The very thought left her petrified.

With years of keeping her emotions in check and being faithful to her responsibilities, she found her fear odd. No one in Branfield knew the truth. Nothing could pose any real threat to this marriage, except her own misgivings and last minute jitters.

Or intriguing blue eyes and a handsome face?

Why was she so reluctant to accept the fact that marrying Norbert Briley was a reasonable solution to her dilemma? It did not make sense. She should have leaped at the chance he offered her. Why didn't she? There was only one answer that made any sense at all to her.

She did not love Norbert Briley.

Despite her dire circumstances and despite the image she presented to the world as a mature and strait-laced widow, she was as susceptible to the sensitive nature of her femininity as any other woman. She simply could not relinquish her wistful, romantic dreams—not easily—and not without feeling a deep sense of regret for what might have been.

Her practical nature and instinct for survival nudged her musings aside. Deliberately ignoring the stranger, she smiled for the first time when Norbert concluded the discussion with an invitation for everyone present to attend the wedding ceremony the following morning at nine o'clock.

Members of the audience stood and formed small groups to continue discussing the issue of sin in literature as the minister made his way toward her. She had not expected any of them to rush over to her with polite or sincere congratulatory wishes, but the fact that they did not still wounded her deeply.

The stranger stood up when she did and smiled again. "May I offer my good wishes now? I'm afraid I may not be able to attend the ceremony tomorrow. It's Mrs.

Welles, isn't it? I'm John Logan. Reverend Briley invited me to the lecture when we met earlier today."

Before Autumn could find her voice, Norbert intruded.

"Why were you late?"

Norbert's tone, as intimidating as the scowl on his face, sliced through Autumn's spirit. "I'm sorry. Mellie . . . Mellie needed me," she explained, although she could have lied and blamed her late arrival on Matsey's daughter who had agreed to watch Mellie after finishing her work at the laundry.

"You spoil your child," he admonished in the same tone of voice he reserved for unrepentent sinners. "All that will change. After tomorrow." He looked past her to John and offered his hand. "I'm pleased you found time to join us for tonight's discussion."

Turning away from John, Autumn tried to hide the embarrassment that stung her cheeks. Being publicly chastised made her feel like a child instead of an adult woman, a strange juxtaposition of her earlier feelings—feelings that only reminded her of how much this marriage would cost her. What did Norbert expect her to do? Leave Mellie to deal with her fears about moving so far away? The man who was going to be Mellie's stepfather was far too dogmatic to be human and too insensitive to her feelings to inspire easy devotion, and her bottom lip quivered.

Norbert, obviously mistaking her annoyance for distress, actually smiled, a benevolent, condescending smile that made her cringe. He put his hand on her arm and turned her around to face the man who had witnessed Norbert's callous reprimand.

Midnight blue eyes flashed with smug appreciation for Norbert's exercise of male authority.

She pursed her lips and took a step away from Norbert whose hold on her arm tightened and prevented her from leaving his side. "Are you settling in Branfield, Mr. . . . Mr. . . ."

"Logan." He paused, one cheek twitching with obvious displeasure that she had forgotten his name so quickly. "Just resting here for a few days before I continue my journey back to Ohio." He covered a series of coughs with his hand, although he could not hide the way his face reddened as he fought to catch his breath. "Nothing serious," he rasped as he loosened his collar.

"You might try stopping in to see Joshua Myndert. He's—"

"We've met. I purchased enough tonic from the apothecary to last my trip home. Just in case I need it that long."

"Reverend Briley? Excuse me for interrupting."

It did not surprise Autumn when Wilma Spakes stepped right into the conversation to lure Norbert away on the pretext of having him speak privately with Widow Brubaker. At eighty-nine, Branfield's oldest matron was confined to a wheelchair which had been placed up front near the podium for tonight's lecture. Widow Brubaker had also promised a sizable donation to Norbert's missionary efforts, and he excused himself with a glance that seemed . . . nervous?

Standing alone with John, Autumn fidgeted with the frayed ribbons on her bonnet. "You're from Ohio?"

"Where I have a tin factory to run. Or to open, to be more precise. Now that I've purchased enough tinware to start my men on their routes, I need to get back to Comfort Bend."

A tin factory!

Autumn's pulse began to race. "I've never heard of a tin factory in Ohio. Most tinware is manufactured here in New England."

"Precisely," he remarked with a self-righteous smile. "The opening of the Erie Canal has created opportunities to move factories west where the market is wide open."

"Yankee peddlers already travel western routes," she countered, as the conversation evoked memories of her brother excitedly describing his travels through western Pennsylvania and New York.

John's eyes widened, turning into twin sparkling sapphires before they darkened into blue slate. "Contracting peddlers to travel hundreds of miles from New England each year cuts into profits. It's more cost effective to center the factory closer to the market—which is exactly why my venture makes sense."

It did make sense to her, and in the time it took to blink her eyes, she glimpsed a future where she would be able to earn a decent living and make a good home for Mellie as well as herself. A future that might preclude sacrificing her dreams.

She moistened her lips and looked across the room to make sure that Norbert was still occupied with Wilma and Widow Brubaker. Convinced that she had time and opportunity, she cleared her throat and tried to rein in the thrilling possibilities that galloped through her mind. "Most people can't afford to buy pewter and buy less costly tinware instead. Unfortunately, it's not nearly as attractive as pewter. Have you given any thought to hiring someone to paint designs on the tinware to increase your sales and give you an advantage over other factories?"

"For a while. Yes, I suppose I did," he answered slowly.

Blue eyes flashed briefly.

Had she detected a sparkle of interest? She pressed him further. "Why did you change your mind?"

An impish grin. "I didn't."

"Oh. Then you've already hired someone," she stammered, chagrined by his evasive wordplay. Was he deliberately baiting her?

"I didn't say that."

A cryptic smile fueled her frustration, but before she could make him explain exactly what he meant, Norbert returned.

Fumbling with his spectacles to push them back up the long ridge of his nose, he took her arm. "It's time to go, Autumn. Godspeed, Mr. Logan. And again, thank you."

Autumn had the distinct impression that Norbert was trying to get her away from John Logan. Her head started spinning with questions. Did Norbert know about the factory John was opening? Was her future husband afraid that if she had found out about it, she would be tempted to seek employment in Ohio instead of going through with the wedding? And just what did John Logan do to warrant a thank-you?

John's voice startled her. "I'm glad to make the donation, especially since we share a deep commitment to following the Word."

She arched a brow and cocked her head. "Mr. Logan made a donation for the mission church?"

Norbert gulped. "Yes. Yes, he did." He tightened his hold on her arm.

Autumn's back stiffened, and she smiled as though his touch were gentle instead of sending a series of painful twinges up her arm. "How very kind of you, Mr. Logan."

John's face tightened. "It was the least I could do. Under the circumstances."

"Circumstances," she repeated as her stomach twisted into knots, although she was not exactly sure why.

Norbert cleared his throat. "Mr. Logan was decent enough—"

"It was the right thing to do. When I purchased the lot of tinware from Klerk—"

Autumn responded without thinking, and her words rushed out in a single outburst. "You bought tinware from Klerk? He declared bankruptcy. I thought the bank took the stock and sold it off to pay the creditors." She took a deep breath and lowered her voice to temper her tone. "All of them except me, it appears."

Norbert glared at her. "Mr. Logan's business dealings with Klerk are none of your concern."

She glared back at him. "I'm only concerned about my wages," she insisted, forcing a gentle tone and taking a side glance at John Logan. "If Mr. Logan paid Mr. Klerk for the tinware, then Mr. Klerk should be able to pay the wages he owes me."

John squared his shoulders. "I didn't know anything about the bankruptcy until I was making arrangements with Aaron Mills to store my wagon at the livery. He told me what Klerk had done. I'm sorry. I truly didn't know that Mr. Klerk owed anyone anything when I bought his stock."

Autumn swallowed hard. "I'm sorry. I didn't mean to imply that you did, Mr. Logan. But Mr. Klerk knew. Why didn't he come to me today and pay me?" Confused, she turned to Norbert who looked more annoyed than concerned.

"Everything has been settled, Autumn. Mr. Klerk, unfortunately, left town during the night. Obviously, he has no Christian principles and took advantage of you. When Mr. Logan learned that you had been cheated out of your wages, he came to me and made a donation to the church to make amends."

Simmering disbelief boiled over into outrage which extinguished the candle of hope that flickered in her heart. She pulled out of Norbert's grasp and glared at John Logan. "You had no right to discuss my wages with anyone but me. No right at all! Those were my wages! Mine!"

Norbert reclaimed his hold on her. "Lower your voice! It's not a woman's place to haggle over money. I handled the matter. Rather well. I thought you understood and respected my feelings on the issue of women in the business world. Yet you continue to step out of your proper sphere . . . and no doubt enjoy making a public spectacle of yourself!"

John edged closer and stepped between them. "Look, I didn't mean to—"

Crackling fire raged through her veins, but she forced her voice to remain calm. "What you did or didn't mean to do is of no consequence now, is it, Mr. Logan? Norbert will see that my wages which you turned into a donation are spent wisely."

Autumn knew she was dangerously close to angering her future husband and she could not afford to push him to the point where he would question whether or not he wanted to go through with the wedding. Forcing her lips into a sweet smile, she feigned an apologetic expression, although it galled her to have to cower to his demands. "I'm sorry, Norbert. I should have trusted you to handle my affairs."

Norbert took a deep breath, looked past her and addressed John Logan. "I think your donation was more than generous, especially considering that it wasn't your responsibility to settle Mr. Klerk's debt. Now if you'll excuse us, I think it's time I escorted Mrs. Welles home."

Autumn nodded weakly and let Norbert lead her out of the Lyceum. She walked stiffly, dazed by what she had learned. The still night air chilled her anger and disappointment, and as they walked down the planked sidewalk, she began to replay her conversations with John Logan.

Was there any chance he would give her a portion of her wages, enough to let her leave Branfield and survive until she found a factory in New England willing to hire her? If not, was there a chance that he had a position for a tole painter in Ohio, or had he simply been making idle conversation, entertaining himself with her when he knew that she had been a painter of tin who had no way to search for a new employer?

These were all questions she had wanted to ask John Logan that had had to remain unanswered because Norbert had interrupted their first conversation, and then had forced her to leave abruptly. She sighed, dismayed that all of her questions seemed destined to remain unspoken.

Unless she found a way to talk to John Logan again. Alone.

It was unthinkable and totally irresponsible, considering the consequences if anyone found out.

It was irrational even to consider it.

As irrational as her dreams?

Her pride burned for the opportunity to remain independent; her mind rained common sense on the flames. But her heart yearned for just one more chance to reclaim her dreams, and she knew that if she had to sneak through the streets of Branfield in the middle of the night on her hands and knees to speak to the man, she was desperate enough to do it.

Chapter 3

Using the back alley door, Autumn slipped inside the kitchen of the Golden Eagle Inn and slammed straight into a hazy wall of heat. Two massive cookstoves at the end of the room were barren of pots and pans, but the oppressive warmth and remnant smells of boiled mutton and sourdough biscuits that had accumulated during the day's cooking and baking hung heavy in the air. Inhaling to take a breath, more for courage than anything else, she approached the corpulent woman who was on her hands and knees, humming as she scrubbed the grease-splattered floor. "Still working, Matsey?"

When the woman's head bobbed up, a frown quickly turned into a toothy grin. "Still got a few patrons left, but I told Mr. Spakes that it weren't my fault Lena's took to her bed with the fever. He can serve 'em hisself. Fourteen hours 'bout enough to make these old bones too heavy to carry." Glancing toward the alley door, Matsey cocked her head. "What you be doin' comin' in the back? Reverend Briley and Mr. Spakes don't be meetin' in the kitchen! They're probably . . ." Her voice trailed off as she got to her feet, and she took a heaving gulp of air to catch her breath.

"I'm not here to see Norbert. Or Mr. Spakes," Autumn responded, her eyes darting to the door that led to the tavern room. Norbert had not mentioned stopping to see Peirce Spakes, and it made her doubly nervous to know that he was here.

A deep chuckle bubbled out of Matsey's throat. Breasts heaving, she shook her head. "You sure done give the tongues in this town more than enough to wag about. Sure wish I'd been able to see the look on Wilma's face when she found out the minister proposed to you 'stead of her." Brows furrowing, she shook a water-wrinkled finger at Autumn. "Best thing you can do now is get yourself married and outta Branfield. Wilma wouldn't make it easy for you here."

Autumn's resolve flickered briefly as hurtful memories echoed the truth of Matsey's words. *The Tin Lady.* That's what the townspeople called her, as though she had no feelings. No heart . . . or soul. Only Matsey knew how much Autumn had yearned for acceptance and friendship, only to become an object of curiosity and gossip. And only Matsey could help her now.

Autumn moistened her lips. "I need to see Mr. Logan. He may have a position for me."

Matsey's voice lowered to a whispered command. "Girl, you best forget the devilment I see written all over your face. There's no use tryin' to support that chile again all by yourself. Get yourself married and let that foolishness go. You don't know nothin' 'bout this man, John Logan."

Autumn's spine stiffened. "I know what I'm doing. I just need your help."

"Hmmph! You know what the minister would do if he found out you came to see that Logan fella? Not even old Matsey could help you then."

"He's not going to find out. That's why I avoided the

front desk. Can you tell me where Mr. Logan's room is? He's not in the common room, is he?"

Matsey picked up the scrub bucket and waddled toward Autumn, her huge frame blocking the younger woman from taking a single step. "Not the way that man coughs at night. Mr. Spakes would have eleven other guests screamin' and complainin' loud enough to wake the dead. He put him in one of the private rooms upstairs. First room on the left." Eyes softening, she cocked her head, shaking it as she spoke. "You best be careful, Autumn. You know it ain't proper for you to pay call on a man in his room. Miss Wilma's back from the lecture, and she'd clap for joy if she could give Reverend Briley a good reason to cancel the wedding."

With an impatient wave of her hand, Autumn dismissed Matsey's advice. "I just want to speak to Mr. Logan. Privately. I'm need to know if he'll give me a portion of the wages Klerk owed to me, or if he's serious about a position for a tole painter in Ohio."

Matsey plopped the bucket on the floor sending waves of dirty, soap-scummed water over the sides. "You sure you know what you're doin'? Way that man coughs, he won't live long enough to pay wages to nobody."

Autumn sighed.

Matsey shook her head. "What do you want me to do?"

Grinning, Autumn gave her a quick hug. "Just help me get upstairs. Where are the back steps?"

Pointing to her right, Matsey grunted. "That stairway right behind you will lead to the second floor. Can't tell you if he's in or not, though. Had his dinner near two hours ago."

"He was at the lecture, but he should be back by now." Glancing at the stairwell, Autumn chewed on her bottom lip. "Will you . . . will you stay for a while and make sure no one uses the servants' stairs? What I have to say won't take long, and I know you've had a very hard day, but . . ."

Hoisting the half-filled bucket, Matsey ambled over to the foot of the stairs and got down on her hands and knees again. "Sure is one dirty floor. 'Specially right here." She winked. "Take all the time you need. Won't be nobody tempted to walk through the slippery mess I'm gonna make. You just worry 'bout the common stairs. A few of the step-boards creak mighty bad, givin' you some warnin' if someone's comin'. Just you listen real good."

"You're a saint!" Autumn gushed as she started up the stairs.

"First time anyone called me that," Matsey grumbled. "Sure will be the last if anyone finds out I helped you, too. Go on! Get up there before anyone has a mind to have second helpin's 'fore I close up the kitchen."

Gathering her skirts with one hand, Autumn gripped the rickety bannister with the other as she mounted the steep, narrow steps. Without a light or candle to guide her, she felt like she was walking through a thick black cloud. Using her sense of touch, she made her way to the door at the top of the stairs, her breath coming in short, nervous gulps.

Placing her ear against the door, she listened for any tell-tale sounds of movement. Silence. When she opened the door to the hall, she sighed, grateful for the single gaslight that illuminated her view. She chanced a peek up and down the short length of the hallway. Polished to mirror finish, two walnut doors on either side of the walkway reflected the dim light from a gaslit sconce mounted on the wall at the end of the corridor. A clean, but foot-worn carpet runner that ran down the middle of the hall would quiet her steps, but there was no place to hide if anyone should enter the hall before she was inside John Logan's room.

Knowing that the family's quarters were on the other side of the inn, Autumn felt confident that neither Wilma Spakes nor her father would find out that Autumn was here. She tried not to think about Norbert. As long as she could avoid running into a paying guest, who might report her presence to the owner, she should be able to tend to her business and be gone without arousing suspicion or gossip.

Glancing up and down the hall, listening for any sounds that would signal someone's approach from the stairs or departure from one of the rooms, Autumn could barely hear or feel anything other than the loud thumping of her own heart. Leaving the door to the servants' stairs slightly ajar, she tiptoed to the first door on the left. Forming a fist, she raised her hand to knock when a loud crash and a garbled expletive inside the room turned her entire body into a block of ice.

Deep, wheezing sounds, as though someone was gasping for breath, pushed caution aside. Instinctively, she reached for the glass door knob and twisted it. As the door inched open, she took two tentative steps into the room before taking a giant lurch backward.

Bedcover and sheets were twisted into a huge, tangled web at the foot of the bed. A small serving tray, its contents strewn hither and yon, was settled upside down on the floor next to a small nightstand. The brackish contents of an overturned apothecary bottle dribbled onto the already stained carpet, mixing with a quickly spreading puddle of water from a smashed ceramic water pitcher. Eyes wide, she lifted her gaze upward and gaped at the bare-chested man sitting sideways at the head of the bed, his stockinged feet braced on the floor.

John Logan?

She barely recognized him. Beads of sweat coated his

upper body and glistened on tight-muscled flesh. Embarrassed to see a man's body so exposed, she swallowed hard and raised her gaze. A rosy flush erased the arrogant confidence in his features that she had found so irritating and so handsome at the Lyceum.

He cocked his head, anger chalking his blue eyes. "Get . . . out!" he snarled. His vehement order set off another explosion of chest-shaking, breath-snatching coughs. Eyes watering, his hands shook as he tried to reach for the overturned bottle of medicine.

Startled, Autumn defiantly pushed the door closed. Within seconds, she had righted the apothecary bottle and carried it with her as she scanned the littered room for a teaspoon. A sharp tug on the side hem of her apron yanked her to the side, and she toppled into the nightstand, groping wildly with both hands to catch her fall.

Horror overwhelmed surprise as the medicine bottle flew out of her hands and cracked against the wall. Swirling around, she bit back a sharp reprimand the moment she saw the look of utter desolation in his eyes as his gaze locked on the sticky, healing substance that stained the wall.

Lips quivering, he brushed gold-streaked locks of hair back from his face and clutched his throat. His breathing slowed, each shallow intake of air obviously requiring a calculated effort to avoid another attack.

"You need water," she gushed, wondering why she felt guilty for breaking the bottle of medicine he so clearly needed.

He shook his head. "Just . . . just leave. You've done quite enough," he rasped. Closing his eyes, he swallowed repeatedly as though trying to ease a tickle in his throat.

"You need help," she argued as she removed her apron, intending to offer it to him to wipe his brow.

Anger flashed through bloodshot eyes, and his lips curled into a smirk. "Try replacing the medicine you carelessly destroyed."

She tossed her apron at him. "It wasn't my fault! I never would have fallen if you hadn't pulled me off balance! I was trying to find a spoon in this . . . this chaos!"

Wheezing, he deftly used one hand to deflect the apron which fell to the floor. "A spoon! Leave it to a meddling female to insist on proper etiquette in the middle of an emergency. Did it ever occur to you that I might need the medicine badly enough that I could have slugged it from the bottle?" His verbal rampage was powerful, although his voice was barely above a whisper.

"Your didn't have the strength to get to the bottle!"

"Yes I did!"

Conceited, arrogant, ungrateful fool! she thought, her fury building to hurricane proportions. Chest heaving, her hands clenched into fists. "Lord knows you don't deserve my help. I should have let you choke to death instead of letting my sympathy override my better judgment."

"Damn near did," he hoarsed. Sitting up, he swung his trousered legs onto the mattress and leaned back against the thick, wooden headboard. "Now run along and leave me in peace before I tell the righteous Reverend Briley you showed up, uninvited, in my room."

"How . . . how dare you!" she sputtered. "I only came here because I wanted an explanation—"

"Explanation?"

"About what I found out at the lecture tonight."

He snorted. "Get out of here before someone finds out you're here. I have no desire to be run out of town."

The hair on the back of her neck stood on end as fear shivered down her spine. She was taking a risk by remaining unchaperoned in John's room, but the time for pretense was long since past. She swallowed any reticence about propriety at this point. The stakes were just too high. "I need to know . . . that is . . . would you consider paying me a portion of the wages Klerk owed to me?"

Her question hung in the air, and she held her breath.

His clipped answer knocked the wind out of her. "I've done my best to right the wrong that's been done to you. If you're so set on recovering your wages, convince the minister to give you my donation. Or at least some part of it."

Her shoulders slumped. Approaching Norbert and asking him for even one coin that had been contributed to the mission fund was tantamount to inviting disaster. She shook her head, plunging ahead to her second and final option. "Were you really serious about a position for a tole painter in Ohio?" she croaked.

He smiled. "I thought I made that clear earlier," he answered in a normal voice.

"As clear as river mud. I don't have time to waste jousting with words. I need an answer. Now."

He looked away, his cheek twitching. When he turned back to face her, his eyes were solemn. He paused and cleared his throat. "I'm fully prepared to offer you a position in Ohio . . . if you're interested."

Autumn's pulse began to race, dreading the possibility that he was only playing a cruel game. She held her breath as she waited for him to continue.

His eyes narrowed when she lifted one brow. "My offer is real. Very real." He eased out of bed and searched through the clutter on the floor.

Her curiosity peaked when he bent down and pulled something out from underneath the bed. Her heart slammed against her ribs when he handed her a dented tea caddy with a design she had used when she first started work for Eugene Hargrove in Waterbury—before Clayton returned home after a two-year absence with a wife he adored and a baby he treated with indifference. Before Clayton and Trina left their darling little girl with Autumn while they looked for a home where Trina's father, Edsel Cameron, could not find them and force Trina to give in to his demands to let Mellie live with him in New York. Before Clayton and Trina were senselessly and brutally murdered. Before Autumn fled Waterbury with the child who had become the daughter of her heart and lived a lie in Branfield to keep Mellie with her. Before . . .

Suddenly, the secrets she had guarded so carefully shoved to the forefront of her troubles, and icy fingers of fear gripped her heart. If John Logan had been able to trace her to Branfield, so could the man she had successfully eluded for the past eighteen months: Edsel Cameron. "How did you know this was my work?" she whispered as she held out the tea caddy. Her voice cracked in a stalwart attempt to sound more amazed than afraid.

"The tinsmith's mark on the bottom helped," he admitted, "but the pastel colors are as distinctive as the delicate wild flowers you captured so beautifully."

The admiration in his voice was clear, and she ventured to look at him again.

Conceit twinkled back at her. "You can't be unaware of your remarkable talent," he taunted softly as he leaned toward her and reclaimed the tea caddy. He walked across the room and sat it on top of a chest of drawers. "I hope that doesn't mean you'll be tempted to negotiate for a better contract offer than I'm prepared to make."

Blushing, Autumn locked her hands together to keep them from shaking. She looked back at the sorry little tea caddy to avoid his gaze and tried to soften his compliment. "I've never overestimated my skill with the brush or been demanding of my employers. I've simply used my tole painting to earn a respectable living," she responded, carefully choosing her words to avoid sounding overly proud.

"Until now."

Unable to deny her failure, she was just as unwilling to entertain any notion of his offer. She needed time to think and time to convince herself that John Logan's offer was legitimate and he was not a clever agent hired by Edsel Cameron to find Mellie. Unfortunately, time was the one commodity she did not have, and Mellie was too precious to risk losing. "I appreciate your time, Mr. Logan," she said quietly. "I can't accept your proposal. I'm sorry."

"You haven't given it more than a moment's consideration! I've searched half of New England looking for you." He shook his head. "Maybe I shouldn't expect you to understand. It wouldn't make sense to most people. Hell, sometimes it doesn't make any sense to me, either."

Lingering doubt about his sincerity made her cautious. "Why didn't you simply approach me with an offer?"

He stiffened. "I don't know. I suppose after I learned you were being married, I didn't have any hope you'd even give my proposal a second thought. Then I felt guilty for what Klerk had done to you and decided simply to make a donation to Reverend Briley before you both left. I'm sorry. I didn't mean to cause problems for you." His eyes turned a mournful blue. "I guess I was selfish. I know I need you and your talent with the brush to make my venture successful. I didn't want to fail. Not again."

His gentle words and painful honesty assuaged her fear that he was working for Edsel Cameron, although she still felt slighted by John's attempt to manipulate her. "In either case, your motives are unchivalrous and deceitful. Wasn't it enough that you helped Mr. Klerk swindle me out of my wages or . . . or that you caused problems between Norbert and myself?" She trembled as her eyes locked with his penitent blue. "Was it pride or greed?" she whispered. Taking a deep breath, she boldly dared him to break eye contact first.

He did not.

Neither did she.

"Not for gain," he argued, his voice growing cold as he held her gaze. "I have responsibilities to other people who depend on me. I have one last chance to see my dreams become reality. To know the satisfaction of shaping my own future. Maybe I went about it the wrong way, but I thought . . . oh, forget it."

His demeanor shifted, and his voice hardened as though he had inadvertently revealed his own vulnerability. "Despite your talent, you're really no different from any other woman. Marry your beloved Norbert and be happy in your new life. I'll find a way to make the Logan Tin Factory the envy of every tinsmith in New England without you," he said before he grunted with disgust.

Speechless, a thousand questions swirled through Autumn's mind, but she could not deny that she believed him. She understood, in an odd, kindred way, how important his business and his dreams were to him. Hadn't she tried to bury her own dreams for the sake of survival? She softened her expression into a smile. "I think . . . I think I understand why you felt so . . . so driven," she offered shyly, warmed by the unusual camaraderie between them.

He grinned and folded his arms over his chest. "I was hoping you would. Now be an intelligent girl and agree to come to Ohio. We can talk about the terms of your contract later."

He grinned.

The arrogant rakehell grinned!

Shocked by his patriarchal attitude and his sudden reversal in tact and mood, all semblance of propriety flew out of her mind. Did he think she was nothing more than a child who could be easily placated, or a simpering female who could be swayed by a handsome face and a sentimental word or two?

She cleared her throat and spoke out loud in a firm voice that echoed in the room. "Save your two-tongued glibness for someone else, John Logan. I have no intention—"

He sprang from the bed.

Strong hands caught her shoulders in a viselike grip that interrupted her. "Quiet down before someone hears you," he said through clenched teeth.

The whisper of ragged breathing filled the room as she closed her eyes. She struggled against his reprimand, but realized his warning was justly deserved. His hands wrapped around her arms, exuding strength and control, and she concentrated on taking one breath at a time.

When and how his iron grip had melted into a gentle caress was a mystery, but there was no denying the warm sensations he created. She shuddered, realizing for the first time that she was in a very vulnerable position. She was a single woman, alone in a room with a half-clothed man! What had come over her? She blinked her eyes open and held her breath. He actually looked confused. Even penitent.

"I apologize. I didn't mean to upset you," he murmured.

Unable to speak, she pulled free and twisted her hands nervously. Inhaling deeply, she stared at the floor. If John Logan was an agent for Mellie's grandfather, wouldn't he simply have confronted her and forced her to return to New York? Edsel Cameron did not have to resort to elaborate schemes; he had wealth, power, and influence on his side. More than likely, John Logan was exactly who and what he said he was. A man motivated by nothing more than his dreams. Driven and unprincipled, perhaps. But not without a conscience.

Or a soul?

Turning to face him, she licked her lips. "I'm sorry I screamed at you, but you don't have any right to do . . . to do what you've done to me."

Blue eyes deepened into the color of a midnight sky, studded with stars of regret. "You're right. I should have spoken to you honestly about coming to work in Ohio instead of trying to bait you." He paused. "If I had been honest with you from the beginning, maybe . . ."

She gazed deep into his eyes, nearly mesmerized as midnight blue softened into sparkling sapphire. Soft, warm sensations raced through her body. How had she dismissed how dangerously attractive he was?

His lips formed a dazzling smile that made her blush. "Could we start over?"

"I—I'd like that," she stammered as she stepped back, intending to find a safer place from which she could continue their conversation.

He tugged on her hand and held her in place. "You could make a good life in Ohio. For yourself and your daughter."

Mellie.

"I have to know more about the position," she said softly. "I need to think about all the possibilities before I agree to come to Ohio. For me as well as for Mellie." His bare chest glistened in the soft light and lifted slightly with each breath he took. Blushing, she turned away. "Maybe you should get dressed, and we can talk about it."

He chuckled. "You can't think right now?"

I can't think beyond the fact that your hand is wrapped around mine . . . and it feels good.

She turned to face him, frightened as much by her reaction to his hand-hold as the seductive sound of his voice. A sharp rap at the door, however, startled her. Before she could turn around, she heard the door creak open. The rustle of skirts. A sharp intake of breath. A hiss.

"I knew it!"

A familiar voice.

The whole room started to spin, and Autumn dipped her head. She broke John's hold and clutched at her skirts as she turned around in slow motion. Yet her heart was beating so rapidly she felt faint. When she lifted her face to the intruder, misty eyes met blazing censure. She clenched her teeth, vowing not to be intimidated by the young woman who stood in the doorway, arms locked across her chest, foot tapping with agitation. Or was it pious satisfaction?

"Harlot! Reverend Briley will find it impossible to forgive you this time, Autumn Welles!" she ranted.

Chapter 4

Peirce Spakes stormed blindly into the room, nearly colliding with his daughter. "Wilma, don't—" His lips moved soundlessly, twitching as his speech sputtered to a halt. Eyes bulging, the flesh on his flatulent cheeks turned a deep shade of purpled crimson. "Mrs. Welles!" His jaw flapped open.

"Autumn!" Quicker than an echo, Reverend Briley's exclamation rang out as he entered the room. He slammed the door shut behind him.

John scowled back at the astonished faces of the three people who had barged into his room, although their eyes were all locked on Autumn Welles. *Five more minutes.* That's all he needed, and he would have been able to put the hem on his fabricated tale and convinced her to accept his offer. He had read it in her eyes! It was written in her tremulous expression, he was sure of it.

Blast these sanctimonious, interfering dolts!

Attempting to hang on to the last thread in the tattered remnant of the previous moment, he placed one hand on Autumn's shoulder in a show of support. "I'm very grateful to Mrs. Welles. She appeared at an opportune moment," he rasped, exaggerating his sickly state by deliberately making his voice sound hoarse. "I'm afraid this spell was worse than the last. I was choking and gasping for breath. I couldn't reach my medicine." He smiled, gesturing weakly at the apothecary bottle that lay amidst the litter on the carpet.

Wilma sniffed her disbelief, indignantly shrugging her shoulders. "Playing an angel of mercy, she no doubt made the difference between life and death. How fortunate for you that Mrs. Welles just happened by, Mr. Logan."

"Indeed," he responded, wondering if any woman could look as self-righteous as Wilma did at that moment. Or as unattractive. Stick thin, with wiry brows and a beaked nose and dressed in a washed-out gray gown, she looked like a starved opossum.

"Didn't you find it odd that she was here? My father reserves the rooms on this floor for single gentlemen. Ladies are never permitted to venture upstairs."

John cocked one brow. "Then why are *you* here, Miss Spakes?"

She sputtered, her thin lips twitching as she edged closer to her father. "I saw Mrs. Welles go down the alley to the back entrance. She was alone. Naturally, I was curious. I knew Reverend Briley had an appointment to see my father tonight. When I came downstairs and saw that they were alone . . . that Mrs. Welles wasn't with them . . ." She tossed her head. "I felt it was my responsibility to apprise them both of what I had seen." Her chin rose defiantly, and she glared at Autumn. "Unfortunately, my worst fears were confirmed."

Autumn flinched. She smoothed her skirts and walked over to the minister, stopping just a few feet in front of him. "I only came to say goodbye to Matsey."

He swallowed hard, his Adam's apple bobbing up and down the skinny column of his neck. "Matsey is a cook. The kitchen is on the *ground* floor."

Anger flashed through Autumn's voice. "Matsey has been on her feet for over fourteen hours. She's exhausted. I offered to bring Mr. Logan his tray while she finished scrubbing the floor." She pointed to the upside-down serving tray on the carpet. "Mr. Logan was suffering a severe spell. In my haste to help him, I dropped the tray."

"You're not a common serving wench," the minister bristled.

"I—I was only trying to help," Autumn exclaimed, her voice choking. She glanced at the mess on the floor and blushed. Turning her back on her three accusers, she knelt down and retrieved the serving tray. She reached out and picked up a pewter mug and a soiled napkin and plate as well as the cracked apothecary bottle, placing them onto the tray.

Wilma stepped away from her father and shook her finger at Autumn. "Nursing a half-naked man who is not your husband in the privacy of his chambers is scandalous, not angelic," Wilma pronounced, her nose lifting haughtily in the air.

Reverend Briley stepped around Wilma and walked over to Autumn, kicking the broken water pitcher out of his way. The pieces smashed against the night stand, and Autumn cringed. The tray in her hands started to shake. He towered over her as she remained on her knees. Her lips quivering, his white-knuckled fingers tilted her chin up to face him. "I want an explanation, Autumn. Miss Spakes is not exaggerating your lack of decorum."

Peirce Spakes chortled. "There's only one explanation, Reverend. At least to reasonable souls." He pointed to the rumpled bed and Autumn's apron which was lying in a heap on the floor. "It's clear that Mrs. Welles intended to spend her last evening as a widow consorting with Mr. Logan. Fortunately, the poor devil was too sick to pursue indecent and immoral pleasures of the flesh with her. He does look much recovered," he added. "I'd venture to guess that we arrived just before—"

Autumn pulled out of the minister's grasp and stood up to confront Peirce Spakes, rattling the contents of the tray. "How dare you make such an outrageous assumption!"

"Outrageous? Your behavior here tonight defies convention! The Golden Eagle has a reputation to uphold, a reputation I depend on for the livelihood of my family. My patrons are decent, Christian people who demand lodging in a reputable establishment, not a brothel!"

"Hopefully, they're less sanctimonious and judgmental than you are," she spewed as she set the tray on the night stand.

John watched as charges, accusations, and countercharges flew back and forth between Autumn and her accusers like bullets. He observed the action with the concentrated eye of a seasoned general gauging his troop's performance in battle and assessing strategy instead of casualties. Autumn Welles was, after all, the Tin Lady. Whether or not she was dented and scraped during the attack did not matter as long as it resulted in a canceled wedding. Before Autumn arrived unexpectedly tonight, he had decided he had no choice but to interrupt tomorrow's ceremony with some sort of scandalous excuse, which he had yet to conjure up. The only stumbling block he had run into before his coughing spell had been Amelia and how to prevent her from witnessing Autumn's public humiliation. Now that the opportunity to avoid a public spectacle had presented itself, shouldn't he let the others stop the wedding and sidestep any blame?

Admittedly, he much preferred to have Autumn accept his offer and move to Ohio as a result of gentle persuasion, but given the unexpected and bizarre scene now taking place, he had no problem turning the job over to the others.

Verbal bullets ceased to cross the room as the battle crested, and the minister's voice sounded calmer now as he talked to Autumn. They stood in the center of the room while Peirce Spakes and his daughter guarded the door like sentries on watch duty.

The minister's voice suddenly rose from a whisper to a sharp reprimand. "Then you admit you lied about bringing Mr. Logan a tray?"

Autumn looked weary, but not defeated. "Yes. I came here to see Mr. Logan and used the rear entrance to avoid being seen."

"Tell me why, Autumn. Why did you come to see Mr. Logan tonight?"

Autumn squared her shoulders. "I had business to discuss with him."

The minister's eyes narrowed. "You promised—"

"No," she interrupted. "You *ordered* me not to see him or speak to him again on matters of business." Taking a deep breath, she paused and lowered her gaze. "We're not married yet. My discussion with John Logan is my concern. Not yours." She glowered at Wilma beneath lowered lashes as though daring her to intervene, and the young woman had the decency to blush and button her lips.

"Any discussion that concerns you is my business as well," he countered.

She sighed. "Not until we're married. I had to speak to him tonight on a matter that did not concern you. It concerned me. And Mellie."

Wilma flew into the middle of their discussion. "That's probably the first bit of truth that you've woven into the rest of your lies. I overheard your conversation with Mr. Logan just before I knocked. You were discussing Mellie and how you had to be sure . . . about something."

Autumn glared at her. "You were eavesdropping on a private conversation!"

Wilma glared back.

The minister looked like he had just heard the date of his death announced as tomorrow. "Mellie?" He glanced at John with wide, bulging eyes. John merely shrugged his shoulders. Looking back at Autumn, the minister cleared his throat. "I think you'd better explain."

John sat up straight, his eyes locked on Autumn's face. Charges and accusations had crackled like kindling during this whole bizarre episode, and he had caught fleeting glimpses of fire in the woman that transformed her features from plain to extraordinary. Intrigued, he studied her closely now, but that familiar mask of detachment and control had slipped back into place. The minister's command had apparently doused the fire before it had a chance to catch.

Still, he remained curious. For whatever reason, Autumn had apparently not told the minister about trying to recoup part of her wages or pursuing a possible offer of work. John could understand why she would have been reluctant to explain it earlier. But why now?

Shaking her head, Autumn frowned. "What we discussed is private."

"I need more of an explanation than that."

"I don't owe you any more than I've already told you. The issue is settled. Mellie and I—"

"You test my patience and stretch my loyalties," he whined. "I demand to know what connection Mr. Logan has to Mellie!"

John's skin began to crawl. With the tide of battle shifting, placing Mellie directly in the line of fire, he quickly reversed his decision to remain a curious but innocent bystander and donned battle gear. "If I might make a suggestion—"

Reverend Briley cut him off again with a glare and shook his bony finger at Autumn. "Well? Do I get a full explanation now or must I demand one tomorrow in the presence of the congregation?"

Autumn gasped and clutched her throat, and John backed down. For the moment. Jumping to her defense now might make him look like her champion, and he had no desire to spare her any discomfort. Not unless the minister switched his tactics and reversed back to Amelia.

"Public confession is more than justified," Wilma interjected as she charged forward. "For the child as well. Perhaps by questioning her, we might learn the truth. Especially since her mother seems to be set on being so mysterious."

Autumn's face turned ashen. "You can't do that to Mellie!" She tugged on the minister's sleeve. "Promise me you won't put her in front of the entire congregation and question her. She's only five!"

Wilma snorted. "And hopefully too young and innocent to lie. At least not in a church and not with a practiced tongue. Just perhaps, *Widow* Welles, the child might shed some light on other matters as well."

Peirce Spakes nodded, stepping up to place a supportive arm around his daughter's shoulders. "You were a stranger in Branfield when you arrived several years back. We accepted you. Welcomed you and your daughter into our community as upstanding, Christian people. After tonight, however, I wonder . . ." He shook his head. "Perhaps this isn't the first time you've entertained one of my patrons."

"It might explain your rather frequent visits to *Matsey,*" Wilma muttered. "Most widows must remarry quickly, yet you've remained independent for several years. You've enjoyed more freedom than God intended for a woman. Perhaps you abused that privilege, turning to the sheets to supplement your meager wages and using poor Matsey as a cover for your escapades."

"I earned a good living until Zebulon Klerk declared bankruptcy and cheated me," Autumn retorted. "Most widows don't have the skills I do."

Jumping on Autumn's poor choice of words, Wilma snickered. "Skills, indeed. Be honest and confess that you turned to fornication to support yourself! It's better than trying to cover your fall into prostitution and inventing a tale that involves your little girl."

"Leave her out of this!" Autumn sputtered.

"*You* didn't!" Wilma countered. "When the truth about your sordid life is exposed, both you and your fatherless child will be outcasts!" Her eyes glittered with condemnation. "The color of your gown is almost prophetic," she spat.

John cringed, noting that Autumn's faded russet gown looked scarlet in the dim light. Should he intervene? As much as he wanted Autumn to suffer, he never expected Wilma Spakes to launch into such a cruel and vindictive attack that might affect Amelia. Surprisingly, neither Reverend Briley nor her father moved a muscle to stop Wilma, and John wondered how much more Autumn could take before she cracked. Or exploded. Pale and shaken, her bottom lip trembled. Were her eyes glistening with tears of frustration or anger?

Apparently, neither.

Autumn blinked back her tears and turned to Reverend Briley. Her voice was calm and steady, but low. "Am I no better than a Salem witch? Condemned by hysteria if I cry innocent and freed if I admit guilt and beg for forgiveness?"

He took a deep breath. "You need to tell the truth. Nothing more, and not a whisper less."

Peirce Spakes laughed. "The truth? We have only to look around us to see the truth. Judge her by what she tells us? For all we know, Mellie is living proof of her mother's disgrace! The child remembers no father. Ask her!"

Her body trembling, Autumn responded immediately. "She was only three years old when her father died!"

"Was he your husband? Or a paying customer?" Wilma chirped. "How better to protect the child than to move to a new town where no one would ever suspect that the respectable Widow Welles is nothing more than a whore and her darling daughter is a bastard child! That outrageous mop of red hair makes her stand out from the others, but her sin of being illegitimate will brand her for life."

"I've heard enough. Be quiet. All of you!"

Four bodies jumped at John's deep-throated command. He rose from the bed, the muscles in his jaw twitching as he put on his shirt. He clenched his teeth as he tried to contain his fury. It was one thing to sit idly by and let Autumn bear the brunt of such a malicious attack. It was quite another when the venom was directed at his daughter. He may not have been there to protect her in the past, but he was here now. He would never allow anything to hurt her, especially the malicious witch hunt that brewed right in front of his own eyes.

Except for Autumn Welles, he was the only person present who knew exactly why she had moved to Branfield. He was the only one who knew without a doubt that she would not tell them the truth. In the space of a week, he had learned one very important thing about Autumn Welles: She would stop at nothing to protect the child she claimed as her daughter. For that reason alone, she commanded his loyalty and his protection now.

He scanned the faces of her accusers, his gaze finally resting on Autumn. "Tell them."

She shook her head.

He glared at her. Obstinate woman! Was she made of steel instead of tin? Why couldn't she just tell them enough to satisfy their curiosity and settle the issue of why she was in his room? Brown eyes hardened into stony resistance that set up a wall of stubborn will between them.

So be it.

If she would not or could not find the courage to tell the truth, he would command a guerrilla tactic that would bring the battle to a stunning conclusion that guaranteed his own victory.

Waging this battle carried heavy risk, regardless of the outcome. If he lost, his five-year quest would be extended until he could return to Ohio for a court order confirming Amelia's true identity and giving him custody of the child known as Mellie Welles and then travel west to find Autumn and force her to give the child up. If he won, he risked violating the terms of Edsel Cameron's will and losing Amelia's inheritance for her.

He refused to consider defeat; as for victory, he had become profoundly Machiavellian in the past five years. The law served many interests, and if Edsel Cameron could find a legal way to force his dictates, John would use the law, quietly and without any qualm of conscience, to undo what had to be done now.

His mind set on victory, he walked over to the chest of drawers in the far corner of the room and picked up the tea caddy he had shown to Autumn earlier. He carried it back with him, holding it out so that everyone could see the remnants of the fine details painted on its scarred and dented surface. He took a deep breath and quickly improvised. "Autumn painted this for my mother nearly six years ago. I've used it to trace her and the child."

Three sets of eyes narrowed with suspicion, but one set of deep, brown eyes widened with apprehension.

"You're right about one thing, Miss Spakes," he continued, stepping alongside Autumn and putting the tea caddy on the nightstand. "Mellie is not legitimate, and Autumn was never married to Mellie's father. But it wasn't because Autumn lived the life of a harlot."

He heard Autumn's sharp intake of breath and watched a shudder tremble through her entire body.

Reverend Briley, however, was the first to voice the question that lit in the others' faces. "How do you know all this?" he gritted, a nervous tic twitching his cheeks.

John took one look at Autumn's face and clasped her hand. It was cold and rigid and he squeezed it, as much to urge her silent cooperation as to make sure she did not try to escape. He did not blame her for being afraid. Tonight's events had gone beyond any rational explanation; conclusions that were motivated by self-righteousness and jealousy had been reached by giant leaps of imagination. Yet all things considered, he could not take the chance that she might resolve her pitiful situation by simply running off and disappearing. Again. Without warning. Without leaving any trace of where she might have gone.

Amelia.

He cleared his throat and scanned the faces that stared at him with expressions that were expectant, if not impatient. His shallow breathing was the only sound in the room. He took a deep breath to clear his head as a swell of emotion, stored deep within his spirit for the past five years, carried loving memories to the surface that washed over him and made it difficult to breath. His heart began to pound.

"I know this," he began, "because I am Mellie's father."

Chapter 5

John's outrageous lie ripped through Autumn's entire being with the force of a lightening bolt. Her knees buckling, only the pressure of his hand helped her remain on her feet. The room began to spin. Was he crazy? Or dazed from his coughing spell? He had said fewer than ten words during this whole fiasco, yet when he finally decided to speak out, he uttered words that literally stole her breath away.

Through lowered lashes, she saw that she was not the only one taken by surprise with John's shocking, ludicrous announcement. Wilma wore a smug expression, while her father had a look of total stupefication on his face. Autumn avoided looking at Norbert, and glanced up at John instead. Head back, jaw set, his eyes were shuttered into two indigo rocks of veracity.

Challenged by the sheer power and strength of will in his expression, she stiffened her spine and set her shoulders. She did not need anyone, especially John Logan, to further tarnish her honor when the charges against her were so blatantly false and her accusers so quick to accept his word and judge her guilty.

"You're lying," she said irritably as she pulled her

hand out of his. "Mellie's father is dead. I don't have to listen to—"

Reverend Briley cut her off. "Let the man speak." His expression hard, she was rooted in place as he nodded to John. "Continue."

John's demeanor instantly shifted from authoritative to meek. Shoulders slightly slumped, he gazed at Autumn. He smiled, a slow, heart-melting smile that triggered apprehension in every bone in her body. What could he possibly say now that would not make matters worse for her? Why did he present himself as a partner to her alleged debauchery? His behavior was more than just meddlesome and interfering. It was outrageous!

Norbert's, too, she decided the minute she caught his self-righteous expression. She had the right to defend herself or leave the room if she chose to, but neither one of them acted like they even gave a thought to that possibility. They were acting like children instead of grown men, each fighting over a prize . . . a prize that just happened to be her! She repressed the urge to lash out and chastise them both for their cavalier attitudes, realizing that neither one of them would be likely to pay her any heed.

The die was cast.

She would let them both square off like two boys in the shadow of the schoolhouse. In the midst of the fray, when they were too busy to notice, she would find a way to slip past Peirce Spakes and Wilma, get home to Mellie, and disappear, leaving them all outwitted!

John began to cough, breaking her current train of thought. When he recovered, he claimed center stage for himself and shocked her even further into disbelief. "Autumn and I lived in Waterbury. We were betrothed. And very much in love." His voice grew wistful as he turned towards her. "I loved you then. I love you now,

Autumn, and I won't let you take all the blame. It wasn't your fault. It was mine."

He should be on the stage in New York!

She fumed as she looked past him at the rapt faces of his audience of three and he continued his performance. Rooted in place, they were shoulder to shoulder, like patrons in the front row of a theater, observing John as though he were about to deliver crucial lines of dialogue at the climax of a dramatic play. Drama . . . or tragedy? She could barely wait to hear the rest of his scripted words, hoping for an opportunity to reveal him as a consummate master of deception before she left them all in a hasty but dramatic exit that would rival the dreams of every stage actress in New York.

She listened closely as he continued.

"I'm a Yankee peddler by trade. When I left Waterbury over five years ago to take to my route, Autumn and I planned to be married in early September when I returned."

He paused and turned to look straight at the minister. "I didn't come back to Waterbury. I—I stayed in New York City after the usual gathering and fell into a life of . . ." He dipped his head and swiped at his eyes. "Drink claimed the next two years. When I finally came to my senses, it was too late. Autumn had disappeared. I've . . . I've been searching for her ever since."

His voice grew distant. "I searched for Autumn and the child she carried when she left Waterbury. Every town. Every village and hamlet. Do you know what that did to me? To know I fathered a child without benefit of marriage, branding the woman I loved desperately a . . . a . . ." Looking sheepish, John smiled. "I saw Mellie on her way home from school, and I recognized her immediately. She's the image of my . . . my mother." His eyes misted. "She passed away without ever seeing her grandchild." His voice cracked. "To imagine my child ostracized as a bastard? I couldn't find Autumn to beg for forgiveness or to plead for a second chance and make things right and whole again. I never stopped looking. Even when I became ill, I promised myself that I would never give up. I made a pact with God. If He led me to my family, I would never again stray from the path of righteousness." He sighed, his expression sorrowful enough to elicit a sigh of understanding from Wilma. "I never thought Autumn would refuse me."

His eloquent confession stung the room with the force of a Shakespearean soliloquy. Autumn's hands formed into fists and her knees locked. She had the powerful urge to kick him in the shins before he added yet another layer of preposterous lies to his tale. A frightful alarm, fueled by the several facts he offered about her background in Waterbury, however, sent her heartbeat galloping and stilled her vengeful instincts. He knew too much about her to be improvising his dialogue. How did he learn all this? More to the point, why? Just to find her and hire her for his factory?

As much as she wanted to scream out the questions that plagued her, she forced herself to hold silent. Rather than interrupt him, she resolved to let him continue, if only to find out how much more he really knew before she made good on her plans to flee from this charade.

Norbert lifted one bushy brow. "Did you and Mrs. Welles discuss this earlier at the Lyceum?"

John nodded. "I begged her to marry me. I have a new life waiting for us in Ohio. I purchased Klerk's tinware as an investment . . . and to prove to her that I was sincere."

Wilma's eyes narrowed with suspicion. "Why didn't you simply go to her home and speak to her when you first arrived?"

"I couldn't properly pay call on Autumn. I hurt her deeply once before. I couldn't risk her reputation, but I could get her attention by purchasing Klerk's tinware. When I learned of her betrothal to the minister, I knew I had to act quickly. I tried to talk to her at the Lyceum. I just had to convince her to believe me, even if it meant incurring her wrath for turning her wages into a donation for the church." He smiled at Autumn. "I counted on your temper and that streak of independence that's fused to your backbone to bring you here tonight."

Autumn clenched her teeth, unwilling to utter a single word which might be construed as testimony that would reinforce his farcical tale. *Temper? You haven't seen my temper yet!*

John looked at the minister again, shaking his head. "Autumn came here tonight and refused me again. Wilma must have heard the end of our conversation when I pleaded with Autumn to reconsider. For Mellie's sake. I guess I can't blame Autumn for saying no. She's found a husband who is trustworthy, honest, and above reproach." His voice lowered to a whisper. "She's found you."

Pride flashed through the minister's expression before it hardened into disappointment when he looked at her. "Autumn? Is it true? Did you lie to me about your widowhood?"

Despite her best efforts to remain calm and coolly detached from the sheer madness that surrounded her, a warm, guilty flush rose up her neck, warming her cheeks. If she labeled John a liar and told the whole truth, what then? Norbert would do more than break their betrothal. He would insist that Mellie be returned to her grandfather, and Peirce Spakes would make sure that Edsel Cameron was notified even if Norbert did not.

In either case, she would lose Mellie, and Autumn

knew it was a price far too high to pay to salvage her own reputation, particularly since she could offer no proof of her alleged marriage. She stared hard at the floor. What about John? Had she been too quick to dismiss the idea that he was working for Edsel Cameron? Probably not, or now he would have simply told them all that he had been hired by Cameron to trace Mellie. More logically John had concocted a tale that would give Autumn no choice but to go to Ohio.

He must be desperate to go to such lengths. Was he really so demented by his own ambition that he would force Autumn to marry him in order to salvage his dream? She swallowed hard and looked up, but Norbert did not give her a chance to voice an answer.

He removed his spectacles to mop his face and brow. "It seems that tonight's lecture and discussion were ordained by God to prevent a gross mistake tomorrow. On my part and yours, Autumn. Your sins. Mr. Logan's sins. Mine. They're all the same. Some glaring, some hidden in the deep recesses of our souls."

Wilma's high-pitched voice rang out. "You're blameless," she squeaked as she approached the minister. "You're the sacrificial lamb in this twisted, sorry little affair!"

He replaced his spectacles and shook his head. "I knew that marrying Mrs. Welles was a mistake, but I refused to listen to God's voice. I should have a wife who will be as dedicated to His work as I am, as willing to sacrifice for others as need be. Autumn is far too headstrong and independent, but my flesh was weak. Lured by her female charms, I acted too rashly, and I was too proud to admit that I had been wrong and break our betrothal. God help me," he whispered. "I must do so now."

Autumn's patience, flowing like sand through an hourglass, finally ran out. There had never been a time in her life when any man had lived up to her expectations. Not her father or her brother. Not either of her two employers. And especially not Norbert. Once again, she was left to her own devices to survive. Could she trust John Logan? Not until the sun froze. "I'm leaving," she announced, picking up her skirts. She took two steps before Wilma blocked her path.

"Step aside," Autumn warned.

"Where do you think you're going?"

"Home. Now get out of my way."

"Really?" Wilma snickered as she braced her feet. "And when tomorrow dawns, what will you do? Canceling the wedding will be scandal enough, but when the whole community learns that your life here has been one huge lie, that Mellie is a *bastard* child, what will you do then?"

Autumn shook from head to toe when she realized that her departure only added credence to John's outrageous assertions. Everyone in the room believed him as surely as they believed every word in the Bible, and she had no doubt that if she refused to marry John, they would take Mellie away from her and give the little girl to John.

Already charged and convicted, she relinquished any hope of vindication and claimed the right to vent her anger. "You'll make sure they know, won't you? Will you stitch a scarlet letter for my cloak? What about Mellie? Are you self-righteous and spiteful enough to make her wear one, too?"

Wilma's father moved to stand protectively by his daughter's side. John edged closer to Autumn, taking her hand and tilting her face to his. "You can't let that happen. Mellie will spend the rest of her life reeling from cruelty and prejudice."

"The sins of the *father,*" she spat, vowing that John would not be spared the humiliation heaped on her and an innocent child. "I've taken care of Mellie by myself before. I'll find a way to do it again."

Reverend Briley placed his hand on Autumn's shoulder. "To err is human, to forgive—"

"Don't!" she bristled, shoving his hand away. "Your constant, holier-than-thou platitudes choke me. They always have."

"You have an important decision to make," he said quietly. "Will you accept Mr. Logan's proposal and right the injustice and sin you've committed? Or will you let your anger and bitterness destroy your child and damn both your souls?"

Autumn gulped back a hasty retort. *Decision? That implies I have a choice.* Her head pounded with the galling realization that Norbert was right. Even if she escaped with Mellie, miraculously finding funds to leave, the scandal would reach them. Eventually. The tin community was spread out, but sooner or later, one Yankee peddler or another would carry this tale of shame straight to her hearth. If Peirce Spakes did not make sure of it, Wilma would.

"What will it be?" John urged softly. "Will you give me a second chance? Will you let me know my daughter? Provide for her? Love her?" His voice trailed off into a plaintive plea. "Help me to right the wrong I've committed."

Autumn stared at him. The light behind him cast a luminous, pious aura around his head, and the illusion made her tremble. Righteousness was truth and beauty. His disquieting image made her furious. While physically attractive, John Logan had a wretched, conniving heart. He was willing to lie and claim Mellie as his child, and marry Autumn, saving them both with a monstrous fabrication . . . to salvage his dreams?

Her earlier assessment of him galled her. A soul?

He did not have one. He had traded it for a tin factory in Ohio.

The distance between Connecticut and Ohio stretched before her like a crooked road to safety. Far enough away to assure that scandal would never find them. But then, neither would Edsel Cameron. She chewed on her lower lip, contemplating the possibilities. While the ultimate solution exacerbated her, she quickly recognized her one last opportunity to keep Mellie safe from her grandfather. Relief, in the form of a single tear, trickled down her cheek.

The ever faithful shadow of sadness descended over her dreams.

She nodded, and within moments, a bustle of activity filled the room. In a trance, she watched Wilma restore the bed to order while her father excused himself long enough to retrieve the minister's Bible. Norbert carefully picked up the pieces of the broken pitcher while John donned a waistcoat and freshened his appearance. Before she realized the full import of her decision, she was exchanging wedding vows.

With John Logan.

Standing tall and solemn beside her, he turned his body slightly so that he could face her. He repeated the words that would bind him to her, although her heart was pounding in her head, and she caught only fragments of his pledge, which faded into a faint echo. "I, John Logan, take thee, Autumn Welles . . ."

His voice, deep and steady. His words crisp. But his eyes! Intense blue panes of glass, like windows to his soul, cracked with a deep pain that quickly changed to stoic determination before a curtain of detachment closed his emotions to her scrutiny.

"I, Autumn Welles, take thee . . ." As she listened to her own words, a shadow passed over her as the seeds of a dream that lay fallow in her heart forever fluttered away in the breeze of her despair. Overwhelming sadness consumed her. She would probably never find a true soulmate, a man who would love her with all her faults and with all her strengths. An equal partner who would share life's blessings and help carry its burdens.

It was hard to let go of her dreams when she had fought for so long to keep them alive. Admirers had stayed distant while she cared for her ailing father, but still she had had her dream. After his death, she took on the responsibility of caring for Mellie; suitors retreated even further when they learned that she was not willing to plop Mellie back into the arms of her parents—parents who never stayed home long enough to get to know and love their own child!

Mellie.

Tears blurred Autumn's vision as she remembered the day Clayton and Trina brought Mellie home with them. Barely seven months old, the infant stole Autumn's heart the moment she saw her. Fretful and thin, the baby soon began to thrive, although Clayton and Trina could not claim credit for the change.

Autumn's accepted this child as her own, body and soul. She rocked her. Cuddled and spoiled her. And when the baby woke repeatedly when she was teething, it was Autumn who made sure the little one had her teething beads to soothe her. It was Autumn who clapped with delight when Mellie took her first steps. And it was Autumn whom Mellie called Mama.

Autumn never understood how Clayton and Trina could have been so detached from their only child. The intensity of their infatuation with one another left no room in their lives for anyone else, even their own child. Autumn's devotion to the child had cost her several opportunities to be courted, but she did not consider any of the men seriously. She clung to her dream of one day falling in love and she kept it alive, despite the unlikely odds it would ever come true. Protecting it. Immersing herself in her painting. Expressing it in her artistry.

Grief for a dream lost forever consumed her. ". . . Until death do us part," she murmured as cued, realizing that Norbert, ironically, was conducting the improvised and hastily-conducted ceremony. No church candles, formal words, or close friends. Her accusers as witnesses. No ring on her finger. A man she hardly knew by her side.

"Since both parties are free from impediment, by the powers vested in me as a minister of the Word, I pronounce you husband and wife."

With those words, Autumn's dream took flight on the wings of Fate and faded into the horizon, leaving in its wake an emptiness that transformed into a rebelliousness that fought back against her despair.

Husband and wife? She wanted to gag. Liar and co-conspirator, perhaps. But husband and wife?

Never.

Marriage to John Logan was pure and utter nonsense.

A travesty of commitment, devotion, and love.

Love for Autumn conjured up only one image: sparkling turquoise eyes and a mane of red curls.

Mellie!

She had failed her own daughter and given her a swindler for a father.

John's earlier plea echoed in her mind: *"Give me a second chance."*

She swallowed hard, envisioning the marriage bed that awaited her. It would be no bed of roses, she vowed. The only second chance John Logan would get from her would be the opportunity to pay her wages and set her free, or spend from here to Ohio picking thorns out of his flesh!

Chapter 6

John jammed the door bolt into place, snapping Autumn out of the reverie that had turned the past hour into a surreal vision. The man in front of her, however, was no dream. His powerful, masculine presence filled the room. Absolutely and completely.

"Could have saved us both a lot of trouble if I'd remembered to do that earlier," he mumbled as he walked past her to the bed.

Autumn whirled around to follow on his heels. "How kind of you to accept some responsibility for what just happened, unless you're insinuating that this was all my fault."

He ignored her, bending down to pull a worn travel bag from beneath the bed. "I'm not insinuating anything. The fact is, none of this would have happened if you hadn't barged into my room tonight. Can you move aside?"

She stepped back as he placed the travel bag on the bed and walked over to the dresser. Disgusted with herself for obeying his offhanded command, she exploded. "Fact? Or fantasy? Based on the incredible fiction that poured out of your mouth tonight, you haven't the ability to tell the difference between the two. You've missed your calling. You'd make a marvelous novelist. Better yet," she taunted, "you really should try your hand at the stage."

"Look, Tin Lady," he grumbled as he walked back and forth between the dresser and the bed, filling the travel bag. "I didn't invite you here tonight. If you'd been able to curb your impetuousness, you'd be safe at home dreaming about your wedding to the honorable Reverend Briley."

"Instead," he continued as he inspected the cracked apothecary bottle and tossed it aside, "the Tin Lady will spend the rest of the night traveling the turnpike heading west to Ohio." The last thing he packed was the tea caddy before he slammed the travel bag closed and belted it securely.

Stunned momentarily by his use of the nickname she had heard townspeople use for her only when they thought she was out of earshot, she was doubly hurt that he would fling it at her without batting an eye. She did not dare hope he would apologize for calling her the Tin Lady, but he should. "Don't wager on it," she sputtered, wishing he would stand still long enough to really listen to her. "I'm going home to Mellie. I'll find a way to undo this . . . this mockery of a marriage in the morning."

"Fine," he countered. "Which lawyer would you like to consult? Wilma's uncle, Malcolm Spakes? Or perhaps—" When she sniffed, he shrugged his shoulders. "There's also the matter of paying the legal fees."

She cocked her head. "You forced this marriage. It's your obligation—"

"Forget it."

"I can't!"

Scowling, he carried the travel bag over to the door and dropped it onto the floor. With three long strides, he walked back to her and took her by the arm. "You still don't want to admit you made a mistake you can't fix yourself, do you?"

Shaking free, she stared at him, wishing she had a stool to stand on so she could deny him the smallest advantage. She stood on tiptoe. "My only mistake was trying to help you."

He ran his fingers through his hair. "There's no time to debate how it happened. It did. In a few hours, when the dew evaporates in the first rays of the sun, Wilma will have half the town drooling for every glistening drop of evil gossip. By nine o'clock, those who haven't heard the news will be gathered at the church for a wedding that isn't going to take place. Reverend Briley, no doubt, will use the opportunity to give a stirring sermon."

His eyes narrowed as he bent forward slightly, and she dropped back onto the soles of her feet. "Which parable do you think he'll choose?" His lips twisted into a sardonic smile. "It won't be about casting the first stone. That's a wager I'd stake my life on."

Gulping, Autumn licked her lips. "I can leave with Mellie on the morning stage at five o'clock. I'll head north to find a new position."

"What will you use for fare?"

"You . . . you could give me my wages."

He rolled his eyes. "You have an annoying habit of bringing up subjects already discussed and settled. Why is it that you can't seem to take no for an answer?" In the blink of an eye, his expression hardened into granite. "And just in case you have somehow overlooked the rather dramatic conclusion to this debacle of an evening, you can't leave with Mellie to go anywhere. Not without my permission. I'm your husband now."

"I don't want a husband!"

"You should have voiced your complaint when you had the chance," he countered, his eyes glittering with curiosity. "In fact, you had several chances to avoid marrying me. Why didn't you just tell Reverend Briley about the position I offered to you in Ohio?"

"It was none of his business!"

He edged closer, and she could feel his breath fan her face when he tipped his head down to stare into her eyes. "What about your late husband? Why didn't you stop me, invoke his name and offer to provide proof that you were really married to Mellie's father?"

Uninvited, tears smarted her lids, and she bit the soft underside of her lower lip as she and John squared off. The unspoken ghost of her past stepped between them.

She shivered. She could not trust John with the truth. She had never trusted anyone enough to share her secret. Not even Matsey and certainly not Norbert. Why should she put her faith in John Logan? Based on what she knew about him now, he would probably be happy to wrap Mellie in velvet with a garland of silk ribbons and deliver her to Edsel Cameron if John ever found out how badly her grandfather wanted her. Cameron could afford to pay a reward handsome enough to finance the dreams of half of Branfield, let alone a fledgling tin factory in Ohio. The reward would tempt any man to sell his soul, and since John Logan had already done that, she'd rather trust a snake!

Eyes locked into a stand off, John's gaze intensified. "Well? I'm curious, *Mrs. Logan.* I think I can claim the right to know about this mystery first husband of yours." He cocked his head. "Did you have a husband, or was Wilma closer to the truth?"

Quickly choosing martyrdom as a lesser risk than being honest, Autumn locked her lips together and froze in place, her body as rigid as a glacier. His brows lifted, then he walked a deliberate circle around her, hands clasped behind his back. When he returned to face her, he shrugged. "Frozen silent. By stubborn independence or the truth?"

She stared over his shoulder at the stained wall behind the night stand, refusing to meet his censuring gaze or respond to his question.

"Stubborn little fool," he taunted. "You can't bear to be held accountable to anyone, can you?"

Disbelief melted the outer edge of her frigid shell. Her lips twisted into a sad smile. He was a greater fool than she thought possible. Then again, most men in Branfield found it easier to blame a woman's behavior on a fickle nature rather than take the time to really understand her.

It was not entirely their fault, she admitted reluctantly as she looked at her own life. She enjoyed a certain amount of distance between herself and other people. It was easier and safer that way. For her and for Mellie.

Safety.

His ridiculous accusation granted her that.

Playing on his assessment of her as a stubborn, independent woman would be wiser than trying to explain her motives. She wrapped herself in his assumption to protect herself from his unending questions. What other choice did she have? "You wouldn't understand," she whispered, praying he would fall victim to her ruse. "It's not easy being a woman and having a man dictate your every move." She sighed. "Every thought, every decision, questioned and settled to suit him."

"Yet you chose to marry and subject yourself to a husband's authority," he murmured.

She nodded. "For Mellie."

His eyes widened, and she felt his gaze as it penetrated to the depths of her soul. Shifting her weight from one foot to the other, she toyed with her hands as beads of perspiration formed on her upper lip.

"For Mellie," he repeated, his words as soft as the

first breeze of summer. "The lioness protecting her cub."

"And you?" she murmured, stepping back to distance herself from his commanding presence. "Why did you enter the fray and take the blame for my alleged sin?" She sighed. "Chivalry hardly seems likely or reasonable. Compassion? You're too calculating to let emotion sway you. Let's think about this," she ventured as she began to pace the room. "If not chivalry or compassion, it must have been your innate sense of fair play. Three saints pitted against one sinner pricked your conscience."

Swirling around to face him, she cocked her head and placed a sweet grin on her face. "Dear me, it couldn't be for your own self-interest, could it?"

Her grin turned upside down, and she planted both hands on her hips as she cast aside the role of helpless female. "You conniving scoundrel! You added extra wood to the fire beneath their cauldron of accusations to make sure of only one thing: to guarantee that the only choice I would have would be to go to Ohio."

He grinned. A slow, aggravating, blood-boiling grin. "It worked."

"What kind of man are you?" she spewed, dangerously close to losing the last ounce of dignity she had left and charging at him. "You'd probably marry the devil to get your own way."

"Or a witch," he teased, his grin deepening.

She stomped her foot. "This isn't funny! For mercy's sake, we're . . . we're married!" Unbidden, her eyes darted to the bed, and she blushed.

"Don't worry," he cautioned as he opened the door and waved his arm in a gallant gesture. "I've packed our marriage certificate with my papers. Even though we have to wait until we reach Ohio, I intend to file for an annulment as soon as we arrive."

Autumn frowned. "Why can't you file for it the minute we reach the next town?"

An odd look covered his face. "Do you really think word wouldn't travel straight back to Branfield? Add that tidbit of gossip to tonight's scandal with the fact that you'd be traveling with me without benefit of marriage and you've almost guaranteed a scandal that would make Hawthorne's heroine look angelic. The towns from here to Ohio are hot beds of gossip and our stops would be difficult . . . even unpleasant."

He shook his head. "Look, Autumn. I don't want this marriage any more than you do, but realistically, it makes our journey to Ohio less . . . less complicated."

She chewed on her lower lip. "I'm not sure. . . ."

He chuckled. "Don't worry. Your virtuous body will remain untouched. I've no desire to permanently chain myself to a woman as headstrong and foolish as you are. This is a business arrangement. Plain and simple."

"This marriage is a mistake!"

His face grew solemn. Pain flashed through his eyes before he shuttered his emotions. He picked up the travel bag and glared at her. "You're wrong. I never make the same mistake twice."

John opened the door to Autumn's home for the second time, stepping aside to let her enter first. After forcing her to stay with him while he carried his travel bag to the livery and loaded it into the wagon, he also demanded her company as they walked back to get Autumn's trunk, returned to the livery to store it on the wagon, and then came back for Amelia.

At this point, he was sure that Autumn was on the verge of physical collapse. Her shoulders slumped, she was nearly asleep on her feet. Docile and submissive, she was a ghost of her former self, and it occurred to him that the Tin Lady was really human after all. Still, he had no choice but to force her to stay with him as he loaded the wagon, he told himself as she wordlessly passed by him.

He shoved aside his guilt. Given the slightest opportunity, she would have taken flight with Mellie, and he would have had to renew his search. Five years was long enough!

He stood to the side as Autumn whispered her thanks to a young Negro woman who had been watching Amelia and ushered the girl past him. He closed the door, careful to keep noise to a minimum. Autumn stood at the door to Amelia's bedroom, her hand poised on the door knob. "The outside stairs are steep. You might drop her," he warned, taking Autumn by the shoulders and leading her over to a rocking chair. "Sit here. I'll get Amelia. I can carry her easier than you can."

Easing back into the chair, Autumn nodded. "The night air is chilly. Wrap her tightly in her quilt. And don't forget Woolly Lamb. She usually has it clutched in her hand, but sometimes . . ." Her eyes misted. "You may have to look for it."

John stared at her, caught off guard by the emotion that gentled her features. He turned away and walked toward Amelia's room. How could she think about wasting precious time looking for something as inconsequential as a toy animal when dawn was less than an hour away? He had to have them safely out of Branfield before the warblings of the birds woke the earliest risers. There was no way he would chance even one cruel remark hurled at them as they left—taunts that would echo in Amelia's innocent mind, confuse her, and make her resent him.

He opened the door and paused to survey the room. Light from the other room cast an eerie glow to the room over his shoulder, and his frame blocked some of the light. He waited for his eyesight to adjust and shook his head when it did. Though orderly, there was little about the room that inspired warmth. A small iron cot. A single wooden chair. One uncurtained window.

The bedclothes stirred, and his eyes riveted on the little mound in the center of the bed. Heart pounding, he tiptoed to the bed and looked down at Amelia. His daughter. His beloved child was only inches away from him! A mass of curls covered her face, and he swept them away, his fingers brushing her baby-soft cheeks. Transformed by the miracle of finally being reunited with his daughter, he held his breath, studying every feature on her little face. His body tingled, anticipating the opportunity to hold his daughter in his arms for the first time since she was an infant.

Hoping that Autumn did not exaggerate when she said that Amelia slept soundly enough to be moved without waking up, he bent and wrapped the quilt around her. When the single sheet caught in the action, he dismissed any thoughts about trying to untangle it.

His hands shook as he placed them beneath the sleeping child and scooped her into his arms. Stirring briefly, she curled into his embrace, her face resting on the side of his neck, her lips caressing his flesh. He felt a surge of love, unbounded joy. They took his breath away, and he stood perfectly still, enjoying the wondrous feel of her little body against his own. Their hearts practically beat in unison, and he smiled.

He felt whole again.

For the first time in five years.

He cradled Amelia tenderly in his arms and made his way back to the outer room. Autumn waited for him, anxiously peering at the child as soon as he reached her. Tucking the quilt tighter around Mellie's form, she folded a flap of fabric over the child's face, leaving a pocket of air between quilt and skin. "It's not good for her to breathe in the night air," she explained. "Did you find the lamb?"

He shook his head. "I forgot to look. It's not important. We have to leave."

Ignoring his order, she opened the makeshift cocoon, her expression quickly turning from consternation to relief. "It's tucked in her hand," she whispered.

"Is there anything else?" he gritted, trying not to lose his temper. "A favorite dish you'd like to pack? A trinket you've forgotten?"

Her eyes widened. "My paints and brushes!" Swirling around, she walked over to the window and lifted up two wicker baskets set below it. When she turned around, her face was more animated that he had seen for the past hour. "Everything else is packed in the trunk."

"Then we're wasting time," he muttered, anxious to get Amelia and Autumn to the wagon and leave.

They walked side by side down the dark and silent streets of Branfield. Moonlight, clear and beckoning, guided their way past blackened windows in silent cottages. The main street, bedecked with shops and several taverns, slept as deeply as the residential area, although it would awaken soon. Unfortunately, the livery was located at the far western end of town, and Autumn seemed to grow wearier and wearier with every step.

But to his surprise, Autumn was able to keep pace with him, although she had to take three steps for his every two and kept shifting her precious baskets from one hand to the other. She also had followed every order he had given her. Admittedly, he realized that she was merely overwrought and tired, and he could expect her stubborn nature to be restored by morning.

When they finally reached the livery, John had to admit that the thought of putting Amelia down and getting a few hours sleep was sorely tempting.

Gritting his teeth, he led Autumn to the peddler's wagon. It was a tall, fully-enclosed vehicle with a driver's box in the front. He nodded with his head. "Take her," he whispered. Autumn set her baskets down, and he gently transferred Amelia into yet another human cradle. He closed the door to the livery and lit a lantern. As the mantle caught, flickering waves of light cast a harsh luminance to the interior. Lowering the flame, he dimmed the light to twilight.

Looking up, his pulse began to race. Autumn's face, serene and loving, lay on his daughter's cheek as she hummed a soft, comforting melody. He swallowed back a lump of guilt. Obviously, the woman had done much more than just provide for Amelia for the past few years. She had devoted herself to the child, made sure she received an education, and took her to church. Autumn Welles was the antithesis of the frivolous, self-centered woman who had given birth to Amelia, and he admitted that Autumn deserved the courtesy of a civil tongue and fewer taunts.

Fool! She stole your child! When Trina and Clayton died, she should have sent the child back to you. Instead, she hid her away in a remote western Connecticut town, claiming the love that belonged to you. You're Amelia's father. Autumn Welles had no right to deny you a place in Amelia's life!

Bitterness replaced guilt, and he hardened his heart against the madonna image Autumn brought to life. Walking over to the wagon, he dropped the hinged back half-wall, rolled up the canvas flap that covered the top half, and secured it. He set the lantern closer to light the interior. The tin peddler's wagon, in which Klerk had hidden his store of tinware, had been easily converted into a vehicle that would accommodate their needs during the three-hundred-mile journey to Ohio. While the wagon normally stored up to a ton of tinware, John had purchased less than half that amount from Klerk. It sat boxed and stored in the front of the enclosed wagon. He had tied ropes from one side of the wagon to the other to prevent the cargo from shifting. The rest of the wagon bed was lined with blankets and several pillows, making an acceptable bed for sleeping.

"Bring her here," he whispered.

Autumn edged toward him slowly, her face skewing into a quizzical expression. "Must we travel at night?"

He lifted his daughter into his arms and nodded for Autumn to climb inside. "We've little choice. Careful," he urged as her skirt caught beneath her knees when she started to climb into the wagon. Once she was inside, he handed Amelia to her. "I've got provisions set aside for the journey," he murmured as he watched her settle the little girl at the far end of the makeshift bed. She placed a pillow under Mellie's head and covered her with another blanket. He put Autumn's baskets into her trunk, closed the back wall and latched it securely before pointing to a narrow box with a lid. "The outside storage compartments contain supplies for the horses and emergency repairs, but I put a supply of goods you might need in there."

He lifted the lid, waving his hand along the contents. "Water. Cider. A tin of biscuits and dried beef. I didn't know what Amelia liked, so I had to guess. We'll take most of our meals at the inns and taverns along the way, but I thought . . . since she's a child . . . she might get hungry before it's time to stop."

Autumn looked at him oddly, and he suddenly felt awkward, resenting the way he had fumbled for words. Did she think he was a total cad, unwilling to accommodate either her needs or the child's?

"Mellie likes cider," she whispered before confusion clouded her face. "May I . . . I'd like to stay with her."

Her simple request touched him and softened his

heart. Alarmed by feelings too quick to resurrect on their own, his voice grew gruff. "Do you think I want you alongside me on the driver's seat? Given the hour, I doubt anyone would notice, but I don't want to chance it. It's best if it appears that I'm leaving alone. Miss Spakes will embroider the details later, but I'd rather not give her any extra credence."

She flinched, his verbal rebuke stinging her cheeks crimson. Untying the canvas drop cloth that stored along the top frame of the back opening, he paused before dropping it into place. "This should help keep out drafts of cold air, and the glare of the sun when it comes up. Sleep well, *Mrs. Logan.*"

As the canvas fell, curtaining the interior of the wagon from light, Autumn curled into a ball alongside her daughter and snuggled close to her. Bone-tired and emotionally exhausted, she welcomed the chance to close her eyes and rest her bruised spirit. She would have been able to sleep on a bed of chopped ice, but reluctantly acknowledged that the travel bed John had fashioned for them was almost as comfortable as her bed at home.

Home.

The word conjured up several images that she reviewed as though they were stored on pages in a scrapbook. She thought of the small but sturdy saltbox in Waterbury where she grew up, tended her father in his sickbed, and welcomed Mellie into her life. The flight to Branfield added two more homes. The first, a tiny, one-room cabin; the second, the dwelling over the tailor's shop. As dissimilar in appearance as they were in location, almost every home she had ever lived in had been the result of her own labor, her carefully-developed skill with the brush that enabled her to be self-sufficient and independent.

All of her homes had one other thing in common,

however. They had all been filled with love, love that she shared with the little girl who now slept through yet another move. She sighed, wrapping her arms around Mellie, enjoying the feel of her tiny body and the sound of her breathing. Mellie was flesh and blood, all Autumn had left of her family. She loved her so!

As the wagon jostled into motion, Autumn tried to let it rock her toward sleep. Her thoughts, however, raced ahead to life in Comfort Bend, Ohio. Another town. Another set of people to meet and know and hide the truth from. Would life in Ohio be like finding the pot of gold at the end of the rainbow? Or was it just another twisted path in her life? The path seemed to change direction more often than the wind shifted as she escaped from the clutches of Edsel Cameron.

Concentrating with all of her might, she chose to bring the image of a rainbow into her mind's eye. As she eased into sleep's warm embrace, the rainbow began to fade, but the glitter of golden coins made the rainbow's fragment look pale. They danced in front of her eyes. Were they for her? Were they forecasting a successful venture that would allow her to care for Mellie by herself?

She groaned in her sleep as the coins began to whirl in frenzied, frantic jerks. The design on the coins turned grotesquely human, and a cacophony of guttural laughs made her shake with fear.

Edsel Cameron.

She bolted upright, lifted Mellie into her arms, and leaned against the side of the wagon. Heart pounding, she tried to dismiss her dream turned nightmare. The gentle clopping of the horses' hooves, the creaking of the wheels, and the gentle tinkering of the tinware reminded her that her decision to be married on Wednesday had been met. She began to shake. She and Mellie were totally at the mercy of a man she barely knew!

One worry thundered through her mind.

The coaching road they traveled could lead to freedom and independence . . . or a heart broken again by yet another lost dream.

Chapter 7

Sunlight, warm and intense, teased and tickled the sensitive flesh on the back of her eyelids, and Autumn stirred beneath the covers. She stretched and opened her eyes slowly to bring the light of day into focus. Disoriented by the lack of motion, she blinked twice as she scanned her immediate surroundings. Woolly Lamb lay on the pillow next to hers, and her fingers trembled as she picked it up. Terror, swift and furious, sent her scrambling to her knees to peer out of the end of the wagon.

"Mellie!"

Her frantic call went unanswered.

She could see the coaching road that led to New Haven straight ahead, framed by low, overhanging branches with autumn-colored leaves. A low cloud of dust hovering just above the surface of the road testified to wagon traffic that had already passed by the dense copse of trees that lay on either side of the tinwagon. Fumbling, she undid the latch and lowered the back wall to make her exit.

Dropping to her feet, she rounded the corner of the wagon in haste, catching her shoulder on the edge. Yelping, she stumbled, stepping awkwardly as she regained her footing and rubbed away the sharp pain that shot through her upper body. Blinking back tears, she stopped and listened for sounds that would lead her to her daughter. The team of horses slurped noisily from a narrow stream, breaking the otherwise ominous silence that surrounded her.

Heart pounding, she ran to the stream, her eyes scanning both directions as she ran. "Mellie! Mellie!"

No answer.

Picking up her skirts, she followed the edge of the stream. Avoiding pockets of soggy moss and trying to sidestep slippery rocks, she made her along the bank of the stream. Crisp, dry leaves and debris crunched beneath her feet. Bramble bushes grabbed at her skirts. Branches from saplings, thin and leafless, whipped at her face. She ignored the pain and fumed at the slow headway she was making. She pushed away tangled tresses that interfered with her vision, her eyes searching desperately for any sign of her daughter.

"Mellie! Where are you?"

Her mind struggled for an explanation that would still her pounding heart. Where could Mellie have gone? Where was John? Hoping that they were together, she continued along the stream until her throat was raw and her breath ragged. There was no sign of them. She panicked, reversed direction, and raced back toward the wagon, her heart thumping with fear and worry. The urge to strangle John Logan the moment she found him grew stronger every second that passed.

Unfortunately, he was nowhere to be found, either.

The horses were still tethered and munched on tender shoots of grass that lined the steam. Running to the back of the wagon, she peered inside, praying for a miracle and desperately hoping to find her daughter asleep in her bed. Her heart sank. Tumbled quilts. Barren pillows. Autumn's open trunk, baskets set alongside, a child's nightdress discarded. Woolly Lamb still lay abandoned.

Stopping for a moment to catch her breath, she heard a wagon creak past on the road. Spinning around, her heart sank when she realized that it was just another family moving west, their belongings packed in a Conestoga wagon. Both parents walked alongside of the wagon with several small children while a young man drove the team of horses. Waving enthusiastically, they smiled.

Autumn gritted her teeth, waved back, and smoothed her hair as they passed out of view. Angry with herself for sleeping so soundly, she was infuriated with John. Did he really abandon her here? How did he escape with Mellie without waking Autumn? Cursing herself as a fool for trusting him and giving in to her exhaustion by falling asleep, she began to cry. Her tears dissolved into fear even as they formed. Obviously, John and Mellie could have joined up with any wagon that passed, leaving Autumn abandoned and all alone.

Her rational self begged for attention. The whole scene just didn't make sense. Why would John go to all the trouble of packing for a journey to Ohio if he intended to kidnap Mellie and abandon Autumn before they had even traveled ten miles? He could have taken Mellie in Branfield with a lot less effort.

Unless he never had any intention of taking them to Ohio.

Her breathing grew shallow as she looked at the Taunton Post Road again with new understanding. It did lead to New Haven, but from there it branched off into two directions. North to upstate New York. Southwest to New York City.

Edsel Cameron.

Was he waiting for John Logan to bring Mellie to him?

Her chest contricted with anguished outrage. Heartless knave! John Logan had tricked her again, but this time she would not be content with delivering a blistering tongue-lashing. This time she would carve his heart into pieces for stealing Mellie away!

Whirling about, she forced back the raging fury and confusion that made her pulse thunder in her head. If she could only think logically, she would find a way to follow John and get her daughter back. Staring at the horses, who were starting to get restless, she swallowed hard. She had never driven a team of horses before, but given the circumstances, decided that now was certainly an opportune, if not fateful, moment to learn.

After securing the back wall of the wagon, she hitched up her skirts and climbed into the driver's seat. Bracing her feet on the sleigh-styled front of the driver's box, she reached for the reins. Too late, she realized that the reins were tied to a tree. She climbed down to get them and then clambered back up into the driver's seat.

Taking a deep breath, she closed her eyes and tried to remember what to do first. How many times had she seen men pass through Branfield, stopping at the livery or the mercantile to load up on supplies and then move on? Squinting, she tried to replay the scenes that had surely been stored in her memory, hoping to recall how the others had done it.

"Are you sure you know what you're doing?"

John!

Her eyes flashed open, and she twisted around to face the direction of his voice. Her eyes squinted against harsh sunlight, visually searching the woods, and her hands tightened on the reins. There! A rustle of leaves. A flash of white linen. The full figure of the wretched man dressed in form-fitting brown trousers, his broad shoulders straining beneath a camel-colored coat, emerged from the woods directly opposite from where she had searched. He was holding hands with a familiar red-headed waif who smiled innocently and waved. Autumn ignored his mocking blue eyes.

"Mellie!"

Autumn scrambled down from the driver's seat and raced to meet them. Swooping the startled child into her arms, she whirled her away from John. "Where were you?" she murmured, pressing the child against her breast. One anxious hand caressed tangled red curls while quivering lips pressed kisses against Mellie's forehead.

"We took a walk 'cause you were still sleeping and . . . and I had to *go,*" she responded, squirming against her mother's tight hold. Lifting her little face, her lips curled into a proud smile. "Mr. Logan helped me. I'm glad you didn't marry Reverend Briley, Mama. Now you can paint again. Mr. Logan said so."

Fear melted into relief that quickly solidified into a core of iron resentment. Swirling around, Autumn glared at John. "You should have awakened me. I was frantic. Didn't you hear me calling?"

Eyes narrowing, he shrugged his shoulders. "I didn't think Amelia needed your help. We handled it. And no, I didn't hear your shrill, harridan voice."

"Her name is Mellie," Autumn corrected as she set the child back on her feet, ignoring his barb that she sounded like a shrew. "In the future, I wish you would leave her care to me. I'm her mother."

"Now that we're married," he responded, the timbre of his voice sending chills down her spine, "I'm Amelia's father. I didn't think I had to ask permission, especially when you were too tired to see to her needs."

Mellie nudged closer to Autumn and tugged on her hand. "Is that true, Mama? Is Mr. Logan really my papa now?"

"Tell her," he urged, the harsh expression in his face daring Autumn to deny it.

Autumn clutched her daughter's hand and felt her pulse begin to throb in her temples. "I want you to go to the wagon and brush your hair," she said firmly. "Mr. Logan and I have something important to discuss."

"Is it true, Mama? Is it?"

Autumn ignored the child's persistent questions and led Mellie to the back of the wagon. Lifting her inside, she pointed to the open trunk. "Find your brush," she ordered. "I want all those tangles brushed out. Mr. Logan and I need to talk."

Slender shoulders set defiantly, Mellie reached for the brush. "I told you I didn't need a papa."

Autumn smiled. "I know."

Turquoise eyes filled with disappointment.

Autumn tried to keep the frustration and anger out of her voice. "I promise that I'll explain everything to you as soon as Mr. Logan and I have a chance to talk."

Nodding solemnly, Mellie began to brush her hair. Autumn leaned inside and gave her a kiss. "Stay here. I'll be right back." Turning, she saw John leaning against the trunk of a huge maple tree just a few feet away. She approached him with determined steps, noting with chagrin that he had probably overheard every word she and Mellie exchanged, and unless they chose another place to have their conversation, Mellie would hear everything she and John said.

Vowing to keep the discussion decidedly one-sided and very adult, she nodded to John who followed her to the edge of the stream. Turning, she arched her back and put both hands on her hips. "Just what do you think you're doing?"

"Right now?"

"Of course!" she spat, frustration too close to the surface to control.

He grinned. "Judging from the look in your eyes, I suppose I'm about to be subjected to a silly, emotional tirade. Can you make it short? We're losing time and—"

"Silly?" She charged forward. "You told Mellie that we were married!"

He cocked his head and scratched the stubble on his cheek. "We are. Why is that a problem?"

Eyes wide, she stood on tiptoe to gain advantage. Nostrils flaring, she dabbed a finger into his chest. "Mellie didn't want me to marry Norbert, and she certainly wouldn't want me to marry you, either!"

He stared her back onto the soles of her feet, a habit she found exasperating. "Like it or not, Autumn, we're married. Just how do you think you could explain traveling three hundred miles with a man who wasn't your husband?"

She tossed her head. "I don't see any reason why you can't simply be someone I hired to see Mellie and me to Ohio."

He edged closer and forced her to take several steps backward. "And what if we have to spend a few nights sleeping in the wagon because the inns are full?"

"You can make a bedroll and sleep under the wagon."

He laughed. "I'm not concerned about where I'll sleep! I'm more worried about a scandal that would affect me, too. I can't have my venture undermined before it even begins. This is too important to me. I thought I made that clear back at the Golden Eagle."

"Pointedly," she answered, grabbing the opportunity to shift the tide of the conversation back to her own purpose, although it still pained her to recall the look of contempt in his eyes when he made his startling announcement. "If I remember correctly, you said you planned to have our marriage annulled."

"Your memory is quite accurate. Fortunately, it's also a tad sight better than your mood, not to mention your appearance." He leaned closer, and she could feel his breath fan her cheeks as his eyes dropped to her bodice. "If you're trying to convince me to change my mind through seduction, perhaps you'd better pick another time . . . when you're more presentable."

Shaken, Autumn followed his gaze and quickly re-did the top several buttons that must have come undone during the night or during her frantic search for Mellie. Autumn pushed strands of her hair away from her face, her hands trembling. When her fingers brushed several welts that criss-crossed her cheeks, tears sprang to her eyes. Blinking them back, her voice hardened. "Far be it from me to try to convince you to share the marriage bed with me," she protested as her cheeks flamed. "I'd sooner bed a viper."

He grinned, the sun reflecting on brilliant white teeth. "Good. At least we agree that neither one of us is attracted to the other. What's your point?"

"Mellie."

His back stiffened. "The girl has nothing to do with whether or not we find our way to the marriage bed."

Autumn shook her head. "You still don't understand, do you? You told Mellie that we were married."

"Why do I feel like we're walking on twice-plowed ground?"

"I'm not talking about us. I'm talking about her. If we're married, that means you're her new papa. A papa she doesn't happen to want." Her voice softened. "She wants everything to be the way it used to be. Just Mellie and me. She knows how important my painting is to me, and she thinks I gave that up to get married. I—I guess I never realized how important it was to her, too."

"Children don't always get what they want or know what's right for them," he responded angrily. "She'll just have to accept me as her father even if she doesn't like it."

"It might take the entire journey to convince her that she can't argue with decisions made by adults. Then you're going to turn around, have the marriage annulled, and tell her you're not her papa any more?" Sighing, Autumn slumped her shoulders. "It's not fair. She's too little to understand that you're only going to be a temporary father."

The look on his face changed from exasperation to something that looked like intense pain. It deepened the dimple in his chin and turned his eyes the color of an angry, churning winter sea. Then it was gone. Cold indifference turned his expression into stone. "I'm not going to have my life decisions dictated by a five-year-old girl. You'll have to find a way to explain it to her later. For now, all she needs to know is that we're married. If it helps, tell her that you'll still be painting. That part's true enough."

"You don't care. You really don't care one bit that she might be confused, do you? I hope it's worth it," she spat.

"What?"

"Your dream," she whispered, mourning the loss of her own dream, recalling the way he had evoked her understanding early last night before the others intruded—and hating herself for falling prey to his charm. She tried to remember his exact words to mimic him. "Shaping the future with your own hands? Meeting the responsibilities you have to other people? At first I thought you might have a soul beneath that conniving, lying coat of honor you wear. I was wrong. You traded it for a factory full of tin."

He took yet another step closer. "Maybe you're only using Mellie to suit your own designs. Is this a plea to make this a real marriage?" he breathed incredulously, his eyes glimmering with humor. "I guess I never considered . . ." He cocked his head. "You aren't proposing that we consummate the marriage, are you, Autumn?"

Her eyes bulged. "Never! I haven't forgotten what you said."

He cocked one brow.

"You never make the same mistake twice. I think that's close enough to a direct quote. Well, John Logan, stand forewarned." She squared her shoulders and tilted her chin. "Neither do I."

John pulled the bandanna up over the bridge of his nose and urged the horses to continue their rhythmic plod. As the morning faded into early afternoon, the number of wagons and coaches along the road had increased traffic to a steady flow. The sporadic parade of wagon wheels and horses' hooves created thick clouds of dust and grime that irritated his throat and tightened his chest even though he had tried to keep back from the other travelers.

A side-glance at Autumn and Amelia confirmed their own discomfort, and he stared at his daughter. Half an inch of road dust covered her thin cloak, and the color of her hair had changed to dull, sparrow brown. Despite Autumn's attempts to keep the child comfortable, Amelia had been restless for most of the morning, whining and rubbing her eyes until she finally fell asleep. Cradled in Autumn's arms, she was now oblivious to the continued assault of the dust clouds.

Autumn sat far enough away that they did not touch, her backbone broom-handle straight, her ribbonless bonnet perched crookedly on her head. Tears from dust-irritated eyes had turned streaks of dirt into grimy patches that stained her cheeks the same color as her brown cape. Stone silent, she ignored any attempt at conversation, staring straight ahead, denying John the pleasure of her company.

Pleasure? The woman was a veritable cauldron of taunts and barbs! He could not imagine a more disagreeable traveling companion if he tried . . . until he thought of Wilma Spakes.

On the brighter side, John admitted that he also was spared a repeat performance of Amelia's stubbornness that she dramatically had displayed when he and Autumn returned to the wagon after their discussion. He recognized only too well the tilt of her chin and the set of her shoulders. She inherited that from her grandmother.

Shifting in his seat, he concentrated on the road ahead, confusing thoughts rolling against the banks of his mind like waves of the ocean at high tide. Autumn's charges that he was being coldhearted and uncaring about Amelia's state of mind crashed with tidal rhythm. He grimaced. Why should he care what Autumn thought about his character or his motives? He owed her nothing, although there was a small part of him that reminded him that perhaps he did owe her something for taking good care of Amelia. There was no way he could tell her the truth without risking the success of the elaborate scheme he concocted to get back to Ohio to prove that Amelia was his daughter.

He gritted his teeth.

If Autumn learned that their marriage violated the terms of Edsel Cameron's will and notified Cameron's lawyers, the veritable fortune left to Amelia would be forfeited. John never would let that happen, and he never would risk Amelia's future by trusting Autumn with the truth. She was too smart somehow not to turn this whole situation to her own advantage. Would she see that Amelia's fortune was lost and then put the blame on John in a ploy to turn Amelia against him?

Merciful heavens! He had married Autumn Welles!

Amelia.

He'd marry a dozen times to get her back.

Amelia's reaction to him, however, hurt deeply. He never really gave much thought to what would happen when he found her, at least from her perspective. The moment he saw her that first day in Branfield, his heart had swelled with renewed love and instant attachment. He always assumed it would be the same for his daughter.

Less than a week later, he knew he had been a fool to think it was going to be that easy. Damn Trina! She stole the child away when Amelia was just an infant. Too young to remember his face or the times when he held her in the middle of the night, nursing her through a tummy ache or a fever while Trina complained about losing her sleep.

He never regretted taking over Amelia's care. In fact, there were times when he was so busy with the orchards during the day that he barely saw her. At night, when chores were done and the fire burned low in the hearth, he looked forward to holding her. Trina whined that he spoiled the baby, although he often wondered why she seemed so detached from her only child.

When Trina ran off with Clayton Welles, John was hurt, angry, and absolutely astounded that she took Amelia with her. The only answer that made sense was that Trina did not want to humilate him. She wanted to destroy him. Their own relationship had grown cold, and John knew that part of the responsibility for that had to be his. He never gave up trying to please Trina, but no matter what he did, it was never enough—or it was always too late. In the end, any love he had for her had turned to bitterness.

Autumn would never get the chance to do that to him. Let her fume, fuss, or, like now, retreat behind a wall of stony silence. In the end, Autumn would have to acknowledge his natural right to claim Amelia. Once the marriage was annulled, he would take Amelia to New York to live on Cameron's estate where he would administer Amelia's inheritance until she reached her majority. Until then, according to the will, he could not marry again, but he would spend all of his energies on Amelia. The child would grow to love him and accept him as her father. It would just take a little longer than he had expected.

Hopefully, no more time than it would take to travel three hundred miles.

In the distance, blurred outlines of a small settlement gradually formed into distinct images of homesteads and newly-constructed stores. Exhausted to the bone, he decided to stop early today. There were already enough miles between them and Branfield now to guarantee that Autumn could not take it into her head to walk all the way back. He peeked at her from beneath hooded eyes. Judging by the look on her face when she sighted the town ahead, she just might not argue with him about stopping early.

It was an argument he intended to win if she did fight him, although truth to tell, he was almost too weary to wage a lengthy battle.

After slowing the horses, he lowered his bandanna. "Looks like this might be a good place to stop for the night," he announced, taking a quick glance away from the road to judge her reaction.

Dull eyes lit briefly, then shuttered. Shoulders straightened. "Mellie and I can travel further."

"Well I can't," he countered. Autumn was as stubborn as he was tired. "Some of us slept during the night while others—"

"I didn't insist on starting out at night!"

"No, you'd rather have left Branfield during the day with your nose in the air, daring anyone to say one word against Amelia so you'd have had an excuse to unleash your wicked temper and defend her just to prove that you can take care of her."

"Mellie."

"What?"

"Her name is Mellie," she repeated without taking her eyes away from the road.

"Amelia suits her better," he spat, clicking the reins to dispel his frustration. "You do have the tendency to be single-minded and easily distracted from important issues. Maybe that's why you didn't find out about the store of tinware Klerk hid from his creditors."

She swung around to face him. "I trusted him to be honest."

"That was your first mistake." He grinned before pushing the bandanna back into place, then realized he would have to raise his voice to make his words distinct rather than muffled. "Don't bother telling me about your second. I was there. It's the next one I'm looking forward to seeing."

Fury darted from her eyes, and John could have sworn he felt the sting of her anger pierce his skin.

"I don't intend to make any more mistakes," she hissed, shifting Mellie onto her other leg. "From now on, you keep your hands and mind busy tending to the wagon and horses. Mellie is my concern, and I'm going to make sure you don't have a single opportunity to hurt her any more than you already have."

His hands shook. He was tempted to stop the wagon, tie Autumn to a tree, and leave her there! "Seems to me you've done enough of that yourself."

Her arms tightened around the sleeping child. "Me? You're daft! You're just looking for ways to ease your own guilty conscience. I've never done anything to hurt Mellie. She's always come first in my life."

How about conspiring with Trina and Clayton to keep

Amelia away from me? Or hiding her from me when she deserved to be reunited with her natural father?

He bit back the words that were on the tip of his tongue. Now was not the time to tempt fate, especially since Autumn was in a position to cost Amelia her inheritance if she found out about the will. "If you hadn't let your emotions rule your actions, you'd be traveling with the righteous Reverend Briley instead of me. You'd have had a real marriage, and Amelia would have had a permanent father." He turned his head to glare at her. "Instead, you've put her in a . . . let's see, how did you put it? A confused state of mind. One day you're betrothed to the minister; the next, you're married to a man who is practically a stranger. Seems to me that you played no small part in all of this. I didn't get caught alone with you in a situation that questioned your virtue. It was the other way around."

"You don't have to remind me," she huffed, quickly covering her mouth as a thick cloud of road dust rose up unexpectedly.

His planned retort was lost in a fit of coughing that left him shaking and wondering if he would ever be fully recovered from his bout with whooping cough. Infernal dust! It covered his clothes, coated his mouth, and clogged his lungs. He fumbled with the reins as he bent down to grab the jug of water he kept close by. Groping with one hand, he leaned sideways, only to be shoved back upright.

"Slow the horses," she ordered. Shifting Mellie to her shoulder, she grabbed the jug of water and handed it to him.

Using one hand, he pulled down the bandanna and drank hurriedly, water spilling down his face and chin. The cool water brought instant relief to his irritated throat and stilled the cough, although he knew that he could not cure the spells effectively without replacing the medicine that had been destroyed.

He handed the jug back to her, readjusted the bandanna, and wiped his brow. "Thanks," he murmured sincerely, grateful that she had helped him.

She nodded. "I'm sorry about the medicine," she murmured. "Do you think you can get more in town?"

He shrugged his shoulders. "Only if the town's got an apothecary."

"I could mix something for you."

"No thanks. I hesitate to even imagine what that might be." He gave her a cautious look. "Poison, most likely."

Indignant, she turned away, mumbling to herself.

"What was that you said?"

She turned and grinned, mischief dancing in watery, red-rimmed eyes. "I said that I would never do that. You'll probably cough yourself into the next kingdom before I get the chance to consider it. Then I'll have the tinware that belongs to me and will tide me over until I can find a position to earn my keep . . . and Mellie might not have to deal with having a temporary papa for much more than a day."

Chapter 8

From what John could see ahead, deep ruts in the Taunton Post Road would lead the tinwagon directly through the town of Glenham. Not really large enough to be called a town, he decided after one long look from the edge of the settlement. It was barely more than a hamlet, its existence obviously spawned by the growing westward movement of families who needed provisions and accommodations along the way. Except for the passing of a few wagons, the town was nearly asleep, with only a few people moving along the sidewalk. Signs on either side of the coaching road, silhouetted by the dropping sun's late rays, swung in the strong breeze that had kicked up only in the last half an hour.

John shaded his eyes with one hand as they continued at a slow pace. Although the lettering on some of the signs was indistinct at this distance, he could easily make out the symbols painted on each sign. He held his breath as he searched for one featuring a mortar and pestle, medicine jars, or apothecary weights.

His eyes shifted from the nearest sign featuring a bed with the head of a dazzling red rooster as a headboard to the next one featuring a horse's head. Two other signs with nearly identical frothy mugs competed for patrons. The only other sign had only crude green lettering on whitewashed wood: BAILEY'S GENERAL STORE.

No apothecary.

He sighed and clicked the reins, pulling around the wagons that stretched ahead of him and headed toward the livery.

Mellie scrambled off of Autumn's lap and knelt down to hang over the front edge of the driver's box. She pointed straight ahead. "Are we going to stop here, Mama?"

"Get back on the seat! Don't let her do that," John shouted harshly through his bandanna. He did not bother wasting time to direct his orders to the child. He was more worried about controlling his galloping heartbeat and the fear that lurched through his chest when Amelia was so close to danger.

Autumn's hands shot out immediately and pulled Amelia back from danger. After settling the little girl on the wooden seat, Autumn wrapped her arms around the stricken child, effectively shielding Amelia from his vision. And his wrath?

He pulled down his bandanna as he halted the team of horses in front of the livery. Turning, he let out a shaky breath. "It's not safe to lean over the edge," he chastised as he peeked around Autumn's body to find huge blue-green eyes brimming with tears. "You wouldn't want to fall and get run over by the horses or the wagon wheels, would you?"

Amelia shook her head, setting free one huge teardrop that fell and clung to the top of her cheekbone. "I held on tight," she answered, her chin quivering.

Autumn hugged her close. "I wouldn't let you fall," she murmured. Turning to John, she frowned. "There's no need to lose your temper and speak so harshly. Mellie is a good girl, and she minds well. Just *ask* her to do something. She'll do it."

"There wasn't time to worry about the tone of my voice," he grumbled as his heartbeat slowed to normal. "The road is full of ruts and holes. One sudden jolt and Amelia would have been trampled or squashed by the wagon."

"Now that she knows how dangerous it is, she won't do it again. Will you, *Mellie?*"

"No, Mama."

Autumn turned her back to him and enfolded the child into her embrace. Soft words of comfort elicited shaky, childish whimpers. The sound of that tiny, frightened voice cut John to the quick, choking off his intention to settle the issue of his right to discipline his daughter once and for all.

He ignored Autumn's insistence on calling the girl Mellie. He was more concerned about Amelia. After getting off to a fine start by having time alone with her this morning, he had managed to alienate her by forcing the issue of this ridiculous marriage, refusing to stop for more than a few minutes to share a quick meal of beef and biscuits, and now losing his temper.

At this point, he realized that the fact that he was Amelia's natural father did not automatically give him the latchkey that would open the door to Amelia's heart and affections. When she was hurt or upset, it was not his embrace that she turned to. It was Autumn's.

Resentment, long stored deep in his heart, burgeoned into bitterness that soured the taste in his mouth. While he had spent nearly five years alone, mourning every moment lost with his daughter, Autumn had molded the child's sentiments and established her guardianship so thoroughly that there was only enough room for one person in Amelia's heart: Autumn.

There was more than one way to open a locked door,

he vowed, conceding that trying to get past the guard and ram the door had been a mistake. Let Autumn think she had the upper hand. He would play on her overconfidence and slip past her. As for Amelia, until he got to know his daughter better, he would have to control his temper and exercise patience. Be attentive to wait for Amelia to open her heart to him by herself. Even if she did not recognize him as her natural father, some innate bond of nature would ultimately prevail over the artificial bond that Autumn had forged to suit her own ends.

Bitterness quickened into consolation that sweetened the taste in his mouth and softened his mood. He climbed down from the driver's seat and extended his hand to Autumn. "Why don't you and Amelia stretch your legs a bit while I see about the horses," he suggested, deliberately making his voice congenial but not overly gallant.

Nodding, Autumn handed the child over to him, but averted her eyes. The little girl stiffened the moment he plucked her into the air, and her knees locked as soon as her feet touched the ground. Shoulders set, she looked up at him, her little features caked with enough dust to make her look like a street urchin. "I'm hungry. Can we get something to eat?"

He smiled. "Sure we can. Let me help your mama get down and see to the horses. They're powerfully hungry, too."

"First we need to wash up," Autumn interjected as she stood and smoothed her hair back from her face. She picked up the useless bonnet, then cast it aside before raising her hand for help in disembarking.

John ignored her outstretched hand and placed both of his hands around her waist. When his fingers met at the small of her back, it dawned on him that her figure was certainly less formidable than her temperament. He lifted her easily out of the driver's box and set her on the ground next to Amelia, more than satisfied by the rush of color his impetuous move brought to Autumn's cheeks.

Before she could issue an order or make a cutting remark, he bent down to his daughter's eye level. "Do you think you could take care of your mama for me while I go inside?"

She nodded, a small grin tickling the corners of her mouth.

"Good. I'm counting on you to do a good job."

Turquoise eyes lit up, and John hoped that by replacing his unintentionally sharp reprimand with good memories, he could erase some of today's mistakes. He stood and pointed at an awning-covered porch lined with barrels and cartons of unpacked goods which ran along the front and side of Bailey's General Store. "Why not see if there's a supply of gumdrops in Bailey's?" He pressed a coin into her hand. "You do like gumdrops, don't you?"

Her fingers clamped tight around the coin before she tugged at Autumn's skirts. "Can we, Mama?"

"You can't eat candy before you've had dinner," she cautioned, sending a frigid glance directly at John.

He almost shuddered. Lord! The woman had a unique way of getting under his skin! "Your mama's right." Scratching his head, he furrowed his brow and winked at Amelia. "Think you could buy a few and save them until after we clean up and have a nice, hot meal?"

Head bobbing hard enough to set her curls rustling, Amelia grinned.

Autumn snorted. "We'll meet you at Bailey's," she announced, promptly leading the little girl away from her co-conspirator.

John stood up and leaned against the wagon to watch them as they made their way up the planked sidewalk made of still-green wood and crossed the street. Once they entered the store, he turned away. Whistling, he patted one of the horses on the rump. Sidestepping the unexpected cloud of dust, he headed toward the livery door.

The look of pure pleasure that had covered Amelia's face warmed his heart.

One hope rejuvenated his aching body: reclaiming Amelia's affections was going to be easier than he thought.

Clutching Mellie's hand, Autumn stepped into the general store and closed the door behind her. Inhaling dust-free air, she recognized the smell of fresh-cut timber at the same time that she felt the tightness in her chest ease from breathing dust-clogged air along the turnpike. She looked around the inside of the store. Unlike the general store in Branfield, now operated in the same building by a fourth generation of the same family, Bailey's was practically brand new. Few stores of goods lined the shelves, and it looked like the owners were still unpacking. Her hold on Mellie relaxed, and the child bounded ahead, racing straight for a wooden counter with glass jars of sweetmeats lined up on the counter top.

"Here they are, Mama. Look!" Too short to see over the top of the counter or to inspect the array of glass-encased goodies up close, Mellie jumped up and down, creating a cloud of road dust that filtered off of her cloak.

A tan and white striped curtain to the left of the counter parted open, and a middle-aged man, sporting a beard that rested on the crest of his round belly, took one look at Mellie and smiled. He lifted her up and sat her on the counter. "There you go, little miss. Take a good long look and decide what makes your mouth water most."

Giggling, Mellie swung her legs beneath her and knelt on the counter top. "Oooh! You do have lots of gumdrops! How many can I get?" she asked as she put her coin on the counter.

His eyes narrowed. "Well, usually that coin would be enough for three gumdrops, but it just so happens that we're havin' a special on them today. Why not pick out four of your favorite flavors."

Laughing, Autumn shook her head as she approached the counter. Did all men find it impossible to deny Mellie anything? "Mind your manners, young lady. Thank Mr. . . . Mr. . . ."

"Bailey. Titus Bailey, ma'am.

Eyes wide, Mellie's exuberant mood sobered beneath Autumn's gentle reprimand. "Thank you, Mr. Bailey."

He chuckled. "Better wait till you've sampled my gumdrops before you thank me."

Putting her hand on Mellie's shoulder, Autumn nodded her approval. "Go on, Mellie. Which flavors would you like?"

Licking her lips, Mellie studied the dozen jars as creases of concentration formed on her forehead. "That one. Red. It's my favorite. And a green one for you, Mama." She cocked her head before turning to look at Autumn. "What about . . . P-Papa?"

The child's slight hesitation made Autumn's heart skip a beat. Her eyes misted. Mellie had called only one man papa, but Clayton had never been a very attentive father. Mellie was so young when Clayton died that Autumn knew the child could not remember that. The little girl did not even remember Trina, her natural mother.

Maybe it was for the best. Trina had been so obsessed with Clayton and so desperate to run from her father so he would not force her to return to New York with Mellie that Trina had no emotions left for her child.

Poor Mellie.

She did not want a new papa, and Autumn felt guilty. It was probably her fault. After trying so hard to be both mother and father to Mellie, it was only natural for Mellie to resent anyone else coming into their lives. Now John had claimed to be her father.

Trying to decide how much to tell Mellie about last night's events had kept Autumn awake most of the night. Obviously, John had given little or no thought to the matter. Why else would he blurt out that he and Autumn had gotten married before they even had a chance to discuss how it would affect Mellie? It hadn't been easy this morning trying to unwrap the cord of dissension between her and Mellie that John had tightened with his ill-timed announcement, although she was mollified a bit by learning that Norbert was not going to be her new papa.

"Yellow?"

When Mellie answered her own question, Autumn snapped back from her worries. "That's a good choice," she murmured as she pulled Mellie's hand back from the jar. "Let Mr. Bailey get it."

"Call me Titus, ma'am. Everybody does." He cut a piece of brown paper, put it on the counter, and placed three gumdrops in the middle. Gentle eyes looked up at Mellie. "One more."

Once again, the little redhead licked her lips with the tip of her tongue. Eyes narrowed. "Mmmm." A brilliant smile. "Red."

Not surprised, Autumn held back a comment and let Mellie hold the tightly corded package when the shopkeeper was finished wrapping it up.

"You stayin' in Glenham for the night, ma'am?"

"Yes we are."

John's voice startled Autumn, and she turned around, her hand tightening on Mellie's shoulder. Struggling with Autumn's trunk, with his own travel valise stacked on top, he used the toe of his boot to push the door closed. His lips formed a tight smile as he put the awkward double load on the floor. "Did it ever occur to you to pack a small bag?"

"I didn't have one, and Norbert said it was an unnecessary expense."

"Norbert probably didn't intend to carry your trunk in and out of three hundred miles worth of inns! What did he think you were going to use when you stopped at the end of the day? A burlap sack?"

Cheeks stinging, Autumn twisted her skirt in her hands. "I really didn't think about it."

He raised his eyes, walked past her, and addressed the shopkeeper. "We need a travel bag. Just large enough to hold a few things for my wife and daughter."

"Sure thing. Got a few real nice ones in the back. Any preference for color?" He squinted, apparently deep in thought. "I think there's a choice. Haven't really unpacked them yet."

John laughed. "Just pick out something sturdy. There's too much dust on the road to worry about color. By the end of a day's travel, everything is coated with road dust anyway."

Suddenly feeling very self-conscious, Autumn lifted Mellie to the floor and looked at her daughter with the eyes of someone who had not been on the road for the past night and half of the day. Poor darlin'! She looked like a ragamuffin. Using her hands, she brushed some of the dust from Mellie's hair and attempted to smooth her cheeks clean with the palm of her hands.

Aware that she must look twice as bad as her daughter, Autumn quietly shook her cape and tightened the knot of hair at the back of her neck. She had the most gnawing desire for a hot tub of water, but dismissed that as a luxury reserved for the wealthy. Ordinary folks just didn't have the time or the funds to pay for a bath when the following day, they would only need another! Still, part of her feminine spirit longed for the opportunity to feel fresh and clean again.

John, apparently, had no concern for either her appearance or her comfort. Crouched low, his whole attention was centered on Mellie who babbled about the treats which she clutched possessively with both hands. Autumn studied him, wondering what sort of man he really was. To be fair, she could not really fault his flare of temper earlier when he yelled at Mellie or his complaint about having to carry Autumn's trunk.

Deep lines of exhaustion etched his face which was divided into two distinct colors by a line created by his bandanna, and she realized that he had not had any sleep for at least thirty-six hours. During that time, he had defended her honor, albeit for his own purposes. He had prepared for their journey, although it occurred to her now that he must have had the wagon packed even before the lecture at the Lyceum. He had driven for nearly the past ten hours. And he was not even well!

The man had stamina, determination, and a streak of guile that made her more wary of him than afraid. Not to mention the darkest blue eyes she had ever seen with incredibly long, thick lashes that looked too heavy to lift easily. Beyond all that, he was clearly his own man, and the fearsome notion that he was Edsel Cameron's agent died a slow, well-deserved death. There was only a small part of her that waited for one final bit of proof that would clinch victory for her intuition. Once he took the fork in the Taunton Post Road that led to northern New York State instead of New York City, she would hammer the final nail in the coffin and bury her suspicions.

Titus Bailey interrupted her covert study. Carrying

two carpet bags, he parted the curtain with his back, turned around, and held them out to John. "How do these suit you?"

John looked up and nodded to Autumn without even looking at the storekeeper or his wares. "You choose one."

She greeted his invitation reluctantly, swallowing the swell of apprehension that made her mouth dry. The larger carpet bag clearly suited her needs since it would easily hold a change of clothing for both Mellie and herself. It also had enough room for her sketch pad which was now resting in the bottom of her trunk and almost impossible for her to get to without disturbing everything else that she had brought along with her. Her fingers practically itched to put pencil to paper again, and she was so sorely tempted by the size of this carpet bag to select the larger one!

The smaller bag was obviously less costly, a factor which was paramount to her. It would do, she decided, uncomfortable with spending any more of John's money than absolutely necessary. "The smaller one will be fine," she murmured, her eyes lingering on the larger bag for only a few moments longer.

John rose to his full height and looked at the bags before his eyes met hers. "Being thrifty is admirable, but sometimes foolish. You'll need more room than that one provides. We'll take this one," he announced firmly, taking the larger carpet bag out of the storekeeper's hands.

He handed it to Autumn, and the shopkeeper smiled.

Placing his hands on her shoulders, John turned her around to face the trunk. The warmth of his touch burned through her cape causing pleasant but foreign sensations to flow through her body. He dipped his head, his breath tickling her ear. "Pack what you and Amelia need for tonight."

Her heart fluttered. Her pulse skipped into a staccato rhythm that made her feel light-headed. *Ninny! You're as susceptible to his charms as a five-year-old being tempted by a gumdrop!* She stepped away from him, shaking off her schoolgirl reaction to him. "The smaller carpet bag was suitable enough," she said crisply.

He smiled a gentle reproach. "There's a fine line between being frugal and being stingy," he commented as he set his travel bag on the floor and opened the trunk. "I know we haven't had time to discuss the details, but we can talk about your contract when we get to Ohio. In the meantime, just consider the bag part of your travel expenses which I can tally and deduct from your first month's wages."

He reached into the trunk, pulled out a small, tin matchbox with each hand, and held them out to the storekeeper. "I presume you'll take these in trade?"

The shopkeeper beamed. "You bet. I'll be back in a jiffy. I think I saw something you might need that would even the exchange," he added as he re-entered the back storeroom.

Flabbergasted into silence, incredulity widened Autumn's eyes till her lashes touched her brows. She could not take her eyes off the matchboxes. Beads of perspiration coated her palms, and she dropped the carpet bag. Her chest tightened. When she had learned that Klerk had sold a hidden store of tinware to John, she had been hurt as well as angry. Seeing the tole-painted matchboxes again, the very matchboxes she had delivered to Klerk just days before he closed the factory doors forever, turned Klerk's betrayal into a mockery of the hours it had taken to create these designs with her own talent and imagination. His declaration of bankruptcy was much more than a sad injustice; it was a personal affront that made her tremble. Again.

"I painted them," she whispered as she stepped forward. She looked up into determined blue eyes. Mellie tugged at her skirts. Disappointment that John would bargain with tinware she had made more valuable because of her own labor washed over her. Did he use the matchboxes deliberately to remind her that he still had the upper hand, or was he truly oblivious to the pain he was inflicting?

"What's wrong?" he asked, his hold tightening on his bounty as she approached. "Autumn?"

She shook her head. Too heartsick to be angry, she also knew that the threads of her future were intricately woven with John Logan's plans for his tin factory. They still had to travel hundreds of miles together. They were going to work together and live in the same town.

She took a deep breath and moistened her lips as she reached out and took Mellie's hand. If the fabric of the future had any strength at all, she had to try to make John understand that she simply could not let any man take advantage of her again.

She glanced down at the floor, drew a mental line in the sand and when she looked up at the matchboxes, she hoped she was doing the right thing.

Chapter 9

Autumn's breathing synchronized with her rapid heartbeat as her gaze locked on the identical design painted on each of the tin matchboxes that rested on John's upturned palms. The intricate details on the vines of red and blue flowers that covered the japanned coating on the matchboxes blurred as Mellie tugged at her hand, but Autumn recognized the colors. Bonnie Blue. Schoolhouse Red. Branfield Brown. She had created and named each distinctive shade. The names evoked subconscious memories and captured meanings known only to her.

"Mama! Mama!"

Fright laced Mellie's voice, shifting Autumn's first impulse away from a discussion with John before allowing time for another heartbeat. She squeezed Mellie's hand. This was not going to be a discussion she wanted her daughter to witness. "Give me a minute. We need to talk," she whispered to him as her primary attention focused on Mellie instead of the man who stared back at her like she was addled. Stepping around the imaginary line she had drawn earlier, she opened the door and led Mellie outside.

Mellie dragged her feet as though sensing something

important was going to happen. Something that frightened and confused her, and yet something she seemed determined to watch. Autumn lifted her daughter up and sat her atop one of the barrels on the porch. Smiling, Autumn deliberately softened her expression. "We have something very important to discuss. I want you to wait here. It will only take a few minutes."

Mellie's little face scrunched into rebelliousness as she tried to scramble down. "I want to stay with you."

"You can't," Autumn cautioned as she put both hands on Mellie's thighs to hold her still. Waiting for the child's tense muscles to relax, Autumn lifted one hand to Mellie's face and curved a finger under the child's chin, tilting her face upward. "I'm counting on you to mind me, Mellie."

Blue-green eyes locked into willfulness. "I don't want to sit here. I'm hungry," she whined.

Ignoring her earlier dictum, Autumn took the package of gumdrops out of Mellie's tight-fisted hold and unwrapped it, placing it onto her lap. "Eat two of your gumdrops."

Delight washed away stubbornness, and Mellie plopped a red gumdrop into her mouth.

Autumn kissed the top of Mellie's head. "Be good," she warned. "And don't move from this spot. I'll be right back."

Once she was back inside the store, prepared to make a stand, Autumn frowned. Titus Bailey was back and stood behind three bonnets which were lined up on the counter. Disappointed by yet another obstacle to having a private conversation with John, she fought to think of a way to make sure that Titus left and stayed in the storeroom for a good while.

At least long enough for the battle to be won or lost.

She ignored John's exasperated expression and walked over to the counter, inspected the bonnets, and shook her head as an idea popped into her mind. "I'm sorry. These are too large." She leaned across the counter and lowered her voice to a whisper. "Have you any patent medicines? My husband has a lingering cough. It's sometimes very bad."

His eyes softened as disappointment quickly changed to concern. "No, ma'am. I'm afraid the peddler with drugs and essences hasn't come through Glenham yet. Least ways, not since I opened the store."

Autumn recognized pity as one of the many emotions in his eyes and seized the moment. She sighed. "I suppose I could mix something. If I give you a list of a few items, could you . . . I mean . . . you might not have them, but if you do . . . Will there be enough left to pay for them after you deduct the cost of the carpetbag?"

He smiled and patted her arm. "Tell me what you need. It'll take a little time to sort through my stock, though."

She whispered a number of ingredients, trying not to smile when his expression grew doubtful.

"I'll be back," he reassured her and disappeared behind the curtain.

Autumn turned around and said a silent prayer that there would not be any more interruptions, such as the arrival of another customer! She was not sure yet what she was going to do or say to John, but she was not leaving this store until he granted her justice and some right to control her own life.

John was leaning against the front wall, one of the matchboxes still clutched in each of his hands. One toe-tapping foot rested on top of her trunk and sent impatience echoing in the near-empty room. Irritation twisted his features into a scowl. "Try as I might, I can't fathom what's so important that you'd clear the store for us to discuss it."

She smiled as she made her way back to the trunk. "I'm curious," she admitted, raising one brow. "How did you get to the matchboxes so quickly? Klerk's tinware is solidly packed in crates and boxes inside the wagon."

He shifted his position and braced both feet on the floor as though preparing for a heated debate. "*My* tinware is stored just like any proper peddler's. The side compartments are stocked, too."

Her brows lifted as she recalled that earlier he had claimed that the side compartments held nothing more than supplies for the horses and emergency repairs. She blended this new information with other details that were just coalescing into a plan of action and pointed at the matchboxes. "Do you really feel no sense of guilt for using them against me twice?"

"Twice?" he echoed.

"The donation," she said softly, "was supposed to make amends for the wages I lost. I assume it's on its way to build a church I'll never see. That injustice is now beyond my control." She stopped just short of the invisible line she had sworn not to cross. Tears stung her eyes, and she blinked them away. "To take tinware I decorated for wages I never received and then use it to purchase a travel bag that I have to pay for out of my future wages is unfair. It's also cruel and unkind. I didn't do anything to you to deserve that kind of treatment."

She took a deep breath and shook her head. "I don't want to be accused of rash judgment or to be unfair to you. Just tell me you didn't realize what you were doing . . . or that you didn't deliberately try to flaunt your authority to hurt me."

The tight set of his jaw relaxed, and he swallowed hard as a guilty look flashed across his face. "I just grabbed the matchboxes. I didn't mean to—"

The absolute look of surprise, mixed with embarrassment, was too real and too quick to form to be feigned, and Autumn realized that John was guilty of only one thing: acting in haste.

"I'm not asking for an apology," she said quickly before he had a chance to say a word in his own defense. "If we're going to travel to Ohio together, I think you should treat me better than you have. I've given you no cause to act like I'm your indentured servant, and I'm simply asking that you deal with me fairly. With courtesy."

She stopped to give him time to respond. Instead of justifying his behavior or his cavalier treatment of her, however, he remained silent. The dimple in his chin deepened. His eyes looked . . . troubled?

"You're right, Autumn. You do deserve an apology. I'm sorry. I should have realized . . . I didn't really think beyond getting a few wares to trade." He took a deep breath and gazed at her. "What do you want me to do now? You need that travel bag."

She swallowed hard. "I'd like to work that out in a written contract."

He tilted his head and cocked one brow. "Now?"

"Now."

She bent down and opened the lid to her trunk. Lifting aside her Bible and the two wicker baskets, she rifled through the clothes to get to the bottom. Her fingers brushed against the packet with Mellie's teething beads, which she had kept as a precious memento. She searched for her sketch pad and pencil. After securing both, she restored order to the trunk and closed the lid. She walked over to a waist-high barrel a fair distance from him, opened the pad to a clean sheet and laid the pad of paper on the top of the barrel. "To begin," she said without looking up at him, "you should absorb all travel expenses for Mellie and for me." She wrote quickly, then raised her head. "Any objections?"

Teeth clenched, he shook his head.

She started writing again. "You'll pay my wages directly to me on the first of every month. Klerk paid me ten dollars. You'll pay twenty. And hold a month's wages separate from your business accounts in case of bankruptcy."

"Double?" He snorted. "And you accuse *me* of being unfair and self-serving?"

She chewed on her lower lip before crossing off her original figure without looking up at him. "You're right. I'll agree to ten, but maybe we can talk about a raise after the factory is doing well. As for the rest, Mellie and I will need a place of our own. A two-room cabin stocked monthly with firewood."

"And a serving maid?" he grumbled.

She glanced at him impatiently. "Mr. Bailey will be back at any moment, and Mellie is probably devouring the last of the gumdrops you insisted she have. Do you want to prolong this or get it done before she makes herself sick?"

"Go on," he snapped. "I'm sure your list of demands is as long as the turnpike to Ohio."

She scribbled her last demand, unwilling to spend precious time explaining her intentions and just as unwilling to engage in an argument. "I'd like final approval of all sketches and designs."

His brows furrowed. "I hired you to create designs and to paint. Why would I try to interfere?" he replied, his fingers tightening around the matchboxes.

"I—I just wanted to make sure that you won't try to . . . I mean, Mr. Klerk always—"

"I'm not Klerk," he said softly. "I know you still don't believe me, but I really do feel badly about your wages. I thought I was doing the right thing by making that donation to the minister. And I thought I was doing the right thing by trading a few pieces so you would have a travel bag." He paused and looked at her. "I'm sorry. I guess I just didn't take the time to think about how you might feel."

Autumn flushed. She expected John to lash out at her or to defend his behavior. She did not expect him to admit that he had been wrong, and it made her take a good long look at her own rash assumptions about him. She did not like what she saw in herself, and her hands started to tremble. "You expended a great deal of time and effort to find me. You *married* me to make sure I had no choice but to accept your offer. If you had only . . ."

He sighed. "We've been through all this before, Autumn. You know how important you are to my venture. A contract seems unnecessary. I'm a man of my word, and I'm not used to having my word questioned. Why don't we talk about a contract later when we get to Ohio?"

"I can't. After all that's happened, I'd feel better if I had a written contract in hand. Are you willing to let your male pride prevent you from putting your name to a contract, or . . . or is there some other reason you seem so determined to have me come to Ohio?"

An odd look blanched his face, and his entire body tensed as though he struggled to contain himself. His eyes narrowed to slits, and his lips tightened into a grim line. He walked over to her, took the pencil out of her hand, and boldly signed the contract without even reading it over. He held the pencil out to her. "Satisfied?"

She signed the hastily drafted document and folded it. "I feel vindicated," she offered, trying to soften her obvious victory. "I'll keep this safe."

His eyes lit with distrust.

She smiled. "You and I both know what the contract says, and I'm not likely to forget my obligations. You, on the other hand, might find it tempting to have a lapse of memory, given your reticence to agree to the terms today. I'm keeping possession of the contract since I might need to use it from time to time to remind you of our agreement."

He snorted. "I doubt I'll be able forget a single detail."

Victory sweetened her disposition and silenced a nagging worry about why he had given in to her demands without more than a cursory argument.

She grinned. "I won't let you."

John signed the register at the Red Rooster Inn, admitting to himself how close he had come to complete and utter panic when Autumn confronted him about a contract in the general store. Expecting a scene laced with hysteria and theatrics, which Trina had practiced to perfection, he was surprised by Autumn's practical and well-reasoned response to his blunder.

He had selected tinware decorated by her own hand on impulse, never fully comprehending how dastardly he had become. Even though Autumn bore little resemblance to Trina in appearance, he unwittingly reacted like they were interchangeable. Sometimes he looked at Autumn and was surprised to see that her eyes were not blue or that her hair shined like melted chocolate instead of the color of summer wheat. The two women were as different in appearance as day and night.

Tarnation! Appearances aside, both women had manged to do the same thing: to take his name and rob him of his daughter!

Signing the register as Mr. and Mrs. Logan unnerved him and brought back memories he would rather forget. The first time he had married, he had been too young to understand that Trina saw life and marriage as a series of adventures and not necessarily events that went hand-in-hand. Spoiled by her father and the attention of far too many suitors, she had probably picked John only because she thought it might prove entertaining. She pursued him openly, and he interpreted her unusual proposal as a compliment. The excitement for her, however, lasted only as long as it took to travel from New York to Ohio. Finding herself pregnant was like having the curtain drop on the final performance of a play that was closing early.

This time, he realized, he had taken the upper hand and forced Autumn to marry him. He fully anticipated that she would be as vain and self-centered as his first wife, or as devious and unscrupulous as her brother, Clayton. Instead, she constantly surprised him by her tenaciousness and her common sense, her selfless dedication to Amelia, and her down-to-earth approach to adversity.

Surprise, however, did not equate affection or allegiance. Neither did it change his determination to have his marriage to Autumn annulled as soon as he arrived home in Comfort Bend.

He finished writing his signature and turned the register back to the proprietor. "We'll be leaving at first light," he said firmly. "Will that be a problem, Mr. Clydesmore?"

A man with his right arm in a sling who was close in age to John's thirty years shook his head. "Not at all. My wife will make sure there are plenty of steamin' hot batter cakes to fill you up before you leave. I'm real sorry about not havin' a private room for you and your family."

John glanced toward the stairs and looked up to see a second floor that offered nothing more than beams, rafters, and studs and the promise of future accommodations. "The common rooms will be fine."

"I was workin' day and night to get them rooms upstairs done, till this happened." He lifted his injured arm away from his body and sighed. "Mara's even got the curtains ready, but the way it looks, it'll be spring 'fore she can hang them."

"It's not a problem. Would it be possible to get some hot water for my wife and my daughter? We've been traveling half the night and all day. They'd like to freshen up a bit before dinner."

"Sure thing. I'll get Mara to take care of that. Then I'll see you get the same."

John turned away from the front desk which was really nothing more than a crude counter of unpainted timbers. Autumn and Amelia stood near the door, waiting for him to finish registering. Amelia looked like she had taken a bath in maple syrup. Poor little thing. Patches of sticky sugar dribbles, compliments of her childish attempt to eat two large gumdrops at the same time, stained her cheeks and lips. Autumn had not even attempted to try to clean her up again, although she did have a word or two to say about who was responsible for the child having possession of the sweetmeats which were now nothing more than a memory. Rather conveniently, Autumn sidestepped the issue of who had given Amelia permission to eat the candy in the first place, and he stored a barb in his memory bank for future use.

When he nodded for them to join him, Autumn took Amelia by the hand and approached him slowly. "Do we have a room for the night?"

"Not exactly," he responded, wondering at her ability to put the scene at the general store behind her so quickly. Maybe it was because she was still gloating at having defeated him so easily.

If she only knew.

The instant she mentioned that he might have an ulterior motive for taking her and Amelia to Ohio, he realized immediately that he would have to give in to each and every one of her demands. What choice did he have? He would rather have her assume that she had bested him than raise any suspicions about his real motive for wanting her in Ohio or the terms surrounding Amelia's inheritance. Satisfied with the rather generous terms of the contract she thought she had extracted from him, she had no reason to doubt that the position was anything other than a very lucrative opportunity.

That misconception was crucial, especially now that he would not even be in the same room at night to make sure she did not try to run away. She had no reason to go anywhere now but Comfort Bend, and he looked forward to finally having a full night's rest, his coughing spells notwithstanding. He pointed to the stairway. "The upstairs rooms aren't finished yet. We'll have to sleep in the common rooms."

Relief, brief but real, flashed through her eyes. "Mellie will sleep with me."

He let out an impatient sigh. "Children always sleep with the women. Mr. Clydesmore offered to have his wife fetch some hot water so you can wash up. We can meet back here say in half an hour to go to supper."

Nodding, she turned and followed the proprietor as he carried her new carpetbag, now filled with a change of clothing and a brown package she had quickly packed and offered to explain later, and led her off to the right. John watched as she opened a door and led Amelia into a large dormitory with a dozen beds lined along both walls. The proprietor placed the carpetbag inside the room, closed the door, and walked back toward John. "I'll see to that hot water now, Mr. Logan. Men's common room is to your left."

Hoisting his travel bag off of the floor, John found his way to the men's dormitory. It was laid out exactly as the one reserved for women and children and was just as empty of patrons. Glad that he had decided to stop several hours before most other travelers would, he chose the bed closest to the door and sat down.

The mattress dipped beneath his weight as he stretched out. Hands behind his head, he stared up at a ceiling of bare rafters made of virgin wood. He closed his eyes, battling the need for sleep against the rumbling in his stomach. Tension eased from his body as he realized that he had nothing left to worry about—at least as far as Autumn was concerned. Although she did not gloat with her easily-won victory, he knew that she derived great pleasure from forcing his hand and making him agree to the terms of her contract.

A contract as useless as a Tin Lady in a town with no tin factory! Or as elusive as his dream of returning to New York and raising Amelia on his own?

He was not sure he wanted to be within a hundred miles of Autumn when she found out that this position in Ohio was nothing more than a hoax perpetrated to one end: claiming his daughter and taking her away from Autumn. He had the feeling that she would not be as rational or as quietly in control as she had been at the general store. Her attachment to Amelia appeared to be genuine, and he did not believe she would give the child up easily. Pity, however, did not mitigate the crime she and her brother had committed against John and did not threaten to weaken his determination.

The Tin Lady.

Her face flashed before him, in all its amazing incarnations. The prim, strait-laced, expressionless matron. The serene madonna who protected her child with the fierceness of an ancient warrior princess. The dignified artisan who protected her rights.

He had seen more emotions flash like quickfire across her features in the past two days than he thought possible. And each time, he caught a glimpse of a woman whose beauty seemed to unfold and intensify with each different emotion, just as nature seemed to use each different season to exhibit the various facets of her beauty.

Autumn. She was a woman who could intrigue a man for the rest of his days, and he paused to imagine what it would be like if the slow, smoldering embers of fire he had glimpsed in her spirit ever flared into the fiery throes of passion. The thought made him shiver.

He had never encountered a woman like Autumn, and he knew he had to control his growing physical reaction to her. He had to shut out the stirring feelings that made him wonder what it would be like to hold her in his arms, touch his lips to hers, and run his hands along the gentle curve of her hips. He was a man, dammit, not a eunuch! Five years of abstinence left him hungry to feel a woman's body again, and Autumn was very definitely woman enough to remind him of what he had missed . . . and what he was legally entitled to savor.

Consummating this marriage threatened more than his future. It would destroy Amelia's. Her inheritance from her grandfather guaranteed a future for Amelia that John could never afford to give to her, and he was not going to jeopardize everything by giving in to temptation.

He derided his weakness as only momentary, and Autumn's presence in his life even more transitory. She would have no choice but to leave Ohio. Not unless she wanted to face charges that she knowingly kept his daughter from him! Once he rekindled his natural bonds to Amelia, he would give a thought to satisfying his needs. He would never have to marry again. Never have to trust his heart to another woman. At least Cameron spared him that. But that did not mean he intended to remain celibate the rest of his life!

Confident that he had resolved his most pressing concerns, he let his body drift into a much-needed nap. Just a short one, he reassured himself. Long enough to take the edge off of his exhaustion, but short enough to guarantee that he would sit down and break bread with his daughter tonight for the first time in five years. After a good night's rest, he would be strong enough to resist the temptation that Autumn presented.

The long and painful quest for his daughter was over. It was finally time to begin the journey home.

Chapter 10

Two weeks later, dawn had barely broken when Autumn ignored John's order and blocked the side door to the livery. "I'm not moving an inch until you agree."

"You don't have a say in the matter," he countered as he lifted her up and set her aside in one easy motion. "I said no. I'm handling the situation the way I see fit, and it's none of your concern."

"Suppose you fall asleep at the reins, and the horses bolt, carrying us all to our deaths. Will it be my concern then? You haven't had more than a few decent nights' sleep in half a month." She fought the urge to stomp her foot and thought better of trying to stand on tiptoe to challenge him. If she was stubborn, as he claimed, he was the most exasperating and obstinate man she had ever met.

Oh, those deep blue eyes of his! Streaked with red, they flashed angrily, like a flag whipped by a brisk wind.

"I said no. I feel fine. Now let's go." He opened the door and swung his arm in an arc. "It's time to leave, Amelia. Scoot inside, and I'll boost you into your seat."

The child eyed him warily as she approached him. "Mama said if you took your medicine, you wouldn't cough all night and have to sleep in the wagon." She scrunched her lips and wiggled her nose. "Does it taste that bad?"

"He wouldn't know," Autumn answered testily before John had a chance to comment. "He won't even try it."

"I don't want it. And I sure as the dickens don't need the two of you making an issue of my health. Lord knows we're wasting time arguing about it when we've lost enough time already. I never should have agreed to stop and let you sketch in the afternoons or collect specimens for pigment, Autumn. We should be using every minute of daylight for travel."

Autumn stood her ground. Literally. "Changing the subject is one of your more insidious habits, but I resent the insinuation that I'm sketching wild flowers or collecting samples to dry for pigment as pure recreation. I've been hired to do a job, and I'm doing everything to make sure that the new designs for the tinware will be unique and distinctive." Autumn tossed her head back. "It also doesn't alter the fact that your coughing spells are interfering with your sleep. I know the tonic I made will help, but you're either too stubborn or too foolish to admit it."

When he scowled, Autumn lost her patience. Talking to this man was like talking to a pillar of stone. "Suit yourself," she spat before grabbing her carpetbag and taking hold of Mellie's hand.

She stepped through the doorway into the livery. The interior of the livery was considerably dark, and it took a moment for her eyes to adjust. When they did, she noted that, as usual, the horses were already hitched to the wagon, and John had everything ready for the day's travel.

"Mulish clod!" she muttered to herself under her breath. John was headstrong enough to cough his way to Ohio just to prove that he did not need her help. Or was it more than that? Although he had joked about the possibility that she might poison him, given half the chance, he really did not think she could do such an awful thing, did he?

It was hard to tell what he was thinking, but one thing was clear: the poor man was exhausted. Deep lines etched the corners of his eyes, and dark circles beneath them added poignant testimony to his severe lack of sleep. It was worse than bad luck to have found neither an apothecary nor a traveling medicine drummer since leaving Branfield. She suspected that John's offer to stop and let her sketch for a time each afternoon was really prompted by his need for a catnap rather than any desire to please her or let Mellie release some of her pent-up energy.

Mellie reached in front of her and tugged at the carpetbag. "Did you put the medicine in here? Maybe Papa will take it later, when he's ready to take a nap."

Autumn smiled and stooped down to meet her daughter at eye level. "No. I have it in my cape pocket, but he has to decide when and if he wants to try it."

Turquoise eyes deepened in color beneath furrowed brows. "You made me take my medicine when I was sick, 'member? Make him take his, too."

"Unfortunately," Autumn chuckled, "grown men don't like to be told what to do, even if it's something they know they should do. Why don't we just wait and see what happens later today? He might change his mind." She tried to sound optimistic, but the likelihood of that happening seemed as remote as the possibility that Autumn would ever recoup one coin of the wages Klerk owed to her.

"Maybe I won't," John remarked as he stepped inside. Autumn shrugged her shoulders, choosing to let the matter drop rather than turn it into another argument. When he lifted Mellie high into the air, her squeals of delight echoed in the livery. Autumn realized that however gradually, her daughter was warming to the man she called papa, due in no small measure to his uncanny interest in the child. Autumn caught him staring at Mellie when he thought Autumn was preoccupied with her sketching, and she had noticed how hard he tried to assuage the little girl's boredom during the endless days of travel.

Nothing seemed too much trouble for John, at least where Mellie was concerned. He sang ballads, pointed out and named all sorts of flora and fauna, and even helped her practice her letters after supper. For her part, Autumn had the unpleasant but necessary duty of being the disciplinarian while he was an adventurous and tireless playmate!

As she watched them together now, Autumn felt a small twinge of regret. When he was with Mellie, John's whole demeanor changed. He was so relaxed and unguarded that Autumn was able to catch a glimmer of the man who had snatched her breath away at the Lyceum. Since that day in the general store when she insisted on having a written contract, however, he had become polite but distant with her, and she finally admitted to herself that she regretted this new gulf between them—a gulf that seemed even wider when she saw him with her daughter.

His attachment to Mellie almost seemed natural, but Autumn discounted it as simply another conscious maneuver to convince her that marrying him and choosing to go to Ohio instead of marrying Norbert was a good decision. A surge of maternal instinct warned Autumn that letting John get too close to Mellie was a mistake, although Mellie did swing from one extreme to another, fascinated with him one moment, and clinging to Autumn's skirts the next. Clearly, the child was befuddled, having had no experiences with a father, at least none that she could remember.

Clayton.

Autumn's disappointment with her brother and his perplexing disinterest in his own child was profound. While she could not deny that Mellie needed a father's presence and love, she could not allow John to claim that place in Mellie's heart for himself—not when he had no intention of remaining her father when they arrived in Ohio! It was cruel and dastardly to toy with the affections of an innocent child, no matter how much he wanted to realize his dreams.

Feeling perturbed by the playful atmosphere that filled the livery only heightened Autumn's own sense of guilt for the role she played in creating this whole situation—a situation that conceivably could break Mellie's little heart.

Autumn cast a hard glance at John who was still tossing Mellie into the air and catching her with exaggerated gusto as the little girl's apron flew up and covered her face. "I thought you were in a hurry," she reminded him. "And unless you relish the idea of wearing Mellie's breakfast, I suggest you stop."

"Charged with yet another crime of poor judgment," John grumbled, setting Mellie on her feet.

Face flushed, Mellie wrinkled her nose at Autumn who led the child to the driver's box with nary another word. She straightened her daughter's attire and stood tapping her foot while John set her carpetbag and his travel valise into the rear of the wagon. By the time they climbed aboard and he clicked the reins, Autumn had set her mind to what had to be done. Starting today, she would make sure that Mellie spent less time with John, and if he did not like it, he could . . . he could find another little girl's heart to break!

When they emerged from the livery, the bright mid-

September sun quickly chased away the early morning chill in the air and softened her mood. As the wagon turned right and they continued their westward journey, she watched the passing fall-colored terrain with only half an eye. They had taken the fork that led through northern New York state nearly a week ago, and she had heaved a sigh of relief as the road to New York City and Edsel Cameron disappeared from view. Thoroughly convinced now that John was no agent for anyone other than himself, she began to relax her guard for the first time in years.

She did not even question John's odd travel schedule. She understood that he started out earlier than the other travelers to avoid as much of the inevitable road dust that irritated his throat.

Within an hour today, however, they were last in a line of half a dozen wagons. They were traveling in silence when suddenly seized by an unusually severe coughing spell, John dropped the reins, pulled down his bandanna and clutched his throat as he gasped for breath. Horror-stricken by his depth of his distress, Autumn was also terrified that the horses would bolt out of control. She grabbed the reins and held them in white-knuckled hands as she tried to take over for John until he recovered. Her earlier admonition now a dangerous reality, she fought the urge to castigate him for not heeding her plea to take his medicine.

As the spell passed, John took frantic swigs from his water jug which Autumn judged was probably half empty already. She held her breath, wondering if the man was now going to admit that water alone was just not enough to stave off his spells. Not any more, not when their safety was at stake. Had he lost his common sense to the constant clouds of dust that exasperated his physical problems, or was he just too proud to accept the medicine she had made for him?

Chancing a sideways glance at him while Mellie was preoccupied with her chalk and slate, Autumn found troubled blue eyes waiting. Watching. Riveting her into place and draining the breath out of her lungs. The anguish in his eyes told her that he knew he had endangered all of them and he was willing to take the medicine. He just could not bring himself to say it out loud.

She took a deep breath. If she ever hoped for a chance to prove him wrong about anything truly important, this was a golden opportunity. He deserved to be upbraided for risking their safety as they traveled, exactly as she had predicted. He merited a swift enjoiner, demanding that he admit that she had been right to insist he take his medicine.

When the color of his eyes changed from midnight blue to simmering sapphire, the soulful expression in his guilt-filled eyes tugged at her heart. Biting back words that would only satisfy her own sense of righteousness, she turned the reins over to him and took the bottle of medicine out of her cape pocket. She handed it to him and reached back into her pocket for the spoon. By the time she turned to give it to him, he was already taking swigs of medicine straight from the bottle. She looked at the spoon and grinned at him as she shook her head. "I guess you don't need this."

Her pulse began to beat faster when he leaned closer and broke into a smile. "Not when I'm riding in a wagon."

Or sitting half-dressed in bed?

Her lips formed a tremulous smile. "Does the tonic help?"

He nodded. "Thanks. It does. I . . . I should have taken it sooner." His eyes clouded and grew distant. "I never would have forgiven myself if anything had happened—"

"It didn't," she murmured, touched by the deep pain that etched his features. "Just keep taking the medicine."

"Yes, ma'am." He grinned. "The taste is rather peculiar, though. You wouldn't want to share the secret of your ingredients, would you? As a patent medicine, it could earn quite a fortune."

Goose flesh. Erratic heartbeat. Shortness of breath. Mercy! His eyes were beguiling, his voice mesmerizing. Hastily, she looked away, catching a last second glimpse of sun-streaked hair that framed his strong, angular features. She stared straight ahead, her eyes focused on the rear of the wagon just ahead of them as she tried to find her voice. At the moment, it was caught halfway between a rasp and a croak, neither of which extreme was close to acceptable. "Peppermint tea," she finally said, relieved that her words sounded quite normal.

When he laughed, she swung her head around to face him, her eyes wide.

"I'm sorry," he apologized as his expression sobered. "I enjoy the flavor of peppermint tea, and this isn't even close."

She shrugged one shoulder. "I also used a number of curative agents which aren't always pleasing to the palate."

"It's not terribly awful-tasting. Just peculiar."

"You have to give it a chance to work. Your spells are getting worse as we travel. If you continue to take the tonic, you should see some improvement. My mother taught me how to mix it," she offered. "It's usually quite effective, and the honey should make it pleasant enough to tolerate."

"Honey," he repeated. A cloud of worry scudded across his face. "It's been years since I tasted its flavor, but I didn't think I detected it in your tonic."

Autumn studied his face, searching her mind for

some reason he should be so concerned about the honey. "I don't understand."

His gaze hardened.

Thoroughly bewildered, she turned toward him, her heartbeat beginning to accelerate, then thudding hard in her chest. "What's wrong with using honey? It's one of the usual ingredients in home remedies for coughs and irritated throats."

He clicked the reins and stared straight ahead. "Nothing."

His cold dismissal bristled at her patience. "Can't you tell me why you're so upset?"

He pulled hard on the reins and brought the horses to a halt. He ran his fingers through his hair. "Look. I'm not finding fault with your tonic. The truth is that the only time I ever used honey, I was covered with welts and scratched for a week."

Autumn swallowed hard, and a lump of fear lodged painfully at the base of her throat. He was sensitive to honey? *Honey?* She felt her lifeblood freeze in her veins. "How much did you take—the time you found out you were sensitive to honey?" she croaked before holding her breath as she waited for an answer.

His expression hardened, the muscles in one cheek twitching. "A spoonful," he gritted between clenched teeth as he started to cough again and reached for the bottle of medicine.

She reached out and touched his arm, her fingers resting on hard muscle. "Please don't take any more. Drink some water for now. If you pull over for a bit, I can mix another batch of tonic without honey."

He tensed and took another swig. "We can't afford another delay. I'm a mature adult. I'm sure I've long outgrown my childish sensitivity to honey."

"But what if you haven't?" she whispered.

He took another swig, put the bottle next to him on

the seat and clicked the reins. "I said it's not a problem, and I don't need you smothering me with your concern. I survived the disease without you, and I can certainly tolerate a few lingering coughing spells until they finally stop. Which no doubt they will . . . now that I have the tonic."

Taken aback by his unwillingness to admit he had a problem or to let her help him, she settled against the back of the seat and let the matter drop. She did not mean to add to the distress he already had. She was only trying to be helpful so the man would be able to drive carefully and get a good night's rest. She hoped he was right and that he had outgrown his sensitivity to honey. Otherwise, he would still be up all night, but he would not be coughing. He would be scratching at hives that would cover his body, if they could penetrate through the plate of armor called his pride.

Hives.

Like patches of hungry red ants feasting on his skin, they covered his torso, arms, and legs. The more he scratched, the worse the confounded welts itched, and John plunged into the chilly waters of a narrow creek with one goal: relief.

Closing his eyes, he ducked below the surface and let the slow moving current numb his skin as he braced both feet on the rocky bottom of the creek. Dark and peaceful, the nether world of the creek blocked out the warm sunshine that irritated the hives and the misery that surrounded this thoroughly humiliating turn of events.

Blasted honey.

He knew he should have discarded the tonic and suffered with using just water the minute Autumn confirmed his fears. She had warned him not to use the medicine and offered to mix a new batch. When he refused, she pleaded with him to listen to her.

Instead, his determination to prove he had outgrown a childhood allergy had erupted into stoic foolishness that plagued him for the past day as he tried to hide his discomfort from her and Amelia.

Why?

As he stood up and broke through the surface waters, he shivered as a light breeze chilled his flesh. The truth echoed in the still and quiet corners of his heart.

He stared at Autumn through a break in the trees that lined the creek. Sketching yet another precious one of her wildflowers, she was facing in the other direction with Amelia asleep beside her. He studied her bent form, the soft brown waves of hair that escaped from her knot and skimmed her shoulders and the gentle curves of her body. Contrasted against a sharp line of boulders, her figure appeared even more delicate and feminine than usual.

He swallowed hard.

He had been so all alone these past years, driven by guilt for his part in the failure of his marriage and frustrated when his goals were constantly challenged and destroyed. He had been left to his own survival, both emotionally and physically. Unwilling and unable to depend on anyone else. Afraid to trust anyone for so long he had forgotten how.

Traveling with Autumn for the past few weeks was a jolting and painful experience for him that nearly overshadowed his relief at finding his daughter. Subtle things Autumn did during the journey were like trip wires that detonated a series of explosions, cracking through his defenses and exposing emotions and needs he had buried deep within his soul. The rustle of her skirts as she prepared a light meal along the turnpike, humming as she worked. The touch of her hand, ever so brief, when she handed him a meal he did not have to make for himself. Quietly solicitous, she refilled the water jug each time they paused for a brief rest and tidied the sleep area in the rear of the wagon where he slept. All with little word of complaint.

And in the process of sharing endless hours together, Autumn reminded him of the comfort and pleasure a man could find with a woman's presence in his life.

He dove beneath the waters, letting the brisk, cold water quickly douse the warm feelings that softened his heart toward Autumn before they had to take to the road again. *If only it were as easy to get rid of the blasted hives!*

He emerged from the creek, dressed and joined Autumn and Amelia. Although he had cleared his mind of all his troubling thoughts about Autumn, all benefits of his therapeutic bath had evaporated, and he could feel his skin begin to tingle again. His resolve to hide his discomfort from both of them, however, quickened. He stretched out on the tree-shadowed face of a boulder, reluctant to sit in the sun. The cold planes of the rock eased through his thin shirt and quieted his itching back that was screaming for attention already. He rubbed against the craggy stone surface, trying to appear nonchalant about his movements.

"Feeling better?"

Autumn's question, the first open reference she had made to let him know she was aware of his physical reaction to her tonic, caught him off-guard. "A swim invigorates a man, especially after being confined for hours on end to the seat of a wagon."

A smile teased at the corner of her lips. "You shouldn't be suffering too much longer. The new tonic—"

He bolted upright. "What new tonic?"

"The one I mixed last night and used to replace the

original medicine," she responded casually as she held the completed sketch close and studied it. "That should help."

His body tensed as a new itching attack gave him the urge to scratch off an entire layer of his skin. His hands clenched into fists. He was *not* going to scratch a single hive. Not in front of her. "The other tonic—"

"—gave you hives," she interrupted. She set the sketch pad down on the ground and turned to him. Her deep brown eyes were dancing pools of controlled mirth, but her lips were taut. "Mellie's asleep. She won't see you scratching. Not that it helps much except to give you some semblance of relief. You really need a salve."

"Another home remedy?" he snapped. Lord have mercy! His back felt like it was on fire!

She paled, and the light went out of her eyes. "I'm truly sorry for what's happened."

"Nothing that happened is your fault," he said through clenched teeth as tingling sensations on his back vied with itching arms for his attention. He stretched his shoulders and flexed his back muscles. "It's not unbearable."

She caught a grin before it stretched into a smile, stood up and walked over to a nearby tree. After selecting a fallen tree branch, she came back and held it out to him. "Try using this to reach the middle of your back."

He stared at her. "I'm fine."

It was a lie, and he knew it.

So did she, obviously.

He snatched the branch, reached over his shoulder and scratched at the flesh along his spine, instantly quelling his physical discomfort, if only for the moment. He scratched with the stick until his flesh was raw. Pain he could handle. It might even take his mind off what was really itching him.

When he reached down to scratch his left leg with his other arm, she smiled at him. A full dazzling smile that transformed her normally-prim features into a beautiful, heart-stopping countenance. Was this the same woman he had called the Tin Lady?

Mesmerized, he held perfectly still and stared at her. Flecks of green shimmered in the depths of luminous brown eyes. She had an incredible dimple in one of her cheeks, and her flawless skin became translucent, beautifying her features beyond all human expectations. He blinked hard, wondering if she had captured the sun and kept it locked up deep inside of her until this very moment when she smiled and let it dawn with such dazzling intensity that he had to look away.

Not the sun, he decided quickly, but a fire. A dangerous flash fire that inflamed his loins and scorched his better judgment. Breathing hard, he switched the stick from one hand to another to scratch his other leg. When he heard her start to giggle, he chanced another look. Wonder-struck, he watched as her radiance intensified and her features changed again. His heartbeat stammered as she was incredibly transformed into such a vivid beauty that her name, *Autumn,* suddenly echoed in his mind with dazzling clarity.

She made him tremble.

She made him ache.

And she stopped his heart in the middle of a beat.

Grace be given. He could not take his eyes off her.

She cocked her head. "I'm sorry. I didn't meant to laugh, but you are insufferably proud and terribly stubborn," she said when she finally brought her giggle under control.

"At the moment, that's the least of my concerns," he grumbled. He did not want to even imagine what he looked like, sitting on a rock in the middle of nowhere, scratching every square inch of flesh he could reach. It was humbling, to say the least, but the sound of her laughter as it erupted again almost made it worth it. It was lilting and magical and . . . terribly contagious. In spite of himself, he started to laugh with her.

"This is ridiculous," he managed between breaths. "I can't imagine why I thought I could get away with using honey and not pay dearly for it."

She reached out and touched his shoulder. "I saved the tea leaves from supper last night and breakfast this morning. Would you . . . I mean, I could—"

"Anything," he urged as the itching grew worse. "Make a salve or a compress or anything else you can think of. At this point, I'd sell the whole wagon of tin for a few hours of blessed relief."

"Would you?" she whispered, her eyes dancing with possibilities he understood immediately.

Fortunately, Amelia chose that particular moment to wake up. "What are you doing?" she asked as she climbed to her feet. She looked at him with sleep-flushed cheeks and smiled.

John blushed. "I'm . . . I'm scratching my back," he mumbled, as uncomfortable with both of them knowing he was suffering as he was with the blasted hives themselves.

"Oh. Are you gonna use the stick to scratch your arms, too? If you rip your shirt, Mama won't like it. She'll have to mend it, and she doesn't like to sew." She walked over to him and started scratching one of his arms with her tiny fingers. "I can help. Do your legs itch, too, like they did this morning when you were trying to scratch them with your boots?"

Dumbfounded, John dropped the stick and gazed into his daughter's eyes as she leaned closer to him. Were his efforts that obvious that even a child could see through them?

"Don't worry," Amelia whispered. "You'll get better soon."

He nodded, unable to speak, and looked at Autumn, who smiled as she tussled Amelia's hair. He would recover. Eventually. But would he ever get over the amazing discovery that within the spirit of Autumn Welles, there was a fire that rivaled the sun for its intensity?

Not a full-raging fire. Just slow-burning, deeply-hidden embers that once fanned, could flare into a bold and dangerous bonfire. Engulf him. Sear his self control so that he would risk everything that was so important for the life he planned for himself and Amelia. And melt the jagged pieces of his heart into wholeness.

Alarmed by feelings that left him shaking, he turned back to Amelia to reach out and touch her still-flushed cheeks. He tensed immediately. "You feel warm. Are you feeling sick?"

"Mellie's never sick," Autumn interjected before Amelia could answer or he could even take a breath. Concern filled Autumn's eyes, however, as she rested the back of her hand against Mellie's forehead. "Just a little too much sun today. That's all." She put her finger under the child's chin and tilted her face upward. "Next time you nap in the sun, wear your bonnet, young lady."

Autumn turned to John and nodded toward the wagon. "We'll be ready to leave in a few minutes."

John followed them back to the wagon, but he could not help but be confused by the fear and quick denial that had filled Autumn's expression when he had suggested the child might be sick.

It matched his own.

Chapter 11

As the wagon crossed through the northern New York countryside, John shivered beneath an oilskin raincoat. Huge gray-black clouds lined up across the horizon, casting an ominous mantle of gloom on the midday landscape and forecasting yet another round of drenching showers that already had left him chilled to the bone.

For the second straight day, Autumn and Amelia traveled inside of the wagon. And for the second straight day, John battled more than just the forces of the natural elements. He fought a melange of conflicting emotions concerning his daughter, struggled against admitting a grudging respect for Autumn, and confronted his nagging conscience, experiencing little success in any of these mental reviews.

Intermittent, childish cries from the inside of the wagon stiffened his concern for his daughter. When the sounds finally stopped, he felt the tension ease from his body then tighten again.

Amelia.

The fruit of his loins. The daughter of his heart, denied to him for nearly five long years until he had miraculously found her again. While his love for this little girl was deep and instinctive, it was more difficult to redeem her affection for him—an experience that rocked the very essence of his soul. She welcomed his attention, yet somehow distanced herself. Her adoptive bond with Autumn was stronger than ever, but her attachment to her *natural* father?

Lukewarm at best.

The wagon jolted through a never ending series of ruts and water-filled potholes, and he tightened his hold on the reins as the sound of jostling tinware echoed in the air. It struck him, quite suddenly and ironically, that the path to fatherhood was as elusive and difficult as maneuvering the wagon safely past mud-mired dangers in the roadbed, shaking his assumption that his reunion with his daughter would be a natural phenomenon, a revival of instinctive, unbreakable bonds preordained by nature. The pain of admitting his error was a stranglehold that squeezed the breath out of his lungs.

He was wrong.

All this time.

Trina.

He had been wrong even about the consequences of her nefarious defection. They could not be undone in a single moment of joyous reunion with Amelia like he had always believed. Too late, he realized that siring a child did not guarantee attachment or love. Amelia's bond with Autumn proved that. The simple process of living together, day in and day out, was stronger.

Extinguishing the burning resentment he had for Trina, Clayton Welles, and his sister for denying him the opportunity to nourish the natural bond between himself and his own daughter was almost impossible. And as likely as relinquishing his claim to his daughter.

Another series of plaintive whimpers disrupted his thoughts. He listened hard, realizing that the sounds of Mellie's distress faded quickly beneath the sound of Autumn's voice as she sang a lullaby. Softly. Tenderly. Her comforting melody was in stark contrast to the rainy weather that vied with the dreary tempest of his own emotions.

Autumn.

A living, breathing paradox more compelling and spiritually disquieting than any he had ever encountered. She was the epitome of motherhood and female devotion in a way that was beyond Trina's interest or understanding.

Damn! He pulled his hat lower as a steady drizzle, blown by torrents of wind, turned into a heavy rain that drenched his face with cold water and effectively doused his initial impressions of Autumn when he first met her in Branfield and replaced them with experiences he had shared with her as they journeyed to Ohio. Independent? Yes. Willful? To a fault. But she was also letting down her guard and day by day, she revealed herself to be a woman of depth and character with a delightful sense of humor that stirred up feelings he thought he had buried long ago.

Autumn's inner beauty notwithstanding, the glow that laughter brought to her features that day by the creek tormented him. Haunted him. So that his nights continued to be sleepless, even though his hives had disappeared.

Remarkably, his coughing spells had stopped, too. Whether or not he owed that to Autumn's tonic, natural healing, or rainy weather that packed down dusty roads seemed almost a moot point.

He was bothered by more important issues. How could a woman like Autumn, whose unpretentious and caring nature was now so apparent, be related to a scoundrel like Clayton Welles? It just did not make any sense to him at all. The enigma that was Autumn Welles, the Tin Lady, became even more puzzling when he tried to analyze her conduct in Branfield. The night she visited him in his room at the Golden Eagle was bizarre—to say the least—and raised even more questions about the woman who now carried his name.

His wife.

He shook his head. Was Autumn merely obstinate to the point of self-destruction? That first night he was sure that she was, yet after spending nearly three weeks with her, he knew that his initial assumptions about her were premature.

Autumn was only unyielding on one very important issue: Amelia. But he was confused now more than ever. Why didn't she defend herself against the outrageous charges hurled against her by Peirce and Wilma Spakes? Was she too proud to admit that she had lied to everyone in Branfield, fabricating a background for herself and Mellie?

Or was it possible that she did not know that Amelia was *not* her brother's child? Did someone find out and threaten her? Is that why she agreed to marry Reverend Briley—to escape? Only a fool would fail to see their union as a curious but obvious mismatch.

He began to shake. Not from the cold or the rain. From the dread that perhaps he had misjudged her, and that she agreed to marry him out of fear. Of what? Or more precisely, of whom?

Scarcely before he finished posing the question, the answer came to him as abruptly as the steady downpour of rain stopped. She would only be afraid of anything or anyone who posed a threat to Amelia, and he realized now that her fear could only have one face and one name on it: his. And a darling, innocent little redhead who never deserved to be caught between the two of them was going to suffer.

A swell of dogged determination flooded his heart. He was Amelia's natural father, and given time, Amelia would grow to love him and accept him into her heart. But what about Autumn? Would Amelia ever be able to forget her or forgive him for sending away the only mother she could remember?

A loud, clanging sound coming from the inside of the wagon jolted him back into the present. He drove the team of horses to the side of the road and brought the wagon to a halt. The clanging stopped as soon as the wagon wheels creaked still, and he bounded out of his seat after securing the reins. As soon as he lifted the canvas drop curtain at the rear of the wagon, Autumn threw aside several tin pots that she must have been banging together and practically pounced on him, clutching at his shoulders.

"We need to stop at an inn. Mellie's not feeling well. It's too damp and cold in the wagon. She needs to be warmed by a fire."

One look at Autumn's worried expression sent John's heart into a series of flip-flops as the cries and whimpers he had heard earlier took on a more ominous nature. "What's wrong with her? She seemed fine this morning. Just a little cranky," he added, remembering how whiny and fretful his daughter had been at breakfast.

"She's flushed and warm to my touch, yet she's complaining of being cold. I've wrapped her in blankets and rocked her till my back and arms ache. I finally got her to sleep, but . . ." Autumn's voice cracked, and her eyes misted. "I know it's only midday, but do you think . . . I mean . . ."

John nodded, looking past Autumn at Amelia's sleeping form. An unusually bright shade of pink stained her cheeks, although she seemed to be resting comfortably with the Woolly Lamb clutched in one of her little hands. Flashes of the night she got sick from eating all of the gumdrops raced through his mind. She had completely recovered by the next day, easing his guilt.

Just last week, when he had suggested Amelia might be ill, Autumn had quickly rejected the idea without taking a breath to consider it. But this time, Autumn seemed truly concerned. Shivering as the rain pelted his back, he tried to keep his own worry from racing into panic. "I don't know how far it will be, but I'll stop at the first inn I come to. Is there anything else I can do for Amelia?"

Autumn shook her head. "Drive safely. I hope I'm not overreacting. It's just . . . I worry when Mellie gets ill. She'll probably be fine once we get her settled in someplace warm."

Autumn's bottom lip quivered, and fear filled her luminous cocoa-colored eyes. John had the most powerful urge to climb into the wagon and hold her. Reassure her that he would not let anything happen to Amelia because he loved her as much as Autumn did. Crush her fears in an embrace. Quiet her worry with a promise from deep within his heart that he would make sure that Amelia would be all right.

His hand trembled as he reached out and cupped Autumn's cheek with his hand. Gently, she leaned into his touch, and he felt the warmth of her flesh against his fingers. It sent off warning bells in his brain that his worried heart silenced with a single beat. "Rest while you can," he murmured. "Amelia will need care when she wakes up."

A dangerous current of warm emotions passed between them, and John pulled away, jolted by the intensity of his reaction to Autumn. What was happening to him? He had lowered his guard too easily, swayed by her devotion to his child and the magnetism of her femininity, letting the allure of this woman pull him too close to her.

Adversaries.

He and Autumn were rivals, he repeated silently over

and over again in his mind. Whether she recognized that now or not, he did, and it was an advantage he was not going to surrender or forget.

Disgusted by his own weakness, which he credited somehow to guile that had to run through her veins as surely as her brother's, he glared at her. She flinched and edged closer to Amelia, a frightened, confused look covering her face.

Message sent and received.

Satisfied, he began to drop the canvas cover back into place. "See that Amelia is kept warm," he ordered. "I'll find an inn."

Several hours later, after being turned away from several inns because the owners feared that Amelia's illness might be contagious and dangerous to other patrons, John stopped the wagon in front of a tollgate and climbed down from his seat. With only a few daylight hours remaining, he had precious little patience left. Amelia's condition had worsened. Her fever now raged even higher, and he was consumed by his failure to find a safe haven for her.

"The tollgate's locked because the stream flooded the roadbed. Try again tomorrow."

John's body twisted around to the right, following the sound of the man's voice that cut through the mist that surrounded the wagon like a cloud that had dropped to earth. Heavy, booted steps crunched on the gravel roadbed, and John waited until a figure finally emerged into sight. An average-looking man in his sixties with sparrow brown hair approached, and his oilskin raincoat was askew as though he had donned it in haste. Gentle brown eyes, however, warmed with apology as he extended his hand. "Lehman Whittaker. I'm sorry for the inconvenience."

John's grip was intentionally hard. "Logan. John Logan. I need to get through. Any chance I might give it a try?"

Head shaking, Lehman broke their grasp and pointed to the horizon. "Still more rain coming. Last my brother checked, the stream was still rising. It probably won't recede for a day or two. Caleb's a bit more cautious about these things than I am, but I trust his judgment enough to suggest you wait at least until the morning." He paused. Wrinkles creased his forehead. "You'd be better off settling in at Four Points at the main crossroads. Nathan's got good hot food there and a fire in the tavern room to warm your bones even if he does water down his cider."

"I can't afford to mince time or words. My daughter is ill. I need help." John let the words hang in the air for a moment. "I tried the Four Points and two inns before that. No one will chance letting us stay. They told me about an inn down this road. I have to try to get there. She's getting worse. Fever is burning her alive."

Confusion turned to curiosity as the stranger looked past John to the driver's seat. "Your child?"

John nodded toward the back of the wagon. "My wife is caring for Amelia as best she can in the wagon, but if I could get the child inside to a dry, warm bed—"

Lehman cut him off. "You'll never get through. How long has she been sick?"

"Just since this morning."

A series of tiny cries coming from the rear of the wagon punctuated his words, and he watched as Lehman's expression filled with pity.

"Got plenty of room right here. My father's in Virginia for a spell, visiting my sister who's about to marry off the last of her brood. You and your family can use his rooms. Turn the wagon around. I'll direct you. The homestead sits a ways back from the road."

Swallowing twin lumps of relief and gratitude, John nodded weakly. "I'm much obliged to you," he rasped.

"Nonsense. Just following the Good Book," he shouted back over a ripple of thunder. "Follow me. I'll lead you there, and we'll get that little one tucked in proper in a warm bed."

In the rear of the wagon, Autumn had eavesdropped on the conversation between John and the other man with a mixture of fear and hope that quickly turned into surprised relief when the man offered them a place to stay. She patted Mellie's back as she rocked her from side to side, soothing her back into sleep. Mellie's face rested between her mother's neck and shoulder, and her fevered flesh was hotter now than it had been just an hour earlier.

Autumn bowed her head and rested her cheek against Mellie's curls. Tears of worry slipped quietly down Autumn's face. Mellie was rarely sick, although when Clayton and Trina first brought their baby home, she had been fretful and prone to colic. Had last year's bout with lung fever returned? Were the little girl's lungs restored and strong enough to survive another attack?

Her heart pulsed with heavy beats as she hugged Mellie closer. John's concern about Mellie last week flashed through Autumn's mind. Had she too quickly dismissed the possibility that Mellie might be getting ill?

Autumn could not lose this child, this wondrous miracle of love. Not now. Not when she was close to achieving a wonderful new life for both of them. Nothing. Neither her talent with the brush nor the position in Ohio meant anything . . . not without Mellie.

Sniffling, Autumn chided herself for being foolish. All Mellie needed was a few days of rest and devoted care, and she would be back to her exuberant self. As the wagon began to roll into motion, she wrapped Mellie securely in several blankets. Autumn ran her fingers through her hair, deftly redoing the knot at the base of her neck before freshening her own appearance.

Minutes later, the wagon stopped, and John lifted the canvas flap and secured it with ropes. She blinked at the bright light that flooded the inside of the wagon, light which emanated from a small stone bungalow only a few feet away.

"Lehman, this is my wife, Autumn," John said quickly without looking at her. He reached inside and scooped Mellie easily into his arms and turned away. Autumn accepted the stranger's assistance and climbed out of the wagon, grateful for the kind expression on his face.

"Sorry about your troubles, ma'am, but don't you worry. Caleb and I will see you have everything you need to get your little one set to rights."

Worried, she glanced ahead as John carried Mellie toward the door to the house. Nodding silently, Autumn rushed after him, stopping only long enough to pluck Woolly Lamb out of a mud puddle. The door swung open and another man, a mirror image of Lehman, stood silhouetted in the back light from the interior of the house.

"Caleb!" Lehman called out. "Get a good fire going in Father's rooms. Looks like we've got company, and they've got a real sick little girl."

Caleb stood aside to let John enter the house, and Autumn followed on his heels. Heart pounding, she clutched Mellie's mud-soaked little lamb. "Please," she prayed softly, hoping that God would hear her. "Please help Mellie."

Chapter 12

"You're still so hot."

Autumn laid the palm of her hand against her daughter's scarlet cheeks and felt the shallow beat of her heart against her fingertips as she touched the girl's temple while she slept. *Fever.* Its distinctive odor permeated the room. It left Mellie's little lips dry and cracked, and it stretched the limits of fear in Autumn's breast.

Seated on an ottoman, Autumn leaned closer to the chaise that Caleb and Lehman had set before the fire in the small, second-story reading room that belonged to their father. She ignored the sleet and driving rain that pelted the windows which were set on either side of the mantel. Like dark glass eyes of death, they stared down at the sickbed.

Shivering, Autumn ignored the gloomy illusion and strained to see the first streaks of the third dawn that would break since they had arrived at the Whittakers's homestead. Would the arrival of a new day, however dreary, also bring with it the end of Mellie's fever?

Wearied footsteps mounted the winders of the staircase that curved sharply upward from the main floor of the bungalow. She looked over toward the landing and trembled. Was he back?

When John came into view, she sighed with relief and felt a strange rush of closeness with this man who was now her husband. Her seamless vigil at Mellie's sickbed had exhausted her to near collapse. He fared little better.

Fingers of light from the fire chased away the shadows from the stairwell as he approached her carrying a bucket of fresh water. Dark circles under his eyes, lines of worry that etched his features, and rumpled clothes all testified to the long stretch of duty he shared with Autumn at Mellie's bedside.

A swell of gratitude caught in her throat. His attentiveness to both of their needs these past three days had never wavered, and he quietly had dedicated himself to making sure that she had everything she needed to tend to the little redhead who lay weak and limp beneath the covers on the chaise. He had forced Autumn to eat a few bites from each tray of food Caleb and Lehman sent upstairs. When she had refused to budge from Mellie's side, even to sleep for a few hours in the bedroom on the other side of the stairwell, he had brought her a pillow and taken his own rest in the chair at the end of the chaise.

As he set the bucket on the floor at her feet and handed her a new cloth, he leaned toward her. "Is she any better?" His whispered voice was strained.

She shook her head, dipped the cloth into the frigid water, then wrung it out. "Her fever should have broken by now." She turned to bathe her daughter's face and lovingly smoothed back matted red curls from her forehead. Blue-veined eyelids fluttered briefly as Mellie stirred then slipped back into stillness, each shallow breath she took barely strong enough to rustle the covers.

Autumn watched as John arranged his chair sideways and closer to the chaise before he sank down into the seat. He stretched his long legs out in front of him and rested one hand on top of Mellie's foot, his thumb slowly caressing her instep. Leaning his head against the back of the chair, he closed his eyes and took a deep, fatigued breath. "I thought the ice bath might have helped."

Autumn cocked her head, amazed by the sound of abject failure that resonated through his words. Remembering the ordeal of the ice bath from earlier that afternoon, she shuddered. Mellie's pathetic cries had torn at her heart, and only John's reassurance and steadying support had given her the courage to continue the treatment. He took over when her waning strength gave out, and Autumn realized that he took the disappointing results of trying to break Mellie's fever as a personal one. "It did help. She's cooler to the touch now than . . . than before," she murmured, hoping that if she said it, then it might yet come true.

Deep blue eyes fluttered opened and flickered with doubt. "She needs a doctor."

"Caleb and Lehman told us that he's back east. By the time you travel to Whitley to the nearest physician, it wouldn't make any difference. Either her fever will break soon or . . ." She let her words trail off, unable to voice the other possibility.

"Caleb and Lehman offered to go."

She shook her head again. "They've done enough." Even though she had not seen either one of the twin brothers who so graciously provided shelter for them all since the day they arrived, she knew that John had kept them informed as to Mellie's condition as he went back and forth between the sloped rooms on the second story and the main floor for fresh supplies. The two brothers cooked meals to sustain them, and John carried a heart-swelling message from both of them that they were praying for Mellie, too. They were like a pair of vigilant guardian angels, and she knew she could never repay them for their kindness, even if . . .

Instead of contemplating what might happen if Mellie did not recover, she concentrated on John, studying him as he sat just a few feet away. How often had she prayed to see Clayton display one iota of interest or concern in his only child? Yet here was a man who had known Mellie just barely a month, and he was willing to travel for miles in disastrous weather to search for a doctor!

The scene in the general store in Glenham when she accused him of having a hidden reason for wanting her to come to Ohio flashed through her mind. Once again, she quickly dismissed his look of stupefaction and anger as having any source other than wounded male pride. John had done more for Mellie in the space of a few weeks than her natural father had ever done, although Autumn was loathe to admit that she was just a little jealous of Mellie's divided interest during their journey west. As this frightful crisis evolved, John had responded with total devotion. He held her little girl when Autumn wearied, although when Mellie woke up, it was only the comfort of her mother's arms and voice that settled her.

Reluctantly, John had claimed a place at the end of the chaise and rubbed the little girl's foot, relegated to being an anonymous comforter or securing a fresh supply of water or a bowl of broth. He chopped the ice stored in the ice house and then packed it around her fevered body just hours earlier, but allowed Autumn to nurse Mellie without insisting that he take turns—just to keep Mellie calm. He had even laundered the Woolly Lamb which now sat on the floor near the fire to dry.

The sting of Mellie's preference for her mother was evident in the subtle slump of his shoulders and the way his eyes turned a mournful shade of blue whenever he looked at Mellie. Mesmerized by the unusual color of his eyes, Autumn compared it to the pale shade of Bonnie Blue she created for her tole painting that was the gentle and carefree color of spring flowers that grew wild and free near her childhood home.

She was close enough to John now to notice that his eye color was even more intriguing and much more compelling and complex than the lighter shade. She knew that she someday she would have to try to duplicate the color of his eyes for her painting. It could have only one name, one that would capture forever the man's tenderness and devotion to her little girl: Logan Blue. As blue as heaven, and every bit as faithful.

He leaned forward, his sudden movement breaking her concentration. "Is something wrong?"

Caught staring, Autumn felt her cheeks warm. "No. I'm sorry. I was just thinking. About how good you've been to Mellie. And to me."

He pulled back, his expression hard. "A man doesn't deserve credit for doing what's right," he countered. "Or what's natural."

"Not all men know what's right or feel emotions that should come naturally," she murmured. Clayton's face flashed in her mind, and she stared at John again to chase it away, wondering how he could be so caring and so concerned about a five-year-old girl now, and then turn his back on her when they finally arrived in Ohio. What odd blend of feelings motivated him now and would justify his actions later?

"Men don't have a lock on queer emotions." His statement hung in the air like laundry frozen to a clothesline in winter as he leaned back into the chair.

"You mean your wife."

He nodded. His expression changed from wistful to pained, and she knew she should refrain from pushing him further about his first wife. He had told her that his previous marriage had been a mistake, but he had not told her how it had ended. Emboldened, she gave in to her curiosity. "How long has it been? Since your first marriage ended?"

He inhaled and held his breath, his chest swelling before he exhaled slowly. "My wife died several years ago." Anguish briefly lit his face before it hardened into a stone mask.

Understanding the quicksilver range of emotions displayed on his face was difficult for Autumn. If he regretted his first marriage, why had his wife's death been so hard to accept? Was it that death eliminated any hope of love redeemed or devotion reclaimed? Or did he merely regret every day of his marriage?

"I'm sorry," she whispered.

He snorted softly, his lips curling derisively. "Sorrow has nothing to do with it. Not for me. She died in the arms of her lover."

Autumn gasped. Her heart thudded in her chest. No wonder he wanted their marriage to be a business arrangement! Being betrayed by his first wife had obviously embittered him toward the sanctity and joy of matrimony, although Autumn had no false assumptions as to why he had married her. In fact, she finally understood now why he had used the institution to his own advantage. It held no sacred or emotional meaning for him.

How could it?

She turned away from him and bathed Mellie's face again, trying to shield any sign of her empathy for his pain and loss. Empathy that he would probably hurl back at her in typical male fashion.

"I don't need your pity."

She froze in place, wondering if he had read her thoughts. The now-warm cloth in her hand shook slightly as she folded it and hung it over the rim of the bucket. "Not pity. Understanding," she answered softly.

She chewed on her lower lip, then sighed. "You don't have an exclusive claim on pain or loss . . . or loneliness."

"I didn't say I did."

"You didn't have to. I could hear it in your voice." The hurt look on his face made her heart ache. Wearied by her concern for Mellie, a concern he shared so completely, her guard slipped lower still. Safely out of Branfield and beyond the clutches of Edsel Cameron, she could not resist unburdening the heavy load she had carried alone for so long, especially to the man who had created the opportunity for her to paint again and make a safe home for her daughter. After all John had done for her and for Mellie, she realized that she owed him some semblance of the truth. The time to match wits in verbal skirmishes or misunderstandings based on assumptions was over. "There's no way I can totally understand how you feel. I've . . . I've never been married."

She looked at him, waiting for the same look of condemnation that Wilma Spakes and her father hurled at her or the censure in Norbert's gaze. John's eyes, however, were warm blue embers. She gulped. "Mellie—"

"—is a love child." He had finished her statement so matter-of-factly that he startled her.

"No," she said quietly.

He sat forward in his seat. "Either you were married before and Amelia is legitimate or you weren't and the child is illegitimate. In either case, I'm not your judge. You have your own conscience to reckon with. No one else's."

She tilted her chin and held his gaze. "I've never been married before, but Mellie is not . . . not a bastard child. She was . . ."

Tears welled in her eyes. She was so tired her bones ached, and her spirit longed for the comfort of another kindred soul who had been wounded by fate. So lonely. So *alone* for the past year and a half, guarding her secret, watching every word, perfecting her cover story to protect the little one by her side. If John knew the truth, would he protect them both with the same level of devotion she had witnessed for the past few days? Had she finally met a man who would not disappoint her or let her down?

Battling back tears was futile, and she swiped them away with the back of her hand. "I can't bear to think that I might lose her. She's all that I have. All that has given me joy and pleasure for the past four and a half years."

She wavered. Should she bare her secret? *Could* she?

"Mellie is the daughter of my heart and soul," she whispered. "I've raised her since she was less than a year old. But . . . but she's not the child of my womb."

His sharp intake of breath startled her. His gaze intensified, impaling her to her seat.

"If Amelia is not your child, why would you claim her as your own? Except for your age, it's not unusual for a single woman to have a ward." Confusion filled his face, but he stared intensely at her, pinning her immobile. "What was that display in Branfield all about? Why didn't you tell Reverend Briley the truth?"

Her back arched with righteousness and determination. "He wouldn't understand. He would make me . . . make me take her back. I can't do that. I won't!"

An alarming chill glazed dark, fathomless blue eyes. "Take her back? Who did you take her away from?"

"Her grandfather, but he has no right to claim her!"

"But you do?" John's hands clutched the sides of the chair, his body as rigid as a glacier about to break free and ruthlessly crush her with implacable consequences. "What about her parents?" he whispered.

"They're both dead."

His eyes widened, the cold hard look melting for a heartbeat before it froze. "How convenient for you."

"And how inconvenient it was for my brother and his wife to die!" Chest heaving, she glared back at him.

"Your brother?"

She nodded and sucked in her breath, twisting her hands on her lap. Unable to bear the shame of admitting that her brother and his wife had been too consumed with each other to give Mellie more than a cursory thought before they plopped her into Autumn's care, she embroidered on the truth. "My brother was a wonderful father. He came home after two years on his peddler's route with a wife he worshiped to distraction and a baby daughter that he adored."

She sighed, gathering the strength to continue her lies and to avert John's penetrating gaze. "Trina's father is extremely wealthy, and he had tried to take Mellie away from them. He didn't approve of my brother as a suitable husband for his daughter or as the father of his only grandchild." She shook her head. "It broke their hearts to leave Mellie with me while they searched for a safe place to settle down with their little girl. Someplace where Trina's father wouldn't find them." Her eyes misted. "They never came home. They were both killed by thieves on a deserted road outside of Boston. By then, Mellie was over three years old, and I loved her like she was my own natural child instead of Clayton's. She loved me. She called me m-mama. And I didn't stop her."

Autumn's voice cracked, and she took deep breaths of air to still her shaking voice and heart as she gazed at Mellie. "I know I should have taken Mellie to her grandfather. He can provide for Mellie and give her the very best of everything, but I just can't bear the thought of losing her. I'm her aunt, and I know that the courts would never understand that Mellie should stay with me instead of her grandfather. But . . . but I'm the only mother Mellie can remember."

She reached out and took Mellie's hand into hers, holding it against her cheek. The warmth of the child's flesh made her tremble. "I—I ran away with her because I knew that her grandfather would never understand that Mellie loved me, too. I found a position in Branfield, hoping that he wouldn't be able to find either of us. As a single woman with Mellie as my ward, I would be far more suspect than a widow with her natural child."

"So you lied to Reverend Briley."

A hushed statement, not a cold accusation. She nodded, grateful for the timbre of understanding in John's voice, yet reluctant to let go of Mellie to face him. "And everyone else in Branfield. I just didn't want to risk the truth. Losing Mellie would be like tearing out my heart. Can you possibly understand now how I felt when Wilma and her father confronted me in your room? Norbert would never have forgiven me for what I had done. Ever. If I defended myself, the truth would have reached Edsel Cameron, and he would have sent someone for Mellie. Or sent someone to snatch her away. Someone," she murmured as she put Mellie's hand back beneath the quilt. "Someone like you."

She had unburdened the guilt she now felt for ever doubting him and opened her past for his scrutiny. Why? To forge some kind of link between them, to let him know that he was not the only one who had been betrayed when placing his heart into someone else's hand? What would she find glowing in those riveting, mesmerizing blue eyes? Windows of pity? Understanding? Or would they be shuttered closed against her?

Taking a deep breath, she chanced a look at John's face to gauge his reaction to her risky confession.

Chapter 13

John stared down at Autumn. Perched on the ottoman at his feet, her eyes were wide with expectation. For one sheer moment, she had dropped the practiced veneer of her prim and proper facade, allowing him a too-rare glimpse of her soul. He felt his heart begin to pound in his chest, amazed by the vulnerability reflected in the depths of her eyes and the scintilla of guilt she carried for not trusting him.

Lines of weariness that were etched in her oval face only added depth to her character, and an innocence emanated so completely from within her that it only intensified her physical loveliness. Gentle fingers of soft, flickering light from the banked fire reflected in the depths of mink colored eyes that made them glow. She was a tawny sylph, a gift of Mother Earth, goodness made human by Nature's hand.

The image startled him, setting loose a barrage of conflicting emotions that ripped through his defenses. Again. More eloquently than the first time. For one fleeting moment, time stood suspended. His heart reached out and touched hers, and he was mesmerized. Captivated. And nearly overcome by the sheer magnificence of the feelings that engulfed him.

His youthful fantasies about the emotion of love shared between a man and a woman, based on pleasures of the flesh, were forgiven and redeemed as easily as the jaded man he had become. This was a woman of promise and destiny, a life partner who could share his hopes and dreams as well as his love.

Revealed too late.

A rumble of thunder followed by a crack of lightning jolted him back into reality and onto his feet. Autumn flinched, grabbed Mellie's hand, and turned away to soothe the restless child. Was it the sound of the crashing, intensifying storm, or his sudden movement that startled her?

He stepped back and studied her closely as though distance would give him a new perspective on his own bewildering thoughts. A sudden bolt of lightning reflected through the window and illuminated Autumn's image. His muscles tensed. She radiated innocence and love, not guile and deceit, he realized, as parts of her eloquent confession echoed in chorus with the now-distant thunder.

Turning away, he walked over to the window and stared through the rain-splattered panes. His hands gripped the window sill, knuckles touching cold glass. Outside, trees hunched in supplication, and dark ominous clouds swept across the sky. There was no mercy in the sheets of furious rain that pummeled the landscape. Was there also no room in his soul for tenderness or compassion? Leaning his forehead against the window, he closed his eyes.

He believed Autumn when she told him that Amelia was her brother's child. Somehow, she had reached into what was left of his heart and claimed his total sympathy when she bared her soul and admitted that she ran away with Amelia because Autumn was afraid of Edsel Cameron. Her motives were pure, almost heroic. As the champion of an orphaned child who needed protection, Autumn was nothing more than a sacrificial victim of fate, a woman who dedicated her life to her brother's small child.

No. My child.

Cold panes of glass pressed against his knuckles and tempered his thoughts. Rooted once again in reality, he turned away from the window. He watched compassionately as Autumn soothed Mellie back to sleep, wondering if Autumn would ever accept the fact that her brother had lied to her, and she had dedicated her life to a child that was not her own brother's flesh and blood.

His gaze rested on Mellie's little face, still so flushed with fever. His chest tightened as an ache, buried deep within his soul, became dreadful, personal pain. Autumn's description of Trina and Clayton as doting parents whose hearts were broken when they had to be separated from their daughter made his stomach churn.

John knew the truth.

Even though Autumn appeared to have been totally hoodwinked by her brother into accepting Trina as his legal wife and Amelia as his natural child, John could not understand why she lied about Clayton and Trina's devotion to Amelia.

John had spent too many sleepless nights wondering who would comfort his baby girl when she was sick or afraid of the dark. It would not have been Trina or Clayton. From what he had learned, they had been too obsessed with one another to give the little girl a thought.

Poor Amelia! She must have been so confused. Did she cry herself to sleep, hungering for the love and comfort of her papa's arms, too young to understand why her mother ignored her and her papa had disappeared?

Resentment quickly turned into anger, but he stored it deep within his consciousness as a reminder of what had been done to him and to his child by Trina, her lover, and compounded, however innocently, by the woman who sat in front of him. He channeled his anger and disappointment into rigid control of his emotions. He had held them in check long enough before he met Autumn, and he could do it now!

Reclaiming Amelia would not be any easier now that he knew that Autumn was a victim as surely as he had been, although he did not dare give her a clue that he had not been fooled by her description of her Trina and Clayton. Let Autumn think that he believed her. It would keep her off guard long enough for them to reach Ohio.

"I'm sorry I doubted you."

"What?" John looked away from Mellie to stare at Autumn.

She blushed, twisting her apron in her hands. "I wanted to apologize for not trusting you in Branfield. If I had . . ." She dipped her head and lowered her gaze. "It seems Norbert may have been right after all. Lies, even when created for good purposes, seem to take on a life of their own."

He exhaled slowly. *Lies?* Hers? Or his?

Was it possible she really did not know that Edsel Cameron had died shortly after his daughter's death, unaware that Amelia had not been left behind with John in Ohio? If Autumn did know, was she also aware of the terms of the will? Would she actually deny Amelia her rightful inheritance rather than give her up, assuming the courts would not allow a woman to serve as the child's guardian?

He cleared his throat. Intrigued by her willingness to trust him, he pressed his advantage to learn more about her fear of Edsel Cameron. "Did you really suspect that I was sent by the girl's grandfather?"

Autumn nodded once before looking up at him. "It

all seemed too good to be true. Too coincidental, I suppose." She smiled, creating that one ridiculously deep dimple in her cheek. "Your hint of an offer was so tempting. That's why I came to the Golden Eagle. I just needed to know if there was any way I could escape marrying the somber Reverend Briley." She giggled nervously. "You didn't like him very much, did you?"

John chuckled. "He's not my idea of a true minister of the Word. What really perplexed me was your decision to marry him in the first place. He . . . well, he didn't seem to quite know how to handle you. Now that I think about it, he and Wilma Spakes seem better suited."

Autumn sighed. "I couldn't find work in Branfield. I thought it would be best at the time and ultimately, better for Mellie if I married him. You're right about our suitability, though. Wilma would certainly agree with you, and so would her father. My guess is that the poor Reverend Briley didn't stand a chance against the two of them after we left. I've even looked back over my shoulder during the trip to Ohio, wondering if we'd meet Norbert and Wilma traveling west." Her eyes grew distant and narrowed in thought.

"That possibility occurred to me, too," John admitted slowly. "Knowing the man, however briefly, I suspect that he and Wilma will avoid confronting us if we do meet. He may be judgmental and rigid, but he is also mollified when sinners repent and do what's right. As far as he's concerned, once he married us, our blackened souls were cleansed. His new wife, if he and Wilma did marry, will not challenge his authority."

Autumn cocked her head. "You don't know Wilma. If she has the opportunity, she'll embroider the whole episode, and although she'll be sure to stitch the ending properly, I guarantee the thread she uses for my part will be scarlet."

Recalling Wilma's venomous attack, John was inclined to agree with Autumn's astute assessment of Wilma's personality. "Godly women seem to be at a premium," he muttered under his breath as he stretched, trying to ease the tightness in the tense muscles of his back.

He glanced at Amelia and felt guilty for having any thoughts beyond her recovery. Reaching to the side and bending forward, he picked up her Woolly Lamb and squeezed it tight to make sure it had fully dried. Satisfied, he knelt down beside the chaise lounge. Lifting the covers, he found one of Mellie's hands and opened it. Placing her treasured possession into her palm, he wrapped her warm little fingers around it. His eyes widened as she tightened her grasp even as she slept. Looking up at Autumn, he was taken aback by the sight of her tear-filled eyes.

"You're a good man, John Logan," she whispered as she reached out to place her hand on his shoulder. "Mellie is lucky to have you for her father, even if it's only temporary."

By mid-afternoon, Autumn could barely keep her eyes open. She wanted to blame the bright sunlight that flooded the room in the aftermath of the storm for making her close her eyes, but she could not convince her fatigued body to agree. With barely more than a few hours sleep snatched haphazardly when Mellie did not need to be bathed, fed a little broth, or comforted, Autumn had passed beyond exhaustion. She was numb and almost asleep on her feet.

John had eventually dozed off while still sitting in his chair, his arm draped across Mellie's legs and one errant lock of golden brown hair lying on his forehead. A swell of emotion lodged in Autumn's throat. Beneath his dangerously handsome appearance lay a compassionate heart and the combination of good looks and loyal spirit, laced with his own pain and vulnerability, almost made her tremble.

She could share her life and her dreams with this man and know the full promise of deep and abiding love once she broke through the barriers erected by his first wife's betrayal. Together with Mellie, they could create a real family. Nurtured by both a mother and a father, Mellie would grow up secure, feeling loved and witnessing the true commitment of a man and a woman joined together in a loving marriage. Brothers and sisters for Mellie, of course, completed this imaginary picture of wedded bliss and familial perfection for Autumn.

The threat posed by Edsel Cameron faded into the background. Convinced that he would never find Mellie once she was formally adopted by her new papa and changed her name, Autumn knew that there was only one problem, one insurmountable barrier to her fantasy: John Logan. She knew that he was committed to only the dream of building a thriving tin business in Ohio, and he had no room in his life or his heart for a wife and child.

Indulging her curiosity, she wondered about the people he said depended on him. Family, most likely, although he had yet to mention anyone other than his mother who had already passed away. Siblings? An elderly father? She could understand those responsibilities, perhaps better than anyone else.

She admired John for his loyalty, but she also knew that devotion and responsibility were cold bedmates. He was a virile, handsome man who could not forever deny his need for a woman in his life. Sooner or later, he would marry again, even if he could not or would not admit it to himself. Could she convince him to consider her? He was already enamored with Mellie, but Autumn could not begin to fathom his feelings about her. They ranged from distrust to admiration, although there were so many in between that she had only a small glimmer of hope that her fantasy might become reality.

He would not make the first move, but for Autumn, playing the role of temptress seemed as foreign and unlikely to succeed as the sun shining at midnight. She did not know how to play the coquette, even if she wanted to try. Neither could she easily relinquish the fear of being disappointed again. She had learned too many painful lessons where men were concerned, and although she was anxious to try for the first time in her life, she was too concerned about Mellie to give it serious thought right now.

John Logan. He was the man she had dreamed about, and later, when Mellie recovered, Autumn vowed to find a way to lay claim to his heart and at long last, find all of her dreams fulfilled.

She sighed. A deep sigh that came from her spirit as well as her body. Feeling guilty for wool-gathering while her daughter lay so ill, Autumn chalked off her fanciful daydreaming as weakness caused by her fatigue. If only she could get a good night's rest . . . .

Standing up, she stretched, arching her back and holding the pose until her cramped back and shoulder muscles protested. Relaxing her posture, she tidied up the room and carried the tray with the remnants of a half-eaten meal on it to the table near the stairwell. She caught her reflection in the highly-polished silver frame of an oil painting and gasped. She looked awful!

Backing away from the frightful image, she realized that she had paid little attention to her own grooming these past few days. After checking on Mellie, whose little face was still flushed with fever, Autumn carried the bucket of water and a fresh cloth with her as she tiptoed past John and opened the door to the bedroom. A large bed, with a thick oak headboard and footboard that sloped outward like a sleigh, sat against the paneled wall. Her carpet bag rested at the foot of the bed on top of a blue and white quilt.

Hurriedly, she closed the door and placed the bucket and cloth on the floor. She looked around, almost relieved there was no vanity or mirror, not that the elder Mr. Whittaker would have need for one. She spied a rattan chair and propped it in front of the door. Satisfied that she would have a few private moments, she undressed, washed quickly with the cold water, and shivered even as she put on a fresh gown and apron. Apparently, the elder Mr. Whittaker preferred sleeping in winter without benefit of a fire which was the reason they had set up a chaise for Amelia in the reading room.

After fumbling through the carpet bag, she found her brush and removed the pins from her hair. Sitting on the edge of the bed, she brushed her hair, carefully removing the tangles before she twisted the shoulder-length mane into a tight knot at the back of her neck.

She stopped for a moment and held very still. Had she heard Mellie whimper? She strained her ears, but heard nothing. Realizing that her hair was pulled painfully tight, she used both hands to loosen it and used her fingertips to shape the soft waves that once again framed her face.

Feeling refreshed and somehow less fatigued, she hurried back to Mellie's bedside, careful not to wake John. He had shifted in his seat, one cheek resting on his shoulder, his face bathed in sunlight. His chest barely moved as he breathed. She was glad that he had finally given in and fallen asleep, although she doubted he was anything less than uncomfortable in the straight-backed wooden chair. She hesitated only a moment before she went back into the bedroom and pulled the quilt off the bed. Returning, she covered John and tucked the ends of the quilt over the back of the chair to hold it in place. Shaken by the feelings that ran through her when she brushed his hair with the back of her hand, she swirled away from him. Closing her eyes, she forced herself to take several deep gulps of air to make her heart beat drop back to a normal cadence.

She was acting like a silly schoolgirl!

Worse, she chastised herself as she dropped to her knees to check Mellie closely. The child still slept, and Autumn studied every detail of her daughter's face. Deep crescents beneath her eyes seemed even darker. Lips cracked from fever were parted ever so slightly. Cheeks once scarlet were ghostly pale as though . . .

Autumn's heart literally stopped beating. She held her breath, reaching out with shaking hands to touch the limp form that lay ever so still beneath the covers. Tears trickled silently down Autumn's cheeks, and her lips began to quiver. "Mellie! Oh, Mellie," she cried as she pressed the palms of her hands against her daughter's cheeks. "Mellie!"

Heart pounding back to life, Autumn leaned forward and rested her weight against the side of the chaise lounge. She loosened and smoothed the cap of sweat-drenched ringlets that clung to Mellie's head. She paused, almost too afraid to breathe as she laid her hand against the child's cheek before tracing the column of her neck. Autumn's eyes were riveted to Mellie's face. Her heartbeat lurched. Fingertips trembling at the sides of Mellie's throat, they stilled for a moment as Autumn felt for the gentle pulsebeat of life.

Waiting. Hoping. Praying.

Then weeping.

Tears ran down her cheeks as she bowed her head and cried openly.

Chapter 14

The fever had broken!

Before the words had formed an elated awareness in her mind, Autumn bowed her head and silently offered a prayer of thanksgiving. Then suddenly, a tremendous weight from behind knocked her off balance and crushed her against the chaise lounge. It pressed against her rib cage, and her knees dug painfully into the wide-planked floorboards. She struggled blindly, instinctively, as a blanket engulfed her upper body and head, pitching her into abject darkness and pulsating fright. Something or someone jammed her face into the chaise making it difficult to breathe. She grew dizzy. Bright lights danced in a frenzy in front of her eyes.

Fear and confusion gripped her heart and fueled a twisting, violent struggle against her unseen attacker. Frantic, she used the last bit of wind in her lungs to scream out. "Stop! Please, stop!"

To her amazement, the weight immediately lifted, and she was free. The blanket was yanked away, and she blinked as daylight intruded suddenly and harshly through a curtain of tussled hair that covered her face. Strong hands pulled her back to a kneeling position, and she took heaving gulps of air as she leaned back on her haunches and pushed her hair out of her face—only to find herself entangled in the quilt with John who was kneeling beside her barely inches away.

He stared at her, his cheeks flushed. "Are you all right?"

His question was almost ludicrous.

"Are you insane?" she spat irritably as she attempted to restore her hair to order. "What were you trying to do to me?"

"Your scream startled me awake. I got caught up in the damn quilt when I bolted to my feet. I thought . . ." His voice dropped off as he looked away from her and stared at Mellie. Autumn felt a stab of guilt for snapping at him and accusing him of deliberately attacking her.

Concern, deep and overwhelming, shimmered in his eyes. "Is she . . . is she all right?" His voice shook.

"Her fever has broken," Autumn murmured, awed by the sudden reversal of her emotions. Embarrassment replaced fear. Then another feeling ran through her, and she recognized it as longing, a desperate, gnawing hunger to share the relief that surged through her own spirit when she realized that Mellie was going to recover. John must have heard her when she cried out Mellie's name and thought . . .

She looked at him again, seeing him in a new light. Dear God, he seemed to be devastated by the possibility that sickness had claimed the little girl he had tried so desperately to help.

Her earlier anger seemed totally without basis now. Instead, a more appropriate feeling, guilt, overwhelmed her as she tried to avoid looking at John and concentrated on disentangling herself from the blue and white quilt which bound her physically to John. She admitted to herself that she was linked to him emotionally even more strongly. She would never forget his kindness to her and to her daughter, and she wondered if she would ever fully understand how this man had come to love another man's child so quickly and so completely.

Impulsively, she wrapped her arms around his waist and laid her head on his chest. "Mellie's going to be fine. I didn't mean to alarm you." She gave him a squeeze. "I've been so afraid that . . . she—she just didn't seem to be getting any better. I was so tired that my eyes kept closing so I tried to stay awake by tidying up. I went into the bedroom to change, and when I came back I saw you sleeping and covered you with the quilt. When I checked Mellie, I realized that her crisis had peaked. . . . I didn't mean to frighten you."

Oddly, she stopped her explanation as her thoughts became ideas that jumbled together, and she was caught off guard when she heard the pounding of his heart against her ear and felt the warmth of his body against her cheek. It felt good, even right somehow, when she realized that he was holding her, too. When had his arms wrapped around her shoulders? Shyly, she tilted her head back and looked up at him.

Her heartbeat fluttered in her chest, and she moistened her lips nervously. His eyes bore directly to the center of her spirit, and she caught her breath. No longer the deep, cynical shade of midnight blue, they were softer and sparkled with the gentle luminescence of beautiful sapphires. The quilt slipped to the floor, and a warm flush rose to her cheeks as he raised one of his hands to caress her cheek, tenderly lifting a tendril of hair off of her face.

Ever so slowly, his thumb caressed her jawline and she tilted her head again just enough to increase the sensuous feelings that waltzed across her face from the touch of his fingertips. The warmth of his shallow breathing fanned her lips making them tingle and ache.

Her fingers toyed with the corded muscles that ran along his back.

Brown eyes searched the depths of dazzling blue mirrors, looking for an explanation of the wonder she felt being enfolded in his embrace. Did he feel it, too? Were they blue crystals of desire glistening in his eyes? Shaken, she closed her eyes and took a deep breath as a maelstrom of conflicting emotions tumbled and stormed through her body like rolling thunderclouds about to burst.

He shifted his position and pulled her closer to him. He kissed her forehead. Her eyelids. The tip of her nose. Each cheek. An earlobe. His lips made a pleasured assault that made her skin tingle. Her heart began to hopscotch an insane, erratic beat that pulsed wildly with anticipation as he ignited her passions.

Eyes fluttering open, she caught one fleeting glimpse of his lips before they parted slightly and mated with hers. Sweetly. Tenderly. Melting the last of her defenses and fanning the flames of her own desires. His kiss became bolder, more insistent. Pulsing sensations fluttered through her body. Growing weak, yet desperate for more, she returned his ardor and pressed against him as she parted her lips, unable to resist the teasing pressure for a single moment longer.

He pursued her, courted her, urged her to respond more fully. Trembling, her hands slid up his back and rested on his neck to toy with the ends of his thick brown hair. Thigh pressed against thigh, hip to hip, his hands pressed against the small of her back to bring them even closer together. She felt his body shudder then tense as he plundered her mouth. Taking pleasure. Giving it twofold. Again and again until the tensions and boundaries of distrust that separated her from him were erased. The intensity was dizzying; the pleasure intoxicating . . . and far beyond the limited possibilities of her naive imagination.

She loved him.

And she knew him now. Just as she knew that the scoundrel and the conniver had been masks he wore, masks that protected a man who had been dreadfully hurt in the past. A man now driven by his dream and his loyalty to his family, yet a man so tender and so caring that she knew she would never find another man who would dare to compare to John Logan.

"Mama? Mama? I'm thirsty."

John froze in place at the sound of his daughter's voice. Awkwardly, he pulled away from Autumn. Breathing heavily, he gazed at the woman who had practically melted in his arms. Face flushed, her lips were swollen and a small patch of skin on her chin was chafed from his passionate assault. Her breathing was ragged, too, and for a moment, he thought he might have lost the last shred of common sense he had left.

Lord-a-mercy, she tasted as sweet as honey.

And she was much more dangerous, he realized, as he watched her turn toward Amelia.

What had possessed him to kiss her? What power did she have over him that made him forget who she was? Was he that desperate for a woman's touch that he had succumbed to her charms so mindlessly?

He slipped the quilt aside and edged around Autumn, careful not to touch her, and wishing he could erase the memory of her sweet surrender and the feel of her breasts crushed against him. He leaned forward and watched as Amelia took a drink of water. Her turquoise eyes were wide open for the first time in days, although she looked especially pale now that the fevered flush was gone. She still looked quite fragile. "Feeling better, Amelia?" he rasped as he squeezed her foot.

"Uh-huh." Her eyes narrowed as she studied Autumn's face, and she pulled her foot away as she clutched Woolly Lamb close to her chest. She used the heel of her foot to push herself closer to Autumn and gripped her mother's arm.

John smarted from the child's open rejection and steadfast loyalty to the woman she called her mother.

"Why did you make Mama cry?"

John cringed.

"He didn't," Autumn purred as she wiped away the tears that ran down her face. "I was crying because I was so happy to see that your fever had broken. We need to get you freshened up, Mellie. Your nightgown is drenched with sweat, and your hair . . ." Autumn turned to John. "I can go downstairs later and heat up some broth for Mellie. First, could you check with Caleb or Lehman? Mellie will feel even better after she's had a good bath and a change of bedclothes."

John swallowed hard. He wanted desperately to scoop Amelia into his arms and hug her tightly to his chest. For three days, he had watched his only child battle a fever that left her tottering on the precipice of death—with the hand of Fate tugging her away from him. When she finally regained her balance and stood solid on the road to recovery, he wanted to be able to hold her and be the one she turned to for comfort. Instead, she drew back from him and clung to Autumn, all the while accusing him of hurting her mother.

He tried to tell himself that it was not Amelia's fault. Dammit! It wasn't his fault, either! And if he dared to be honest with himself, it wasn't Autumn's fault either.

He stood up slowly, unable to deal with the ache in his heart. "I'll check about a tub for bathing," he murmured and went downstairs without looking back at either Autumn or Amelia. By the time he reached the bottom of the curving staircase, he knew he had to do something to change his relationship with Amelia. Fast.

He could not bear another four weeks of watching her strengthen an already close bond with Autumn while holding him at arm's length.

He paused on the bottom step, staying hidden in the shadows of the staircase. Frustrated and hurt, his heart grieved for all the years he and Amelia had been kept apart. He longed to share this heartache with someone.

With Autumn? God's mercy, he could not shout out the truth that Amelia was his daughter any more than he could trust himself to keep his hands off of Autumn for very much longer. But it was time to admit that he needed someone else's help.

He closed his eyes and shook his head. Was there no way out of the pain of his dilemma? He would sell his soul to be in Ohio right now.

Twice.

There had to be a way to get to Comfort Bend without spending four more weeks with his hands tied to the reins and his eyes glued to the roadbed while Autumn and Amelia continued to enjoy one another's company, and he was left all alone to deal with the awful truth.

He breathed slowly and deliberately as he made his way to the kitchen. Before the wagon wheels on the tinwagon rolled a single inch, he would have to find a way to get to Ohio quickly.

He did not have a choice.

Not if he wanted to get home before he lost his heart to a woman he had no right to claim. A woman who had been manipulated first by her brother, then Zebulon Klerk, and finally John. A woman who deserved much more than he could ever offer to her, especially when his first gift would be the truth about Amelia that would break Autumn's heart.

With a glimmer of an idea, John strode through the kitchen and out the back door, heading for the tinwagon. There was a map stored in one of the side compartments, and if he was right, he could easily alter his travel route and complete this journey home via canalboat and steamship.

He could also make one very important stopover in Buffalo where he could consult with the one lawyer John knew he could trust to make sure he did not act foolishly and risk Amelia's inheritance: Raphael Linderman.

If only someone could tell him how to safeguard his heart.

Chapter 15

Deep in thought, Autumn stood on the rooftop deck of the *Mary Louise* in the first week of October as the passenger packet slowly headed west on the Erie Canal. With an artist's eye, she took a good long look at the canvas of her personal life. It was a watercolor, with gentle hues that were as translucent and tranquil as those she mixed for her tole painting, yet somehow the colors were quite ordinary, devoid of passion and depth. John Logan added emotional, striking colors that transformed the illusion. Using brushstrokes that were bold and sensuous, he gave her a glimpse of a future that could be a masterpiece in oil, a work of art that was suffused with all the dramatic colors of love between a man and a woman.

John Logan.

He was the man of her dreams, and confident that Mellie had completely recovered, Autumn was now ready to try to lay claim to his heart. Could she really find a way to be alone with him so she could break through his resistance, ease the ache in his heart left by his first marriage, and convince him to give love a second chance?

Still unsure of herself, she turned away from the railing to watch Mellie playing a game of jackstraw a few yards away with her new friend, Wilby. Each of them was trying to remove a straw without disturbing the rest of the pile while Wilby's widowed mother, Doris Foulke, watched over them from her seat on a nearby bench. Autumn studied the young widow out of the corner of her eye. Younger than Autumn, Doris had haunting eyes—eyes that were far too old for her youthful face. The fear and distrust in Doris's eyes reminded Autumn of the life she had left behind, and she swallowed a lump in her throat.

In the past few days, Doris slowly had become a friend, even though Autumn still knew very little about Doris and her son. A friend, however, was something Autumn desperately needed right now.

Taking a deep breath, Autumn walked over and sat down next to Doris, enjoying the early morning sunshine that bathed the rooftop deck. "The children seem quite preoccupied," she commented. "I'm so happy that Mellie has a playmate. Traveling by wagon was a difficult and lonely journey for her. She missed being with other children. I have to admit that I'm also enjoying spending time with another woman."

Doris smiled shyly. "We're grateful for your company, too." She looked around the deck, her becoming expression wary. "Mr. Logan doesn't mind?"

Autumn raised one brow, surprised by the liquid fear in Doris's eyes. "John and I only recently married, and I'm afraid the only thing he minds is that we've had very little time to ourselves. Without Mellie." Truth to tell, John did not seem to mind at all; in fact, he found one excuse after another to avoid spending time with her now that they were on the packet.

When Doris looked at her oddly, Autumn smiled. "I think he's making the best of it by spending time with the other men while I share part of the journey with you and the children. Once we finish our journey, it will be different, but I'm sure he'll still encourage me to have friends of my own."

"That may depend," Doris whispered, her face clouding with apprehension.

Had Doris's husband objected when she tried to form friendships with other women? Was that pain in her eyes caused by unhappy memories or by the grief and uncertainty of widowhood? Feeling guilty for discussing the problems of newlyweds with a woman who was probably still in the throes of grief, Autumn frowned. "I'm sorry. I didn't mean to add to your troubles. I know how hard it is to be alone, especially when you have a child."

Doris stiffened. "I manage."

At that moment, Mellie jumped to her feet and started racing toward the rail as a freight packet loaded with farm produce passed by, interrupting the conversation. Wilby followed hesitantly after gathering up the straws and storing them inside a drawstring bag. As he walked over to the rail, one of his legs dragged across the deck, the scrape of leather against wood a harsh, telltale sound that indicated a brace of some sort was hidden beneath his trousers. A shock of wind-tousled baby fine hair, the color of blanched almonds, hung in his eyes while his lips tightened with gritty determination to catch up with Mellie.

Standing side-by-side, the children waved to the freight handlers, and Autumn's heart swelled with compassion for the boy. "Wilby is a wonderful boy," Autumn offered. "It must be hard to know when to let him . . . I mean . . ." Autumn cleared her throat. "It's hard to curb my own protective nature. When Mellie was sick a short while back, I was so afraid. I—I still am."

"It's easier now," Doris responded. "Wilby's father always accused me of coddling Wilby."

"Did you?"

Chin tilted defiantly, Doris stared straight ahead, "No."

A thousand questions, not a single one of them a question she had any right to ask, swirled through Autumn's mind like heavy snow flurrying in a sudden squall.

Doris bowed her head. "George had a mean streak as wide as this canal. He never came to grips with having a son who was less than perfect. He was too full of hurt to find any tenderness for his own son. . . ." Her words ended in a strangled gasp.

Autumn reached out and laid her hand on Doris's shoulder. "I'm so sorry."

"Sorrow and regret won't ever let Wilby run like a normal boy, but he's better off now that his papa is gone. I thank God that he can't ever hurt my boy with his bitterness again."

Tears filled Autumn's eyes. For Doris. For Wilby. And for the joy of having John Logan in Mellie's life. "Are you going home to your family?"

"There's no one to take us in. I'm taking Wilby to Buffalo. It should be easier to find work there." Doris sighed. "To be honest, I don't have the funds to go any further, not if I set aside enough to last us until I find a position."

Envisioning the life that waited for Doris and her young son in spite of the determination in her voice, Autumn shuddered. She knew what it was like to shoulder the responsibility of caring for a child, alone and without the support of family and friends. She knew only too well. Feeling guilty for her own stroke of good fortune, Autumn felt compelled to help the young woman. "John is opening a tin factory in Ohio. Maybe . . . maybe you can come with us."

Excitedly, Autumn described the process of tole painting and the workshop in the tin factory that John tentatively planned for women whom Autumn would train. Taking a deep breath, she waited for Doris to respond to her invitation to come to Comfort Bend to work.

Doris's brows furrowed. "Will the wages be enough to support the two of us? Where will we live?"

"I don't know any of the details, but I'm sure John can answer your questions."

Doubt filled Doris's eyes. "He might not like it that you discussed this with me before asking him. Maybe it's best if I just keep to my plans."

"Fiddle faddle! John would be thrilled to have you work for him. Any woman who has to support her little one will be a good, dependable worker. He's already met you and Wilby, and Mellie will be quick to plead a good case, too."

"I don't know. I'm not sure. . . ."

Autumn took her hand. "Let me talk to John. Please. I don't know anyone in Comfort Bend, and it would be a great comfort to have a friend nearby."

With a shy smile, Doris nodded her head.

"Let me see what I can do," Autumn suggested as the shadow of a plan took shape in her mind—a plan that just might benefit both of them. If it worked.

From the stern of the packet, John studied Autumn as she made her way down the steps from the top to the main deck. With cheeks flushed and a dazzling smile on her face, she was more breathtaking than ever.

For half a heartbeat, John's vow never to take her into his arms again turned into an overwhelming need to touch her. Hold her. Kiss her until he was dizzy.

Was he crazy?

No. He was in love with Autumn, a realization that struck him senseless with the wonder of it. Wonder? It was preposterous. He was in love with the Tin Lady? How ludicrous! And miraculous enough to take his breath away.

He held perfectly still as she made her way toward him, struggling against his desire for this fascinating woman. Unable to control the racing of his heart, he turned around, braced both hands on the wooden railing and studied the wake of the packet. Traveling by canalboat to Buffalo with forty-odd passengers offered little chance for him to be alone with Autumn, but her presence, once a disquieting comfort, churned his emotions into a whirlpool of needs he fought minute by minute.

His hold tightened on the railing when he heard her approach and she stepped alongside of him. The sweet scent of jasmine filled the air, and he swallowed hard. Had she always scented her hair or had he just started to notice? "Where's Amelia?" he rasped, still staring hard at the water in the canal.

"Doris took the Mellie and Wilby to the captain's library to look for a book," she responded, renewing their gentle banter over Amelia's name. It was a subtle clash of wills, but one that John had no intention of escalating when he had greater issues to battle.

Autumn leaned against the railing and brushed his arm. "I thought I might go for a walk on the towpath and look for wildflowers. Would you like to join me?"

Red flag!

"I don't think that's a good idea," he cautioned as he looked at her.

Disappointment flashed briefly across her face as she attempted to hold onto her smile. "It's perfectly allowed. Other passengers—"

"Other passengers who have managed to jump off and back onto a moving packet boat weren't wearing skirts." His mouth went dry with the thought of having a brief glimpse of her ankles.

She laughed. "That's why I invited you to come along. To make sure I keep my balance."

"What about mine?" he mumbled under his breath. How could he maintain any sense of emotional equilibrium if he accepted her invitation and in the process of jumping off the packet, she were to stumble and fall into his arms?

"I beg your pardon?"

He loosened the collar of his shirt. "I said, what about . . . what about getting back on . . . assuming you manage to disembark discreetly?"

Her eyes began to twinkle. "I saw several passengers jump back aboard from one of the low bridges. It looked like fun."

"Fun," he repeated, shaking his head. Was this the same woman who lived such a prim and proper life in Branfield that the very notion of fun seemed antithetical to life? His voice hardened. "It's dangerous and out of the question."

Autumn's face fell, and her expression turned grim. Had he managed to put out the gently burning embers of her spirit with a few cold words? When her cheeks paled and her eyes deadened, his chest tightened. "Why don't you work on your sketches up on deck?"

"It was just a thought," she whispered as she turned away. He watched her as she walked toward the side of the packet and justified his flat refusal as proper, if not absolutely necessary for the sake of his own peace of mind.

He was about to turn back to the railing when his eyes widened in disbelief. Autumn stood at the break in the railing, squared her shoulders and gathered her skirts in her hands before she took a short leap onto the towpath.

Her skirts billowed in the air, and John froze in place. Eyes narrowing and focusing like binoculars on a distant prize, he saw them. Shapely, trim ankles. Sweetly-curved calves. God's grace! His heart thudded in his chest, and his traitorous eyes coveted seeing even more . . . until Autumn landed quite solidly on the towpath and her skirts dropped like a theater curtain cutting short a stunning performance.

His pulse pounded a thunderous ovation; his mind reeled. The woman openly had flaunted his wishes, and before he quite realized it, he had marched across the deck, leaped onto the towpath and caught up to her with several long strides. "You aren't usually this defiant," he grumbled as he took her arm and guided her over the tow ropes and past the hoggee who was urging the tow horses to maintain a steady pace.

"You aren't unreasonable. Usually," she countered as she stepped over a puddle in the path.

"I warned you about being indiscreet," he said firmly. He clenched his jaw, trying to forget the sweet vision beneath her skirts and ignore the warm feel of her arm pressed against his body. His eyes fused with hers, and to his immense satisfaction, her cheeks flamed.

She pulled away from him. "I asked you to come along."

"And I told you—"

"No. You *ordered* me," she whispered, shaking her head. "I was only trying to . . . it doesn't matter. I'm sorry if I embarrassed you."

She was so quick to apologize that John wondered if other men had denied her simple requests in the past as coldly as he had just done. Did her brother treat her unkindly, or was it more recently Zebulon Klerk or Norbert Briley? John did not like being in any of their company, even figuratively. It wasn't Autumn's fault that he was struggling with his feelings for her—feelings he had no right to have or expect her to return. "You didn't embarrass me, Autumn. If anything, you surprised me."

She looked at him askance, the corners of her lips trembling. A lump of regret caught in his throat. "I should have agreed to come along," he admitted. "There's very little you ask me to do."

Her eyes misted. "I'm trying not to be too demanding."

"Demanding?" He shook his head. "You tend to be a bit headstrong at times, but I've never thought of you as demanding. Did . . . did Klerk or Reverend Briley?"

She broke their gaze and looked off into the distance. "Mr. Klerk was quick to remind me that workers have no right to demand anything at all. Norbert had very strong ideas, none of which allowed me to ask for something, let alone demand anything."

John frowned. "And your brother?"

She squared her shoulders. When she spoke again, her voice was hushed, like it came from a place stored far away and deep inside of her. "I adored him while I was growing up. Even when I realized how irresponsible he was, I still loved him. He was my brother." Her bottom lip quivered. "When he came home with Trina and his baby, he treated me like . . . like a servant instead of his sister."

Her voice choked with emotion, and the anguish in her face forced John to look away. "He trusted you with Amelia," he suggested.

"It had nothing to do with trust and everything to do with convenience. Clayton was too preoccupied with his wife to waste a moment on his little girl, but he had a host of demands for me so he and Trina were free to . . ."

John's brows lifted. "Demands?"

She moistened her lips. "Clayton was quick to remind me that it was my responsibility to care for Mellie. My *responsibility?*" Her eyes glistened. "I loved her, and I wanted to take care of her. Clayton and Trina didn't want Trina's father to have Mellie, but they didn't really want her, either, so they left her with me. I thought Clayton would at least send funds to help me. Not half a penny. So I painted. Day and night. During the off-season, I even took in laundry and sewing to make sure Mellie had everything she needed."

John felt like Autumn had taken a sledgehammer and smashed every carefully conceived notion he had ever had about her—ideas that were built on a foundation made of lies and excuses for Clayton Welles. She had always defended her brother, painting his image with words of praise, but now that illusion burst, and in one thunderous instant, his assumptions about Autumn exploded, undermined by the simple, eloquent truth of what she told him now. He swallowed hard. "Why? Why did you lie to me before about your brother?"

She turned to face him, but this time, there were no tears in her eyes. Only regret . . . and shame? "It's not easy to admit the truth to myself, let alone anyone else."

"So you invented a fairy tale."

Brown eyes flashed rebelliously. "Wouldn't you?" Her footsteps quickened. Skirts rustling in agitation, her words tumbled out in a rush. "The townspeople in Waterbury knew the truth, and when I left, I swore that never again would I have to see pity reflected in anyone's eyes. Not for me. And certainly not for Mellie."

The sledgehammer hit again with a force that made his head spin, and he took several deep breaths.

Autumn slowed her pace and paused to study a patch of goldenrod. She looked up at him and chewed on her bottom lip. "I wasn't really honest when I asked you to come with me so I could collect wildflowers. I—I wanted to talk to you about Doris."

"Doris?"

Autumn nodded. "Her late husband was apparently a fiend who couldn't bear to have a son who was less than perfect. Now that he's gone, Doris has a chance to make a good life for Wilby, but she needs your help."

John's heartbeat leaped into a gallop.

"It's never easy when a woman has to fend for herself," she explained. "That's why I told Doris I would speak to you. Can she come to Comfort Bend to work for you?"

John nearly choked. "Were you recently released from a lunatic asylum? The factory is nowhere near ready to start hiring the women! I can't pay wages to . . . to a female simply because she's destitute. In case you've forgotten, I have responsibilities to a lot of people. I also happen to own the factory. *I* hire the employees, if and when I'm ready, not you or Doris."

Chest heaving, he stared at Autumn who responded by twisting her hands together. Feeling responsible for luring her to Ohio under false pretenses when it was clear to him now that she did not deserve to be tricked, he simply could not shoulder the additional guilt of making empty promises to a woman like Doris who already had been treated harshly by her own husband. Even if it did mean hurting Autumn and denying the fact that her concern for Doris and her son made Autumn threateningly endearing to him.

"Please don't be angry with Doris. I took it upon myself to mention the position without speaking to you first, and she was worried you might be upset."

"At least Doris's thinking is headed in the right direction. She should go home to her family," he admonished, too flustered to do much to temper his tone.

Autumn's voice cracked. "Doris doesn't have anyone

else to help her. I can't bear to think of her in a strange city all alone without anyone to help her until she finds a position. What will happen to Wilby if she doesn't? Besides, once we get to Ohio and our marriage is annulled, Mellie and I will be all alone in a strange, new town. It would be a great comfort to have a friend."

John arched his back and squared his shoulders. "No. It won't do at all."

Autumn's eyes glistened. "I know you have a lot of responsibilities, but I was hoping—"

"Don't. Forget it."

"I can't," she whispered. She looked up at him, swallowed hard and took a deep breath. "If you're unable or unwilling to help Doris, then . . . then I will. According to my contract, I'm entitled to a two-room cabin. Doris and Wilby can stay with Mellie and me. At least they'll have a place to stay."

He threw his hands up into the air. "Your contract! I knew that was a mistake."

Brown eyes flashed a warning before Autumn started toward the canal bank. She paused at the edge to wait for the packet that was just approaching, gathered her skirts and looked back over her shoulder. "I'm going to ask Doris to come, even if you won't promise her a position," she said quietly before she jumped onto the packet, effectively cutting off any response he might have.

As she made her way up to the top deck he stared at her back until his vision blurred and his spirit ached. He felt like an angel, a fallen angel who had managed to keep his immortality, but was destined to spend eternity guarding the fiery gates of hell that contained every lie he ever told Autumn.

If he took a chance, bared his soul, and told Autumn the truth, would she believe him? If he also told her that he had fallen in love with her, but could not claim her as his wife because of Edsel Cameron's will, would she laugh in his face . . . or slap it?

He stood very still, and his heart filled with the desperate longing for love—Autumn's love. He felt soul-wrenching yearning that surprised and overwhelmed him in a single, breathtaking, pulse-stopping moment.

Love, however, had more than a single essence, and the image of his precious little daughter flashed through his mind's eye. Amelia. How he loved her! And now that he had found her, he knew that he could never turn his back on his responsibilities to her. He was her father. He had to protect her inheritance, safeguard her future, and guide her into adulthood.

Alone.

How ultimately unfair it was, he decided as he walked toward the packet, that he had found love only to be forced to let it slip away.

Chapter 16

On their last night aboard the packet, Autumn parted the burlap curtains that separated the common sleeping quarters for women and children from the rest of the main cabin. Behind her, the other women were busy with nighttime ablutions that were complicated by cramped quarters, whining children and a dismal lack of fresh water. Mellie and Wilby were already tucked into bed, and Doris had agreed to watch over both of them while Autumn met with John before the men assembled their bunks for the night.

She stepped into the room through the space between the curtains, her pulse racing because she was half an hour later than she had promised. The pungent odor of pipe tobacco, along with remnants of distinctive suppertime aromas, laced the air. While an odd assortment of men bunched shoulder-to-shoulder at the long dining table, quickly converted to accommodate gambling, others formed small groups in the far end of the narrow room, their conversations peppered with exclamations in German and English.

She spent five frustrating minutes scanning the room. Had John given up waiting for her and assumed that she did not want to resolve their stalemate over bringing

Doris to Ohio? Autumn was half-tempted to let the curtain fall back into place and seek the relative comfort of her bunk, as though comfort were anywhere close to describing the narrow, stiff band of canvas that stretched between two wooden frames and squeaked every time she took a breath. If the thoughts that tumbled through her mind were any sort of omen, she knew that she would find little peace or rest unless she found John and they were able to put this new source of conflict between them to bed.

"Looking for anyone in particular?"

Startled, she glanced back over her shoulder. John stood alone, lounging in the corner, obviously in a position to observe her as she searched the room for him. "You might have made your presence known," she chastised as he walked toward her.

"I thought you had forgotten all about me," he drawled, taking her elbow and guiding her across the room to the door.

As likely as forgetting to breathe.

His touch sent her pulse into double time, but she smiled demurely as they passed the gamblers and he ushered her through the doorway. "Are you sure it's safe to go outside? It's grown awfully dark," she whispered as her eyes struggled to adjust after leaving the brightly lit cabin.

"Dark, but private," he said quietly as he steered her over to the steps that led to the rooftop deck. "We need to talk, and unfortunately, there isn't a square inch of privacy to be found unless we take to the upper deck." He urged her gently up the staircase. "We're on a flat now. There won't be any dangerous low bridges overhead."

Autumn mounted the steps slowly. The only bridge that was important to her was the one that separated her from John. Would he meet her in the middle and compromise about Doris, or was he going to try to convince Autumn to cross over to his side?

When they reached the top deck, she turned and searched his face for a clue to his intentions, but his features were nearly hidden in the shadows of the gleaming twilight.

His hold on her arm tightened. "You've been avoiding me," he murmured.

"I've been busy with Mellie," she lied, knowing full well that he was right.

"It's not like you to sulk to get your way."

Autumn gulped and dropped her gaze. "I'm not sure I like being the topic of this conversation. I thought we were going to talk about Doris."

"We are." He led her to a nearby bench and sat down next to her. She waited while he took a deep breath. "I wanted to apologize for losing my temper when you told me about offering Doris a position in Comfort Bend, but it wouldn't have flared so quickly if you had consulted me first before talking with her."

Autumn toyed with her skirts, only too aware of his presence as his thigh pressed lightly against her leg. "Does that mean she can have a position?"

He exhaled slowly and raked his fingers through his hair. "It means that . . . hell, Autumn, I don't know what it means. I haven't gotten back to Ohio to find out if the factory is ready. I don't even know if all the journeymen have arrived. Everything is still very tentative."

"You hired *me.*"

"And others as well. I take my responsibilities seriously." His voice became strained. "Everything I own is committed to this venture, and I just can't assume responsibility for Doris and her son when there's no guarantee of work for her. Not right now. Maybe later. If you had given me the chance to explain this to you before, we might have been able to avoid arguing about it."

For the first time tonight, Autumn was grateful for the deepening darkness. It hid her own embarrassment. Touched by his own apology, she had no excuses for her own behavior. "I'm sorry, too. I was so caught up in the excitement of actually being able to offer Doris a position that I didn't stop to think about what I was doing. It wasn't my place. Not without consulting with you first."

Cold air rushed against her skirts when he moved away and settled against the back of the bench. He stretched out his legs and gazed skyward, arms locked behind his head. "Amazing."

Alarmed by the way her heartbeat quickened at the sound of his voice, she stood up and stared at the starless sky. Moonlight filtered through a thin layer of passing clouds, and the only amazing thing about the sky was that it was almost precisely the color of his eyes. "'Tis pitiful. There aren't any stars."

He chuckled and pulled her back down beside him. "Not the sky. Us. We're actually having a pleasant, civil conversation."

A bubble of giddiness burst into nervous laughter. "I never deliberately force an argument. It just seems to happen," she offered, finding the topic of their discussion slightly too unnerving to be called civil. Even in the semi-darkness, his very nearness sent every fiber of her senses into full-blown, heart-racing alert, and she longed for the touch of his lips against hers.

"I seem to have given you cause. More than once," he murmured, his voice low and seductive.

She trembled and folded her hands on her lap to keep them still. "I graciously accept your second apology."

He sat up so quickly that he startled her. "Good. Then let's compromise. Talk with Doris and tell her that you made a mistake. She'll understand—"

"That doesn't sound like a compromise," she protested.

He smiled, flashing white teeth. "You didn't let me finish. Offer to correspond with Doris, and if I'm able to hire her later, you can write to her. I just want you to be careful. Don't raise any false hopes and have the woman waiting for a position that might not come."

"But—"

"You can't mislead her, Autumn. It wouldn't be fair."

Autumn debated whether or not to concede and accept his compromise. It made absolute sense, but truth be known, there was another reason she wanted Doris to come to Ohio. She hesitated. She couldn't tell him the truth, not without risking her heart. "I'd still like Doris and Wilby to come and stay with Mellie and me."

A deep cloud of a sigh hung between them.

"Haven't you been listening to anything I've said?" He paused and shook his head. "I didn't want to tell you this, but I had to sell the tinware to finance our own travel. There's some surplus, but I can't afford to use it for Doris and Wilby. Not when we might need it."

Autumn looked at him, her mouth agape. "You sold the tinware?"

He nodded awkwardly. "I didn't have a choice. I needed the funds. Until I get back to Ohio, I can't be responsible for Doris and Wilby when I'm not sure I can provide for you and Amelia. Once the factory is in full operation, the tinware can be replaced."

His profound sense of frustration and responsibility softened her disappointment, in spite of the fact that he had misled her about the wagonload of tin being shipped to Buffalo on a lineboat since there was no room for freight on the packet. Feeling guilty for assuming that John had an endless source of funds on hand, she reached out and laid her hand on his cheek. "I'm not asking you to take responsibility for them now.

Doris has enough funds to travel with us. Once we get to Comfort Bend . . ."

He stiffened, and she dropped her hand. She stared at her lap, doubly mortified by her boldness and his quick rebuff. Was her touch that insufferable, or was it the touch of any woman that disturbed him? Was there no way to penetrate the hurt that armored his heart? She moistened her lips and chanced to look at him. "Once we reach Ohio, you're going to annul our marriage. Mellie and I will be all alone, and Doris and Wilby would help to ease being surrounded by strangers. Unless . . ." She swallowed hard, unable to bring herself to ask him outright to reconsider his decision to end their marriage, even though it was still a marriage in name only.

"Unless what, Autumn?"

His question, as gentle as the sound of the water lapping at the packet boat, unnerved her. Surprised that he would pursue what she had left unsaid, Autumn leaned back and closed her eyes, listening to the sound of her own heartbeat as it kept cadence with the persistent pulse of her dream. She loved him so much she thought her heart would burst, and she loved him enough to risk suggesting that she wanted to be his wife. Not because she was forced into their marriage, but because she loved him. His first wife's betrayal, however, had left deep wounds, and she wondered if the key to his heart lay elsewhere.

She opened her eyes, turned and gazed deeply into his eyes. For several long and desperate heartbeats, neither spoke. Moonbeams gave her a glimpse of his anguish, and when he turned away, she sighed. "Mellie has grown up without a father. I used to think that it didn't matter. Mellie had my love and my devotion, and I thought that it would be enough." All the rationalizations she had made in the past about loving Mellie enough to make up for not giving her a father seemed shallow when she finally gave them voice. "Mellie needs a papa . . . like you."

John leaned toward her and tilted her chin up. "Are you asking me to forget about the annulment? For Mellie's sake?"

He had just claimed her heart again, and he probably did not even realize it. He called her little girl Mellie. Not Amelia. Mellie. Autumn's spirit sang with the priceless gift he just had given to her—a gift she wanted to share with him more than anything in the world: her love. She pressed her face against the palm of his hand. "It's not just for Mellie. It's . . . it's for me, too. I could help you realize your dreams, and I would try to be a good wife to you."

His hand began to tremble, and he pulled it away. "I told you from the beginning that this marriage was a business arrangement. Nothing more," he said hoarsely.

Stunned by his rejection, Autumn bowed her head. "I understand," she whispered, battling the tears of shame that stung her eyelids. "I had no right to ask anything more from you, and I—I apologize for thinking . . ." She blinked hard and cleared her throat. "I have a contract to work for you for one year, and I will. If you can't hire Doris later, I'll understand, but for now, she wants to come. I want her to come. And I want you to know that I'm very grateful to everything you've done for me."

She smiled when he furrowed his brows. "You kept me from making a terrible mistake and marrying Norbert, and you gave me the opportunity to put a world of distance between Edsel Cameron and Mellie."

Her thoughts trailed off into a future where her dream had come true. It seemed as far away as the moon which peeked out from beneath the gauzy layer of clouds to bathe them both in iridescent moonbeams.

She gazed into his midnight blue eyes, searching for a glimpse of the tenderness and need she had seen that day in Mellie's sickroom when he held her in his arms and kissed her—emotions he had locked away beyond her reach ever since.

For one stunning moment, she saw them before a shutter closed the window to his soul. It was just long enough to reassure her that John Logan was not as immune to love as he thought.

His back was against the wall. Literally.

Lying on the middle tier of bunks, John stared into the darkness. A cacophony of snores, squalling babies, and the pounding echo of deckmen's footsteps overhead filled the room, but he barely heard them. All he could hear was Autumn's voice, her words, some spoken, some unspoken. They echoed in his mind, over and over again, chasing away sleep and challenging him to take a good, hard look at his life, his goals and his dreams. His heart filled with a desperate longing for love—Autumn's love—a heartrending yearning that surprised him and overwhelmed him in a single, breathtaking moment when she had reached out to him, nearly bared her soul, and asked him not to have their marriage annulled.

Not just for Mellie's sake.

For her. For Autumn. *She loved him!* He saw the wonder of it in her eyes, felt the joy of it when she touched his face. Lord! It wasn't fair. He didn't want to find love. Not now. It was too late. Cameron's will forced him. . . . Damn the will and double damn the man who wrote it!

The love John had for Autumn came too rarely in any man's life to be tossed aside for the sake of an inheritance. If the inheritance was his to decline, he would do it in a heartbeat. But it was not his fortune. It belonged to Amelia, and as her father, he was responsible to see that she received everything she was entitled to have under the terms of Cameron's will.

Is that what he had to do—choose between the love he had found with Autumn and the responsibility he had for his daughter?

He clenched his jaw and stiffened his spine.

For five years, he had driven himself to the point of exhaustion learning how to scheme and lie to get the information he needed to track Trina and Amelia. It suddenly occurred to him that those lessons were not easily forgotten, nor should they be.

He could use those skills again to suit *his* needs, not Cameron's.

He could challenge Cameron's will, convince the courts to set aside the condition that forbid him from remarrying and still claim Amelia's inheritance for her.

A surge of energy shot clear through his body. If he could not defeat a jumble of words on a sheaf of paper, he did not deserve the love that lay waiting for him in Autumn's heart. Once he broke the knots and untangled the lies that threatened to strangle the life out of any future he and Autumn could share, he would court her until she could not resist him. He would make her fall in love with him. Again.

He had several advantages over Autumn, who seemed reluctant to confront or challenge Edsel Cameron. Hell, she did not even know the man was dead! But John knew the strengths and weaknesses of the man who had risen from a sea of immigrants to captain a vast economic empire. Cameron had been shrewd enough to use his money to make up for his lack of formal education and breeding, and no doubt had hired the best legal minds in the East to draw up a will that could prove the adage that the pen was mightier than any sword that might rise up to strike down his will.

Challenge the will?

Only a fool would even consider going up against Cameron or his lawyers.

A fool?

No. He wasn't a fool. Just an ordinary man with the opportunity to claim the love of an extraordinary woman like Autumn. With the help of one man in Buffalo, Lord willing, Edsel Cameron's will was about to be rewritten.

And if John failed?

The thought was unbearable. Almost as unbearable as traveling the rest of the way to Ohio with Autumn and not being able to tell her that he loved her and celebrating that love in a passion that would bind them together forever.

Chapter 17

John walked back into the hotel room in Buffalo, took one glance at the opaque privacy screen as Autumn finished dressing, and scowled. Was it his imagination, or did the gas lamp on the dressing table, also behind the privacy screen, actually create a more titillating vision of her body than if there had been no screen at all?

After completing the packet journey and spending three days here in Buffalo trying to book passage on a steamship, he realized that getting to Ohio with Autumn without bedding her was going to be more than unbearable. Now he knew that unless he traveled on a different ship, it was going to be downright impossible.

He slammed his eyes shut and turned away. It didn't help. He could still see the outline of her full figure, the long, gentle curve of her legs. Damnation! "The coach is waiting. How much longer?" he asked through clenched teeth as he tried to ease the now tight fit of his trousers.

A whoosh of skirts. A stifled giggle. "Almost done. I'm sorry I had to change at the last minute, but my gown—"

"It doesn't matter now. Just be quick about it. I have

to see you all to the ship, attend one final meeting, and get myself aboard before departure."

"I'm hurrying," she gushed. "Did Doris and Wilby get word—"

"They're in the coach with Mellie," he grumbled as he turned around. When she finally stepped out from behind the screen, his heart thudded in his chest. Eyes wide, he stared at her, nonplussed by the gripping image of the young woman he once irreverently had called the Tin Lady. It was not just the new gown she wore that took his breath away. It was the dazzling smile and the excitement in her eyes that overwhelmed him.

She blushed, twirled around, and held her arms out at her sides. "Do you like it?"

Is the blaze of a fire hot?

He gulped and loosened his collar. "New gown?" he croaked.

She grinned and lifted out her skirts. "Old gown. New collar and a bit of lace. Doris helped. I don't have much flair for dressmaking."

"It becomes you," he murmured, too overcome by the startling transformation to fashion an untruth or to hide the admiration in his voice. A wide collar of ivory lace and matching trim at the waist turned the severely-tailored russet gown she had worn the night of their wedding into a creation that accentuated every feminine curve. The sculpted edge of the collar rested on the tips of her breasts, and a narrow band of lace hugged at her waist.

His mouth watered.

When she took his arm, her touch burned through the fabric of his coat. "Are you ready?" she purred, her eyes brimming with an invitation that made his pulse race.

If he did not know her as well as he did, he would have sworn that she was deliberately trying to captivate him! That very notion left him speechless, but desire pulsing in certain parts of his anatomy made it painfully clear that the last thing he wanted to do was to leave the room before he tasted every one of her sweet charms that were packaged so delightfully it made his loins ache.

He led her to the door with only one consoling thought in mind. If this last meeting went as well as he expected, he would not have to wait much longer to make Autumn his wife in the truest sense of the word. And when he did, he would make sure she wore this very same gown so he would have the privilege of peeling it off her body, inch by delectable inch.

And if the meeting didn't go well?

It would take a lifetime just to erase the erotic fantasies that seared his imagination.

John sat across from Raphael Linderman in his Buffalo law office, more than anxious to find out if John's decision to challenge Edsel Cameron's will and Linderman's offer to help him was more than an impossible dream. The smell of richly-grained leather, the faint trace of beeswax that left a mirror shine on the top of the massive mahogany desk, and the musty odor of ancient tomes engulfed him, bringing back memories of the office Linderman had kept when he was a professor and John was his student. A fire crackled in the hearth, chasing away the damp chill of a rainy fall evening and warming his hopes for the future.

Now a twice-retired lawyer, Linderman had explained that he inevitably returned to his law practice more out of boredom than any need to line his pockets, and he seemed to be a perfect choice to orchestrate John's inquiries to Edsel Cameron's New York lawyers. Classical legal expertise and uncommon decency, combined with a reputation for a strong sense of justice, set Linderman outside the coterie of lawyers John had met who regarded the legal code as either stone commandments mandated to protect the wealthy or a checkerboard designed to play the law like a challenging game of chess.

Gray, wirehair brows hooded deep-set hazel eyes that sparkled with energy. "Good news, John. The telegram authorizing your advance arrived earlier today," he announced as he handed an envelope over to John.

Putting the money away in the inside pocket of his frock coat, John heaved a sigh of relief. He had more than enough funds now to finance the rest of the journey home, even if he had to provide for Doris and her son. Although Autumn had told Doris there was probably no hope of finding a position at John's factory, Autumn had convinced her friend to come to Comfort Bend for an extended visit instead of moving there permanently, a compromise that satisfied him, at least for the time being. As a new bride about to arrive in a town without family or friends, Autumn had explained that it might be easier for her if Doris came along for moral support.

If she only knew.

John could not fault Autumn's argument, not when he would have family and friends by his side. Didn't she deserve the same? Although he felt no guilt for misleading Doris, he did feel better knowing that he now had the funds to send the woman and her son on their way when it was time.

John shook his head. "I can't believe it was that easy."

The lawyer cackled. "McClain and Hitchcock is one of the most prestigious law firms in New York. Invoke the name of one of their wealthiest clients, and they can't be more accommodating. As administrator of your daughter's inheritance, you have every right to request funds to make your move to New York as comfortable as possible." He leaned forward and knitted his hands together, discreetly stilling the tremors of old age. "They were probably relieved that you finally decided to meet the terms of the will, although I'm quite positive that their relief is bittersweet. The firm reaps hefty fees by administering the estate in your stead."

John cocked his head. "Wait until they find out what we're going to do. Are you sure it's legitimate to use funds from Mellie's inheritance to challenge Cameron's will? Somehow, it just seems like it should be illegal."

"Just unusual," the lawyer answered with a wink. "But no more unusual than using an out-of-state lawyer to handle your affairs."

John smiled. "There's a lot to be said for living in small towns, but keeping secrets isn't one of them."

"Lawyer-client privilege—"

"Doesn't always prevail," John said quietly. "I don't want everyone in Comfort Bend to know about the will —or my attempts to circumvent it—unless I win my case, and I certainly don't want Autumn to be subjected to any kind of scandal. What else were you able to do for me?"

Linderman shuffled through a pile of papers and pulled out the list of concerns John had drawn up on his first visit. Squinting down the length of his bulbous nose, the elderly man concentrated for a few moments before smiling. "For the annulment, you need an in-state lawyer. Paul Yost is the nephew of a good friend of mine, and you can trust that his work will be discreet." The lawyer's demeanor suddenly lost all hint of informality. His expression hardened. "Are you sure that you want the grounds for the annulment to be coercion? It's not exactly flattering to your case."

John straightened in his chair and swallowed hard, recalling his second meeting with Linderman where he had insisted that before John started legal proceedings to challenge the will, his marriage to Autumn had to be annulled. It was necessary, Linderman argued, because if the court found out that John had brashly remarried before filing suit and waiting for a decision to be rendered, it would predispose the court to rule against him.

When Linderman had detailed carefully the grounds for annulment, John had been stunned. Why hadn't he realized that a marriage could never be valid if either party had not entered it freely and willingly?

The lawyer addressed him again, apparently interpreting John's silence as an invitation to offer an alternative. "Might be simpler to cite the usual: nonconsummation."

Frowning, John shook his head. "Autumn was forced into this marriage, and that should be part of the official record. The least I can do for her now is be honest." He did not want to add that he was so close to consummating this marriage that it would be foolish to risk having papers drawn up that might not be valid. If he did in fact make love to Autumn, which was becoming harder and harder for him to resist, he did not want to jeopardize the annulment process, even if that made him feel lower than dirt.

"Then give these papers to Yost. You and your wife simply have to sign them."

John stared at the annulment papers. "It's that simple?"

"Not quite. Yost will have to file them with the court. All routine. I've taken the liberty of wiring an old compatriot of mine, Judge Claybourne. Princeton, Class of '08. Or was it '09?" He chuckled. "Well, it doesn't really matter. Claybourne will sign the annulment decree the day the papers arrive on his desk which coincidentally will be the day you deliver the papers to Yost. He's married to Claybourne's granddaughter—"

"Is there anyone you don't know?" John laughed out loud.

A smile lifted the tips of the lawyer's mustache. "Expect there might be. The old guard is dwindling." A series of chest-rattling sneezes cut him off.

John waited for the lawyer to catch his breath before broaching the topic that had kept him sleepless for more nights than he cared to remember. "What about proving that Mellie is actually my daughter?"

"Based on what you've told me, I don't foresee any problems. You say you have a daguerreotype showing you and your first wife holding the baby?"

"My mother has been safeguarding it for me."

"She's willing to testify as well, I presume?"

John dropped his gaze. "She was heartbroken when Trina ran off with Mellie, and she wants her granddaughter back where she belongs—with her family. My sister, Grace, and her husband can also document the truth."

Linderman shrugged gaunt shoulders. "Then you don't really have a problem. Claybourne will schedule a hearing in his chambers as soon as you contact him. Once your wife, or your ex-wife as the case will be, sees the daguerreotype, she'll recognize Trina as the same woman Clayton Welles presented as his wife and Mellie's mother. Add the proof of Welles' travel itinerary that makes it impossible for him to have fathered the child. . . . I think your case is irrefutable."

A bough of regret wrapped itself around John's heart. The pain was piercing. He knew how dreadfully hurt Autumn was going to be, and it seemed ironic that when all he wanted to do now was to fill her heart with love, he would quickly become the scourge of her heart when she learned the truth. Would there be enough left to ever forgive him? Someday?

"Is there . . ." He stopped to clear the lump in his

throat, still uneasy about the option Linderman suggested at their first meeting which would keep Autumn in Mellie's life as her governess. It seemed a logical way to circumvent Cameron's will if the courts ruled against him. But at what price to Autumn? "Are you sure that there's nothing in the will that prevents me from choosing a governess for Mellie?"

"Nothing. At least that's my professional opinion based on a careful reading of the will. Can I make a suggestion?"

John nodded absently, certain that there were no quick and easy solutions to his predicament.

"I've got more than a few good reasons to go to New York City, not the least of which is seeing a great-grandson who's my namesake. While I'm there, let me see what I can do. The first unwritten rule of law is rather simple. No lawyer has yet to devise a document that can't be undone by a smarter lawyer. In this case, hopefully, that's me."

Hope flared in John's chest. "Do you really think there's a chance you can help me to break Cameron's will?"

Caution flashed back at him. "All I need to find is one loophole wide enough to let you win the heart of that young lady of yours and protect Mellie's inheritance at the same time."

Autumn paced the small but elegantly appointed sitting room aboard the steamship, *Sun Dancer,* by the dim light of a single sconce. Thick, red carpet, identical to the lush floor carpeting in the adjoining bedroom, cushioned her steps.

Maybe she should not have asked Doris to keep Mellie tonight so there would be time for Autumn to be alone with John.

But she had, and for very good reason.

Actually, the idea first occurred to her in Buffalo when she realized there was so little time left. In a few short days, they would all be in Ohio, and unless she did something to change John's mind, he was going to file for an annulment of their marriage. Realistically, she had only two choices: wait and see if John would reconsider or . . . or make the first move herself.

She toyed with the ribbon on her nightdress as she slowed her momentum. She made the first move earlier today by wearing her restyled gown because she knew in her heart that John was not going to change his mind about ending their marriage. Why should he? When they had talked alone that night on the packet and she boldly had suggested that she did not want their marriage to be annulled, she had not had the courage to tell him that she loved him. Instead, she had used Mellie, her own daughter, as reason enough for him to stay married to Autumn.

She swallowed hard, knowing that she had betrayed the love she had for John as surely as his first wife had been unfaithful to her marriage vows. No, Autumn did not spurn him in favor of another man. She did something just as devastating—she rejected John as a man who inspired a woman's love and devotion and asked him to be her husband because her little girl needed a father.

Not because Autumn had fallen in love with him. Not because she wanted him or needed him to make her life complete. What greater hurt could there be for John, a man who had been so dreadfully wronged in the past?

Autumn had realized her mistake even as she made it, but she was not willing to let that mistake go uncorrected and sit idly by as this man, the love of her life, slipped away from her. Not without a fight. There was only one way to convince John that she loved him and wanted him to be her husband—in name and in deed—

now and forever. She could not just talk to him like she had originally planned. She would have to show him, convince him with her heart and her soul and her body—seduce him. The outrageous idea made her tremble.

Was she out of her mind?

No. She was simply a woman with a dream so real that she could reach out and touch him.

Wasn't seduction devious and immoral?

"Not between man and wife," she murmured to her shadow as she made her way into the bedroom. Light from twin sconces on either side of the filigreed headboard was reflected in the glass-paneled door that led to a small balcony and danced softly on the white satin bed cover. She walked over to the balcony door and stared up at the diamond-studded sky. The rains that had drizzled the area for the past day had stopped, and the moon shined majestically again as gentle winds chased away reluctant cloud cover.

She opened the door and stepped outside. After making her way to the corner, she leaned against the balcony and welcomed the light breeze that cooled her flushed skin. Now that the ship was underway, John would be here soon. She shivered as the breeze grew stronger. She really should go back inside, but she was reluctant to give up the glorious view that took her mind off what was going to happen, for better or worse, in the next few hours.

Lost in thought and in the cover of darkness, she wrapped her arms around her waist and prayed for the wisdom to know what to do or say when John finally arrived. A clicking sound made her pause, midthought, and she turned back to the door. For a fleeting moment, she caught the shadow of a figure as it moved away from the door. Immobilized for several seconds, she realized that John must have arrived. But what was that sound she heard? She reached the door in seconds and turned the handle. When she pulled at the door, it did not budge. Horrified to think she had been locked outside, she pounded on the door as she peered inside through one glass panel. The bed covers had been turned down and a pitcher of water with several glasses had been placed on a small table next to the bed.

Obviously, the shadow she had seen was not John's. It was the maid's, who had come to prepare the suite for the night . . . and locked Autumn outside on the balcony!

She pounded at the door with both hands, hair and gown frantically flying about. "Let me in!" she wailed, praying that the maid was still in the suite and would hear her.

No response.

She pounded at the door and cried out for help, again and again, until her fists ached and her throat was raw. *This can't be happening. Not now. Not tonight!*

After several incredibly long minutes, she realized that the maid must have left the suite. There would be no rescue—until John arrived.

Teeth chattering, Autumn huddled in the corner of the balcony next to the ship's wall. A strong breeze whipped at her hair and lashed her thin cotton nightdress. She wrapped the gown around her legs and rested her forehead against the top of her knees.

The wind's fury doubled, raising gooseflesh on her already frozen limbs. With one hand, she caught flying strands of hair that had broken free and stung her eyes. Blinking away the pain, she smoothed them away from her face, bunching the tresses at the back of her neck. With the other hand she pushed at her nightdress that billowed up to her thighs. She struggled with the hem until it was caught tight in her fist.

As she stared at the balcony door, tears streamed down her face, and she cried until there were no more tears. Thoroughly miserable, she hiccoughed. Bowing her head in defeat, she was convinced that her guardian angel had either taken the night off or turned her sorry case over to a fledgling who had no experience with a woman desperately in love.

John made his way through the crowd and down the long expanse of the main salon that ran through the middle of the steamship from bow to stern. Melodious strains of piano music whispered in the background of gay conversation and the vibrant rumble of the paddles as the side-wheeler made its way down the Ohio River. Flickering light from crystal chandeliers cast a glimmering glow on opulent decor. The trim on handcarved panels in the domed ceiling matched white filigree accents around windows and doors which led to sleeping chambers. Murals depicting pastoral innocence and splendor contrasted with the decadent wealth of the passengers' costumes and jewelry, and it occurred to him that the entire dichotomous scene illustrated the virtues of both of his wives.

City-bred Trina: the dazzling debutante whose beauty stirred his youthful loins to bewilderment and left him unable to understand the difference between lust and love. Village-reared Autumn: the quintessential model of virtue who gentled his aching misery and stirred the passion in his soul, a passion that promised the union of body and spirit in a love that defied imagination.

Two totally opposite women. Two different worlds.

If given the choice, which world would he choose for his daughter? He swore under his breath. He would never deny Mellie the fortune that rightfully belonged to her. He was a man whose own family had experienced and risen beyond pinching poverty and he had seen what economic dependence had meant for Autumn. He was also a man strong enough to guide his daughter through the maze of artificial values that would surround her in New York.

Pausing, John flagged the attention of a waiter who was carrying a tray of drinks. "Suite thirty-five?"

The waiter grinned. "Straight ahead, sir. On your right. Enjoy the . . . voyage."

Chafing at the man's conspiratorial smirk, John hurried on his way. A bridal chamber! Could there be any more ironic accommodations for a couple who had a marriage of convenience and traveled with a five-year-old? If he hadn't been absolutely desperate to get back to Ohio as soon as possible, he would have waited for another ship that had two separate staterooms!

The annulment papers, still safely secured in his coat pocket, pressed against his chest, and he was doubly grateful for Mellie's continued presence on this phase of their journey to help reduce the opportunity to consummate this marriage.

He approached the door to suite thirty-five slowly. He unlocked the door and turned the handle. He stepped into the suite, nodded his silent approval at the accommodations and walked directly to the bedroom. One quick glance at the bed sent him rocking him back on his heels. The bed was empty. At nearly midnight? Mellie should have been tucked in hours ago. Where was Autumn? Had she left her common sense at the wharf and decided to visit with Doris? Or did she have some other reason not to be in the suite? And where was the cot he had ordered for himself?

Grumbling to himself, he hung his frock coat and vest in the closet next to Autumn's and Mellie's gowns which were arranged in Autumn's unique manner by color instead of size. Pausing, he reached out and touched one of Autumn's gowns. Memories of their travel together tumbled through his mind, and he turned away.

He was tired, too tired to go chasing all over the ship

after Autumn. He would have plenty of time to demand an explanation when she finally returned.

He undressed quickly, laying his pocket watch next to Autumn's hairbrush on a small, built-in dresser. He pulled off his shirt and cravat and tossed them on a side chair. Sitting on the edge of the bed, he removed his shoes and socks. Impetuously, he bounced up and down twice, wondering what it would be like to make love on a spring mattress, a luxury reserved for bridal chambers, or so the advertisement claimed.

Relegating that thought to ashes, he stood up and walked over to the balcony door. He checked the bolt to make sure it was in place, wishing he could lock out the disturbing thoughts of what it might be like to actually share a honeymoon suite with Autumn.

For tonight, however, he had to figure out a way to get a good night's sleep. Without a cot, he would have to make do with the floor in the sitting room—not an unpleasant thought since it would put a little distance between Autumn and himself when she was dressing . . . or undressing.

He slid the bolt free, stepped out onto the balcony and stared at the sky. A sky full of promise and hope, romantic enough to satisfy any poet's dream. He turned away and froze in place.

"Autumn!"

She stirred and slowly raised her head. "John?" she groaned as he lifted her to her feet and pulled her inside the room. Shaking uncontrollably, Autumn thought her bones would shatter. Judging by the look on John's face, however, he would no doubt enjoy a good stomp on the splinters!

"What the blazes were you doing out there? Where's Mellie? Do you know what time it is?" His eyes widened. "My God, you're blue!" he exclaimed, lifting her into his arms. As he carried her across the room, she clutched at his bare shoulders, her fingers aching with cold.

Blessed heat. Warmth. It emanated from his body, and she snuggled stiffly against him. Her cheek rested in the hollow of his shoulder, and her lips tingled as they pressed against his throat. "M-M-M-Mellie . . . with D-D-D- . . ."

"Doris." He finished her valiant attempt to speak and in one frantic motion, pulled down the covers and laid her on the bed.

Groaning softly, she curled into a ball and yanked the covers to her chin. Oddly, she noticed that the mattress began to shake as shivers racked her body. She closed her eyes and inched closer to the center of the bed.

The room began to spin. From a distance, she heard the echo of oaths. Clothes dropping to the floor. The creak of the bed springs. Then strong arms pulled her into an embrace. Relief! His body was a cradle of warmth, offering her a respite from the gnawing cold that left her unable to move without jerking or speak without making her teeth chatter.

He smoothed the hair away from her face and pressed her closer to him. "You're frozen through. It's going to be all right. Let my body help to warm you."

She nodded, her chin poking his chest, and she concentrated on letting her tense muscles relax as he wrapped his bare legs around hers. Hip to hip, he pressed his body against hers, stroking her back and murmuring softly. "That's it. Try to relax. You'll feel warm soon."

Pain shot through her head as several strands of hair at the nape of her neck caught beneath his arm. Tears sprang to life again as she tried to release them.

"No. Stay still," he warned as he adjusted his position.

The pain immediately ceased, and she braced her

hand on his chest. As warmth chased away her chills, her body began to tingle and throb. Then she yawned. A gaping, loud, very unladylike yawn.

God, he must think I'm a loon!

"Go to sleep. I'll hold you until you've completely thawed out. Then we'll talk."

Her eyelids drooped as the ice in her veins slowly melted. "S-S-Sorry. S-S-Sorry," she stammered as she felt her body weaken and she began to nod off into a world devoid of pain or embarrassment, even color.

"Rest," he countered. "When you wake up, you can explain what the deuce you were doing out there."

Autumn kept her eyes closed, welcoming the blackness. A circle formed in front of her eyes. No. It was not a circle, she realized, as the shape became more focused. It was a wheel with thousands of spokes, each a different color of the spectrum. It flashed, then started spinning rapidly like a wheel in a game of fortune. The colors whirled together, then became distinct again as the wheel started to slow down. Like a desperate gambler, she held her breath, waiting to see whether or not she had won her wager.

Stop at sapphire blue, she prayed, a color that would foretell understanding from the man who held her in his arms, and not scarlet, the color of humiliation and failure.

Chapter 18

A surreal drumbeat. Steady. Primal. Rhythmically sensual. Autumn stirred. The drumbeat quickened and changed cadence again as it intertwined with the measured pulse of her heartbeat.

Consciousness peeked slowly over the horizon of her reverie, invading the warm cocoon that enveloped her and gently awakening her other senses. A heavy weight rested across her legs. Warm flesh molded against her torso. Tufts of hair tickled her cheeks, and a hand cupped the back of her neck. Scents: male and female.

John.

His heartbeat. His body.

She moistened her lips and kept her eyes closed, prolonging—what? Overwhelming, sensual pleasure, or the inevitable confrontation, she supposed, swallowing what was left of her pride and her half-baked scheme. If she kept perfectly still, maybe . . .

"Feeling better?"

The deep resonance of his voice vibrated against her cheek, and she nodded ever so slightly.

"Are you able to talk now?"

She managed another nod, stronger than the last.

His fingers toyed with strands of her hair. His simple

gesture seemed far more intimate than the fact they were lying together in bed with barely a stitch of clothing between them.

"I'm a good listener," he murmured.

She gulped, wondering if evaporating into thin air was humanly possible. Since that seemed as likely as being able to turn back the hands of time, she gathered every precious ounce of courage she had tucked away for an emergency and opened her eyes. A soft, seductive glow of light emanated from the wall sconces over the headboard and danced on the white coverlet, a sea of silk that covered them both. Dark shadows hid the rest of the room.

With her head resting against his chest, she could not see John's face. Instead, the firm muscles of his upper arm were in her direct line of vision, and she concentrated her gaze on a small jagged scar, pale against his bronzed skin. "I suppose I should start by saying thank you," she began, realizing for the first time that her arms were still wrapped around him and not quite sure how to change that.

"You're welcome."

Awkward, still silence. The steady rise and fall of his chest. The frantic pounding of her own heartbeat.

"Mellie is spending the night with Wilby and Doris."

"So I gathered. Was that your idea or Doris's?"

She almost wished his question had been accusatory instead of merely inquisitive. It might have given her reason to blame this whole scenario on Doris, who thought she was playing Cupid for newlyweds who had had no time alone. "It was mine. All mine."

Silence again.

The back of his hand stroked her cheek.

Why didn't he push her away? Didn't he understand what she had done . . . or at least planned to do?

"I'm sorry."

He chuckled softly. "I guess you are! Hiding on a balcony with winds strong enough to blow you away while gowned in nothing more than a filmy nightdress is either an act of lunacy or desperation."

"I wasn't hiding," she sniffed. "I was on the balcony. Trying to think. Then before I realized what was happening, the maid came in and inadvertently locked me outside."

"You can't think when you're fully dressed?"

"You're horrid! Of course I can!" She pushed away from him just far enough to raise her head so she could glare at him, and she remembered the night at the Golden Eagle when she had been too distracted by his state of undress to think clearly.

Her mouth went dry as he toyed with the high collar on her gown. "But you think better when you're dressed for bed."

I can't think at all when you're holding me!

Butter could have melted and sizzled on her cheeks. "I suppose I should explain—"

He kissed her silent. A gentle nip of a kiss that stole her breath and scattered every single thought in her head.

He kissed her again. "Explain what?" he whispered as he nibbled at her lips. "That you were going to lure me into your bed?"

She gasped, and he took stunning advantage by claiming her lips in an insistent assault that overwhelmed her senses and tilted the axis of her being. Then he released her. Suddenly. Without warning.

The world stopped spinning as his eyes darkened. "Why, Autumn?" Pain, deep and piercing, etched his face. "For Mellie?"

She placed two fingertips on his lips. "Not for Mellie." His breath fanned her fingers, and she gazed at him until she was drowning in miraculous sapphire pools.

"For me. I wanted to be alone with you . . . to see if I could convince you that I love you enough to erase the bitter memories. The betrayal. The loneliness you must have felt after your first wife . . ."

When he stiffened, she paused and cradled his cheek with her hand. A day's growth of whiskers teased her palm. "I love you, John Logan. I want you for my husband."

"So you decided to seduce me."

She dropped her hand and lowered her gaze. "Yes." Her bottom lip quivered as he tilted her chin so she had to look at him. A weak grin tickled the corners of her mouth. Her heart stood still as she waited for him to react to her confession. She deserved whatever condemning words he might use. Harlot came to mind first and she flinched, wondering if the rest of her life would be long enough to erase the memories of the worst mistake she had ever made in her entire life.

He sighed and lifted her hair away from her back, letting it slide through his fingers. "I've thought about a lot of things these past few days."

She took a deep breath.

His expression sobered. "There's a great deal I need to tell you, but I'm not sure—"

"You don't need to—"

"But I do," he insisted. "Do you know where I've been these last few days?"

She furrowed her brows. "At meetings arranging some final details for the factory."

He clenched his jaw and shook his head. "I met with an attorney, Raphael Linderman."

Her heart skipped a beat.

"Tonight he gave me the annulment papers for us to sign. They're in my coat pocket."

Every nerve ending in her body began to scream, and she could feel her lifeblood literally freeze in her veins.

The papers to end their marriage were in this very room! She could not have made a bigger fool of herself if she tried. When she moved to push away from him, he held her fast.

"Let me finish. Please."

Heart pounding, she searched his face, confused by the combination of tenderness and regret in his expression.

"I love you, Autumn. More than I've ever loved any woman. It scares the hell out of me, and it certainly makes me feel like an utter monster for the way I've treated you. And tonight . . . when I knew you were warm again, I kept you in my arms, longer than I had any right to."

He loves me!

"You're not a monster!" she gushed. "It was my fault. You must think I'm a . . . a . . ."

His gazed hardened. "After what I did to you in Branfield, I can hardly find fault with you."

"We've both made mistakes."

He stiffened and molded both hands on her shoulders. Supple flesh beneath the thin nightdress caressed his palms as beads of sweat dotted his forehead. He stared at her, and the expression in her eyes tugged at his soul. Luminous. Shimmering with emotion he did not deserve to see, let alone claim. The fire in his loins burned hotter, threatening his resolve. "I can't make any commitment to stay married to you." He blurted out the words before his courage failed him and his body betrayed him. Lord-a-mercy, he wanted her. In his life. In his heart. In his bed. Not for one night—forever. Fervent need dueled with his conscience. As much as he wanted to claim her as his soulmate, he knew he had the duty to tell her the truth before . . .

Hurt twinkled briefly in her eyes, and he felt like he

had just stabbed her in the heart. "When you learn the truth, you probably won't want to be my wife."

Understanding replaced the hurt. "I know everything about you that I need to know. I trust you with my heart. I trust you with Mellie. There's nothing—"

He sat up and turned his back to her. "Get dressed," he gritted. "I can't think straight when you're pressing your body against me and staring at me with lovestruck eyes."

She giggled and raked her nails gently down the column of his spine.

He ran his fingers through his hair. "Don't do that!"

"What?"

"It's not humorous."

No. The ache centered between his legs was too painful to even acknowledge and if she didn't stop . . . he shivered away the sensations that skipped down his spine and sent decency out the window. God, he wanted her!

She pressed a kiss against his back.

"Damn!" He turned around and glared at her. "You're playing with fire, Autumn. Be careful. Get out of bed right now and get dressed before it's too late and your whole world turns to ashes and scatters to the wind. I won't make love to you unless—"

She flinched and scrambled out of bed, and he swallowed the rest of his words as he watched her walk over to the closet. Heaving a sigh of relief, he leaned back against the headboard and closed his eyes. Thank God she had the common sense to get away from him. He heard the creak of the closet door. Hangers moving. Clothes rustling. Footsteps fading into the next room and then returning.

Judgment hour had arrived.

God help them both.

"John?"

He opened his eyes, prepared to take one final look at the love in her eyes before it disappeared. She stood at the side of the bed—still in her nightdress! Soft, brown waves of hair lay provocatively on the gentle mounds of her breasts, rising and falling with every breath she took. So beautiful. Desirable. And fully within her rights to make him suffer. But this . . . he exploded. "Are you deaf or simply defiant? I asked you to get dressed. I can't talk to you when you're—"

"Sign this." She held out a sheaf of papers and a pen.

Dumbfounded, he grabbed the annulment papers. "Where did you get these?"

"You told me they were in your coat pocket. Sign them," she repeated as she pressed the pen into his hand.

Unbidden, the memory of another time when he had signed her contract in the general store in Glenham flashed through his mind. Was the woman going to make this a habit? Flipping through to the final page, his eyes widened as her signature stared back at him. "Did you read this?" he huffed as he penned his name.

"Only enough to know that they're papers that annul our marriage."

"And the grounds?" he grumbled as he scribbled the date. Fortunately, she had already dated her signature because at the moment, he had trouble remembering anything more difficult than his name.

"I didn't read that far."

He shook his head and thrust pen and paper back at her. "Aren't you even curious? What if I had listed grounds for an annulment that you found distasteful?"

She put the papers next to his pocket watch and walked back to him. "You trusted me when you signed my contract. I'm trusting you now not to do anything to hurt me deliberately." She paused to moisten her lips. "I'm not your first wife, John. I'm me. Autumn. I love you to lunacy, perhaps, but I love you. I'll always love you. With or without a certificate that binds you to me."

He folded his arms over his chest in a self-protective move designed to do one thing: stop him from pulling her into his arms. Glowering, he snorted. "You have no idea of who or what I am."

She walked around the bed slowly, deliberately, as though marking off territory or setting a boundary. His curiosity grew with every step she took, and the sway of her hips made his mouth go dry. "What the blazes are you doing?"

"Making a mark."

"A mark." He groaned and slammed his fist into the mattress. "It's the middle of the night. No, it's nearly dawn. You're cavorting about in a nightdress that's nearly transparent while a man—a naked man who may or may not remain your husband—ogles himself silly, and you're making an invisible demarcation in the proverbial sand?"

She stepped inside the imaginary line. "That's the past," she said softly, pointing behind her. "This is the present. Just you and me. Not your first wife, not even Mellie exists. I love *you.* Arrogant, gloriously bullheaded, secretive John Logan. Tomorrow when the dawn breaks and we both step over that line, we can deal with the past and plan for the future. Tonight," she whispered as she untied the ribbon on her gown, "tonight is a precious moment when we can pledge our faith in one another."

Her words, sugar-sweet and seductive, coated his spirit with the thick nectar of pure and natural love. He let it pool at his feet, gathered it, and then bound it at his side, sheathing the sword he would wield to destroy Edsel Cameron's will. Autumn might be angry when John revealed the sordid truth that brought them together, but he would win her back. In a day. A month. A year. He would win back the love that shined so brilliantly in her eyes and claim her as his wife forever.

She was right.

The path they chose tonight would somehow lead back to one another's hearts. Yet as decisive as she had been in forcing his hand, she now retreated. Waiting. Hope burned bright in her eyes as she eloquently relinquished the power she held over him and waited patiently for him to make up his mind.

Ever so still, Autumn waited.

The drumbeat began again. Beating faintly and slowly at first. Then harder. Faster. And this time, Autumn recognized it as the sound of her own heartbeat as she waited for John, mesmerized by the sapphire glow of promises that lay in the depths of his eyes. Too afraid to breathe. Too afraid to admit that even if he turned away from her now, she would love him every day of her life until he kept those promises, until . . .

In the next heartbeat, he rose from the bed. Strong, powerful arms molded her body against his lean, masculine frame. She wrapped her arms around him and clung to him as her heart swelled and pulsed with the miraculous wonder of being welcomed into the heart of this incredible man.

His lips nuzzled her neck as he whispered her name, sending a litany of sensations shimmering to every part of her body and fanning the embers of her love for him into a glow that carried heat to her most private places. She pressed closer to him, shivering as the tips of her breasts crushed against his chest, kindling new flames of pleasure. Being held in his arms was so breathtaking, so thrilling that the room began to spin, and the sheer magic of love expressed in physical desire overwhelmed her.

Gone were the doubts and the fears that she would

ever be able to ease the ache in his heart. She could hear it beating as strong and wild as her own. Gone were the empty days of loneliness—for both of them.

Placing her hands on his shoulders, she tilted her head back, and he pressed kisses against the tender underside of her chin. Her flesh tingled, and her pulse beat even faster.

When he pulled away from her, she gazed deep into hooded, passion-filled eyes. "Love me," she whispered, feeling very wicked as she caressed the outline of his lips with her fingers.

He groaned and scooped her into his arms. His breath came in ragged gulps that caressed her face. As he carried her the short distance to the bed, hungry kisses devoured her lips. He tugged at the ribbons of her gown. Her nightdress slipped down to her waist. As he lowered her garment and laid her against the bed, smooth silk chilled her back. His warm, sensuous flesh covered the front of her body and chased away her modesty.

She shuddered, and he raised his head to smile at her. Eyes glazed with passion and need gazed down at her and rendered her speechless. "So beautiful," he murmured as he trailed the tips of his fingers across her breasts and sent desire skimming through her veins. He lowered his head, and she arched her back as he began to suckle first one aching, pulsing breast and then the other until she was whimpering with pleasure.

She closed her eyes, taking mercifully short gulps of air as he brought her to the peak of pleasure with his lips and his hands. The sheer joy of his ardor left her trembling. She groaned as the colorful palette of long-suppressed emotions burst into exciting new shades of passion. When he kissed her mouth, urging her lips apart to accept him, the hues exploded into a kaleidoscope of breathtaking patterns that burst with wondrous brilliance before her very eyes as he teased her. Courted her. Claimed her as his for now and forever. His hands molded against the curve of her hips, fondled the sensitive inner flesh of her thighs, and each tender caress beckoned her into a world of ecstasy he created for her.

For them.

John opened his eyes and stared at Autumn. Aglow with the blush of passion, her body pressed beneath his, she tempted him beyond rational thinking, beyond reason. He had thought her plain at first sight, but when he had seen her smile, a full, dazzling smile that stretched across her face, he got a glimpse of the fire that burned deep within her spirit and she became beautiful.

Now, as she lay beneath him, with all her wondrous charms a feast for his eyes, she transcended beauty. Radiant in the throes of passion, the fire in Autumn was like a carnal inferno, blistering in its intensity as her love for him scorched away all the hurt and the pain and the agony that once had filled his soul.

He bent down and kissed each of her eyelids. When they fluttered open, she smiled and kissed the tip of his chin.

His breath caught in a lump that lodged in his throat as he nudged apart her legs and slid gently into her satin sheath. She clung to him, matching his rhythm as he carried them both to the pinnacle of human love and over the crest into eternity. He never took his eyes off of her face as he plunged deeper still, uniting them together and sealing their commitment to one another with a celebration of love's greatest gift. A bonfire of pleasure engulfed them both.

The next morning, Autumn stood once again on the balcony. She stared at the landscape as the *Sun Dancer* journeyed south. Marveling at the spectrum of verdant colors in the tree-covered, rugged hills of eastern Ohio, Autumn leaned against the balcony railing as John stood behind her. She tilted her head back to catch the early rays of sunlight that promised fair weather and signaled a new day.

Would it be the start of the new life she dared to dream about in Branfield or something even more splendid? Would she be able to win John's heart so that the wonder and joy of their passionate night together created a bond that was truly strong enough to overcome whatever problems the past contained?

John's hand, cupped lightly at the back of her head, trembled slightly. "It's time to go," he murmured before he dropped his hand and stepped back from her. "Doris and the children are waiting for us."

Had Autumn detected a slight tinge of regret in his voice? She turned away from the railing, her gaze resting for a brief moment on the corner where she had huddled from the cold wind only last night. As she walked back into the sleeping chamber, she deliberately avoided looking at the bed. Memories of that impossibly romantic night swept over her, however, and she gathered them into her heart and stored them safely away. Like a true bride, she finally had a hope chest, but it did not contain the usual variety of household treasures. Her treasures were intangible, made not of cotton or iron or tin. How did one package love and preserve a special moment in time?

Stepping quickly, she made her way through the sitting room. When she reached for the door handle, John's hand closed over hers. "Wait."

Her heartbeat stammered as he took her by the hand and turned her around to face him. Thick-lashed blue eyes stared down at her and nearly stole her breath away.

"Before we join the others for breakfast . . ."

She stood on tiptoe and steadied herself with one hand poised against his chest. She pressed her lips to his, tenderly and ever so briefly. She felt his hand move to her waist and heard the soft intake of his breath. Reluctantly, she dropped back onto the soles of her feet and smiled. "I love you," she whispered. "The future is ours to claim—when you're ready."

A cloud of pain changed midnight blue to black. "I never meant to hurt you," he said as he toyed with the ribbons on her bonnet. His fingers shook slightly as he brushed her throat, although his face grew stern. "Promise me you'll let me explain, that you won't . . ."

When she sighed, he dropped his hand.

"Of course I'll listen. It's not unmanly to ask me to do something instead of issuing an order."

He glared at her. "You have no idea how hard this is going to be for both of us."

Her gaze softened as she recalled the moment when she had finally told John the truth about Clayton and how hard it had been for her. "Yes, I do."

Confident brown eyes caressed blue uncertainty as silence settled between them. She took his hand and laid it over her heart where her precious memories were stored. "What I feel for you is as certain as a heartbeat. I promise to listen to you, and then we'll deal with the past. Together. I'll wait until you're ready. For as long as it takes."

He swallowed hard. "There may not be enough tomorrows. I can't ask you to wait forever."

She pressed a finger to his lips, wondering if he could ever understand the depth of her feelings for him. Was the pain of his first wife's betrayal still buried so deep that he could not trust himself to believe in love again? "I'll wait," she whispered.

Sapphire blue eyes filled with doubt, but beneath the

doubt, she saw the promise of a love too special to be chanced to impatience or misunderstandings.

She could only pray that the promises were real and not just an illusion that reflected her own feelings instead of his.

Chapter 19

After spending two interminably frustrating nights on a cot in the sitting room while Mellie shared the bed with Autumn, John welcomed their arrival in Cincinnati with profound relief and a sense of dread he never anticipated nearly five years ago when he left Ohio. Following directions from the owner of the livery to the home office of Paul Yost, he maneuvered a rented buckboard through the bustling streets. His chest tightened. Where was the joy and fulfillment he had expected to feel each time he had dreamt of a triumphant return with his daughter?

Those feelings lay smothered under a blanket of responsibilities that might force him to break the heart of the woman who sat beside him. The woman who loved Mellie as much as he did. The woman who was innocent and had played no role in the plot to rob him of his daughter.

The woman who had stirred his passion, soothed his angry spirit, and stolen his heart.

The buckboard bounced through a series of potholes, jostling John's immediate thoughts back to the task at hand and setting off squeals from Doris and both of the children. "Sorry," he mumbled as he took a furtive side-glance at Autumn.

She smiled, a damnably innocent, trusting smile that made him feel like he was about to slaughter a lamb.

Irritated by the guilt that lassoed and strangled the breath out of his lungs, he clicked the reins, guided the team of horses around a wagon unloading grain and rounded the corner. As the street narrowed and wagon traffic thinned, he spied the two-story brick colonial home of Paul Yost that the livery owner had described. He heaved a sigh under his breath as he parked the wagon under the shade of a giant, yellowing buckeye oak and secured the brake and reins. "One last stop," he explained in answer to Autumn's raised brow.

This time, her smile seemed halfhearted.

"Will you be long? The children are anxious to put an end to their travel."

Only long enough to break your heart.

He paused to take a deep breath, praying that Linderman would find a loophole in Cameron's will so that ultimately, John could ask Autumn to marry him again and come to New York as his wife—and Mellie's mother. Until he had a favorable solution to the problem that Autumn could not even fathom in her wildest nightmares, however, he saw no need to give her false hope, even if he was only hours away from destroying the love she had for him.

"The papers have to be filed," he whispered, catching a brief flash of pain in her eyes before they warmed again to that soft shade of mink that melted his heart. He would have done anything not to annul their marriage, but Linderman had been quite adamant that the annulment was absolutely necessary if John wanted to challenge Cameron's will successfully. "I won't be long."

Mellie jumped up from her seat and stood next to

Autumn. "I wanna get outta the wagon. Can I go with you, Papa?"

"Stay with your mama. I'll be back before you can count to twenty and back."

"Wilby will help you count," Doris interjected and started both children off while nodding for John to take his leave.

John hurried up the shrub-lined walk and sounded the brass knocker. The door opened, and a young man with a gray-streaked beard that contrasted with his dark brown hair greeted him with a smile.

"John Logan. I need to see Paul Yost."

The man extended his hand. "I've been expecting you, Mr. Logan. Please, come in."

Although the man's handshake was firm and businesslike, John also felt compassion in Yost's grip, and he followed him into a small office directly across the hall from the parlor. Yost paused at the doorway, indicating for John to take a seat in one of two heavily-upholstered arm chairs that sat in front of a window that faced the street. A small desk sat in the opposite corner of the room, and although floor-to-ceiling bookcases on either side of the desk held standard legal reference books, their stark formality was broken by an impressive array of china figurines and crystal vases.

Soothed by the decor, which held few of the standard trappings of law offices he had visited, John removed the annulment papers from his jacket and sat down.

Yost closed the pocket doors. "Mr. Linderman stressed the need to be discreet."

John nodded, distracted by the faint sound of the children's voices as they counted in unison and wondered if he would be able to keep his promise to be quick. "I appreciate your help." He handed the papers over to Yost. "Autumn and I have already signed the papers," he volunteered as Yost carefully reviewed the document. "You'll see that this is sent directly to Judge Claybourne?"

Yost looked up, his expression almost pained. "The signatures aren't valid without being witnessed."

John's back went rigid.

The lawyer waved one hand in the air. "It's not a problem. You'll simply have to sign again now. I'll witness your signature, and if you can bring your wife in here, I'll have her sign in my presence, too."

John's mouth went dry. "Is that absolutely necessary?"

The lawyer straightened in his chair. "Beyond the delicate nature of the annulment and Cameron's will, there is the importance of being letter perfect so that the annulment isn't challenged later, either by Cameron's lawyers or perhaps, even your wife's lawyers."

John clenched his jaw so hard he thought his teeth might crack. Just telling Autumn that he was filing the papers had been hard enough. To force her to sign the document again was tantamount to a slap in the face. Or was it, more fittingly, a form of double punishment for him? Maybe fate had orchestrated this whole mistake so that he would have to witness Autumn's suffering as one way to atone for his trickery with more pain of his own.

He rose to his feet and nodded stiffly. "Autumn is waiting outside. I'll bring her in. Before I do, I want to make it clear that she has no idea that I'm Mellie's natural father."

"I understand."

John glared at him. *Do you? Do you know how I've wronged this woman?*

Yost cleared his throat. "Once the papers are properly signed and witnessed, I'll send them over to Judge Claybourne. As soon as he returns—"

"Returns?" John felt a blood rush redden his face.

"He's in New York," Yost stammered as he bolted to his feet.

"New York!"

"On his honeymoon." Yost blushed. "Outlived two wives and claimed he couldn't live alone. Married a rather remarkable widow—"

"I don't care who he married!" John ran his fingers through his hair. "Mr. Linderman assured me that the annulment decree would be signed the day I delivered this to you."

"I'm sorry. There was nothing I could do. When Mr. Linderman's wire reached Claybourne's office, the judge had already left. He's expected back in about two weeks. I promise you that the annulment will be his first order of business when he returns."

While his pulse struggled to find a normal rhythm, John nodded and mouthed a quick apology. "It's been a difficult time," he said quietly.

"Of course." Yost's expression softened as he led John over to the desk where he signed his name again directly below his first signature. Memories of the events that followed when he had signed the papers for Autumn left his hand shaking as he handed the pen back to Yost.

"Why don't you bring your wife inside, and we'll get this part of your ordeal over? As soon as Judge Claybourne signs the decree, I'll wire you in Comfort Bend. I notified your family that you'd be arriving, just as Linderman instructed me to do."

As John ushered Autumn into Yost's office, he could hear Doris's voice as she led the children through another round of counting. From the doorway, he watched Autumn as she leaned over the desk and signed her name. He wondered if she was overcome by memories, too, and if she already had begun to regret trusting him so blindly.

When she finished, she turned and approached him, shoulders straight and back rigid. Her eyes were downcast, but when he took her arm, she gazed up at him, her eyes brimming with tears that she valiantly tried to blink away. Her bottom lip quivered, and he could feel the muscles in her arm tremble.

"I love you," she whispered. A tremulous smile, a squeeze of his hand. "Let's begin the journey to tomorrow."

John deliberately skirted the main settlement at Comfort Bend to avoid friends and neighbors and postponed his reunion with his mother, his sister, and her family, who all resided together on a neighboring farm. He needed time alone with Autumn, just a little time, but long enough to confess to the whole truth about who he really was and to admit that he had tricked her into coming to Ohio. He did not want anyone else to tell her, even inadvertently. She deserved to hear the whole story from him. Every painful detail, including all the wicked lies he had concocted—lies that would change his heartfelt declaration of love into an abomination no ordinary woman could be expected to forgive.

Even though he knew that it would destroy the affection she claimed to feel for him. Even though it would break her heart.

What about Mellie's?

What about yours?

His body stiff with anticipation, he drove the buckboard through the back yard and beyond the kitchen door to his home. Five years. He stared at the one-story home he had built with his own hands. Neglect had coated it with a down-in-the-heel appearance, although it was evident to him that his brother-in-law, Daniel, had kept his promise to keep the roof repaired and the clapboards nailed tight. Peeling white paint, blistered by inattention during too many hot summers and equally cold winters, puckered the outside of the house. Deep green shutters, however, were latched open, and evidence that his mother and sister, Grace, had readied the house for his arrival could be seen in the freshly-weeded rose garden that Trina had dismissed as quaint, but too plebeian to suit her.

The rose bushes were bare of blossoms, but fuller than he remembered. The house seemed smaller, somehow, perhaps because the trees around the house were so tall now, towering above the roof. He realized at that moment that nothing ever stayed the same. He felt different than he had five years ago, relieved and somewhat surprised that he *was* a different man than the one who had left to find his wife and daughter. Even so, he expected to be overwhelmed with memories of Trina: their happy first days together, the gradual disintegration of their affections, and his last-ditch attempt to save the marriage—an attempt that came too late. Trina had run off, taking Mellie with her when she fled, leaving John an angry, embittered man.

As he scanned the buildings, he found that the memories that remained were simply that: memories. The anger and bitterness, the hurt pride, and even the guilt had dissolved. What was left was regret—and a fervent desire to start living and loving again. He was older now, and perhaps just a bit wiser.

He looked away from the house. The chicken coop was empty, the barn unnaturally silent. As he turned the wagon toward the closed double doors on the barn, he brought the horses to a slow stop, climbed down to open the barn doors, and led the horses inside where he saw that good, reliable Daniel had stocked the barn with a few bales of hay and a bucket of oats.

As soon as the wagon stopped, Mellie and Wilby clambered down from the wagon and raced outside into the mid-afternoon sunshine. Once he had Doris on solid ground, he reached up and put both hands around Autumn's waist and lifted her to the ground. She blushed as his hands rested on her hips. He pulled away. "Feeling stiff?" he asked nonchalantly as he put each of the horses into stalls already lined with fresh hay.

"Bruised is more like it," Doris answered. "I thought traveling by packet was uncomfortable, but I should eat my words after spending five hours bouncing in that wagon."

Nodding her head, Autumn groaned as the two women walked outside. "It doesn't seem to have affected either of the children. They're still full of energy."

John quickly finished feeding and watering the horses and eventually caught up with everyone else. When he got outside, Mellie and Wilby were chasing one another and running about in circles around the water pump. Between the two of them and Wilby's brace dragging in the dirt, they raised a cloud of dust big enough to choke a team of horses. "Hold on, you two," John bellowed over their playful whoops. "If you have that much energy, Doris can use your help in fixing dinner." He looked at Doris. "There should be fresh supplies in the kitchen. Would you mind watching Mellie while Autumn and I have a few minutes alone?"

Doris and Autumn exchanged questioning glances before Doris clapped her hands together. "That's enough. Both of you. Straight to the pump so we can wash you up. Then into the house." She barked her command like a seasoned officer and paraded her two charges to the outdoor pump.

Autumn waited, her brows lifted expectantly.

"I wired ahead to have neighbors open the house. We

need to talk," he explained as he took her hand and led her past the outbuildings and beyond fallow fields that once had been bountifully resplendent with summer corn and winter wheat. He stopped at the edge of a narrow, high-arched footbridge that crossed Soldier's Creek, a wide expanse of shallow but fast-flowing water that separated the orchards from the rest of the farm. He eyed the weakened structure carefully, quickly noting the rotten boards that would need to be repaired before the bridge could be safely used.

"Be careful," he urged as he led Autumn along the right side of the bridge which seemed to be the sturdiest part of the structure. Her hand tightened in his as she followed him to the other side of the creek. The fragrant aroma of tree-ripe apples grew stronger as he walked her through the orchard, carefully avoiding the fruit that had fallen to the ground and started to rot. Bending beneath heavy branches that were badly in need of pruning, he was breathing hard and wondered if he would be able to salvage any of this year's harvest. Would he even be here long enough that it mattered?

"It's a little like the Garden of Eden," she exclaimed, breathless wonder in her voice.

"Just before the Fall," he muttered to himself.

"What did you say?"

"Nothing," he assured her as they emerged from the orchard and worked their way up a small rise. At the crest, he paused to catch his breath and steady the growing apprehension that made him too nervous to enjoy the view.

Autumn turned to face him, reaching out to brush a leaf out of his hair. He caught her hand, and pressed a kiss to her palm. His heart began to pound as he stared at her, trying to capture the look of trusting love and innocence that shimmered brightly in her eyes.

Just one more time.

He smiled and felt his throat tighten as he chanced one last kiss, a kiss that would have to sustain him in the long and lonely days ahead. Days that would be even more difficult than the darkest hours of his desperate search for Mellie.

Autumn's lips were warm and yielding, and he broke their kiss with a heavy heart. "I love you," he whispered. "Enough to make you keep your promise."

She cocked her head, her breath coming in short spurts. "Promise?"

"To listen."

She chewed on her lower lip and nodded.

John took a deep breath and knew exactly where he had to start: at the beginning.

How ironic. The beginning?

This was going to be the moment when everything he had ever wanted came to an end.

Chapter 20

Autumn held her breath. John was clearly troubled and yet as much as she wanted to ease his journey from yesterday into tomorrow, she knew that it was a road he had to travel in his own way. Clouds of black anguish hid the promises that had sparkled deep in his sapphire eyes. Didn't he know that she loved him enough to accept and understand whatever tormenting ghosts of the past he revealed?

When he looked away from her, she took his hand and stood beside him. "You didn't tell me about the farm," she began as she surveyed the rolling landscape below where apple trees bent in supplication under the weight of unharvested fruit. In the distance, smoke curled above a sprawling farmhouse. Twin silos stretched to the sky. Further to the east, the outline of a small town nestled in the bend of a wide roadway that led north. "Comfort Bend?" she asked, tugging on his hand and lifting it to point.

Without answering, he pulled her around to face him. His eyes narrowed, and he looked as though he was about to say his final farewell before being led away to the gallows. "You're not making this any easier by prattling on about the landscape," he murmured.

She blushed. "I'm sorry."

He stared at her as though he expected her to turn away from him when he revealed his lurid past, and he was trying to memorize her features.

"I love you," she whispered, standing on tiptoe to kiss away his frown. When he did not return her kiss, she dropped back to the soles of her feet. Dismay rippled through her body, or was it closer to alarm? He looked so forlorn, so bereft of any hope that love alone would be strong enough to bridge the past to the present that she wanted to weep.

A brief spark lit in his eyes. "Love," he said quietly as he reached out to trail his fingertips across her lips. "I never knew. . . ." His voice cracked, and he dropped his hand.

Apprehension filled her soul. Was their devotion to one another too new or too fragile for him to trust her and to realize nothing that would ever come between them?

"You're so griefstricken," she noted, gently trying to ease his pain as well as his uncertainly. "Can't you trust me?"

A mask slipped over his features, as though he had to protect himself from revealing his emotions. He did not answer her. He just stood there, deeply silent, and stared at her. The wind tousled the ends of his hair so they caught the sunlight, creating a golden aura around his face that only accentuated the darkened depths of his pain.

Once before, when he nearly lost control of the wagon, she had seen him struggle to find words that never came to explain how devastated he was that he had put them all in danger. When he had been unable, she had voiced her understanding of the words he could not say.

This time, however, she knew that it was John's place

to express whatever troubles lay between them. Since she had no inkling of what they were, she could not even try to help him, and even if she could, John needed to do this on his own. She loved him too much to take that away from him, so she waited.

Seconds stretched into interminable tension, and unable to bear it any longer, she nudged his reticence with an attempt to lighten his burden. "I'm trying to be patient, John, but you're acting like . . ." She paused to think and then blurted out the most preposterous thing she could think of. "Like you're about to tell me that Edsel Cameron is waiting for me back at the farmhouse."

"Edsel Cameron is dead."

The mask on his face crumbled as shock and disbelief forced her back a step before a melange of even more powerful emotions paralyzed her. Relief that she no longer had to fear Cameron as a threat to Mellie quickly changed into anguish over the events in Branfield that led her to accept Norbert's proposal and the harrowing confrontation at the inn. All the ugly accusations from that night echoed in her mind, and every fear she had that night reverberated so powerfully through her body that she began to tremble.

She looked at John, pleading with him silently with all the love she had for him in her heart, to tell her that he did not know anything about Cameron that night in Branfield and had not used that knowledge to force her into their marriage. "How long . . . how long have you known?"

His lips tightened into a harsh line. "Several years."

Her heart leaped in her chest. "Why . . . why didn't you tell me you knew him? Why did you let me believe—"

"Because . . . damnation, woman! I wanted to start at the beginning."

Autumn swallowed hard and tried to let her love for John still the fear that raced through her frame. "The beginning," she repeated in a voice as soft as the breeze that rustled her skirts. She looked up at him, sensing the answer to the question she was about to ask before she even gave it voice. "Where is that? In New York?"

He nodded grimly. "I met my first wife there seven years ago." With clipped words, he detailed the events that led to his first marriage, his move west to Ohio to join his family, and the unhappiness that replaced any affection between him and his wife, although he failed to mention her by name or to demonstrate any link between them and Edsel Cameron.

She listened carefully to everything John said, although she felt like she was hearing him from someplace very far away instead of here, standing right in front of him. When he paused to take a deep breath, Autumn's love for this man deepened. She admired him for not placing all the blame on his wife; he claimed more than half for himself. But she needed answers about his connection to Edsel Cameron to quiet the apprehension that nibbled at her trust in John.

She pursed her lips, biting back the urge to rush John's explanation. She had told him she loved him and trusted him, and she was not going to betray her words by giving in to impatience or baseless fears.

When he started speaking again, his voice was wistful. "I knew we weren't suited. Not living here. On impulse, while I was in New York on business, I bought a home and came back to surprise her with the news that we could move back to New York City. I wanted to save my marriage more than anything else in the world."

His eyes misted briefly, and caught with him in the obvious pain of his memories, Autumn depended on the love she and John had declared for one another to soothe his anguish. "You tried your best," she offered, hoping he would fight as hard to hold onto their love as he had done once before in his first marriage.

"I was too late. Trina had already gone when I got back," he said, his voice as stiff as his body.

Trina? Did he say Trina?

Panic raced through Autumn's veins and pulsed faster when John's expression grew sorrowful. "Trina ran off with a Yankee peddler. When she did, she took the one thing that mattered as much to me as she did: our daughter." He paused, cleared his throat and gazed at her with tears welling in his eyes. "I've spent five years searching for my child. Mellie . . . Mellie is my daughter, Amelia. Edsel Cameron was my father-in-law."

Stunned, Autumn gasped. Every ounce of blood drained from her face and pooled in her feet. Her heart throbbed painfully in her chest, and her vision blurred. Jolted beyond thought, she struggled against his stupefying declaration. She blinked repeatedly to regain her vision, and when it cleared, the world had lost all of its color. The lush green and red orchards, the pale blue sky, the lace white clouds—all of them turned muted shades of brown, creating a sepia universe where color's passion did not exist.

She staggered toward him and shook her head. "You're mistaken. Mellie is not your daughter. Clayton was Mellie's father. Not . . . not you," she murmured. Her eyes misted with tears, and her heart filled with tremendous sorrow that John had spent so many years searching for his child . . . only to claim the wrong one. "You're mistaken," she said softly, wondering if he would ever be able to find his own child.

He shook his head. "No, Autumn. I'm telling you the truth. Mellie was only a few months old when Clayton came to Comfort Bend peddling his wares and lured my wife away. I spent three years tracing him, trying to find Trina and Amelia. When I found him with Trina, it was too late. They both had been killed, and I had to face the fact that I had failed. There were no second chances for Trina and me, but I kept going, searching for Amelia. She was all I had left." His face turned ashen. "I can prove that Clayton was in New York making love to a bottle, not my wife, when Mellie was conceived."

Stupefied, Autumn watched the sepia images in her colorless world turn to gray as an endless, silent river of tears coursed down her cheeks. *It can't be true!* Every beat of her heart denied what John said, but every question, every condemning thought she ever had for Clayton and his failure to be a loving father came alive again with astounding force. Conflicting feelings for Trina surged anew, and Autumn reached out and clutched the one emotional anchor in her life before she had fallen in love with John Logan: Mellie.

Denial, swift and sure, rose to her lips. "I don't understand how you could have made such a terrible mistake," she groaned, wrapping her arms around her waist, "but you have."

He sighed. "The one mistake I regret above all others is that I failed to tell you the truth in Branfield."

She shook her head. "The truth is that you were a desperate man looking for relief from the demons of your past. You had been betrayed. You were hurt. And angry. Why can't you admit that you've made a mistake? A terrible mistake?"

He squared his shoulders. "You're wrong, Autumn. I am Mellie's natural father, and now that I've got her back in Ohio, I'm going to prove it."

"No," she cried, taking a step back from him.

He started forward and reached out to her. "Please, Autumn. I'm not deliberately trying to cause you pain. I love you. I want you to—"

"Don't," she warned as he got closer to her, stifling a sob that ripped through her heart and soul. "How can you claim you love me and then hurt me like this?" She tilted her head back to look into his eyes. "There's no factory. No position for me, is there? Was it all a lie? Every promise, every kiss meant to keep me off guard so I'd never suspect that you never really loved me at all? That you were luring me to Ohio so you could claim Mellie as your long lost daughter?"

"I never lied to you when I told you that I loved you," he groaned. "I didn't know how much I could love a woman until I met you. But I love Mellie, too, and I have responsibilities to meet. She's my daughter."

The foundation of her love for him shaken, Autumn's knees began to buckle and the world started to spin. Strong arms grabbed her shoulders, but she pulled out of his embrace. Her trust in John and her love for him had been rocked to the point that she could not think clearly. How hard she had prayed for the chance to find love, only to have her dream stripped away before it ever had a chance to truly grow! Love, once again, seemed forever out of her reach. Except for the love that she had for the daughter of her heart.

Mellie.

God, please God, no! Don't let him take her away from me!

Autumn turned and started running back to the farmhouse, running away, too, from that part of her that told her to stop and listen to what John had to say. Driven by fear that she would lose Mellie, she kept running. She had to get Mellie and leave. Now. Before now! Her footsteps were clumsy and her toes got caught in the hem of her gown.

"Autumn, wait!"

John's voice steadied her gait, drove her, spurred her to run faster. Down the hill, through the orchards. She slipped on a decaying apple, wrenched her back as she steadied herself, and grabbed onto the gnarled trunk of a tree.

Sobs, originating deep within her soul, tore from her lips. "Mellie," she cried. "Mellie." She just could not be the child that John thought was his daughter! Autumn pushed away from the tree and started running again, ignoring the slap of a low hanging branch or the punch of a cluster of apples.

Finally clearing the orchard, she saw the fields and outbuildings on the other side of the bridge and raced forward straightaway. *Mellie. I have to get Mellie and get away!* She repeated this thought over and over in her mind, ignoring the stitch in her side and the clawing tightness in her lungs. The wooden slats of the bridge creaked beneath her weight. She ignored the warning and charged ahead as the sound of John's footsteps grew closer.

Faster!

Keep going!

In a split second, her forward motion abruptly stopped. As if caught in a time warp, Autumn heard the splintering of wood, experienced the feeling of being suspended in thin air, and then dropped hard through the bridge.

Pain exploded throughout her body. A wooden beam jammed into her rib cage, knocking the breath out of her lungs. Her right foot, wedged in the V of one of the bridge supports, grew numb while the toes on her other foot skimmed the surface water of the creek. Splinters tore into her palms as she struggled to hold onto one of the railing posts.

Nearly disoriented, she tilted her head forward to rest it on thick, splintered wood. "Mellie," she groaned and closed her eyes. A vision of dancing turquoise eyes in a face framed with beloved red curls flashed before her eyes, spurring Autumn to try to extricate herself before John caught up with her.

"Autumn!"

John's voice rang out in alarm as cautious footsteps sent the bridge groaning again.

It's too late to escape.

Jaw clenched, she managed to move her right foot so that her weight rested on her heel. With barely any feeling left in her foot, she pushed up with her leg muscles and pulled with her arms until she was able to lean forward, her waist level with the floor of the bridge.

"Hold still!"

She ignored his order and braced both palms on the wooden bridge. Her arms trembled and shook as she tried to push herself out of the hole. She felt her elbows begin to buckle and closed her eyes, expecting to land back down the hole with a thud. Instead, she found herself being lifted into John's arms. She stiffened. "Leave me alone," she croaked as she struggled to get free.

"Keep that up, and we'll both land in the creek," he snarled as he tightened his hold and proceeded cautiously along the edge of the bridge.

"Put me down!" she insisted when they finally reached solid ground.

"You're hurt," he argued as he ignored her request and quickened his pace.

"Please put me down."

He ground to a halt, set her onto her feet, and folded his arms over his chest. She turned away and tested her right foot, swallowing the pain as she tried to put her full weight it. Jaw tight, she held out her palms and winced as she pulled several thick splinters out of her flesh. "Almost as good as new," she remarked, ignoring the pulsating pain that thudded along the side of her rib cage. Pretending concern at the rip in her bodice, she touched her side and winced again.

"I've seen enough," he announced and scooped her off her feet. Again. "If you're too stubborn or juvenile to admit you're injured, then you deserve to be treated like a child. Now hold still. When we're back at the house—"

"I'm not going into that house. Mellie and I are leaving," she argued and stifled a cry of pain when her side jostled against his chest.

"You'll do as you're told."

"Is that an order?"

"Yes. And like a dutiful wife, you'll obey your husband," he warned as he turned the corner of the barn and headed straight to the house.

She felt the blood drain out of her face. "You're not my husband any more. Or have you already forgotten that you filed the annulment today?" she whispered, too shocked and too hurt to find a stronger voice.

He rocked to an abrupt halt and stared down at her. "Like it or not, you're still my wife. At least until Judge Claybourne returns to sign the decree. That should be in about two weeks."

As the door to the house swung open, he paused and looked up. His eyes widened, and his mouth dropped open as his hold on Autumn tightened.

Curious to see what or who had rendered John speechless, Autumn turned her head to the side. In the doorway stood an elderly woman of at least three score with pale white skin and bright red hair swept up into a chignon. Wide-set turquoise eyes, sparkling with familiar clarity, stared back at Autumn who felt her heartstrings tighten. The face. The color of her hair. Those distinctive eyes.

John's arms went slack. "Mother," he whispered.

Autumn fainted in the space of half a heartbeat.

Chapter 21

"Mellie."

It was the first word Autumn whispered out loud as she came back to consciousness. Through half-opened lids, she realized that she was lying in a double bed in a room she had never seen before. Alone. She opened her eyes completely and peered at her surroundings, softly muted by the sun's last rays. Light poured into the room through sheer lace curtain which hung limp and lifeless on an open window directly across from the side of the bed and etched a fancy shadow on the bare wide-planked floor.

She looked away from the intricate design because it reminded her of the elaborate web of lies that John had woven to get a child he thought was his long lost daughter back to Ohio. Her eyes filled with tears as every vehement declaration that Mellie was his daughter came roaring back at her. *"Amelia suits her better."* His seemingly innocent but curious insistence on calling Mellie by her formal name was no longer simply a point of contention between them meant to remind Autumn of John's authority as her husband. *"Her name is Amelia."*

"No! Her name is Mellie!" she cried out loud as she

rolled her head from side to side on the pillow to silence the ghostly horrors of the past and present.

Not me. He never wanted me.

Grief for love once glorious and now lost to her forever left her devastated and feeling more alone than she ever had been in her whole life. She blinked back the tears that blurred the image of the masculine-styled wardrobe and dresser lined up along a whitewashed wall.

As she lifted her head and shoulders, she groaned and dropped back to the pillow. The right side of her body from midsection to toe felt like it had been a stomping ground for a herd of wild horses. "A rotten, blasted bridge," she muttered to herself as she used one of her throbbing hands to lift the single sheet that covered her.

She took one look beneath it and gasped. Instead of her gown, she wore but a white nightdress and through the thin lawn, she could see bandages wrapped around her ribs and her right leg from knee to ankle. A strip of cotton bound four toes together.

She dropped the sheet and took a deep breath as she lifted her injured leg to the top of the sheet. Stabs of pain stopped the minute she grew still. Apparently nothing was broken, except for several of her toes, and although she was relieved not to have more serious injuries, the sight of bruised, angry purple flesh on her instep made her cringe.

She avoided thinking about who had undressed her and tended to her injuries and pulled herself up into a sitting position, surprised by the beads of perspiration that dotted her upper lip when she had finally managed to arrange the pillow at the small of her back and pulled the sheet up to cover herself.

She cocked her head and listened intently, but there were no voices or sounds of movement that would indicate that anyone else was inside the house. Where was Mellie? Had John taken her away? Concern overrode common sense, and she carefully inched her legs over the side of the bed. As blood rushed to her bandaged toes, they started to throb. Fueled by sheer determination to reclaim her child, she wrapped the sheet around her upper body and edged her bottom forward, grabbing the top of the headboard for support.

The smooth wood pressed into tender flesh that smarted. Instinctively, she loosened her grip and waited for the pain in her side to fade to a dull ache before trying to stand up. She had to move quickly, not like a snail! If everyone else had gone from the house, Autumn had to make good use of her time alone. If she could only find the strength to get dressed, find her travel bag, and load it into the wagon! When John did bring Mellie back, Autumn could exaggerate her injuries and beg him to let Mellie stay with her. Then later that night, when everyone else had fallen asleep, she could make an escape.

With one good leg?

On hands and knees if she had to.

She put her weight on her left leg and pushed up, tottering briefly to the side.

"Don't be too quick to test your strength."

She plopped back onto the bed and twisted sharply around. Pain knifed through her side and turned a shocked answer into a plaintive plea as she struggled to keep herself covered with the sheet. "Please leave."

John stood up from the chair he obviously had been sitting in all the while she had assumed she was alone. He walked over to the bed, his pained expression tugging at her heartstrings. "Mother said you wouldn't sleep very long. Are you in pain?"

How much does a broken heart hurt?

His midnight blue eyes darkened and set her to wondering how she had ever thought she had seen any promises there at all. They had been illusions—illusions that were shattered the instant she had seen the undeniable familial resemblance between Mellie and John's mother and then fainted before arguing otherwise.

"Let me try to help you with the pain you're feeling."

She turned away from him and tried to blink back the tears that welled in her eyes. "I don't need your self-absolving pity, nor do I consider any excuse you might offer as worth a single heartbeat of my time," she choked. "And I don't want your help."

"You once told me that your love for me was as steady as a heartbeat."

One tear escaped and slid silently down her cheek. "I—I lied. Just like you did."

Before she could wipe away her tear, John walked around the bed and slipped her back into it. He pulled the sheet up to her chin and sat down beside her. "No. I didn't lie when I told you that I loved you, but I was wrong not to tell you the truth in Branfield. I'll regret what I've done to you for the rest of my life." He reached out and cupped her cheek. "You promised to listen to me. Why did you run away before I had the chance to—"

"Because I knew you were wrong. I *know* you're wrong. Mellie is not your daughter," she blurted, unable to push aside the gnawing possibility that maybe, just maybe . . .

John bowed his head and sat statue-still for several intense moments before he got up, walked over to the dresser, and opened a drawer. Moments later he returned to her bedside and held out a daguerreotype. "Look at this."

She shook her head.

He placed it into her hands and walked over to the window. He stared outside. "A few months after Mellie was born, just before I went to New York, Trina and I posed for a drummer during the celebration of the founding of Comfort Bend twenty-five years earlier. He took this photograph, and for some reason, Trina left it behind." His voice choked, and he stopped to clear his throat. "Maybe she wanted me to have a reminder of what I had lost." He shook his head. "It's all I had left to keep Mellie's face from fading from memory."

Autumn clenched her eyes shut. "Take it away."

A deep sigh. Slow deliberate footsteps as he returned to the bedside. "What are you afraid of, Autumn? That I might be right? That I might be able to prove to you and to everyone else that Mellie is my own flesh and blood? Or that you've been wrong, sorely misled by your own brother's lies, all these years?"

Her eyes flew open. A stream of complaints meant to upbraid him for being selfish and callous fell by the wayside when she gazed into his eyes. Love, unbidden, swelled her traitorous heart, and she looked away quickly, catching an unwelcome glimpse of the images staring back at her from the daguerreotype. Her fingers shook as she picked it up and brought it closer to her.

A young family posed stiffly beneath a gaudy banner: Silver Jubilee. Comfort Bend, Ohio. April 18, 1825–1850. Only months before Clayton came home with his new family! She recognized the man in the daguerreotype immediately, despite the sepia tones that drained away the magnetism of his personality. It was John. Standing tall, shoulders erect, his expression too formally posed to be called anything but picture grim. A child—no—an infant lay cradled in his arms. Autumn studied the miniature face, but it was too young to know if . . .

She looked away and studied the image of the woman who stood next to John in the photograph. Petite, with pale ringlets that framed beautifully chiseled features.

Wide-set eyes seemed too large for such a tiny face. Lips pursed with irritation in a way so singularly familiar that Autumn's hands started to shake, and she began to cry.

She could no longer deny that what John had claimed to be true was indeed the truth.

"Trina."

Autumn covered her face with her hands and sobbed salty tears that stung her wounded palms. Grief surged from deep within her soul and wracked her body. She cried for so many: Clayton, a brother who had stretched the meaning of selfishness and cruelty. Trina, who had betrayed her legal husband and used her child as a weapon to punish him. Mellie, the child of her heart, who had been taken away from her natural father.

Most of all, however, she cried for John and herself. How difficult it must have been for him, the shame he must have felt, the terror and overriding fear that he might never find his runaway wife and little girl. And despite it all, he had an overwhelming goodness in his soul that would let him forgive his wife and plead for a second chance, a goodness that drove him on when all he had left were memories of a tiny infant who once had carried his name but always had kept hold of his heart.

It made all her endless days of labor and all her endless nights of worrying about Edsel Cameron, all the hours she had lain awake trying to find a way to make up to Mellie for her alleged father's indifference and her natural mother's coldness, seem so small by comparison. However innocent Autumn might be, for being one of a trio of people who had kept Mellie from the man who had given her life, guilt filled her spirit, too.

Autumn knew that there would never be enough tears to grieve the loss of her dream. Her heart ached, and she knew that her anguish was far greater for having loved, however briefly, the man she thought had been the man of her dreams. When the reservoir of her tears had drained temporarily, she wiped her face and wrapped her hands around the dageurreotype. Somehow that simple action made her feel more secure, as though by shielding the faces of that young family, she might be able to think more clearly.

"Have you told Mellie?" She stared at the sheet, unable and unwilling to look directly at John.

His response was strained. "No."

"Your not-so-deceased mother knows—"

"That I've found her granddaughter."

"And me? How did you explain . . ."

John's fingers tilted Autumn's chin up so she had to look at him. "For now, all she knows is that you've been caring for Mellie since Trina's death. You agreed to accompany Mellie back to Ohio with me to make her adjustment easier." He paused, his eyes misting. "I didn't see any need to complicate matters. For me or for you. . . ."

His words trailed off, and Autumn moistened her lips. "Telling her that you married Clayton's sister, you mean?"

He dropped his hand and looked away. "That's part of it."

Her heart began to race. "Isn't that enough?"

He swung back to face her. "Ever since Clayton and Trina . . . well, let's just say that in a small town like Comfort Bend, Yankee peddlers have received a cold welcome. Not many people have forgotten what Clayton did. If they threaten to tar and feather a tinman if he doesn't clear the town limits by sundown, how do you think they'll treat you?"

"Like I carry the plague, or like I'm some mystical sorceress determined to break up some poor fool's marriage," she murmured, praying that she had fallen through the bridge and landed in one hell of a nightmare. Wasn't anyone going to wake her up?

She sniffled. Some sorceress. She could not even divine a way to keep John as her husband, let alone induce some other man to leave his wife for her. She was tempted to cry again, and if her side had not started throbbing again, she might have. "What about Doris? She knows we're married, although the poor woman would faint if she knew what was really happening between us."

He smiled. "Doris won't say a word. I talked with her before she left."

Autumn's eyes widened. "She left?"

"She's staying with my sister, Grace, who's about to deliver my fourth niece or nephew. They opened the house for us and Grace's husband, Daniel, brought my mother here at the first sight of smoke rising from the chimney. Doris can be a big help to both of them right now."

Autumn swallowed hard, her voice barely above a whisper. "What about Mellie? Can I see her?"

"Of course you can. But right now, she's down at the creek. My mother thought it might help calm Mellie down if she could see where you fell."

"What happens now?" she ventured, too unsure of her own thoughts to trust herself to look at their situation objectively. How odd that the love triangle she had thought she had battled had not included John's first wife after all; instead, the other woman turned out to be one precious little redhead whom they both loved.

"First, you're going to get a good night's sleep. Mother mixed some Dover's powder for you. We'll talk more in the morning." John pressed a glass to her lips, and she swallowed the medicine he offered, chasing away the medicine's taste with several sips of fresh water from another glass.

Her eyelids drooped, and she protested only weakly when John eased her down into a flat position. "I don't want to sleep. I want to see Mellie." She winced as he brushed her side when he pulled a cover up over her.

"You're bruised and battered. You need rest. Mellie will be here when you wake up. I promise."

She closed her eyes, letting the medicine work its magic as a gentle peace erased the pain in her body.

"You promise," she repeated.

A single tear trickled down her cheek, and she sighed as all the other promises she had seen in his eyes faded from sapphire blue to midnight. "You promise," she whispered, praying that this would be his one promise to her that he would keep.

John carried Mellie into Autumn's room, his bare feet padding noiselessly on the floor. "Hush now, little one. You'll wake your mama," he whispered, hoping to quiet the little girl and get her to stop crying by taking her to see that Autumn was really all right.

"I want my mama!" Wails quieted into whimpers as Mellie scrambled down out of his arms and raced away from him.

Candlelight flickered on the bedside table, casting a soft glow onto Autumn's sleeping form, and as Mellie stood at the head of the bed, the light revealed flushed cheeks and puffed, reddened eyes. Without waiting for his approval, she climbed into the bed, still sobbing, and curled her little body next to Autumn's.

"Hold on," John cautioned, easily lifting the child to Autumn's uninjured side and tucking Mellie under the covers. "That's better. You don't want to hurt your mama." He sighed with relief as Amelia's cries finally ceased. "Do you think you can go to sleep now?"

She nodded. "Mama can, too," she said sleepily as she put Woolly Lamb into Autumn's outstretched hand and closed her fingers around it. "Will you sleep here with us, too?" she asked just before her mouth opened wide with a yawn.

John swallowed the lump in his throat. How could he tell Mellie that he would probably never share a room with them again? "Not just yet. You snuggle down now and get to sleep. You have a big day tomorrow. Grandma needs your help, remember?"

Another yawn.

"Uh-huh,"she mumbled as she closed her eyes.

Minutes later, the sound of her soft even breathing echoed with Autumn's, and John resumed his vigil, choosing to stand rather than sit in the chair in the corner. He raked his fingers through his hair. After four unsuccessful attempts to quiet Mellie and get her to go to sleep in an adjoining bedroom, he had finally given up. He tried to tell himself that Mellie was merely overwrought by Autumn's accident, although he wondered if somehow Mellie had sensed that something monumental had happened today—something far too complicated for any five-year-old to understand.

In the final analysis, if he were unsuccessful in his efforts to break Cameron's will, all Mellie would eventually believe was that her papa had sent her mama away.

Twice.

He shifted his stance, and he could almost feel the weight of the sword of love he naively thought would slice through all the legalisms and find justice. At the moment, the sword hung heavy at his side, like it was made of stone.

"I'm only a man, not a miracle worker," he muttered as he ran his fingers through his hair again. What kind of man was he to tear apart the woman and child who lay together before him? What kind of God forced him into this position?

Not God.

Edsel Cameron.

His anger at his former father-in-law made his pulse pound, but try as he might, he found no solace in anger. Nor did he find solutions. For the first time in years, he dropped to his knees, bowed his head, and in the darkest hour of his despair, just before the break of dawn, he prayed for a miracle.

One small miracle would dry up the river of distrust that flowed between him and Autumn and on the riverbed that remained, flowers like the ones Autumn loved so much would grow—flowers that would blossom with the understanding that he needed to stay with his child, guide her as she grew up, and protect the inheritance that would guarantee that she would never be vulnerable to any man. Ever.

Wasn't that what a father was supposed to do?

Was that asking too much?

At dawn, Autumn woke up to the sound of birds celebrating a new day, and she wrinkled her nose at the strong aroma of apples that wafted through the open window. She winced as the pain in her side seemed worse instead of better. She opened her eyes and gasped out loud. "Mellie!" she cried as she hugged the little girl close to her. One of Mellie's hands gripped the bandages wrapped around Autumn's ribs, and she carefully loosened the child's fingers, smiling through her tears. Woolly Lamb lay against one of Mellie's cheeks, its face buried in a mass of red curls.

Autumn pressed a kiss against the top of Mellie's head, and out of the corner of her eye, caught the silhouette of John's head resting on top of the mattress. Curious, she realized that he must have fallen asleep while kneeling at the side of the bed.

Kneeling?

John Logan bowed down to no man or woman, and

the idea that he had dropped to his knees to pray struck a chord of compassion for him that resonated throughout her spirit and left her trembling. She closed her eyes and swallowed hard, knowing that even as she judged and condemned him for lying to her, she hid behind a righteous wall of glass. She had done nearly the same as he had to keep Mellie from Edsel Cameron. She had lived a lie in Branfield. Lord, she had almost married Reverend Briley and eventually did marry John Logan to preserve that lie!

Admitting the similarities in each of their behaviors made her shiver behind that wall of glass. She wondered if she had the courage to step in front of it, or if she was prepared to see it shatter when she dug in her heels and cast the first stone.

Chapter 22

Autumn hobbled to the front door, crossed her arms over her chest, and stood erect, leaning carefully on the heel of her right foot to steady herself. "I told you I wasn't going, so you can sit there all day in that buckboard for all I care."

Stone faced, John never even acknowledged her. He just tipped his hat back and stared straight ahead. The horses whinnied, and one of them stomped its foreleg as if reinforcing John's refusal to budge. If she did not know better, she would have sworn that John was as good at puppetry as he had been at trying to manipulate every move she made since the accident.

"Suit yourself!" She turned around and started a torturous limp back to the sofa. John's mother, Hannah, sat in a chair and seemed oblivious to the tense standoff since the rhythmic sound of her knitting needles clicking together never lost a beat.

Mellie, on the other hand, who was sitting on the side arm of her grandmother's chair, seemed to find the whole situation intriguing. Humor glistened in her eyes, and she grinned as Autumn plopped herself back down. "Papa said you'd give up and go to the doctor before supper."

"Your papa was wrong!" Autumn snorted. "He's the most stubborn, single-purposed, arrogant . . . ugh!" She pounded her fist on the cushion. The older woman smiled without even looking up from her work. She stopped and fingered the blue trim on a pair of cream colored booties she was just finishing for her newest grandson, John Logan Clarke, who had been named for the uncle who had returned just days before the child's birth.

Autumn felt guilty, knowing that Hannah Logan should be staying with her daughter and the new baby instead of playing chaperone for John and her. The woman must have been torn between staying with her newest grandchild and getting reacquainted with Mellie, although she never uttered a syllable of complaint.

"John is worried about you," Hannah said as she looked over to Autumn. "He just wants to have the doctor take a gander at your foot. It's been a week since your accident, dear. What harm would it do to humor him?"

Turquoise eyes softened with sincere concern and shimmered in the early afternoon sunlight that poured through a bay window. Autumn lowered her head, still undone by the color of Hannah Logan's eyes that was so remarkably like the color of Mellie's. "My toes are healing perfectly well," she whispered.

It's my heart that's never going to mend.

"Maybe you should think about the example you're setting for a certain young lady."

Was reminding her of her responsibility toward Mellie a Logan family trait? Autumn's head snapped up. A sharp retort died on her lips the moment angry brown eyes locked with sympathetic turquoise. She moistened her lips and tilted her chin up a tad. "Running off to the doctor for every little complaint makes no sense."

"I always like to err on the side of caution, especially

when it comes to a body's health." Hannah put down her knitting and put her arm around Mellie. "Why don't you and John go into town to see Dr. Blake? While you're gone, Mellie and I will whip up a good hot batch of apple fritters."

"Mama hates apples," Mellie blurted, "but I don't."

"Mellie!" Autumn blushed, realizing that her lifelong aversion to the taste of the fruit was tantamount to heresy in Johnny Appleseed's home territory where apples were the staff of life for most farmers.

Hannah laughed so hard that she shook her knitting to the floor. "I suppose we overdo it just a bit, don't we?" she admitted as she wiped the tears of mirth from her cheeks.

Autumn groaned. "Apple pancakes for breakfast. Apple butter spread on hot bread for supper. Applesauce for dessert. Unless you prefer apple pie or apple fritters. It's enough to make a person who dislikes the flavor of apples go loony!"

"That's why you have the appetite of a child half Amelia's age! Why didn't you say something?" The older woman leaned forward in her chair, her lips pursed with reprimand.

Autumn felt her cheeks flame and imagined they were as deep a shade of scarlet as her gown. "I don't want to cause any more trouble than I already have."

"Trouble?" The woman slapped her knees and stood up. "Young lady, I don't know whether or not you hit your head when you fell through that bridge, but trouble you're not. John and I both owe you a great deal for what you've done for Mellie after . . ."

She glanced at her granddaughter, paused, and then walked over to Autumn. She winked and nodded her head toward the child who was busy picking up the knitting off the floor. "I don't know what's going on between you and John. It's none of my business," she stated, her voice barely above a whisper. She held up her hands when Autumn opened her mouth to interrupt. "I do know that he's worried about you. Can't you humor him? Just this once? Besides," she added as she reached out to take Mellie's hand, "the ride into town will do you good. Might even give you and John the chance to talk things out."

Without waiting for Autumn to give her an answer, Hannah led Mellie toward the kitchen. Her tall, stately silhouette towered next to Mellie's. "We better take a look in the cupboards. Maybe we can find something special to make that doesn't taste anything like apples."

Halfway into town, one of the horses started to limp, and John stopped the buckboard under a stand of buckeye oaks that vied with apple trees for dominance in the landscape. After removing a small stone that had embedded itself in the animal's right hind hoof, he swatted the horse's rump affectionately. "Good as new," he pronounced as he avoided the dust that filled the air and climbed back up into the driver's seat. He grinned at Autumn as he picked up the reins. "Foot trouble seems to be an epidemic these days."

"My foot's fine," she gritted, grabbing onto the seat as the wagon jolted forward. Instinctively, her feet pressed against the floorboards, and bright lights danced in front of her eyes as her right foot quickly proved her protestation premature.

"Doc Blake can tell for sure."

"It's *my* foot!" she cried. "Can't you just leave well enough alone? There's nothing you can do for a broken toe except wait for nature to take its course."

"You have four."

"Three," she argued, upset that he had made her physical recovery the primary topic of every conversation. "Can't we talk about something else?"

"How's your side?"

She swatted at his arm. "Stop it. And stop this wagon right now."

He brought the horses to an abrupt halt and turned in his seat to face her. "Well? Aren't you going to threaten to hobble back to the house if I don't do exactly what you want? I don't like to play tug-of-war for power."

"It's . . . it's not about power," she gushed.

"It's about Mellie."

She nodded her head. "I can't help it. I have a lot of questions . . . questions that have answers only you can give me, and the only thing you want to talk about are my toes or my ribs!"

John's mouth went dry. He should have answered her questions days ago, but he was so worried about her injuries that he did not have the courage to add more pain to her life. "Ask. I'll answer you as honestly as I can. Where do you want to start?"

Autumn shifted in her seat so that she faced him. "Edsel Cameron."

John's heartbeat went into a skid before it charged forward into a gallop. Reluctant to sever the guarded and tenuous peace that existed between the two of them, he realized that Autumn deserved to know that her fear of Edsel Cameron was justified and that his dictates far outlived the man's physical existence.

"When did he die?" she prompted.

John looked away. "Two years ago. Not long after Trina died. A sudden fever. At least that's what his lawyers told me." He swallowed hard before meeting Autumn's gaze again. "I was in New Hampshire when I heard he died. When I got back to New York, his lawyers confirmed that the old man was dead. He never suspected . . . well, he knew that Trina had run off, but he assumed that Mellie was with me. Every letter his lawyers sent was more forceful than the last. Cameron wanted Mellie to come to New York to live with him."

Autumn's eyes filled with tears. "He never sent anyone to look for Mellie?"

John nodded his head. "I wasn't about to tell him that Mellie was missing after Trina died. I spent too many days and nights on the road, learning the peddler's routes and following every lead to the elusive Autumn Welles to have him send out a score of detectives who might bungle the job and scare her into hiding."

Shadows of leaves from the overhead trees danced on the pallor that covered Autumn's face. "He never sent anyone to look for Mellie." Her voice was flat, her eyes dulled with anguish. "There was no reason to be afraid of him," she murmured, and John could see that the years of living a lie to protect Mellie from her grandfather had not been easy for Autumn. The future, however, was going to be even more difficult unless Linderman found a way to break the will and John found a way to rekindle Autumn's trust as well as her love.

"If I had known the truth . . ."

"You didn't. Don't you think I know that?" He reached out and picked up her hand. It was cold, and he squeezed it. "Neither one of us can afford to stay buried in the past."

Her hand started to tremble. "The future is too frightening, too uncertain."

He wanted to pull her into his arms, hold her tightly, cling to the wavering affection she held for him, and feel the beating of her heart. He couldn't, not yet. Not unless he could offer her a future that would be the one he dreamed about every night. And not unless their affections were based on truth and honesty.

Instead, he tightened his hold on her hand. "There's a will," he began and slowly detailed the inheritance left to the child they both loved as well as the conditions attached to the will that forced Mellie to live in New York and precluded John from remarrying until Mellie reached her majority. He studied Autumn's reactions and watched as her mink brown eyes misted briefly before they muddied into the color of river clay.

When he explained why he had filed for the annulment of their marriage, he swallowed hard. "I had no choice in the matter," he pronounced. Reluctantly, he let her pull her hand away. "Unless Linderman finds a legal way to destroy the will, Mellie and I will be going to New York to live."

"For the inheritance," she whispered.

"For Mellie. To make sure that she receives everything that is her right to claim."

Autumn paled. "Is there any room in Mellie's future for . . . for me?"

John felt deep pain slice through his chest. "I hope with all my heart that the lawyers will find a way to break the will, and we can spend the rest of our lives together—as man and wife." Could he say the rest? He had to. "If not, you could still stay with Mellie . . . as her governess."

"Her governess?" Autumn's eyes deadened, as though he had extinguished the fire in her spirit forever. "How . . . how will you explain that to Mellie?"

"She'll just have to deal with it. It's best—"

"Best for whom?" Autumn sighed. "Does your mother know?"

Defensively, he steeled his back ramrod straight. "*I* make the decisions concerning Amelia's welfare."

"Your mother has spent five years waiting to be reunited with her granddaughter, and now you're going to spirit the child away to New York?"

"At the moment, I don't have any other option," he argued.

Sadness etched her face. "You can give Mellie a wonderful life in Comfort Bend. She's surrounded by family, people who love her, not servants who have to be paid to be attentive to her needs. We all have choices. Some are just more odious or more difficult than others."

"Choices?" His voice softened. "Like deciding whether or not you can stay in Amelia's life and come to New York as her governess instead of her mother?"

Autumn's bottom lip quivered and her cheeks turned scarlet. He would have given his soul to Satan to have her believe that his only dream was to have Linderman disqualify the conditions of the will so that they could all stay together as a family.

She swung away from him, rearranged her skirts, and sat facing forward. "I'll always be her mother. Not Edsel Cameron, not even you can erase the bond of love between us."

"It's as steady as your heartbeat," he murmured as he picked up the reins and clicked them. He did not expect Autumn to respond, but as his own pulse slowly returned to a normal cadence, he wondered if he had any right at all to hope that whatever affection Autumn held for him might find a way to survive.

The town of Comfort Bend huddled on either side of a wide dirt roadway that led northeast to Columbus and south to Cincinnati. A fair distance from the latter gave the settlement a perfect location for wearied travelers; hence, a half-dozen inns and rooming houses bordered the road at the crux of the curve, their brightly painted signs competing for patrons.

Autumn edged away from John as he drove the buckboard down the middle of the street past the inns, and she scanned the rest of the businesses looking for Doctor Blake's office.

John was too busy tipping his hat and waving back at

shoppers and shopkeepers alike to pay any attention to her as the townspeople shouted hearty welcomes and one man even ran over to the wagon, running alongside to shake John's hand.

"Knew you'd find your little girl. Too bad about the missus, though. That the girl's nanny?"

John grinned. "Autumn's here for a visit while Mellie and I get reacquainted. See you later at Dillon's."

"First whiskey is on me!" came the huffed response as the winded man dropped back from the wagon.

Autumn was grateful for the way John avoided disclosing her real identity, but she could not decide which one would be more scandalous: the woman who was Clayton Welles' sister, the woman who claimed to be Mellie's mother, or the woman whose secret marriage to John Logan was soon to be annulled.

Before she could fathom an answer, John had tied up the horses and lifted her down from the wagon. He set her down carefully on the planked sidewalk and nodded toward the open stairway behind him that led to the second story on the corner of a whitewashed building. "Should I offer to carry you or can I assume that you intend to climb the stairs by yourself?"

Autumn looked up the steep staircase and gulped. "I'll climb."

"Thought you might." With a back wave of his hand, he stepped back out of her way, and she limped to the bottom of the steep staircase. She lifted her skirts with one hand and gripped the railing with the other. *One step at a time,* she told herself as she inched her way higher. By the time she reached the top landing, she was out of breath and reluctant to face John and admit that her pride and willfulness had exacted a higher price that she had expected to pay. Her left hand was nearly numb from gripping the railing, and her right foot ached so badly she might not argue too vehemently if Dr. Blake wanted to cut it off.

John stepped around her, opened the door to the doctor's office, and tipped his hat. "I'll be back in an hour. Wait for me here," he said quietly and descended the stairs without saying another word.

Autumn had the distinct impression that she had been dismissed as quickly and easily as yesterday's fashion plates. She gritted her teeth and stepped through the doorway into the office.

John swallowed a second whiskey and put the shot glass down onto the bar top. "That's enough for me. I've got to get over to Doc Blake's."

A chorus of disappointed groans from the small crowd of men who surrounded him filled the interior of Dillon's Saloonery and coalesced into a chant. "One for the road! One for the road!"

John laughed, comforted by the support of neighbors and friends who had gathered for an impromptu celebration. They had listened with rapt silence as he recounted his search for a runaway wife and kidnapped daughter, cheered when told of Clayton's demise at the hands of hoodlums, and looked away when informed that Trina had shared in his fate.

Quickly changing the topic to Mellie, John had carefully explained how Autumn had cared for the child until a relative came forward to claim her and lauded Autumn's insistence that she would accompany Mellie to Comfort Bend to make sure that the child, who was too tender-aged to understand what had happened between her mother and father, made an easy adjustment to her new home.

"One for the road! One for the road!"

John acquiesced to the boisterous chant and lifted the refilled shot glass to his lips. Before he could tilt the amber liquid into his mouth, Bertram Grill, an old acquaintance rather than an old friend, barreled through the doors to the saloon. "Got us a Yankee peddler!" he exclaimed. "Saved a piece of the mangy bastard's hide for ya, John."

Whiskey sloshed over the rim of the glass and stained his fingers as John slammed the shot glass to the bar top. Shouting angrily, the crowd filed outside, and John had to push his way through them to get a good look at what was happening.

What he saw made his stomach lurch. Next to a tinwagon with a damaged wheel, a peddler who was unconscious and sprawled in the dirt lay with his tinware dumped at his feet. The poor devil's face had been pummeled into a bloodied pulp.

John did not recognize the man who stepped out of the crowd, pulled the injured man over to the wagon, and propped him up against the damaged wheel which looked like it had been dented with nothing less than an iron mallet. After putting a tin pot upside down on the man's head, the stranger hit the pot with his fist. "Let the poor devil live to spread the word to all the others that we don't cotton to wife-stealing, child-robbing Yankee peddlers in Comfort Bend!"

Foot stomping cheers rose immediately, and John stared at the unconscious man who had become the scapegoat for all the misery that Clayton Welles had planted and that each townsman had taken to heart as though an insult to one of them had been an insult to all. John also realized that his homecoming had stirred up all the passion and outrage that apparently still simmered after nearly five years. John had returned and now it boiled over into mob insanity.

There was a time, he admitted ruefully as he edged forward, when he gladly would have added a blow to the many others that had already been struck against this innocent peddler. After following peddlers on their routes, sharing their triumphs and their sorrows, he knew better than to stereotype an entire group of hard-working drummers based on the actions of one man, especially when that man was Clayton Welles.

The crowd grew silent as John bent over the victim, tossed away the tin pot, and pulled the man up to a standing position. With one arm around the man's back, he held him up by wrapping the man's arm over his shoulder and grabbing the peddler's wrist. "The time to take vengeance and spew anger is past. This man did nothing to warrant an attack except have the misfortune to arrive in a town where five years ago, another peddler, Clayton Welles, charmed my wife into leaving me and taking our daughter with them."

He paused to look at each man in the crowd while he shifted his burden. "Instead of blaming Clayton or even Trina, maybe we all have to look a little closer." He stopped to clear his throat. "Did it ever occur to any of you that if I had made Trina truly happy, Clayton would never have had a chance to turn her head and convince her to run away?"

John started dragging the man toward the sidewalk. "Take a look at yourself. Ask yourself if you've been a good husband, attentive to more than just putting new shingles on the roof or food on the table. When's the last time you tried to make your wife as happy as you did when you courted her?"

A belligerent voice rang out. "Happy? She's lucky to have a man to provide for her!"

A few men in the crowd nodded in agreement, while others grew pensive. John searched their faces until he spied Bertram Grill, who at least had the innate decency to wear a red face. "See that the man's wares are stored back inside the wagon. Then get someone to help you get it to the wheelwright's to be repaired and tell him I'll settle the bill later."

Bertram nodded, and John made his way through the crowd as it parted to let him through. Cleve Enderview, a good friend who lived on a farm on the opposite side of John's farm from Grace and Daniel, stepped out of the crowd and gave John a hand with the still-unconscious peddler. "Doc Blake's?"

John nodded grimly, and as he stepped up onto the sidewalk, he spied the hem of a scarlet dress. He lifted his gaze and swallowed hard, knowing that the eyes he would find gazing back at him would be dark brown.

Had Autumn witnessed this whole lousy debacle, or had she been there just long enough to hear him bare his soul to his friends and neighbors and admit that if he had been a better husband, Trina would not have left in the first place—not with Clayton Welles or any other man?

Why hadn't Autumn waited for him at Dr. Blake's? Couldn't she do one thing he asked? Frustration chased away his embarrassment, and his mood blackened. He scowled at her. "Why didn't you wait for me like you were told?"

Gentle understanding flared back at him. "You were late."

"I always am," he grumbled.

Despite the curiosity of everyone in the crowd who witnessed their exchange, he knew that they had no idea that his words referred to a far more serious topic.

He did.

So did Autumn.

Chapter 23

Autumn placed a basket laden with food on a bedside table in the bedroom next to John's and picked up the breakfast tray, quickly surveying its contents. She laughed. "You're getting better," she pronounced with the relief of a nurse who was caring for a slow-to-recover patient.

Isaac Mandelbaum's lopsided grin was accompanied by a shiver of pain as he winced and held a bruised hand up to his face. "Got my appetite back, that's for sure. Best meal I've had since leavin' my Lena back in May." He paused, as though it was just too painful to continue speaking. Crescents of pale purple swirled with a garish shade of yellow undershadowed both eyes that were nothing more than slits in clouds of puffy flesh. Both of his lips were still cracked and oozed blood each time he tried to talk or eat, although the swelling had gone down considerably. "I appreciate your kindness, ma'am."

Autumn shook her head. "John deserves the credit for stepping in and sending the crowd away with guilty consciences."

Isaac closed his eyes for a moment, and when he opened them, they were misty. "Good man. *Good* man.

It takes a healthy dose of decency and courage to stand up for a man he don't even know, especially with me bein' a tin peddler and all. After what happened to John, I guess I wouldn't have blamed him if he added a few blows of his own."

The tray started to shake, and Autumn gripped it harder. "You know?"

A lopsided grin formed again and stopped halfway between a full smile and a smirk. "Hannah told me the whole ugly story. She raised one fine son. That she did. Told her so, too." The smile drooped as he ran his good hand across the bandages wrapped around his chest.

"Are you in a lot of pain?"

"Not much," he gritted. "How many days has it been?"

"Five. No, today makes six," she replied. "Dr. Blake said you were lucky that your ribs were only cracked and not broken."

"Lucky? Yes, ma'am." He chuckled and clutched at his side. "With my kind of luck, a fella might consider himself cursed. Lady Luck sure hasn't been too kind, but I keep hopin' she'll take a hankerin' to someone else real soon and forget all about me."

Shifting his position, he shrugged his shoulders. "Lena's been tellin' me for thirty-five years that I don't have the good sense the Lord put in a pebble. The minute I saw the fire blazin' in those men's eyes, I should have put whip to horseflesh and made for Cincinnati. Got greedy, pure and simple," he confessed.

Autumn shuddered as he continued talking with her for the first time since his ordeal. Apparently, he needed to talk, although he must have also shared his experiences with Hannah, who obviously had told him about Clayton and Trina to help the man understand that nothing that had happened to him had been his fault.

"I just needed one more passel of townsfolk to sell the rest of my tinware and pocket enough to last the winter," he continued. "Could have gotten a fair price for the wagon in Cincinnati, too, before I headed for home."

"Your wagon has been repaired," Autumn blurted, trying to add a little hope to the despair that seemed to consume the peddler. "I'm sure John told me the wheelwright was going to repair it and store it for you until you recovered."

Isaac's eyes widened. "I can't afford to pay for that!"

"No need to worry about that."

John's voice startled Autumn, and she stood mute while John approached the sickbed. "You're looking . . ."

"Human again, I hope." Isaac extended his hand. "Much obliged, John Logan."

John smiled as he shook hands. "My mother tells me you're anxious to leave for home."

"I'm already a month later than I should be. Lena will be worried half to crazy."

"Then a few more days won't hurt, especially if I send her a wire that you'll be heading back soon. Dr. Blake is supposed to stop by this afternoon while we're at my sister's to celebrate my newest nephew's arrival." He peeked into the basket of food Autumn had brought and grinned. "There's enough fried chicken and apple pie in here to keep a man twice your size satisfied till dinner."

Autumn jumped knee deep into the conversation. "Are you sure you're feeling up to being left alone? Maybe I should stay with you, just in case you need something," she added, groping at any chance to avoid a family get-together that would only remind her of the family she had never been able to give Mellie. Her panic collided with a deep desire to see Doris again and apologize for involving her in Autumn's troubles.

The disappointment that flared in John's eyes turned to relief that traded places with her own disappointment when Isaac shook his head. "Got a good meal and a comfortable bed. You go on and have fun." He yawned.

For good measure?

Autumn swallowed the last hope she had of avoiding the inevitable, and with only a slight limp as she favored her right foot, she followed John out of the room.

Shooed out of the kitchen, Autumn wandered around the rear of an enormous log cabin and followed the sound of laughter and cheers that echoed from somewhere close by. Grace and Daniel's farm had less acreage than John's, but their home was quite a bit larger and more rustic than the house John had built.

With four children to feed, Daniel obviously had put more effort into the soil than he had into building a home, although Grace had softened the cavernous dwelling with ruffled curtains and colorful quilts that held special, loving memories in each handcrafted square.

Skirting the open yard between the cabin and the barn, Autumn edged along the trees that formed a natural windbreaker and provided shade during sweltering summers. Now at the end of October, only a few stalwart dried leaves clung to nearly barren limbs, and the warm sunshine that filtered through onto her head was a welcome complement to the crisp fall air.

As the corral behind the barn came into her view, she paused, reluctant to join the children and their fathers who were having a grand time without her. The children lined up along the fence with Daniel who stood next to a man Autumn did not recognize. The stranger's arm rested on the shoulders of a tall, gangly boy who looked too old to be Daniel's son. She walked a little closer to see where Mellie and John were, carefully watching the ground to avoid twisting her foot on a tree root. When she looked up again, her heart thudded to a halt.

Mellie.

Wearing dungaree pants and bouncing up and down on the back of a champagne pony, her red curls jiggled like coiled springs and shimmered like red gold in the bright sunshine. Wilby sat behind her, his brace awkwardly sticking out from one side of the horse and his arms wrapped around Mellie's waist. Mellie's eyes were wide with wonder, and she smiled so broadly as John led the pony by the reins that Autumn wanted to cry.

Father and child.

It was a picture that etched itself into her soul, and she stored it in the hope chest of her heart along with other memories far too precious to ever let fade away.

She blinked away her tears and realized that John had kept all of his promises to himself concerning his daughter. But what about the promises he had made to Autumn? Would he someday keep those, too?

Not if he went to New York. Not if he set aside those promises with the mistaken but well-intentioned notion that Mellie needed anything more than he could offer her right now: a safe and secure home, a wonderful, loving family, and two parents who loved her dearly.

Wealth. Status in society.

Both were so superficial and fleeting that Autumn wanted to scream. Couldn't John see that true wealth was measured not in coins, but in family?

She loved John Logan. She would always love him, but she would never understand how he could deny the yearnings of his heart and sacrifice the love he claimed to have for her in the name of duty. John had rediscovered fatherhood as they journeyed from Connecticut to Ohio, but in his fervor to make up for the past five years, he missed one very crucial truth: A father's love could build a foundation for a child that would far outlast the coins that lined his pocket. No one could predict the future or protect investments against the whims of the business cycle, let alone guess the favors of a whimsical and fickle social elite. But neither could anyone ever deny the natural power of love. It transcended all else.

Autumn turned to leave before anyone would take notice of her, certain that her love was not strong enough to dislodge John's misguided sense of duty to his daughter. "Doris!" she exclaimed, her heart pounding with surprise. "How did you get out of the kitchen, too?"

"Grace and Mrs. Logan decided to play matchmaker and ushered me out the door as soon as they realized that Thaddeus had arrived with his son."

Autumn blinked back surprise. "Matchmaker?"

Doris's face skewered into a shy grin, and Autumn noticed that Doris had lost that haunted, pained look in her eyes. "He owns the general store in town. He brought his son with him when he delivered supplies a few days after I arrived." Her eyes softened, and she reached out to take Autumn's hand. "He's a good man. Hardworking. God-fearing. And a widower." She laughed nervously. "Now *I* sound like a matchmaker, don't I?"

Autumn squeezed her friend's hand. "What about Wilby?"

This time Doris's smile was practically stretched from ear to ear. "Thaddeus is afraid that Wilby will keep his promise."

"Promise?"

"Wilby told Matthew, Thaddeus's son, that he would be his eyes if Matthew would run for him. Matthew is blind," she added, her voice breaking. "Thaddeus accepts his son's cross, and he treats Wilby kindly."

Alarmed by her friend's whirlwind of a courtship that curiously was devoid of any hint of romance, Autumn hugged Doris. "What about love? How do you feel about Thaddeus?"

Doris gave her a squeeze and pulled away. "I respect him, and I know he has a good heart. Love doesn't always come first, but at least with Thaddeus, I know that it has a chance to grow. My husband's only been gone for a few months, and . . . well, Thaddeus and I have time to get to know one another before we . . ."

Autumn laughed nervously. "My planned apology for bringing you all the way to Ohio is as useful now as icing for a cake that somebody else ate while it was still hot from the oven. I'm happy for you. For both of you," she said quietly, chastising herself for the fleeting jealousy that she felt.

Doris hooked her arm with Autumn's, and they started back to the cabin. She slowed her pace when Autumn started to limp. "Now all we have to do is find a way to convince John Logan to tell everyone else that you're married."

A sea of contented faces surrounded the long trestle table in the kitchen as Autumn and Doris cleared away the remnants of a meal fit for royalty. Hannah Logan had spent days preparing enough food to feed the town of Comfort Bend, or so Autumn had thought at the time. Judging by the few pieces of fried chicken and empty bowls of mashed potatoes, however, appetites in rural Ohio were almost as large as the growing legend of Johnny Appleseed.

While Autumn wiped up a gravy spill in front of Mellie, Doris placed the last of three pies into the center of the table. "Dessert," she announced proudly. "I hope you all left room."

Autumn rolled her eyes. She did not have to ask. She knew that the pies were all chock full of sugar, cinnamon, and apples. She turned away from the table, intending to start washing the pyramid of dishes when Hannah Logan called out to her.

"Do have a seat with us, Autumn."

She swung around, prepared to mumble an excuse for avoiding dessert when Doris opened the basket Hannah had carried on her lap for the entire ride here and lifted out a dessert that made Autumn's mouth water. A mountain of fluffy white frosting covered some sort of cake, and Autumn was deeply touched.

"Honey cake. I made it especially for you, and if a certain person even tries to steal a whiff, I guarantee he'll regret it."

John broke into a fit of laughter, and before Autumn knew it, even the children were giggling and young John Logan Clarke added a chorus of wails.

Grace lifted her newborn son from her lap, quickly put him up to her shoulder, and patted his back until he quieted. "Poor John. Remember the time Mrs. Hadley made you eat a piece of her blue ribbon pie? You scratched for a month."

John's eyes locked with Autumn's, and she could almost feel the memory of the honeyed medicine come back to life, and it flowed between them. He looked away first and reached over to swipe a bit of frosting from the side of the cake as Autumn held her breath. "I think my allergy to honey might be something I've outgrown. Almost. Just a few weeks ago—"

"John, don't you dare!" Autumn's cheeks flamed.

Grace clapped her hands. "Do tell, brother."

"Yes, do," Daniel insisted.

John winked at Autumn, and she was tempted to turn

the sweet confection on top of his head. "I made a honeyed syrup for John's cough. I didn't know," she protested, taken aback when laughter erupted again among the adults and unsure why she did not tell everyone that it was John's stubborn refusal to stop taking the medicine that caused most of his problems.

"It wasn't that funny at the time," John remarked as he offered the stolen frosting to Mellie.

"No. I'm sure that it wasn't," Hannah agreed.

"What happened?"

Her face beaming, Mellie chimed in before Autumn or John could answer. "Papa scratched and scratched and scratched!"

Howls of laughter again.

"That's going to cost you all," John snorted as he claimed an entire apple pie for himself.

Everyone grumbled and then quickly quieted down as they devoured the desserts as quickly as Autumn and Doris could cut slivers of cake or wedges of still-warm pie. Autumn relaxed and found herself enjoying the gentle bantering and warm camaraderie of the family and friends gathered round the table. Thaddeus and Matthew seemed equally at ease, and Autumn admitted that Doris had been very fortunate to catch the eye of a man who would be good to her and to her son.

Stephen Clarke, at age six the oldest of Grace and Daniel's children, licked the last of the frosting off his fork. "Can we open the presents now?"

"Stephen!" Daniel cast his son a hard expression. "Where are you manners?"

"Presents!" Twins Carol and Faith, three years old and born on Christmas Eve, clapped their hands. "Presents!"

"Not for you, loves. For your new baby brother," Grace admonished. "Now rest your lips and if you're very quiet, Uncle John can give you each a present to open for the baby."

John got up from the table, walked to the other room, and returned carrying four packages, one of which he placed in front of each of the children. The fourth he put in front of his sister.

"Stephen, you go first," Daniel suggested.

Small but determined hands carefully unwrapped the gift Autumn had made for the baby. She held her breath, wondering if what she had done might bring back memories better left buried. Grace's smile, however, quickly changed Autumn's qualms into pleasure. "It's exquisite," she exclaimed as she reached out and lifted the small tin drinking cup for everyone to admire.

"Turn it around, Grace," Autumn urged, anxious to see if Grace would like what Autumn had painted on the other side. In addition to creating a delicate vine of pale blue flowers that hugged the bottom edge of the cup, Autumn had spent days mixing different combinations together to get just the right shade of blue to letter the child's name and birth date.

Logan blue.

The color of John's eyes—more than appropriate for his namesake whose deep blue eyes promised to be the same color as his uncle's.

Grace's eyes filled with tears. "Thank you," she murmured, passing the cup to Daniel who nodded and gave it to John. Autumn did not even realize she was holding her breath as he ran hid fingers over the tole design that transformed an ordinary tin cup into a treasured keepsake.

When he smiled, she bit her bottom lip. "You're more talented than ever," he whispered, and she finally drew a deep breath.

"Open mine! Open mine!" Carol cried, her little hands squeezing the large envelope in front of her.

"Go ahead, but be careful," Daniel warned as he guided her fingers. Carol pulled out a piece of paper that looked like an official document everyone else in the family seemed to recognize.

"You didn't have to continue the tradition," Grace admonished her brother.

"I won't be able to if you and Daniel keep up this pace!"

Hannah laughed. "No one said you had to give each niece and nephew an acre of orchard as a birth present, but once a tradition is started, it can't be broken."

"An acre of land?"

John looked embarrassed by Autumn's question.

"Each year the crop is harvested, I invest the profit from an acre for each of my nieces and nephews. It doesn't amount to a whole lot, but by the time they're fully grown and ready for the university or need resources to purchase their own farm, the funds will be there for them. Unfortunately, I've fallen a bit behind," he said sheepishly as he looked at the twins who had been born in his absence.

Touched, Autumn moistened her lips as John's thoughtfulness added yet another layer to her understanding of the very complex man she had fallen in love with. The sights and sounds of Faith opening the package that contained the booties John's mother had made faded as Autumn battled emotions that threatened to overflow into tears she did not want to explain to anyone. She wondered if John realized that once he moved to New York, the tradition would be pointless unless he hired someone to run the farm.

Grace got up from the table, put John Logan Clarke into a cradle, and returned to the table. "Traditions," she murmured as she opened the last gift.

Curious to know who it was from, Autumn pushed her troubling thoughts away.

Hannah beamed at Grace. "Unlike your brother, dear, I have no doubt that this is one tradition that will continue no matter how many grandchildren the good Lord chooses to give me, Your father, bless his soul, was a generous man, and every time I make a new teething necklace, I remember how very wonderful he was. Outrageous at times," she admitted, "but I think he'd be very pleased to know that I kept my word."

Intrigued, Autumn leaned forward for a better view.

"I told him," Hannah continued, "that a rope of pearls that hung from my neck to the floor was a luxury that would embarrass the Queen of England. He was so proud of finally selling his patent that he insisted!" Her eyes filled with tears. "I told him that I would use the pearls to remind all of our children and grandchildren that they should never forget their roots."

Autumn's eyes widened as Grace lifted a necklace of pearl teething beads into the air. A single wooden bead sat between each series of three perfectly-shaped pearls in a design that sent shivers down Autumn's spine. Her heart thudded in her ears, and the room began to spin. Autumn gripped the edge of the table top so hard that her knuckles ached. "They're real," she murmured, blinking her eyes repeatedly.

"An extravagance that gives me great pleasure," Hannah explained. "The wooden beads are carved from the wooden trunk my grandparents used when they came here from Germany." She narrowed her gaze and looked at Mellie. "I suppose I'll just have to make another one for you, too," she said quietly.

"No! I have it," Autumn blurted.

John's eyes locked with hers.

"I still have it. Mellie was wearing it when . . ." She paused. "I mean, I found it among Mellie's things after . . ."

"You never sold it?" John asked.

"I never even considered that the beads might be real pearls," she answered, recalling an argument with Trina over the teething beads that seemed only odd at the time. Now Autumn wondered what she would have done with the pearls after Trina and Clayton died. If she had sold them, there would have been no surreptitious flight to Branfield. No need to labor day and night to support Mellie. No squabble over Klerk's trickery. No need to marry Norbert or John.

And no opportunity to see the promises in her husband's eyes—promises that were going to be broken forever and leave her heart in pieces small enough to fit into a thimble.

Chapter 24

Today? Today? The question flapped back at Autumn each time the wind caught a garment hanging on the clothesline to dry. She pinned up the last of the laundry and brushed away the tendrils of hair that had escaped from her chignon. As she headed back to the house with an empty basket, John's mother met her halfway.

"Will you take this to John? He's been working since sunup without a bite to eat."

Autumn did not have the heart to say no. How could she explain that she was literally walking on pins and needles waiting for the telegram to arrive that would confirm the annulment of her marriage when Hannah did not even know that a wedding between John and Autumn had even taken place?

One day shy of two weeks had passed since she and John re-signed the annulment papers, and Autumn knew that tomorrow was the day John had said the decree would be signed. She also found it increasingly difficult to wait for news from the other lawyer that would settle the issue of whether or not John was going to take Mellie to New York.

Torn apart by the prospect of losing the daughter of

her heart, a prospect that seemed ever more likely as days passed without word from New York, Autumn felt like worrying about John's hunger as much as she worried about the next meal for herself. "I promised Mellie that we would—"

Hannah's face reddened. "Mellie's halfway to Grace and Daniel's. Thaddeus stopped by on his way, and I didn't think you'd mind. He promised to have her back by dinner."

Swallowing back the growing realization that she was no longer the center of Mellie's world, Autumn smiled weakly as she exchanged the laundry basket for one filled with a picnic supper. "Is he still working on the bridge?" she asked, half hoping he was anywhere but there, as memories still too raw came rushing back.

"Said he'd be done with half a day's labor," Hannah responded as she patted Autumn's arm. "Go on. I'll finish the laundry. And don't hurry back. Isaac and I are going to put his wagon to order now that it's all repaired and David brought it all the way out here for him. You two might want some time alone together."

As much as we might be tempted to share a honeyed apple.

After mumbling a less than sincere thank you, Autumn wandered her way past the barn and still fallow fields. The rhythmic sound of hammer on wood echoed in the distance, but she knew her way without having to follow it. As she approached the bridge, John looked up from the other side. Sweat beaded and glistened on his bare chest, and she sucked in her breath. Snug, hip hugging jeans stretched across the lower planes of his hard stomach and outlined firm, tightly muscled thighs. Streaks in his hair had lightened from burnished gold to pale blonde. When he smiled, he took her breath away. Literally.

"Almost done," he said as he shifted the last section

of railing and began to nail it into place. As he worked, Autumn relived the day she fell through the old, decaying structure and wondered if the process of rebuilding the bridge, board by board, was in any way similar to reconstructing her life. Did she have to rip away the splintered past and build a new life, day by day?

Where would she start?

With Mellie, of course.

No. With herself. She loved Mellie all to pieces, but Autumn also knew that John loved the child, too. Other than the sublimely ridiculous solution of splitting the child in half, there was no easy remedy.

Solomon.

She wondered what might happen if he stepped out from the Biblical pages of history. Would he know what to do?

John would never let Mellie go. That was as much an understatement was saying that apples grew in Ohio. No. It was up to Autumn. Did she have the courage to let Mellie go? A knife sliced through her heart. Not yet.

Not ever?

After tomorrow, Autumn was not even legally entitled to half a say in Mellie's future, and Autumn knew that mounting a legal case to win custody of Mellie was tantamount to expensive tomfoolery.

And caught in the middle of the tug-of-war: Mellie.

"No," she murmured as she sat down on a patch of grass. She was not thinking about Mellie now. Autumn took a good honest look at herself. She loved John Logan as much as she ever had. Maybe more, as impossible as that might seem. How could she go to New York, cloak her relationship to Mellie under the mantle of being her governess and live with John without being able to be his wife? She could not bear it, and she knew that sooner or later, she would weaken and succumb to the loving passion that bound them together irrevocably in a way that no legal document could ever destroy. What would she do if she found herself with child?

What will I do if I'm carrying John's child now?

She shuddered and channeled her thoughts back to Mellie. She was too young to understand that she could not call Autumn her mama any more. Lord have mercy, Autumn was not sure she even understood it herself! It would be easier for Mellie to simply forget Autumn. No, not forget. Autumn prayed that Mellie would never forget her mother. Just learn to live surrounded by love from John, and his family when they visited.

Even if Autumn could bear to live in New York as Mellie's governess, what kind of message would that be sending to Mellie? That money and social position were more important than family ties?

And deep in her heart, Autumn knew that even if John's lawyers eventually broke Edsel Cameron's will so that she and John could remarry, the resentment she tried so hard to resist against him for not being able to choose between keeping them all together as a family in Ohio or claiming Mellie's inheritance for her would eventually destroy the very strong love Autumn had for him.

"No," she repeated.

"No?" John stood next to her holding the basket. "Isn't this for me?"

"Oh-h. Yes. I didn't realize you had finished working." She started to get up, but John put his hand on her shoulder and kept her in place.

"This is as good a spot as any to eat. Hungry?" he asked as he settled down beside her and lifted away the red checkered napkin on top of the meal.

"No. Where's your shirt?"

He grinned and bit into a thick sandwich oozing with cinnamon colored apple butter. "Can't think when I'm not fully dressed?"

Her cheeks flamed. "I already had breakfast," she snapped, choosing to respond to his first question and ignore the second.

"This is supper."

She wrinkled her nose. "Not for me."

He stopped eating and looked at the sandwich. "Guess not." He peered into the basket, cocked his head, and handed her a sandwich of bread and pale creamy butter.

Outdone, she took a bite and made the process of eating an art. Slowly, with small, measured bites, she managed to delay finishing the sandwich as John wolfed down three more of his own. He opened a jug and gulped down a fair amount before handing it over to her.

She shook her head. "Cider."

He shrugged his shoulders and emptied the jug. "How do you like the new bridge?" he asked as he sprawled out beside her and leaned back on one elbow. "Care to test it out?"

She bit her tongue as she tried to polish off the last bite of her sandwich. "No," she managed as pain boomeranged from one side of her tongue to the other.

"Don't you trust my handiwork?"

She stared at him. "Don't you consider it a bit obnoxious to be so blasé about tomorrow? Doesn't it bother you at all?"

His playful mood quickly banished, his eyes darkened. "Of course it does, but I'm still optimistic," he replied.

Autumn's heart plummeted. "Pardon me if I feel otherwise. I've never really been divorced before, and the idea that—"

He sat up and touched her arm. "It's an annulment, not a divorce. It's only temporary. With any luck, Linderman will find a loophole in Cameron's will and—"

She stiffened and carefully lifted his hand away. "I'm

not a doll you can take down from the shelf when you want to play. I'm real. I have feelings. And I can't sit idly by, living a lie, while you wait for a battery of legal experts to make up your mind for you. Pardon me again," she whispered, "if I happen to think that the love two people have for each other doesn't swing on a hinge made of legalisms."

He flinched. "If you'd only be patient, everything will work out for us."

"And if it doesn't?" Tears, gratefully, did not come, and Autumn spoke softly without a tremor to her voice. "I love you, John Logan. I love Mellie. I always will, but I can't live through endless days and nights while you wait for someone else to make up your mind for you. You can choose to keep us all together as a family, or you can—"

He raked his fingers through his hair. "I may not have to make that choice. Let the lawyers—"

She got to her feet and looked down at him, shaking her head. "Hang the lawyers and burn the will. Everything a person could want is right here."

"You don't understand," John countered as he stood up. "As Mellie's father, it's my duty to make sure she receives her inheritance. If I put my needs before hers, I'd be selfish . . . and acting no better than Trina and your brother. What's worse, Autumn? Using a child as a pawn to hurt someone and then abandoning her for the sake of lust or denying a child her rightful inheritance because two people are so selfish—"

"Making a life for ourselves here with Mellie will give her a home and a family. That's not selfish," she whispered before she started back toward the house.

John caught up with her and blocked her path. "You can't walk away from me now."

"You can't stop me. After tomorrow, you won't have that right." She watched as his eyes crackled with a surge of sapphire light that disappeared like a falling star into a sea of midnight blue.

"You said you loved me."

"Always and forever," she whispered as tears filled her eyes.

A twitch in his cheek, a groan. "And you love Mellie."

Her eyes filled with tears. "You know I do."

His expression softened. "I love her, too."

Autumn waited until she battled successfully to find her voice which had tangled with a lump in her throat that pulsed with her heartbeat. "Do you?"

"John! Autumn!"

Isaac's voice sliced through the wall of silence between Autumn and John. "Wait till I tell you. No—you have to see it for yourselves!" The peddler made his way slowly toward them, waving them back toward the house. "Hurry! It's a sight that will warm your heart."

Puzzled, Autumn walked next to John as they caught up with Isaac, who needed little more than a day or two before he was recovered enough to start home.

"Take it easy," John warned as Isaac turned and started rushing back to the house.

"I might look like I'm two blows from death," the peddler shot back, "but I'm feelin' like a cat who just found a tenth life. Get a move on, you two!"

Increasing her pace to keep up with the two men, Autumn celebrated her own full recovery by looking ahead instead of studying the ground before taking a single step. Horses whinnied in the distance, and as the trio grew closer to the barn, the sound of men's voices and wagon wheels creaking grew louder and more distinct.

When she rounded the corner of the barn, she plowed into John who had stopped unexpectedly in front of her. Hands on hips, heels dug in, he stood there seemingly unaware that she had knocked into him. She peeked around him and gasped out loud. "Apples!"

They were everywhere!

Several wagons pulling into the yard groaned with barrels and baskets of the ripe fruit. Two men, both of whom looked familiar to her from the ghastly episode in town, were unloading crates of apples from a wagon parked near the barn doors. Another wagon full of apples, with a grinning Dr. Blake in the driver's seat, sat in line to be unloaded.

John snapped out of his trance. "Bertram. Cleve. What the deuce is going on here?" he barked as he made his way to the two men.

"Started in your south orchard. Thought you might need a hand," one man replied as he put down a basket of red ripe apples. He extended his hand and shook John's. "Most of us already finished harvesting our crops. Thought we might try to salvage some of yours before it's too late."

John's eyes lit with the same sapphire glow that always made Autumn tremble. "I don't know what to say."

"Saying somethin' won't unload these wagons," the second man spat. "Care to lend a muscle?"

As the men joked away the embarrassment in John's face, Autumn slipped back to the house. Every mile between Branfield and Comfort Bend had been filled with questions, fears, and hope that life in Ohio would be good. As she stepped through the doorway and into the kitchen, she realized that it was all that she had ever hoped to dream, or would be, if John had the wisdom to see it, too.

John tiptoed into the darkened bedroom to check on Mellie before he found his own bed. Or was it the opportunity to see Autumn again that brought him here?

He stopped at the window and pushed back the drapes that covered it. Moonlight flooded the two figures in the bed, one capped with red curls, the other with a halo of thick brown waves.

His heart started to beat faster as he knelt down beside the bed and studied their sleeping faces. Mellie. The child he had loved from the day he knew she had been conceived. He smiled as he reached out and put Woolly Lamb back into her hand. He loved her more now that he could ever have imagined. Autumn. The woman who forced him to look deep inside of himself, to face the demons of the past and to reach out and create the promises of the future.

He lifted a strand of her hair off her cheek and held it to his lips. When he detected the light scent of apples, he choked back a bubble of laughter. She might not enjoy the taste of the fruit, but the scent clung to her. No doubt because she had peeled enough apples that afternoon to choke a herd of wild horses—or to make enough pies to feed the army of Good Samaritans who had shown up to help him—which she had done without complaint.

He had not had a chance to talk with Autumn again after their conversation at the bridge, but as he worked alongside his friends and neighbors, he had had plenty of time to think about what she said. Even when he had gone into town and made his daily trek to the telegraph office, her words had haunted him.

"I love you," he whispered as he bent low and kissed her lips. Gently, so as not to wake her. As he pressed his lips to hers, the copies of the telegrams he had put into his pocket made a crinkling sound. He paused and held his breath as Autumn stirred, and he held very still until she settled back into sleep.

"There's still tomorrow," he promised before he slipped back to his own room.

* * *

Autumn woke up. Something was wrong, very wrong. She lay very still and strained to listen again for the sound that had stolen through her sleep. There! She heard it again and eased out of bed. She walked over the window and looked outside. Hadn't she pulled the drapes before going to bed?

Under the light of a full moon, Isaac emerged from the barn with several pieces of tinware and walked back toward the house.

He's leaving!

She swallowed a healthy dose of panic.

"Not yet. I need a few more days. I'm not ready," she whispered as the outline of the plan she had been considering for days took final shape.

No. Now. Or never.

She rushed to the wardrobe and dressed as quickly as she could. She tried not to think beyond each passing minute and packed her travel bag with fingers that shook and eyes that dripped tears onto the few things she would take with her. Sketch pad. Brushes. Her paints.

When she picked up Mellie's teething beads, she let them slide between her fingers, each bite mark on the wooden beads a memory she would treasure forever.

She bit her bottom lip and walked over to the bed where Mellie was still sleeping. "I love you. For now and all your bright tomorrows." She choked on sobs that threatened to strangle her and placed the beads over Mellie's head. They barely fit, and Autumn stifled a half-cry, half-laugh, remembering a time when the beads reached down to Mellie's knees.

She kissed Mellie only once and left unsaid all the things she planned to say as she picked up her travel bag and slipped out of the room. She did not have to leave words with Mellie; she had left part of her heart. And even if she only had a little piece of it left, she would never regret sparing Mellie the confusion and pain of living a lie in New York with Autumn as her governess instead of as her mother.

I can't leave you.

I love you too much to stay.

Autumn tiptoed down the hall, through the parlor, and into the kitchen. Just as she suspected, Isaac had placed a few parting gifts on the table along with a scribbled note of appreciation. She hurried outside and went straight to the barn.

Isaac's wagon was gone.

Thwarted, but determined, she raced back outside and looked in both directions. A telltale cloud of dust sent her scurrying south. Toward Cincinnati. And then to . . . where?

It did not matter.

Regardless of where she went, Autumn would always treasure the love she had for John Logan, protecting it and keeping it safe from being destroyed at that fateful moment when he looked into her eyes and told her he was going to New York.

Chapter 25

Autumn's head began to bob in cadence with the plopping of the horses' hooves as she sat next to Isaac on the driver's seat of the peddler's wagon. Her head jerked back and snapped painfully as the wagon veered to the side as the wheels caught in a deep rut in the dirt roadbed.

"Hang on tight," Isaac shouted as the vehicle tilted to a dangerous angle farther before righting itself with a thud and setting off another musical measure of tinkling, rattling tinware. He mopped his brow and grinned. "Better slow it down a bit. No rush. Cincinnati's no more than an hour away. Be there by noon," he predicted as he studied the overhead sun.

She rubbed her neck and returned his smile. "That soon?"

He raised his hat and scratched his head. "Any reason you're wantin' to make it take longer?"

She swallowed hard. "No."

He put his hat back on and shook his head. "I should never have done this. Not to John Logan."

"I didn't give you any choice," she said softly. When he looked up at her with a pained expression, she reached over and patted his arm. "It's not like what happened before. Trina was his wife. I'm not."

Not anymore.

"You're runnin' away from the man."

Autumn dropped her gaze.

He didn't stop me.

Unable to speak, Autumn waited for her heart to stop racing as she admitted to herself that part of her had hoped that John would come after her. The other part knew that he would not do that. He had done that once before when Trina had left—to no avail. He would not or could not do it again.

"Mellie will miss you."

"She doesn't need me any more. She has her father and her grandmother, not to mention a slew of cousins."

"Horse feathers! Every child needs her mother."

Autumn's head spun to the side. "I'm not . . . I'm only . . ."

His eyes stared back at her until she thought her cheeks were hot enough to kindle a fire. "You're her mother. That's all she knows. Don't matter if you brought her into this world or kept her safe in it."

"She'll do just fine without me," Autumn sniffed.

"Sure she will." Isaac brought the horses to a standstill. "What about John Logan? Will he be better off alone, too?"

When Autumn opened her mouth to speak, he held up his hands. "I know. He has Mellie and his mother and a whole brood of nieces and nephews." He frowned. "It's not the same thing as having a woman who makes you whistle on the way to bed."

Autumn swirled away, stood up, and picked up her skirts. "I won't be troubling you any further." She turned around to back down from the wagon seat when strong arms grabbed her. He urged her back onto the seat. "Don't be too quick to run away from your problems. They have a downright nasty habit of tagging along."

"You have no idea what the problems are between me and John."

"Nope," he agreed as he picked up the reins and urged the horses forward. "None of my business."

"That's what John's mother said."

"Quick, smart woman. How come her son's so slow?"

Autumn's chest puffed out. "He's . . . he's confused. He's not really sure what he wants."

Her mind screamed a disclaimer: *Why are you defending him?*

She ignored it.

"Then he's a fool."

"No!" she argued. "He's . . . he's—"

"A fool. End of discussion."

The sternness in Isaac's voice brooked no further argument, and Autumn settled back into her seat, more confused by her own emotions than ever before. Hoping that time and distance would prove her decision to leave wise, she concentrated on the passing landscape as they neared their final destination. She really was not quite sure what she would do once she reached Cincinnati, but as sure as the sun had climbed to its noonday peak, she would find a way to earn passage back to New England where she would be able to find a position with yet another tin factory. Maybe Isaac would put in a good word for her? No. She had to do this on her own.

She closed her eyes and felt the wagon rock as the roadway curled sharply to the west, and when it straightened again, the wagon slowed down and stopped.

"Look at that!"

Her eyes flew open, and she felt her entire body go

numb. She blinked her eyes and gripped the edge of the seat as Isaac climbed down from the wagon. A crooked white line stretched across the road in front of a crudely lettered sign that had been planted in the middle of the roadbed. It had only one word on it: YESTERDAY.

After Isaac removed the sign, he climbed back aboard. "Waste of good whitewash," he muttered.

Already close to tears, Autumn let them fall as the wagon proceeded and the hurts as well as the faces of people from the past flashed before her. Clayton, whose irresponsible behavior hurt so many innocent people. Trina, whose betrayal went beyond scandalous. Mellie, a precious little baby who gave meaning to Autumn's life. All-consuming sadness over Clayton and Trina's senseless deaths and fear of Edsel Cameron, which spurred Autumn's clandestine flight to Branfield, came washing over her.

When she blinked her mind's eye, she saw Matsey and Doris. Good friends. Klerk. A conniving snake. Mellie. Now a young child whose very smile made all the world look right again.

John.

Autumn tasted salty tears and saw, once again, a man with midnight blue eyes who was determined to win her away from Norbert Briley. A man whose journey home had softened his eyes to sparkling sapphires that held all the promises Autumn had ever dared to dream about.

As she scanned the roadway ahead, she wiped her face with the hem of her dress, too afraid to breathe for fear she might wake up at the beginning of a wonderful dream. "Look!" She pointed straight ahead, and Isaac dutifully slowed the horses down again as they approached a second sign, just as crudely lettered as the first, although this sign had a paper tacked on it, too.

When the wagon stopped, she read the word on the sign out loud. "Today."

Autumn scrambled down from the wagon and ran up to the sign, too excited to worry about walking through another scraggly line of fresh paint that crossed the road in front of it. A telegram tacked to the sign fluttered in the breeze. She held it flat with both hands and read it quickly:

TO: JOHN LOGAN, COMFORT BEND, OHIO
FROM: R. LINDERMAN, NEW YORK CITY
NO NEWS STOP SUGGEST PROCEED WITH ANNULMENT STOP
NEED SEVERAL MONTHS STOP ADVISE STOP

Hope battled despair as the words in the telegram kept echoing in her mind. Was John going to all this trouble to tell her that there was no quick or easy solution to his dilemma? Was he so incensed that she had left with the tin peddler that he was going to punish her by raising her hopes and then dashing them into despair?

Maybe.

She stared up the road.

"No!" she cried as she started running toward yet another sign behind yet another crooked white line. She was nearly out of breath by the time she crossed the line and reached that sign. She ripped two papers off the sign, and her hands shook so hard she had to read the first one twice to make sure she had not misread it:

TO: PAUL YOST,. CINCINNATI, OHIO
FROM: JOHN LOGAN, COMFORT BEND, OHIO
WITHDRAW ANNULMENT STOP ADVISE CLAYBOURNE STOP
RESPOND STOP.

A gust of wind nearly tore the second telegram in half as she read it.

TO: JOHN LOGAN, COMFORT BEND, OHIO
FROM: PAUL YOST, CINCINNATI, OHIO
ANNULMENT WITHDRAWN STOP CONGRATULATIONS STOP
WILL RETURN PAPERS BY POST STOP.

She read it again and cried openly as she dropped it and started running down the road. Faster. Harder. Her feet flew over the roadbed as she looked ahead and from side to side for John. Faster still as she neared another sign. She panted as she removed a small, dark blue velvet bag that had been tacked to the sign. Her fingers shook as she untied the drawstring and turned the bag upside down on her palm. When she tossed the bag away, she stared at her hand and started crying even harder.

A wedding ring.

Clustered with sapphires and pearls.

She slipped it onto the third finger of her left hand. It fit perfectly, like it had been crafted for her and her alone.

"John! John!" Her cries carried on the wind, but as she whirled about and searched frantically for him, all that came whispering back to her was the sound of trees swaying in the wind.

She walked forward, hope resurrected when the road curved again. On the other side of the bed, would there be another crooked line? Another sign?

"John!"

He stood alone on the other side of a line and next to another sign, hands at his side. Tears blurred the lettering, but she knew with every beat of her heart that it said "tomorrow." She slowed her pace to a walk and painted his beloved form in her mind as she walked.

Tall. Broad shoulders. Sun-streaked hair. A tremulous smile. "John," she murmured as she stood in front of him. More than a crooked line separated them, however, and she suddenly grew shy.

He smiled nervously and reached out to take her hand. "Will you forgive me?"

She nodded, too overwhelmed by the feel of his pulse tapping at her fingertips to speak.

"Will you step into tomorrow with a man who doesn't deserve to expect you to do that? I love you Autumn, and I want to share my home and my life with you. Here. In Ohio. With our daughter." His shining blue eyes filled with so many sparkling promises, she thought her heart would burst. "I was a fool to ever think I could let you go," he whispered.

She started to cry and tugged on his hand until he stepped over the line to stand beside her. "I love you. Today and always," she murmured as she stood on tiptoe to kiss him.

He kissed her back. Slowly. Gently. Then hungrily until she was breathless. She took his hand and nodded toward the line. "We'll face tomorrow best if we do it together."

Grinning, he scooped her into his arms and stepped over the line. When he gazed down at her, she cupped his cheek and stared deep into his eyes. They sparkled like the rarest of blue sapphires and glistened with new promises—promises of a love that was strong enough to withstand the joys and sorrows, the thrills and challenges of the future in a world of tomorrows.

"I can't believe you went to all this trouble. Why didn't you just tell me . . . before I . . ."

He kissed her so hard she thought she might faint.

When he broke their kiss, he smiled. "I would have, but you slipped away during the night."

"What if you had been too late? What if Isaac and I had reached Cincinnati before you caught up with us?"

As if on cue, Isaac's wagon rounded the curve, and the peddler shouted, "Everything settled with you two?"

John set Autumn back on her feet and waved. "Great! Thanks for your help."

Autumn looked up at John, down the road at Isaac, and back at John again. "Help? Did Isaac—"

John tilted her chin up, his finger resting gently on her chin. "I've been too late for a lot of things, Autumn, but I wasn't going to take any chances. You're important to me. I couldn't risk losing you because I was such a fool." His gaze deepened, and he changed the timbre of his voice to a gentle caress. "I love you, Autumn. I want you. By my side. In my arms. For now and every tomorrow."

Tears glistened in Autumn's eyes. "Are you sure this is what you want? What about the will? What about taking Mellie to New York?"

He caressed her cheek with his thumb. "I don't know what Linderman will be able to do about the will. If we win our suit, you and I can talk about what's best for all of us. Maybe we can spend winters in New York so Mellie could have the best of both worlds. If not, there are any number of charities that will benefit. It's too early to predict the outcome, but I'm certain of one thing. The greatest gift I can give to Mellie is a father and a mother who love each other as much as they love her."

"You're asking me to stay with you for Mellie?"

He shook his head. "Mellie needs you more than an inheritance, but this isn't about Mellie." He paused, took a deep breath and gazed deep into Autumn's eyes, his soul reaching out to touch her. "When I found you gone I knew that I needed you more than I need air to breathe or light to guide my way. You are the fire that sears my heart with love and joy."

Autumn cupped his face with her hands. "I love you so much, John Logan."

"Show me." he whispered softly and pulled her into his arms, vowing to rekindle the fire of Autumn's love so that it would burn brighter than ever before.